JILLIAN DAVID

EVERNIGHT PUBLISHING ®

www.evernightpublishing.com

JILLIAN DAVID

DEDICATION

To Hubs, who staunchly believes that a blue and red plaid shirt goes perfectly with olive-drab forest pattern camo pants, despite what his wife says.

JILLIAN DAVID

SILENT COMRADE

Project Morpheus, 3

Jillian David

Copyright © 2023

Chapter One

Too many voices blinded Red.

Alfred "Red" Newman leaned against the Savannah College of Art and Design (SCAD) hallway and gritted his teeth as the faux-leather jacket material rasped against the white walls, the sound creating sparks in his vision. Warmer than typical attire for March on the college's Atlanta campus, but this wasn't a typical situation. A guy had to hide tactical gear somehow. He hunched his tall frame into itself and ducked his head, trying something—anything—to drown out the noise but still maintain his ability to focus.

He needed to preserve his exceptional hearing without losing his mind. Hell of a two-edged sword. Hell of an advantage, no question. Made working around explosives a real bitch, but fantastic for tracking down tiptoeing insurgents. Unfortunately, every time the damned experimental Morpheus Virus that had given him his supersonic hearing revved up, he lost a little more sanity. He rolled his neck, wincing as the deep cracking sound ricocheted in his skull. With effort, he loosened jacked-up muscles—muscles ready to fire, to strike, to propel his fists forward as he beat the hell out of something or someone. He shifted the stupid tote slung over his shoulder, all part of today's costume along with the fake glasses that made the bridge of his nose itch. He straightened up against the wall, careful not to press against the hidden Sig holstered at the small of his back.

Students now exited classes, their chatter flowing like a summer flood burbling down a dry creek bed until it rose to a growling rush of sound. A narrow-eyed glance from a passing maroon blazer-clad student made him reset his slumped posture. A quick brush of one leg against the other allowed Red to inventory the guns in both ankle holsters. He reached in his deeper-than-normal jeans pocket to the hole inside and probed with a finger. Knife strapped on the thigh, right where he'd put it.

Like most of the Morpheus Squad members, Red didn't rely solely on weapons. He rolled his free hand into a fist and tried not to be obvious with his systematic assessment of this space's ingress and egress points, as well as its weaknesses that Lequire's men could exploit. He tallied hypothetical casualties in real time.

Keep your shit together. This is an arts college, not the Middle East, and not a team drill. Blend in. The assignment is more of a precaution.

Unrolling his fingers, Red fished in his jacket pocket and squeezed the tiny silicon earplugs, debating. Sacrifice his edge or sacrifice his sanity? The rushing water sound of chattering, closely packed college students rose to a flooded-waterfall tumbling roar. He shook his head, as if doing so would dislodge the sound. That wouldn't give him what his body craved. What it hated. What it loved.

What Red really needed was a shot of antidote. The synesthesia had increased. But, no, he'd had zero time to stop and inject and take the necessary half day to recover, thanks to his target's constant motion. Would it kill this woman to stay put for more than fifteen minutes? He still couldn't figure out when this freaking Energizer bunny slept.

Speaking of Britt McNeill, she'd almost gotten away from him. Embarrassing for a specially trained Special Forces tracker like Red.

Now he needed to get to a pretend class and take pretend notes while he pretended to enjoy discussions about textiles and cuts of clothing. Red pulled the edges of the beanie down over his ears, to hide his bright orange hair. He crushed the fabricated transfer paper in his hand and flinched as the harsh crinkle knifed through his temple.

The mission. Stick to the mission. The skin between his shoulder blades twitched. He glanced around, expecting to see armed thugs aiming guns at him—or worse, aimed at his mission target. Who had again flitted away from his exceptional tail. Red had been one of the best trackers in the military. He lightly tapped his ear through the yarn. Especially after his change.

Even more reason that Britt's evasion pissed him off.

Not evasion, because that implied she knew he followed her. She had no idea. Oh, no. This woman was naturally talented at being nowhere and everywhere, all at once. If only that innate ability could help the situation.

Britt had no idea of the evil that wanted to hurt her. Had no idea if Red lost her trail, not only would the guys back at base never let him live it down, but in a far more critical matter, her life would be in jeopardy. All because Britt's sister had uncovered the truth about their brother Brady's death, putting the entire McNeill family in danger. Red and his team were involved because Brady had been their teammate in Special Forces. Therefore, his team would protect the McNeills like they protected one another. Simple. With luck, Red could concentrate on keeping an eye on her. If only he could stop his ears from absorbing every damned sound in a half-mile radius. He ground molars together, but winced—softly. The virus balked at the restraint and made every muscle prickle.

Heaving in a lungful of air, he held it until he tamped down the need to rip off his own head. Or anyone else's head. In. Out. In. Out. Like he'd learned years ago, when so-called home life had become dire. Before Special Forces. Before the virus. In. Out. In. Out. A familiar exercise.

The fight-or-flight response eased along with the tension in his shoulders.

See? There. All better.

As if sixty seconds of circular breathing fixed his terminally warped nervous system. Close enough.

He shoved away from the wall and joined the flow of students, keeping his shoulders hunched. Couldn't exactly hide 6'2", but he sure as hell could appear less like a military operative and more like a … fashion student. He had the whole getup, meticulously curated by Stumpy and Gonzo. Apparently they had the fashion chops or at least enough Google images to get appearances right: stiff leather-esque jacket, baggy shirt with a subtle striped pattern, organically sourced yarn beanie, edgy ankle boots, stupid-ass leather wrist thingy, literati glasses, dude tote bag. Whole nine yards. He'd drawn the line at skinny jeans. His balls clenched at the thought. Yeah. With his muscled legs, he couldn't rock slim-fit denim without losing circulation somewhere vital.

Three quick, light steps preceded his five-foot-nothing mission target careening around a corner and burying her forehead in his ribs.

"Crap!" With a flurry of flannel and limbs, Britt windmilled backward, likely off-balance due to the backpack that sagged from her shoulders like it contained half her body weight.

He rocketed a hand out and almost picked her up off the ground. Adrenaline hit Red like a crashing wave, blocking out everything else around him as he laser-focused on Britt. He quickly dialed his grip on her arm back to "support" instead of "hoist."

That little intake of air she inhaled? He tasted that auditory pop of sweet pecan sound. His gut tightened as did other areas, and he thanked God once more for looser-fit pants.

The second she was no longer at risk of falling on her cute ass, he let go of her. Had to. Not before he caught a whiff of coffee and … he inhaled … hibiscus? It was a subtle, sweet, and old-school scent that made him think of potted flowers. Maybe. He wasn't an aroma savant like his teammate, Doc.

"Ah, I'm sorry," she said with a sweet yet sharp lilt.

A devilish blink of her intense electric-blue eyes outlined by dark liner damn near sucked the oxygen out of the room. She was no Southern belle—more like a Goth pixie who had gleefully dismembered a Southern belle.

"I won't break." He pitched his voice low. Relief at being back in visual contact with his mission objective loosened his shoulders.

Then all his internal monitoring systems went on high alert. *Protect.*

Her fingers fluttered over his chest, the tiny sounds of fingertips brushing the cotton-polyester blend tickled but did not hurt his ears. Thank God he hadn't worn a chest holster today or she'd be tracing it.

A blink. Dark-mauve lids flipped down and back up to reveal that bright-blue stare again. "You? Break? Uh, doesn't seem like it, no. You're not super fragile." *Pat pat.* "At all. Look at you, all there. Um." Her elfish features shifted into to a sweet, sheepish grin. He felt more than heard her gulp.

His face creaked with an unnatural movement. A smile? He fought the urge to puff out his chest and flex beneath her flapping appreciation, and instead stayed in character and kept his shoulders hunched. As if he spent a lot of time thinking about socially responsible art and had deep literary discussions over coffee. Whatever that kind of dude was, Red tried to project that appearance.

No question, if those short and sparkly—he squinted—lime-green nails ever dragged across his bare skin? He'd blow way more than his mission.

Stay professional, damn it.

The freaky sprite in front of him confused him. Granted, he had assumed the role of a fake fashion student for the purpose of his mission, but even a straightlaced military dude like Red knew a fashion *don't* when he saw it. As an older-than-typical-aged college student of twenty-six, maybe she was creating her own new trend. Purple highlights glinted in the chestnut, chin-length hair that framed her pale, delicate neck. A silver hoop winked on the side of her nose. Two more hoops encircled the edge of an eyebrow.

The unbuttoned navy flannel shirt that covered her thigh-length floral knit dress seemed like more of a nineties look, though he was literally no expert. Toughening up the ensemble? Knee-high black tights and Doc Martens. Even with the thick-soled shoes, Britt only came up to mid-chest height on him.

The entire incongruent package worked for her. It worked for him.

"Hello?" she asked.

Damn it, how long had he been staring? He peered down the hall. Fewer students hurried to classes now.

"I'm Britt McNeill," she said, holding out her hand.

How shocking was her voice now? Low and mellow, her words sounded like bourbon tasted— caramel and smoky and tart, all at once. But with an effervescent brightness that contradicted the dark elements in her appearance.

Her hand disappeared in his, and he reeled in the urge to clamp down, pull her closer, tuck her into his chest, and kill anyone who attacked her. *Whoa, there, boy.*

"Re—Al Neubert. Call me Al." After one carefully controlled shake of her delicate hand, he let go. Had to.

A quick frown made the light glint off the silver eyebrow hoop. "Okay. Al." He resisted the urge to fidget as her gaze narrowed. "Um, so I gotta …" She jabbed a thumb over her shoulder.

"Me too."

With a tilt to her head, she asked, "You're new here?"

"Transfer from main campus in Savannah," he

lied, the backstory flowing like he'd been born with this history. He took a breath in, out, in, out. "Granny is ill here in Atlanta so SCAD let me transfer midsemester."

Ah yes, SCAD, Savannah College of Art and Design, where he was pursuing his fake dream of getting a fine arts degree so he could work in the fashion industry as a trend forecaster. Sadly, he couldn't tell the difference between acid-wash and stone-wash, and God help him if he needed to coordinate colors. Red and pink went together fine. Right?

His sum knowledge of fashion came from the crash course his teammates, Gonzo and Stumpy, had put together before Red left the team compound four days ago. Plus, Red had grabbed a bunch of magazines at the local bookstore a few days ago to read while on stakeout. Cargo pants were out—who knew? World truly was coming to an end. If he pulled off this role, he should get an Oscar.

A sympathetic frown creased the skin between her dark brows. "Oh, that's too bad about your granny. Hope she gets better. Ah." She toyed with the hem of the flannel shirt. "Need help finding a class?"

No, because he could follow Britt to her class, which magically happened to be the same class on his fake transfer papers. Funny how that worked. But he stayed in character and uncrumpled the sheet so she could review the schedule he had memorized.

"Oh, that's easy. Follow me. Hurry, or we'll be late!" The *shush* of skirt fabric brushing against her tights-clad thighs dried his mouth out in a hurry, but he followed her like a cooperative if not uninformed transfer student.

If Britt found out the truth about Red, she'd take one of those ridiculous Doc Martens and cram it where fashion sits...

Chapter Two

Britt might not be a genius, but she knew when things fit and when they didn't. When pieces put together worked well to create a cohesive look. Or when someone was trying too hard to be effortless. Something about Al didn't add up … like velvet and tulle sewn together—it made no sense.

The way he carried himself, hunched and insecure, ran contrary to the tight, hard muscles on his chest and his quick reactions. Polyester-cotton-spandex-mix shirt, if her fingers told the truth, which meant the material should be fitted. What about the horizontal stripes on the shirt? For a guy going to fashion school, he should know better. What she'd give to restructure his … wardrobe. A flutter deep inside sent a wave of heat through her chest.

Not a relationship. Nothing permanent. No connection. Nothing that could make her get hurt. Those were the rules that made life uncomplicated, if not a little lonely. What about enjoying something short-term? Could be fun to … makeover … Al.

She caught a glimpse of him out of the corner of her eye as they hurried down the hall. His look came across as deliberately contrived. The boots were rugged but expensive, and probably had never seen off-road terrain. The glasses hid those warm hazel eyes, and the tan Oakley satchel had a strap that had no smooth wear on it. Hey, nothing against any piece of clothing, but these items seemed more expensive than an average college student could afford.

She swallowed a nasty acid taste. Some students here could easily afford the $40,000 tuition fee, plus living expenses. Other students, like Britt, cobbled together financial aid, grants, the SCAD Challenge Scholarship, and loans to pay for school. Usually it was clear which students were which.

She couldn't put a finger on it, but Al's ensemble didn't work. *Quit playing critic.* People could wear what they wanted, as long as they were comfortable and happy.

Nothing about Al seemed comfortable.

A muscle in his tight cheek popped. Nothing about Al seemed happy, either.

A few fine lines next to his hazel eyes hinted that his age was closer to Britt's and he wasn't the typical eighteen- to twenty-two-year-old student.

Sure, she liked the doesn't-realize-he's-hot-introvert-intellectual-in-a-beanie look, same as any gal. But the way he scanned the hallway and whipped his head over at a noise down the hall, like a Doberman on sudden alert? Out of place.

The denim over his sturdy legs? Too distressed. Too symmetrical. Faux shabby. He was trying too hard.

Using her teeth to toy with the silver hoop on her lip, she sighed. She could judge him, or she could cut the guy a break. His grandma was ill, and he had picked up and moved from Savannah to Atlanta. That situation would make anyone uncomfortable. He probably didn't even have all his clothes unpacked yet. She glanced again. That made the most sense. No fresh clothes. Because if this was a deliberate choice? Phew. He'd need remedial studies before he was allowed to graduate.

"Here we are, Al." She pointed at the number next to the classroom door.

Murmurs and chair scrapes from her classmates taking their seats in Fashion Design: Concept Development filtered out into the hallway.

His big hand spread out on the door, holding it

open for her to enter. She had to step way too close to his broad chest to pass by him. A hint of pine and aftershave tempted her to inhale again.

Murmuring stopped. All eyes shot up.

Britt's cheeks heated as she motioned to get Professor Durban's attention. "New guy," she mumbled, then hurried to an open seat on the far side of the room.

Professor Durban batted their eyelashes and fawned over Al, right along with half the class. The top of Al's neck turned red as he stood with his shoulders hunched. He still took up a ton of physical space.

Even several rows over, Britt fielded the usual nasty glances from Jenna and her crew of fashionista clones. Jenna had on a denim jumper cinched with a metal belt. Hey, just because someone could afford Nordstrom's clothes straight off the rack didn't automatically make them a trendsetter. Anyway, it was easy to be cutting edge when your daddy was the mayor of the wealthiest Atlanta suburb, Alpharetta. Jenna probably had name-brand toilet paper for her 24-karat gold hiney that she demanded everyone kiss.

One of the clones looked over at Britt, then rolled her eyes as the squad tittered and whispered. Good grief. Just like high school, only now Britt was in sixteenth grade. Didn't matter that Britt was a good four years older than Jenna and her friends. Mean girls didn't appear or disappear at a certain age. At least Britt's anxiety was well-treated nowadays. Thank God.

Jenna's ruby-red Revlon snarl turned into a come-hither simper when Al slunk into a seat next to her. Jackpot for Jenna.

Only he didn't slink. Not really. Britt tapped the edge of her scratched laptop. Maybe he did slink, but somehow it was a deliberate action. Which made no sense. A tall guy with broad shoulders like that shouldn't be lacking in confidence. He glanced back and over at Britt, his dark-orange eyebrows rising as a quick, wry grin curled one corner of his generous mouth. Her heart flopped.

Yep. He was confident enough.

Nope. Time machine back to high school or not, Britt had no time for men, dating, or anything extracurricular. Time to concentrate on school, because no way would she *not* graduate this time. Not after years of wandering, trying out colleges and majors, taking semesters off to work and figure out what the heck she wanted to do, all while trying to bolster the crumbling life around her. Britt had finally gotten mental health assistance, and then decided on a destination.

Britt had promised Mom a year ago, that she'd finish her degree. Now Britt had a senior project to finish and a graduation to accomplish. No fashion misfit, hazel-eyed hottie who couldn't make junior sales associate at Banana Republic would prevent her from finally reaching this goal.

Jenna could go right ahead and sink her gel nails into him. Britt snorted. If Entitled Barbie's lip-licking foreshadowed the future, Jenna *would* have Al ... for lunch. Soon. Poor guy, he would never know what steamrolled him. For a second, Britt felt bad for the guy.

Not my problem.

Britt rested a hand on her temple, blocking out her line of sight to Al. It helped.

Some.

Chapter Three

At the age of twenty-five, Red was already way too old for this shit.

He tried to concentrate on the professor's lecture while the unnaturally natural blonde next to him kept turning her head and flipping her hair. Then she moved to coyly tapping her pen on her glossy upper lip, the sound bursting like a cold, damp bubble on his face. Based on her progressive flirtation, he'd bet money on her giving up her digits, or outright asking him on a date. Great. He groaned inwardly.

Red might be the so-called baby of the Morpheus Squad. Didn't mean he had missed out on his fair share of life experience, including some fun and games. He rubbed his ear. If anyone could call a life-changing experimental virus "fun."

No, the fun part was how Uncle Sam had tested the team members like lab rats, all in the name of God and country. Those testing facilities came complete with nice, locked, luxury cells with a daily dose of pain and suffering. Even now, as part of Morpheus Squad, operating in the shadows, Red risked recapture if he blew his cover. The government hadn't finished their experiments. Freedom and his work as a team member came at a price.

His extra abilities meant that he could use his skills to help others or he could hide forever.

The only way he could pull off any mission was to remain undetected.

The muscles between Al's shoulder blades twitched. What he'd give to sit up straight and stretch. Instead, he ignored the student next to him who was busy weaponizing seduction, and he continued hunching like his cover depended on it. He glanced at the ridiculous Fossil watch, useless with its complete lack of digital readout or satellite connection: 9:20 AM. Time to do a threat assessment.

He made a mental blueprint of the classroom, noting the locations of ingress and egress. Windows worked on a rotary latch system, but only opened a few inches. He could easily break the hinges with a well-placed kick. Red had already estimated the distance to the ground: twenty-three feet. A bit high for comfort. His knees creaked when he shifted position. With the virus amplifying his reflexes and strength, he'd still limp away from a jump from that distance.

He wondered what the rest of the team was up to. Rivera and Pele were in similar field ops protecting Britt's father and sister, probably blending in way better than Red.

Unfortunately, when they needed a covert operator to play a college student, the former Special Forces team depth chart ran thin. Red was as close as they would ever get to "youthful."

Up at the front, the professor droned on about concept design, and Red pretended to take notes on a computer tablet. The only concept Red wanted to focus on involved getting out of this kill box with his surveillance target within arm's reach. He sniffed and rotated slightly to assess other people in the room. Students wore everything from monotone black to every shade of the tropics, and that was just the hairstyles. No telltale signs of weapons bulges. No skittish actions.

Good. Reassess in ten. He hunched toward the front of the class once more.

That blonde student one seat over winked at him again with a sniff of her too-perfect nose. He groaned again.

To do his job, he needed to get rid of this woman with the fake nails that she would not stop tapping against the desk. Like a guitar pick against a washboard, but less metallic-tasting of a sound. He rubbed his cramped neck. He needed a mandated rest, but that wasn't happening anytime soon if he wanted to keep up with Britt.

Sound crept through his defenses, unbidden, waking his ability up in a hurry. A heavy, gummy sensation of clomping boots came from the hallway. Automatically, he assessed likely body structure based on pace and stature given the depth and timing of the thuds. About 5'9" and 140 pounds. He sat up straight. *Slouch, damn it.*

The virus wanted more input. More sound. More targets to evaluate. More threats for Red to neutralize. His hand shook as he gripped the stylus as the viral vortex pulled him into the depths.

Senses blending as his hearing acuity increased, he picked up every audible signal around him. With the right amount of breath control and concentration, he could focus his abilities instead of letting viral impulses take over. That was always the goal: use the virus's power to succeed. Not let it get out of hand to where he went insane and lost control.

Papers rustled around him, crisp and bright, tasting like sun tea. One hundred and fifty fingers tapped on keys or scratched notes on paper all around the room in an industrious background patina that rubbed his nerves like dry leather. He scanned the room as much with his eyes as his ears.

The professor's heeled shoes made a snapping scuff as he paced in front of the room. Red glanced at the pronouns on the top corner of the whiteboard. Not he. *They.* Noted. The soles on the shoes were irregular. They must have walked on rocks or gravel before coming to class. One leg was slightly longer, judging by the slower, more solid sound when that left foot made scratchy contact with the linoleum floor.

Someone in the class had asthma, as a slight pinching wheeze came from a thin guy up on the front row.

The most interesting sound? It happened again, laser-focusing his attention. A tiny intake of breath. The scrape of air through pursed lips dragged over his ears like featherlight touches. The descending tone that followed was soft and heated, and no one but Red could hear.

Pretending to crack his neck, he glanced over his shoulder and across the room at Britt. Both of her hands rested on the laptop keyboard, eyes focused ahead. Her darkly tinted lips were open. Breathing. No law against that action. But every time the combined air and sigh happened, it set his nerve endings on fire. The virus needed to get close to that sound.

Red damn near stood up. He stopped himself. Re-hunched. That strong of an impulse had never happened before. There was always a chance the virus would mutate or behave unpredictably. No one knew what the virus would do, long-term. Today was not the time to find out.

"Mr. Neubert?" the professor asked again.

Red jumped at the lemon-sour tone of voice. "Pardon."

Laughter around him pinged against his brain, sleet against hard vinyl. He winced. Damn synesthesia. He needed an antidote soon.

"Do you have a comment to add on the utilization of textiles in postmodern expression? Because by that daydreaming look on your face, you must have lots of ideas. Right?"

Busted by the professor on day one. So much for incognito.

Metallic-tasting scrapes sounded as chairs shifted. The entire class focused on Red. Damn it. He had hated attention in school during his crappy childhood in foster care, and he sure as hell hated attention now during an undercover op.

Time to see if Gonzo and Stumpy's research paid off.

"Textiles in postmodern expression?" He cleared his throat, stalling. Reaching deep into the crash course he'd crammed over the past three days, Red fought the urge to swipe sweat from his brow. Light, warm fog clouded his glasses, but no way would he remove them. He breathed in, out, in, out. "Well, sure. If you believe that postmodern is still relevant—and some experts do not—then the concept of bricolage becomes key—the use of disparate materials on hand to draw attention to the individual different components in the artistic expression. But the act of doing so creates a cohesive product, which at its core stifles the postmodern non-unified aesthetic as it's being constructed."

Did that bull come out of his own mouth?

Were those complete sentences? Did the words make sense? Hell if he knew. He was regurgitating one of many fashion theory word salad concepts that Stumpy had drilled into him.

Silence. Dead, ear-ringing silence. No cough. No chuckle. No typing on keyboards. Red literally heard a cricket in the far corner of the room.

The professor cleared their throat. "Well, I suppose they did teach you something useful back in Savannah after all. Thank you, Mr. Neubert."

Like a vise had been released from his chest and

ears, he exhaled, picking up all the little rustling noises, shifts in seats, and a sense of the students resettling, like a flock of birds had landed on the lawn. He tried to disguise the moment when he rubbed that bead of sweat from his upper lip.

That specific breathy sigh coming from Britt had him checking her, and he caught her quick smirk and scrunched nose. Then she faced forward, studiously ignoring anyone but the pacing professor.

"That was amazing," the hair-tosser next to him whispered, resting her hand on his wrist. Her too-long nails scraped with tiny pings over his jacket sleeve. "About time someone put Professor Durbin in place. You're *so* smart. Maybe you could tutor me."

He pulled away, leaving her to tug on a strand of hair. For real. Here, in this classroom, had she pulled out that line? He tried for a polite and curt nod, hoping she'd get the point. A few seconds passed.

"Well?" she said.

He tried waving her off. "Chat later," he whispered.

The woman sat back, raking her eyes over him. Hell, she looked like a cat about to lap up a bowl of cream.

The guys back at base had said this would be the easiest of the assignments. Those guys had Kevlar for brains. They wouldn't survive a minute in the minefields of this hostile environment. Threats everywhere.

A half-hour later, class ended, and Red tried to time his departure with Britt's. Anything to maintain contact with her to help make his mission easier.

"I'm Jenna. Jenna Woodruff." The hair-twirler drawled the name like it meant something.

"Hmm?"

She stepped in front of him, blocking his way as

she tipped her head up toward him. "Of the Alpharetta Woodruffs?"

He shrugged. "Nice to meet you."

"Oh, I would have thought someone with expensive taste in clothing would know my father, Mayor Woodruff."

"Sounds like a busy guy." He pointed toward the door. "I need to get to my next class."

The woman's scowl briefly creased her perfectly portioned features as she glanced toward her posse hovering nearby. Red was about as comfortable as a goldfish in a shark tank.

Britt had walked near where he stood. A pause in her quick steps, and her electric-blue gaze cut up to him then back down.

With a dip of his head and a lift of a palm, Red tried to appear as if he needed help, a stretch for his acting ability, but he knew he nailed it when Britt said, "Want more schedule assistance, Al?"

"As a matter of fact, yes." He tried to sidestep the Great White in front of him.

Jenna mirrored his movements, then she spun toward Britt. "I'll help him find his next class. Besides, don't you need to finish your little project?"

"We both have senior projects to complete. But yes, I'm working on it later this week, thanks for your concern," Britt mumbled, wrapping two hands around one backpack strap and twining her fingers together.

Jenna snorted. "First off, you'll have to get more discount material at JOANN Fabric." Her lurking friends joined in the polite laughter with a hard edge. "That's going to be the dumbest fashion collection, ever. Unless 'teenage runaway chic' was the look you were going for. Am I right, ladies?" Jenna raked a nail down Red's forearm, the sound of acrylic on leather sandy and harsh.

"You should check out *my* collection. It's all about the glam of high-fashion New York. It's going to be ah-mazing."

Holy shit, he heard the tympani pounding of Britt's heart while a hot, red flush stained her neck and cheeks. Forget Red protecting her from Lequire's cronies who wanted to kill or kidnap her, she had plenty of threat from these frenemies in front of her. Right as he curled his hands into fists and prepared to shove past the catty jerk, Britt inhaled with a sigh, that sweet sound bringing him to heel. He honed in on every note and decibel.

Rather, the virus honed in on her.

Legs shoulder-width apart, Britt rose to full height, still a few inches shorter than Jenna, but topped with a big helping of *hell-if-I-care*. Then Britt smiled, the expression terrifying. There was a flash of hurt, and then it got buried behind the icy glint in her eyes and a chin thrust. Red recognized the kindred ability to push down the pain and fake some confidence.

Her mellow voice remained calm, controlled. Too controlled. "I bargain shop, true. But at least I have earned all that I create. Earned it by myself with skill, not money. Created something original. Nothing was handed to me on a silver platter. No one hired seamstresses to do my work for me." Only Red would have caught the uncorrected tremor in the tone.

Red wanted to hear more. He knew all about the lack-of-silver-spoon status.

"See, here's the thing, friend," Britt continued. "Even after you finish your show and the crowd stands up and cheers for you, you'll never be sure if it was really for you. Or if the cheers are for your daddy's money that he donated to get you into SCAD. Or for all the work you outsourced. You'll never know if you created the magic or not. For that, I truly feel sorry for you."

Jenna gasped, her mouth a rosy pink O on a pale face.

Red crossed his arms. Fantastic job.

With utter efficiency, Britt pivoted fifteen degrees on her heel and strolled out of the classroom, leaving a gaping Jenna doing her best impression of a catfish drowning in pure, clean air.

Jenna ran a hand over her hair and tugged on another strand, recovering quickly as she batted her eyelashes at Red. "She's, uh, more of a charity case here. Doesn't know how lucky she is."

"I see it quite the opposite." He tried to step around, but Jenna clutched at his arm.

"So, can I give you my number?"

He pried her fingers off his arm and grinned, jaw tightening. "Sure, you can give me your number." His words dropped like lead sinkers in a stagnant pond.

The crew around Jenna gasped.

Not that he'd ever call. Ever the peacemaker, Red allowed her to type her info into his phone. Took forever, what with him needing to follow Britt.

Hurrying out of the classroom, he scanned up and down the halls. A glint of purple hair disappeared around a corner, providing him direction and purpose. Doing his level best to appear hunched and tentative while maintaining relentless forward progress, he wove between the students and followed Britt.

Anything else out of place here? Damn it, he hadn't reassessed before bulldozing down the hall. He was distracted.

Of course, he knew that Britt had another class. He knew her entire schedule. Knew her patterns—erratic at times, but she did have some structure to her day. God knew how that woman got so much done all helter-skelter during each twenty-four hours.

Catching up with her outside the next room, he called out, "Britt?"

Her back stiffened. When she spun around, the shimmer of a tear made her bright blue eyes glow. A tiny and imaginary knife twisted in his chest. He wanted to hold her, protect her. He couldn't afford to be blinded by emotion. Distractions meant death in his line of work.

Chapter Four

If it wouldn't have gotten her kicked out of school, Britt would have gladly sacrificed a few knuckles to shut up Jenna. That old-money suburban princess wasn't worth the risk of personal injury. But still, her words hurt.

Here Britt stood, Al bearing down on her. She put her armor on quickly. She tried to do a quick exercise the therapist had taught her to ground herself and reduce her swirling emotions.

He called out, "Britt?"

Okay. Exercise over. Did this overgrown Boy Scout give up? Anyone could see that she didn't want to chat. Before she could answer, his warm hand touched her shoulder and turned her, sure and steady, but relentless all the same. Before she could hide her feelings, he saw her face. Damn it.

"Yes?" Too bright. Too perky. He'd better not comment.

Forced happiness was all she had to work with right this minute. That, and a solid dose of citalopram. Thank God she had learned several years ago never to skip a dose of the anxiety medication.

He paused and tilted his head, staring at her behind those glasses like he was studying a map or planning a recipe. She didn't have time for reflective introspection or deep thoughts. She had real work to do before the semester ended, and it didn't involve Al. She sighed audibly.

His nostrils flared. Pupils dilated. He leaned forward with his head tilted, like he was listening carefully. Weird.

"So, um…" She pointed to the room.

Waving his schedule, he shrugged. "Me too."

Same class. What were the chances? Well, he was a transfer student in a similar major.

They entered the class, but this time he sat right next to her.

All throughout class, she observed him. Okay, not directly, because that would be creepy and rude. Chalk it up to curiosity and the McNeill sisters' most unmarketable skill: identifying when something didn't add up. Britt used that skill to guide her fashion choices, not that it had gotten her any jobs or money. Well, she had gotten the coveted SCAD Challenge Scholarship with her design, so that counted for something.

She watched Al.

Sure, he took notes on his new-appearing tablet. If she didn't know better, he was jotting down gibberish while staring at the room. Could be his Grandma being ill had him distracted. Maybe he didn't dig the Contemporary Issues in Fashion Merchandising class. The lecture topic today *was* dry.

Then there was the jumping.

Not jumping, exactly. More like, any noise no matter how small had him whipping his head around and focusing on the source of the sound. Was he startled? Not exactly. The guy's movements remained measured, deliberate. Every action had a purpose, unlike Britt who doodled fashion designs on her Sketchpad app during class. No. His response to sound was more ... hyperalert. Could be he was neurodivergent and sounds bothered him. That made more sense.

What didn't make sense? The whole time he was not listening but responding to sounds, Britt had the uncanny back-of-the-neck sense that he was concentrating on her. His big frame, crammed into the seat and slouched over the computer, remained rotated slightly toward her. Like he was monitoring her. Which was ridiculous, right?

Right?

She had to be imagining things. The stress from finishing her senior project, juggling work and school, and taking down rich bullies had all caught up to her. Somehow, she had projected her hang-ups onto this hapless, innocent new guy in school. Who had a tiny bit of bright orange hair peeking out from under the edge of his beanie, near his covered ear.

When the instructor concluded class, Britt packed up and slung her backpack over a shoulder. "Have a good day," she called to Al.

"Wait a second. Please." He fiddled around with his own Oakley shoulder tote, taking forever to put individual pens and the laptop and his book away. Every item had a specific slot.

She gritted her teeth and waited. Patience. So not her thing, at least according to her therapist. What about a cute, neurotic guy in a beanie? Also not her thing.

Most college students were several years younger than her twenty-six, what with her failure to launch and all. So he was probably early twenties. She peeked at him. Only, the set of his jaw and seriousness in his gaze suggested he'd lived through some stuff. Maybe he was a nontraditional student like Britt. Age compatible.

No. Quit it. She had a senior project to finish, college graduation, a last wish to fulfill, and family to finally make proud. Heck, she needed to shop for ideas and materials soon, all in the name of getting the collection completed—not that she wouldn't also enjoy the heck out of the retail activity. No way would any person stand in the way of her goals, regardless of how the light made his hazel eyes dance.

She sighed again when he took his sweet time

zipping up the bag. He whipped around, head tilted, like he'd heard her. She swallowed.

No one else remained in the room. Not that he scared her. He made her nervous, but not scared. Big difference.

A quick smile lit up his earnest face. "Any chance we could meet up tomorrow? Coffee. I'd like to thank you for helping me out on my first day here."

One: Why didn't his casual tone match his serious and alert expression?

Two: Coffee? What a big spender.

An immediate smear of shame squashed that last thought way down to the basement. Britt had no room to talk. Look at her, passing judgement. Had Mom been alive, she'd be very disappointed in Britt's presumption. The guy was new in town. He didn't know anyone. He was trying his best. What if all he could afford was coffee?

With him standing there, broad shoulders slumped, acrylic-frame glasses pushed up the bridge of his nose, wearing last decade's striped shirt, and sporting an eyebrow-raised pitiful expression, what woman could say no? Hell, Britt's ovaries couldn't decide if they wanted her to nurture him, jump him, or run for the hills.

Either way—*down, girls.*

Coffee. Ironic choice, considering her part-time job. Britt had access to all the coffee she could ever consume. That wasn't the point.

Sure, she could take some time out of her frenetic dash to the finish line of her college career to sit down and chat with Al.

"Okay." She named a café nearby that she *didn't* work at. "Ten tomorrow morning work for you?"

"You bet."

Air and silence filled the space between them.

"All right, then," she managed. Her tongue stuck to the roof of her mouth. "Um, see you then."

As he followed her out of the classroom, an aura of safety clung to him. Something in the way he moved that big body of his, kind of like a mountain lion, quiet and graceful and smooth, keeping a low profile, but ready to spring into action at any time.

Okay, truly she must be losing her mind romanticizing him as a stalking feline predator.

Britt didn't have time for distractions. Discussion over.

Chapter Five

Sure as shit, Red was the biggest tool around.

He should be at the coffee shop, chatting up Britt and earning her trust so he could get closer to her. Should be.

Instead, Red was breaking and entering at Britt's apartment during the precise time of their coffee date. It was the only decent opportunity when Britt and her roommate were both out of the apartment at the same time. Her roommate was visiting family for a few days, and planned to be back late this morning.

He would know. He had accessed both of their cell phone calendars and text messages. He had also checked those of the tenants on either side of them in this apartment building. Stumpy and his amazing tech wizardry came in handy yet again.

Adjusting his fake cable-company uniform hat, Red kept his sunglasses on as he passed a tenant on the concrete stairs. He glanced at his watch. Best guess was he had about a half hour before the window of opportunity closed.

The exposed, open-air stairwell made his skin crawl, and he brushed his hand over the hidden sidearm on the hip. As if a gun would help. Long rows of open passageways invited Lequire's guys to set up sniper nests in any number of buildings across the street. The odds were stacked against Britt and anyone else they targeted.

Time to even up those odds. He schlumped along with his fake, weapon-filled paunch down the row of apartment doors to peer down the next stairwell. Forget one point of ingress and egress—this place was a literal choose-your-own-kill box.

No way could he secure the building or even a

single apartment. The best protection Red could offer was surveillance cameras and a ring of perimeter security alarms to give him a head start if Lequire or his people went for her.

Actually, no. The best chance he had was if Lequire ignored Britt altogether and focused on her sister, Reagan, or the McNeill sisters' father.

Better yet would be if Lequire gave up his vendetta against all the McNeill family and shoved his corrupt ass back under the rock he'd slithered out from. Red couldn't hitch his mission success on that lousy hope.

As for Britt's safety now, Red was only one man. More boots were needed on the ground to provide adequate protection. The Morpheus Squad was spread too thin. Like his Special Forces brothers, Red would improvise.

Not only had he planted cameras at her workplace, the Mellow Bean, but also at the other café where she now waited for him. He swiped on the screen of his cell phone. A sharp color image of the shop filled the screen. He focused on Britt, a small figure sitting alone at a small table, toying with her phone and glancing at the door every time a customer entered.

A nasty acidic taste crawled up his throat. He couldn't care how she felt, as long as she survived. Britt's safety was all that mattered. Not her feelings.

He had to keep Britt safe from the goons working for Beaumont Lequire, the nasty CFO of Fallen Comrades, a fake charity that siphoned millions in donations into Lequire's pockets. Britt's sister, Kiera, had discovered the truth about Lequire, and now that asshole Lequire wanted revenge. The bastard had tried to kill Kiera two nights ago. Luckily, Kiera and her baby survived.

Kiera had the goods on powerful and politically connected Lequire, and if she made that information public, Lequire and his complicit Senator father would be ruined. Lequire would do anything to silence her, include leveraging her family members' lives.

Britt.

If one believed the threats—and Red had zero reason not to—then the next McNeill that Lequire targeted would suffer.

The thought of Britt's face, twisted in pain, while that sick bastard hurt her? He stopped short of putting his fist through the wall. *Breathe*: in, out, in, out. The humming tones in his head faded away to allow him to focus and filter natural sound in his environment.

Time to finish this surveillance project so he could go back to being in physical proximity to Britt. He'd also have to eat some crow for standing her up.

He knocked loudly as the cable guy, then used his pick device. A quick flick of his wrist gained him access to the small apartment. After another glance across the front door walkway balcony, ridiculously exposed to the parking lot, he eased into the living room.

Every color of the rainbow assaulted him from every corner of the space. Mismatched pillows of all textures adorned a threadbare love seat. He ducked into one bedroom and gasped. If he wore pearls, he'd be clutching them. It was a scene straight out of that hoarding TV show. What he'd give to discard items and organize the space. Color and fabric combinations assaulted him. Pictures and art hung everywhere. Bare wall was a rare commodity.

At least he could easily hide a bug. God knew what else could hide in the wall-to-wall towers of moveable plastic storage. The space was clean, but cluttered. Quickly he planted a device under a lamp base, tucked one into a window frame, and another on top of the closet. Red backpedaled out of the space.

The next room? Total opposite.

Neat and tidy. Sparsely furnished. The quilt on the bed appeared lovingly made but worn. Homemade floral curtains hung from a plain metal rod over a small window. On a wood laminate nightstand sat a picture of Britt with her two sisters and her brother, Brady.

Family. Something Red had never truly experienced. Oh, sure, his teammates made for a motley group of brothers, but it wasn't the same as growing up together. The ever-changing foster siblings didn't count. He stared at the picture of four similar smiles.

Brady. He was a wounded vet and Red's brother-in-arms, who Lequire had killed for uncovering the truth of the Fallen Comrades charity.

A prickle on Red's shoulder blades accompanied a flash of anger, but he easily regained control over the impulse. At least he'd finally taken his regular antidote dose last night and slept for a few hours. The antidote was a bummer for his hearing acuity, but better for his self-control.

His cell phone rang as he planted a device high on top of a doorjamb. No way five-foot-nothing Britt could reach up there.

He thumbed to answer the video call. "Yeah."

"Ready to link up?" Stumpy's goateed face, lit in eerie blue light by monitors, filled the screen. Computer genius and handsome bastard, but wounded in combat. Badly. Didn't affect his ability to work miracles with a surveillance system, though.

"Roger." Red walked to the living room and attached a tiny button microphone to the back of a printed and plexiglass-framed Mia Vesper NYFW picture filled with brightly clad models. "How's the feed working?"

"Give me a sec. I'm doing this from a makeshift setup. We only occupied this space a few days ago."

"Hunt told me." Hunt. Their Special Forces CO both before and after the entire team had been inoculated. "The Bryson City compound was reduced to rubble, I heard."

"Great fun for demo man, Curly." He rubbed his dark facial hair with one hand. "Got it." He pointed at the screen, his illuminated face turning up, down, and side-to-side. Then Stumpy sat back. "Multiple feeds are online. Good job there, Red. Almost as good as I could do." He whistled low. "Holy fuck, that other room is a mess."

"You're not wrong. At least things hidden there will stay hidden."

"For sure."

Red snorted as he pressed another bug to the top of the compact refrigerator. "Hey, how is Kiera and her new baby? No ill effects from…"

"Kiera being drugged and sedated? The baby coming early? They're doing surprisingly well. That child has even our crusty ol' CO wrapped around her cute little finger."

"It's good for him." Red froze. "But Jake's baby is … okay?" Their teammate had conceived this child.

"Doc says she's as healthy as a six-pound bundle of joy can be." Keyboard clicks accompanied Stumpy rolling his lips together, the two parts of his goatee meeting in the middle. "No issues from Jake's virus that we can tell."

"Thank God."

"Got that right. How's the mission with Britt?"

"Exhausting. This woman doesn't stop moving. Ever." Except for now. He pulled up the feed. She sat in

the café, chin on her hands, staring at the table. *Damn it.*
He flipped back to Stumpy's face.

"If she can wear you out, then that's saying a lot.
How'd you get uninterrupted access to the apartment?"

"Uh. Stood her up for a date."

"My man, that's cold." A gleam lit the computer
expert's narrowed eyes as he leaned closer to the screen.
"Hmm."

"What?"

"You feel bad about that, don't you?"

A wash of heat poured through Red's chest. "It's
a nasty move to pull, yes."

"But—"

"But nothing, Stump. I have a mission to
complete. This is business."

White teeth flashed on the screen. "Methinks he
protests too much."

"Bug off." Red chuckled. "Or bug on, as the case
may be." He glanced toward the front door, imagining
Lequire's men right outside, waiting. Egress, ingress. He
catalogued time and distance, over and over. "All done?"

Another series of clicks, and Stumpy nodded.
"We're set. You should be able to see the feeds on your
devices as well."

He did a quick test to confirm. "Good. I gotta get
moving." He patted his legs, hip, and lower back.
Weapons secure and accessible. As if he needed to
check.

Stumpy turned his head and hollered over his
shoulder, then turned back to Red. "Hold up, Hunt's
here. Stay tight, my man." He gave a two-fingered salute
and disappeared.

"You too." Hunt's lantern-jaw face with the salt-
and-pepper flattop filled the screen, and Red instinctively
snapped to attention. "Sir."

"Sitrep."

"No discernable activity from Lequire's camp here. Team status?"

"Operational." He rubbed his square chin with the palm of a meaty hand. "All's quiet with Rivera and Pele right now. That doesn't reassure me." His grinding voice sounded like gravel falling into a pit.

"Roger that. No activity I can detect here. Thought maybe I heard something yesterday, but it was my ears getting too sensitive."

Hunt squinted. "You staying on top of your antidote?" Right. Because Red was the fastest cycler on the team when it came to how frequently he required temporary suppression of the virus.

Doc and Hunt had theories as to what would happen if the soldiers missed the absolute cutoff times for their antidotes. Theories that no one wanted to test. Best guess: you didn't come back once the virus took you over the edge of sanity. Red scrubbed his face. "Yes, sir. Plenty of supply here. I'm on top of it."

"Good, because you're it until we get things buttoned up here. Christ, we're rebuilding our entire world. It's going to be weeks before we're fully operable and secure. Pele's got his hands full wrangling the other McNeill sister, and God knows how many drinks and card games Rivera will have to endure if he's going to stick close to their dad."

Red shook his head. "What if things get FUBAR down here?"

"Improvise. Remove Ms. McNeill from the situation if necessary."

"With respect, that move would go over like a ton of pissed-off bricks. Also, our team doesn't exist, and kidnapping is illegal."

"You're not there to be popular. This whole op is

gray." Hunt's next words iced Red's blood. "You have one objective: keep that woman alive."

Chapter Six

That rat.

That unfashionable bag of crap.

Arrgh. Britt flexed her fingers while she walked, imagining her hands around that jerk's thick neck. Over an hour she had wasted, sitting at the dumb coffee shop, not ordering coffee. A dull headache throbbed behind her eyes. Figured. Now that she headed back to her apartment, she needed caffeine.

Stupid. How dumb could she be?

Britt had even taken the time to select an outfit for the not-date. Something that conveyed less edgy poor student, more feminine and pulled-together adult. The brown loafers and brown tights paired well with a deep-blue shirtdress, belted at the waist. Topped by an unbuttoned brown cardigan, Britt figured she looked as close to "professional" as a gal like her ever could. All dressed up…

Well, with the effort she'd put into her attire and the lousy results, it looked like a sign from God: concentrate on graduating and avoid any dumb distractions. She didn't have time for a punctual guy in her life, much less a tardy son of a gun.

Checking her watch as she climbed the stairs to the apartment, she grimaced. Not enough time to do everything: study, lunch, nap, and class. Her stomach rumbled. Lunch was the priority. Another twinge flitted across her forehead. Okay, maybe fix the caffeine deficiency first, then lunch. She nodded at a tall, muscled man in a black button-down shirt and jeans whistling as he passed her on the stairs. She glanced back. The guy strolled away, an upbeat tune fading away into the sounds of late-morning traffic.

Damn her for falling for Al's, *aw shucks I'm new*

in town, schtick. To think, she had helped him. Enough. Not like coffee with Al would have led to anything else.

As she turned the key and opened the door, a hint of pine and aftershave wafted past her. What the actual heck? Now she hallucinated his scent.

Britt was making a sandwich while still muttering to herself when her roommate popped out of her bedroom, wearing leggings and a semifitted geometric-patterned blouse.

"Hi, honey! Ooh, love the outfit." Tachi flipped mahogany waves back over her shoulders and flashed her perfect smile. Her tall, shapely presence commanded attention, even when she wasn't modeling.

Tucking her chin, Britt glanced down at her nonexistent chest. Oh, hell. How could she get mad at the nicest roommate in the universe? Britt indulged in one second of self-pity, then pulled herself out of it. "You're back! How were the parentals?"

"Good. The usual. Good ol' Kimiko and Juan with their usual twenty questions about my love life … which is nonexistent, bee-tee dubs. Am I getting three squares per day? What about my career? When am I going to become successful? What's next if modeling doesn't work out? They are lovely people, but exhausting."

"Oh my gosh!"

"I'm used to it." Her friend's dark eyes glowed in her flawless face. "But speaking of career, guess what? I just got booked for *Atlanta Magazine*!"

"That's awesome!" Britt stood on tiptoes to give her roomie a hug. "Was it a 'My Style' article?"

"I wish." Tachi stepped back. "Tibi has a new line of handbags. Someone has to show them off, and they picked me for the spread. The bags are gorge! I might get to keep one!"

"Wow! You're going to blow everyone away with fierce pictures. Just remember us little people when you make it big, okay?"

"For you, I'll make an exception and won't block your phone number." She stretched her back gracefully. Too bad her friend was super nice. Made it hard to hate her for being so effortlessly beautiful.

That smile fell. Dark lashes framed her narrowed eyes as she crossed her arms. "Spill it, Britt. Now."

Crap. "What? Nothing. Just a little moody." Britt sidled over to the countertop to complete the sandwich.

Tachi's elegant hand caught the refrigerator door and eased it closed. "I know moody. This is more than moody."

"Thought you were an art school graduate, not a psychologist," Britt grumbled. Her friend didn't move an inch. "Fine. New guy in school asked me for coffee and then no showed. End of story."

"Uh-huh. What else?"

"Nothing else." Britt played with the hoop on her lip. "I'm stressed. Jenna friggin' Woodruff is acting extra privileged and pissy these days. Senior collection is next week. Work is … work. Gotta show up if I want money." She blew out a long puff of air. "I'm tired of being a perpetual student." She hated not measuring up in her family of solid, focused, hardworking people. Also, she wanted to fulfill Mom's dying wish that Britt graduate.

Man, she missed her mom. And her dad and sisters. No time to visit, with the crazy end of the school year. Hopefully they could attend her senior show next week. What she'd give for Mom and Brady to still be alive, to see what she'd done. Britt would give just about anything to hug them once more. A bubbly, sad hiccup hit her below the ribs. God, the past few years had sucked so badly.

"All right, darling." Tachi leaned a hip on the counter and tilted her head. "Then what can I do to help? Kick a boy's butt? Cheerlead? Ply you with alcohol? What?"

"How about let's burn off some steam tonight? Dancing!"

Tachi's mouth drooped. "Can't. Have to work." She leaned back against the counter, her long legs taking up the scarce room in the kitchen area. "Need the tips from the pole, or my part of the rent and the monthly student loan payment isn't going to happen. Slave to the grind, so to speak."

A giggle burst from Britt. Her friend raked in good money. "Sounds fair. I should work on my collection anyway."

Tachi didn't meet her eyes. "Got your models lined up?"

"Yes. And for the millionth time, it's teen fashion. Don't get all bent out of shape. You're not exactly a sixteen-year-old's image of … well, actually, you *are* a sixteen-year-old's dream. But the theme isn't 'excited teenagers.' It's more about teen confidence."

Tachi waved her buff nails. "Sure, sure. You couldn't afford my fees anyway."

****

After a not-so-exciting afternoon class on marketing, without the new guy in attendance, Britt spent several long hours in the fashion lab. Her corner table sat away from murmuring classmates, near a window. Her little nook was surrounded by forms draped with various fabrics. Pins winked on several outfits. Britt rolled her shoulders as she scooted the stool up to the table so she could guide material through the foot of the Singer. The sewing machine chugged along, dropping straight seams into the fabric. The rhythmic noise was mind-numbing, but satisfying. It felt good to bring a concept to life with her own two hands.

Pacing the work space, she added new ideas to the project board and adjusted the order of the show. She built the theme in a more organic manner. The first two models would start out with the more muted yet trendy clothes, then the colors and fabrics would become brighter, the clothing cuts edgier through all six looks. Even though each senior collection was a small part of the larger SCAD fashion show, Britt pretended that this was all her own fashion show. Britt even had her dream lineup of music including Sia, Lizzo, Little Mix, and a healthy helping of Beyonce, all playing through her earbuds on repeat. Anything to stay in the creative mood.

Her heart leapt as she considered next week's event. The SCAD fashion show typically attracted the Who's Who of Atlanta fashion. Students had launched entire careers with their collections. Pull this project off, and it could open doors for Britt that she couldn't even begin to imagine. Screw it up … she'd be serving a lot of coffee. Not that being a waitress was bad. It wasn't. But it didn't fulfill her dream of designing for HaMo or Always Youth lines. Heck, designing for anyone.

A wave of uncontrolled anxiety hit her so hard, she staggered back on her heels, thoughts of failure whirling through her brain. Her hands shook, heart raced. Throat closed up. Air wouldn't move. She stood facing the window so the other students in the lab wouldn't notice her having a standing heart attack.

What should she do? She was going to die. A tiny voice in her mind said, *You won't die. You can be okay.* Okay, she sucked in a lungful of air. She could take care of herself. Britt had the tools. Thanks to several years of therapy, she knew what to do to abort the panic. She had practiced so many times with the therapist and on her own.

Britt stood utterly still, hands pressed to her sides, letting herself feel how solid and stable the ground was underneath her feet. She was safe. This location was safe. She loved working in the fashion lab. No one would ever hurt her here.

Safe place. Breathed in.

Safe place. Breathed out.

Feel the ground. Breathed in.

Solid. Stable. Breathed out.

Then she anchored herself by identifying things based on her senses. What could she see, smell, and touch?

She opened her eyes and stared at the whiteboard bolted to the wall next to the window. Inhaled the clean cotton scent of cloth and the light oil smell of warm, working sewing machines. Crumpled the hem of the brown cardigan in her fists. Knit material. Soft. Familiar.

Safe.

After a few more minutes to breathe and anchor, and Britt had come out of the worst of the panic, thank God. She wiped her cramped, sweaty hands on her cardigan and turned back to the table.

A few hours later, after completing another outfit, she leaned back, rubbing her forehead and rolling her tight shoulders and neck. Only a few students remained in the lab. Twilight outside. She checked her watch: 7:00. Wow, no wonder her back ached and her eyes burned. Her stomach growled. Time to go home.

Early morning shift at work tomorrow, then midmorning classes. Classes with Al and Jenna. Fabulous.

After tidying up her workspace, she pulled on her long-discarded loafers and her cardigan and slung the backpack over a shoulder. With a wave to the remaining students still working in the lab, she ducked out of the classroom.

"Hi."

Britt yelped and jumped back, nearly dropping her backpack.

Al looked up from where he leaned against the white hallway wall and stowed his phone. A flick of his gaze over her, and his eyes narrowed behind those black-framed glasses. The ghost of a wary smile curved his mouth.

Her stomach took a nosedive. No. That reaction wasn't interest, it was jitters. Also, she was pissed that he'd stood her up. She was anything but…

Then he did that puppy dog eyes thing with those dark-red eyebrows, somehow making her feel guilty for being grumpy. Unable to stop herself, she smiled back at him. Then went back to what she hoped was a mean scowl.

"Britt, I'm sorry about earlier today."

"Huh." Not the first words she had expected to come out of his mouth. She crossed her arms. "Go on."

He ducked his head. Goddamn how the beanie and—she squinted—the uncreased tan t-shirt and stiff brown denim jacket made him appear casual but pulled together at the same time. Still seemed like too much effort to look effortless.

She rubbed her gritty eyes. Wow, did she need sleep.

Shoving his phone in a pocket, he said, "Granny had some issues this morning. I had to help her get to a doctor's appointment and then bring her back home."

Some excu—what? She studied his earnest expression. Her lungs deflated, along with her pride. Well, crap.

"Your granny?" she managed to spit out.

A half-smile. "I would have called you, but..." He patted the pocket. "Somehow didn't manage to enter your number, because my life is a complete mess."

Not ready to give up, she pressed him. "What was wrong with your granny?"

"Uh, she was having trouble with her diabetes. Feeling weak. Needed help adjusting medications and then picking them up at the pharmacy. While I was at her house, I fixed some electrical stuff."

"Now you're an electrician?"

His gaze hit hers, then slid away. "I have some skills in that area, yes."

"No way."

"I wasn't always a fashion student, you know." Why did that statement sound proud and wistful and cagey? He waved a hand to cut off her next question. "Enough about me. I was waiting here, hoping to apologize and make it up to you."

In a flash, Britt went from irritated to intrigued. Mostly, because her brain projected every permutation of "make it up to you" in vivid panorama. A piece of what he said penetrated her hazy mind. "You were waiting here?"

When he rubbed his neck, the movement drew her attention to the cords of lean muscle not hidden by the jacket. He shrugged. "It's late, huh? You must be working hard."

"Wait. You've been out here for how long?"

"A while."

"Like a stalker?"

"Hell, I hope not." He fished for his phone and thumbed through a few screens. "Here. Proof of Granny." A picture of a smiling gray-haired woman filled the screen.

"This could be anyone."

"My God, you're making me sweat." He took the phone back and swiped a few more times. "Try this one." The odd angle of two selfie faces greeted her. Al and his granny.

She rocked back on her heels. Didn't Britt feel like an idiot. He had been telling the truth all along. "So why didn't you come into the lab?"

"Didn't want to bother you. Also, kind of chicken. Figured I was in the doghouse after earlier today. Interrupting you might have ended my life." Another sheepish grin. But there was an intensity behind it that didn't quite fit. Like he was trying too hard to be meek, while also assessing everything around him.

He *was* trying to apologize. And the pictures counted for something, right?

Uncrossing her arms, she hooked a thumb under a backpack strap. Mom had always said to give people grace. Britt could be cautious and give grace at the same time. "Okay."

"Um, okay what?"

A smile stretched her cheeks. "Okay, I'll spot you this one. Sounds like your granny needed the help today."

He stared at the floor. "You have no idea." He propped a booted sole flat against the wall. "Dinner?"

"Sure, what day?"

"Tonight?" It wasn't a question.

Chapter Seven

At the rate Red had to duck out to "run to the restroom" at the restaurant, Britt probably thought he had a nervous bladder or a prostate the size of a honeydew. Couldn't be helped. His damn phone kept buzzing in his pocket and he needed to see what triggered the alarms.

As he flipped through the security camera images while standing in the bathroom stall of the Asian fusion restaurant, his muscles twitched. Compulsively, he rechecked the weapons hidden on his lower back and legs. Antidote onboard or not, his body responded to threats of danger. How much of his response was due to the way the virus had changed him and how much came from Red's own internal constitution, he didn't care to evaluate.

Bottom line: Lequire's men were now casing the neighborhood. He had visual proof as of a few hours ago. Red had no backup. Not like he didn't have experience managing on his own business, but this was more than one man could handle.

Damn it. There were multiple trained mercenaries out there, fueled by a desperate man with unlimited financial resources. There was only one Red. The math did not favor him. He would have to get creative in his protection duties.

He exited the restroom and peeked from behind the waiter's station. Britt couldn't see him without craning her neck around. Red narrowed his eyes as he studied the few remaining patrons. Their quiet conversations tapped like a gentle rain on a metal roof. The peppery clink of utensils on plates provided light percussion. No other abnormal sounds came from inside or outside the restaurant. Still, anyone might threaten

Britt.

Pissing him off the most was the glass front of the establishment, and the straight-line shot that gave anyone wanting to hurt her. Not like he could dissuade her choice of restaurant after he had thrown himself at her feet and ate proverbial crow. Still, this open location wouldn't be his first choice.

If the images from his security monitors and the texts from Hunt were to be believed, then Lequire had gotten over his Sunday night Morpheus Squad-sponsored ass kicking at his headquarters only a few miles from here. Today was Tuesday. Lequire would likely respond soon. Closest target: Britt.

Next problem: Red not only had to get her safely home, he then had to stick to her like glue. Easier said than done, as he was still in the doghouse from his Granny-excused absence earlier today. He rubbed his neck, the short hair at the nape and the beanie fabric making shushing cotton sheet noises against his skull. Twenty-four hours since his last shot. Amazing how quickly his hearing rebounded. Damned virus wanted to get right back out there and play some more.

He was cycling faster nowadays.

At some point, the antidote wouldn't be enough. Then what?

Later. He'd deal with things like insanity later.

Ensuring his phone was on silent mode, he eased into the seat across from Britt. He hated having his back to the window, but at least he could physically obscure her as a target. The prickles over his neck urged him to sit up straight, place his body in the way of anything that threatened her, and keep her safe.

The mission required that he stay in character. Shoulders remaining slumped, he flashed her a quick smile. The fluttering uncertainty in her gaze as she toyed with an earring made his arms twitch with the need to wrap around her.

Feelings had no place here.

All that mattered was the mission.

"This was a nice meal," he mumbled. God knew what they'd talked about, he'd been so distracted. He put some twenties in the little black folder and pushed back in his seat.

"Sure. Thanks for dinner." No smile. She didn't mimic his motion with her chair. Instead she leaned forward, eyes narrowed. Uh-oh.

Asking the question was both terrifying and necessary. "Something wrong?"

She crossed her arms. *Oh, shit.* "Why did we come here tonight, Al?"

"To make up for my missing coffee earlier. And you picked the place."

"That's not what I meant."

He had no spit to swallow, but he tried to wet his lips anyway. "Not sure I understand the question."

"We're *here*, together. But you're not here at all. You checked out a while ago. What's the deal?" A metal hoop winked in the low light as her brows drew together.

"There's no deal. Just tired after a long day."

"Then why not wait to have dinner after you got some rest?"

"I don't follow." Strange zaps of irritation popped him like a million mosquitoes. "Look, I apologized for missing you earlier, and here we are now. I wanted to make things up to you. End of story." He patted the table as if to go.

Britt didn't budge. "There's something weird about you."

"I'm a fashion student. We're all a little quirky."

She stared at him for way too long. "Not sure I

buy that."

A drop of sweat rolled down the hollow of his lower spine near his holstered Sig. "Britt. Look, we're both tired. You worked hard today at the shop and then at school." *Time to go home and rest, okay? Let's get you out of this particular kill box.*

Her sharp intake of breath sliced through him. Color leached out of her face, making her electric-blue eyes glow. "I never told you about my job."

Fuuuck. "One of your classmates mentioned it."

"Which one?"

He mentally went through data files like a rat in a desperate maze. "Saleisha, I believe. Sits in front of you in History of Fashion."

"Hmm." Arms stayed crossed. Eyes remained narrowed. Her dark-plum lips parted, like he imagined they magically would right before he kissed her.

Only this wasn't a fairy tale and he was no Prince Charming.

"Name your three favorite designers," she said.

"What?"

"Do it. And explain why you like them."

More mental scanning. "Wow. Uh, hard to pick just three." Scanning. Scanning. At least Gonzo had given him data to work with, thank God. "Rohit Bal, Stella McCartney mostly because I don't like animal cruelty. And although some would disagree, Kenzo Takada, because"—he grasped for the info Gonzo and Stumpy had given him—"of his work with color and textures and a joyful approach to fashion."

"Those are really all over the map."

"Is that a crime?" Because literally everything else he was doing to keep her safe was indeed a crime. Citing fashion mavens was a fucking pastime in comparison. "Someone can't like diverse designers? Or maybe I don't fit the mold of someone who should enjoy fashion." Truth: he kind of hated it.

"Um."

He kept rolling, getting her on her back foot. Covert-ops Civilian Management 101. Keep the objecting party off-balance. Then direct her toward safety.

"Why the interrogation, Britt? I'm just a guy who's new in town who wanted to take you out for dinner. I'm sorry Granny got sick. Bad timing." He pulled what he hoped was a sad guy expression. "A simple 'thank you' would work fine." He rubbed his forehead and huffed for good measure. "Man."

Her lips dropped into a frown. "Wow." She blinked a few times and pulled her head back. "Hey, I'm super sorry. That was all very judge-y and that's not like me at all. It's—you were acting strange and stuff."

Forcing a smile, he said, "How about we chalk everything up to us both being tired and stressed for various reasons, and then let me take you home?"

Her facial expression did another deer-in-the-headlights move.

He put up his hands. "Just seeing you safely home, I swear. Nothing more. Perfect gentleman here."

After giving him another flop-sweat inducing stare, she stood and handed him her heavy backpack. "Okay, then." He slung the bag over his shoulder nearest Britt, so he could keep his outside hand free to grab a weapon or respond to a threat. Awkward positioning, but he'd make it work.

Once they exited the restaurant and strolled on the lightly traveled city sidewalk, Red's senses went into overdrive. Every sound translated into a potential threat, and God help him, there were a lot of sounds. The humid, cool evening air didn't calm him. Cars rolled down the street, taunting him to identify make, model, and trajectory based on engine rumble. A duller roar tasted tangy and smelled of asphalt, indicating the nearby interstate exchange.

Damn it, there weren't enough security sensors to protect Britt. He needed more boots on the ground, and that was the one thing he didn't have.

Walking between Britt and the street, Red asked about her upcoming senior collection.

After ten minutes of animated explanation, she finished describing the teen-friendly theme. "It's going to be great!"

If he had even a small aptitude for fashion, her enthusiasm would have inspired him to start sketching. He shifted her backpack on his shoulder, the scent of hibiscus drifting over him from the material.

"Best of all, it will be done-done. Nothing will stop me now!"

"What do you mean?" he asked.

"Um, nothing."

"No, please go on."

She huffed. "It's just taken me a while to get to this point in my life. That's all."

Only, that wasn't the whole story and Red knew it. "I think there's more."

A pause. "Once I figured out what I wanted to do with my life, this"—waving her arms around in the general Atlanta buildings and street next to them—"fine arts degree was the path to my dream career. For that to happen, I have to show my senior collection."

"You're still planning to participate?" Terrible idea. The one place less secure than her apartment was a large gathering around an open stage with random people all over the place and no control over ingress and egress points. "Wow, you're really into it," he mumbled.

"Why wouldn't I be?" She continued talking, but his attention shifted elsewhere.

A scuffling noise as they passed an alley made every muscle in his body go tense. He almost stood up straight and half-pivoted into a fighting stance before catching himself. *Come on, man. Slouch. Stay in character.*

"Are you okay?" she asked, silver winking as her brows shot up. The streetlights and shop signs in twilight's glow gave her face a yellowish-gray cast.

"Yeah, fine." On instinct, his hand drifted to rest on her lower back, urging her to walk faster.

They passed another block and another alley. No abnormal sounds this time.

Britt stopped. "What's going on with you? For real? You're super jumpy." She turned and faced him squarely, feet planted. "What's the deal?"

Why were they stopping? No stopping. He had to get her to safety.

She crossed her arms and planted her feet.

Shit.

He hated dishonesty, but mission first. Failure in his duty could lead to her death. Simple as that. Praying he could keep up with the lies blended with half-truths, he said, "Part of my college tuition is paid by the GI Bill."

"I don't under—oh." She studied him. "*Oh.*" When she faced him, the light behind and above her cast her features into haunting shadow. "You're jumpy, because…"

When in doubt, stick to as much truth as possible and pile on emotional baggage for believability. "Yeah, I served in the Army. Ground troops." *Fact.* "Faced serious action." *Fact, although his most recent action was when his lab-rat ass evaded capture by Uncle Sam.*

"Saw some, uh, bad things." *Fact, if you considered the injuries Britt's brother Brady sustained on a team mission. Stumpy's accident. Every tortuous task the military had asked the Morpheus Squad to do.* "Since returning stateside, some ... effects of my deployment have lingered." *Also fact, though it was splitting hairs. The virus didn't so much linger as threaten his entire existence. Close enough.*

"Wow. I'm sorry. I had no idea."

"No need to be sorry." Time to pull the heartstrings. He laid the bull on thick. "I'm here, which is more than I can say for some of my buddies." He let his words fade into the night air and gave a small shake of his head for good measure.

"Thank you for your service."

He followed the line of her throat as she swallowed.

"I know bad things can happen overseas." She stared at the concrete for a second.

He tried for a lighter tone. "But we're here now, right?"

"So, fashion major?" A hint of a smile and a twinkle in her eyes eased the rapid switch in conversation.

He nudged her shoulder to get her walking again. Anything to move her closer to relative safety. His neck itched with imagined laser sights targeting him. "Hey, I got tired of OCP."

"OCP?"

"Operational Camouflage Pattern. Didn't bring out my tones and highlights. Sure as hell didn't do anything for my figure."

The laugh that bubbled out of her knocked him down like an Abrams Tank and then lightly rolled right over him. He wanted to feel that sound more. He wanted to be the reason she laughed.

"Rebelling against a frustrating camo pattern might be the weirdest reason for pursuing a degree, but I can't argue your logic." She paused and peered at him. "So, you're more of a nontraditional student, then?"

"In every sense of the word." Also facts. "Unlike most of the students, I'm a wizened twenty-five-year-old."

"Don't feel too bad, Gramps, I'm twenty-six."

Of course he already knew that.

He offered an arm. The brush of her fingers against his forearm made his stomach drop like the plunge from a tower rappel. He drew her closer to him as they walked. "We make good company as the resident old folks."

"Hmm," she murmured as they strolled far too slowly in companionable silence for another few blocks.

Turning into the apartment complex, he spied a flicker of movement near the corner of a building. His phone buzzed in the hip pocket pressed next to Britt. Damn it. Couldn't answer.

He reached out with his hearing, focusing beyond the rumble of traffic and the gritty crunch of their shoes on pavement. Someone in a shadow breathed, harsh and deep. Quick rasps. Like they had run here. Sounded like larger lung capacity, so probably male or tall female. The *thump* of a pulse filled the space like a sweaty bass drum. Every thud tasted like salt.

"Earth to Al."

He barely registered the tug on his arm. He straightened his bent arm and she removed her hand. There was a cold place on his skin where her palm had been. He needed that contact, grounding him.

Another heartbeat sounded, closer and lighter. Britt's rapid pulse. "We're here. Ah, thank you for dinner." She motioned toward the backpack he held.

"I'll walk you to your door." He gritted out, separating sound input from the shadows and from the woman in front of him. Too many signals. Too much danger. The virus drove him to surround her with his body. Anything to protect her.

A hand fluttered over her face. "This isn't, um, an invitation to come up. Or…"

"I'm not asking for … I've been taught to see a woman safely home. All the way home." Sort of true. Years ago, he had made sure his foster siblings got home, for all the safety that had waited for them there. "Ladies first."

When she preceded him up the stairs, the line of her hips swaying gently beneath that dress distracted him. Or was it those delicate limbs in the tights? Hard to say.

At the door of her apartment, he handed her the backpack and she fished in it, pulling out keys. "Thanks, Al. This was a strange but nice night."

Extending his senses, he couldn't detect anyone else in the immediate vicinity. No heavy footstep on nearby concrete. No rasping deep breath coming closer. "I agree. Maybe we can do this again sometime."

There was no mission-based reason to desire her.

Tap, tap. At that butterscotch-sweet patter of her pulse so close, he licked his lips.

All that remained was hunger.

Before Red registered the movement, he grazed her cheek with the pad of his thumb. The click of her swallow bloomed a pinkish-red color in his mind. He followed the smooth line of her neck with his fingertips. In the external corridor lights, her pupils pushed back the irises until they became thin disks of dim color.

Keeping his hand on her neck, he bent down until

the cotton-candy sound of her breath rasping through her lips tempted him.

The virus begged to come out and play. It wanted to feast, to mark, to encircle her.

Red's brain short-circuited at her tiny sigh. "May I?" he whispered. So close.

"Me first. Age before beauty." She slid a hand up his chest and around his neck, drawing him down the few inches to meet her mouth. The soft rasp of her lips brushing against his brought a bright white pop of light and mint color to the sound. Delicious.

The act of stroking Britt's sweet mouth turned his entire body into a detector for every little noise she made. Each new audio input set his nerves on fire and ramped up the virus. Soft. She was so soft. His fingers shook as he held back viral urges as he caressed her face. Carefully, so carefully. He traced the rings in her eyebrow and lip with his mouth. Well, almost everything about her was soft. The contrasts of gentle and fierce, pliable and hard, came together perfectly in Britt.

No problem maintaining his slouch now. He had to lean over to reach her mouth. Gliding hands down her back, he eased the backpack off her arm and onto the stoop. He settled his grip at her waist, spanning her easily. Right at the moment when he considered how fragile she was, Britt growled and nipped his lower lip between her teeth. The rough brush of her tongue over his? The sound bounced off his eardrums in a major chord of pleasure that tasted like honey.

A rush of need floored his inner accelerator, and he shifted, pressing her against the exterior wall, spreading his legs and bending his knees to reduce his height and lean against her, going hip to hip and chest to chest with Britt. To avoid her finding his concealed weapons, he laced his fingers with hers and pinned her hands over her head.

The higher pitch of her moan as he changed the slant of his mouth. Sure as shit, it sounded like angels eating cupcakes.

He left her lips long enough to taste his way down her neck to the hollow at the base of her throat. Delicious. He'd like seconds. And thirds.

The mission.

He needed her trust. He needed her safe. What would be safer than him wrapped around her? Naked, in bed?

Damn it. What else was happening within this field of operation? He had no idea.

His mission objective had become his biggest barrier to success.

Easing her hands back down to her sides, he kissed her one more time and then stepped back.

"Okay. Wow," she breathed.

His chest rose and fell like he'd rucked ten miles uphill. "You can say that again."

She licked her lips, then grimaced. "I'd ask you in, but my roommate…"

"That's not why I kissed you." Liar. Too soon. Too much. Too … not what he was here for. Conflict of interest was the least of his concerns.

Nodding, she blinked once. Twice. "All right, then." Her hand shook as she fumbled with the lock on the door and picked up her backpack. "Good night."

Before she could turn the door handle, he caught her by the upper arm, his hand easily wrapping around the limb. "Britt."

He dropped another mouth-scorching kiss on her lips until they were both panting.

Stepping back, he brushed a thumb over his own mouth, savoring her taste. "Good night."

With a wobbly smile, she slipped inside the apartment. The lock clicked.

Chapter Eight

Britt closed the door and leaned against the hard surface. Her lips tingled. Her legs trembled. Had she almost?

Yes, she had happily *almost*.

Al. What an odd guy. He went from shy to confident and back in the blink of an eye. He spewed fashion info like an expert, but couldn't pair fabric blends to save his life.

She slumped onto the couch with a creak of old springs and flicked on the lamp. A nasty taste settled in the back of her throat. Fashion snob much?

The guy had missed out on a chunk of fashion timeline while deployed. For all she knew, he might have been too busy staying alive to keep up with trends. Now he had a chance to follow his own dream. Nothing wrong with that, aside from her judgement of him. She sighed and rubbed her neck, still feeling his firm but gentle touch.

"That you?" Tachi drifted into the living room and paused, unwrapping the towel around her damp hair. She wore an oversized AC/DC sleep shirt over boxers which did little to conceal her long legs. "Oh." She paused and squinted, typical nearsighted Tachi without her glasses or contacts. She snagged her cat-eye glasses off the kitchen table, tossed the towel on the floor, and sat on the love seat, facing Britt. "That's a dreamy look. Do tell."

"Nothing to tell."

"Nuh-uh. I've known you since Zandrew introduced us after his show four years ago." She shook out wet waves with her fingers. "Your neck and cheeks are bright pink. And if I'm not mistaken, that's a patch of stubble burn. Spill, darling."

Warmth climbed Britt's chest and worked up into her face at the memory of *those lips*, mere minutes ago. Busted. "Even if there was something to tell, the story doesn't go anywhere. I have a degree to finish and a senior project due that can make or break my career. I *will* finish it all." She sighed. "There's no time for anything or anyone else."

One dark eyebrow rose. "Your smoochy-looking lips suggest that you've freed up a little extra time on the schedule."

"Fine." Britt sighed. "His name is Al and he's the new student in school. We had dinner and a kiss afterward. End of story."

"That story is insultingly short on details." She sniffed. "Wait. Is this the guy who stood you up for a date? Because I hope there's a chapter about you chewing his ass out for that."

"I did, actually."

"But?"

"He stood me up because his granny was sick."

Tachi fanned herself. "Well, there go my ovaries. I assume you gave him credit for the granny assist?" She gave an unabashed broad laugh, and Britt couldn't help but smile back. "Of course you gave him credit! Right on the lips."

"That's maybe not exactly how it went down." She swept a finger across her mouth, skin still tingling from his possessive kisses.

"Yeah, no. I'm going to need more than that."

"Really, that's all. I'd love to make more time for him, but I have to finish my degree. Tachi, I can't fail again." Her eyelids prickled. Tears now? She blinked hard. Chalk the reaction up to stress, an emotional roller coaster of fulfilling Mom's last wishes for Britt, plus finally having the finish line in sight. "For once in my life, I have to complete what I started, and no guy is going to distract me from that goal."

"Could you do both? The guy and the goal?"

Britt snorted a laugh. "I'm all for multitasking, but I'm not going to risk it. School first. Try to land an internship or position with one of the big houses. Then if there's time left, I can check out Al."

"What if he's not around by the time you accomplish all of these things?"

"Quit threatening me with FOMO! Not going to work." Britt's head lolled back on the cushion and she grimaced. "First of all, I want to prove to my family that I'm not the flighty one who can't complete any task or life goal."

Tachi paused, wistful expression on her face. "You want them to be proud of you."

"Of course." Rubbing her eyes with the heels of her hands, she tried to scour the image of Al blocking all the light as he filled up the space around her. Wow, how her body had responded to him. She crossed her legs. "Second of all, if he's the right person, then he'll still be there later." She held up a hand as Tachi took a breath and opened her mouth. "I don't have the bandwidth for a new relationship right now."

Her roommate shook her head and whistled low. "You really are the bomb, girl. Wish I had a spine half as stiff as yours."

"My spine wasn't always this stiff." She waved off the protest. "And believe me, you do just fine sticking to your own priorities. You get what you want by sheer force of will if necessary." Tachi's confident, take-no-prisoners attitude made everyone sit up and pay attention.

Her roommate's laugh filled the room. "I like the sound of that!"

They chuckled in the quiet evening until Britt glanced over. "Hey, know what helps with life dilemmas and trying to ignore hot guys?"

Furrows formed between her dark brows as she held up her hands. "No. Come on, Britt. Not shopping…"

"Yes, shopping!"

"How do you have the energy? Mall's not open at this hour."

"Tomorrow evening after school. It's research. Last-minute inspiration. For real I need some supplies."

"Actual work, or are you justifying your addiction?"

"I resemble that remark." Britt huffed. "Brainstorming fabric pairings to polish the collection."

"Likely story." Tachi got up and tugged her shirt down. "I have to work tomorrow, but thanks for the invite, darling," she said over her shoulder as she yawned her way back into the bedroom. True, Britt did appreciate the rent and grocery money her roommate brought in dancing. Crazy good talent and equally amazing good looks could support the bulk of a two-bedroom apartment in downtown Atlanta.

Britt sighed. Soon, she'd have a full-time job that paid all the bills. Soon.

Before then? Shopping!

Chapter Nine

How much could a human being shop?

If the human's name was Britt McNeill, apparently she could shop like endurance athletes ran ultramarathons. Red indulged in a momentary stretch of his back, then returned to his affected poor posture. It had been a late night yesterday, what with the dinner, the kiss, and afterward patrolling the apartment premises until dawn—covertly of course. Staying awake in today's midmorning classes had tested his military training.

Fast forward ten hours, and here they were still shopping into the evening.

He patted the cell phone. No abnormal triggers from his security cameras in the school or around her apartment today. That wasn't necessarily good news. The latest update from CO Hunt indicated that Lequire's attention was focused on Reagan who was up in the mountains, not on Britt, but Red wouldn't take any chances.

He looked up from his mindless perusal of brightly colored summer separates and scanned his surroundings once more.

He could barely see Britt's head over the top of the racks, even with her wearing those thick-soled Doc Martens. The accompanying black tights and black cardigan made the color consistent, but then an unexpected burst of a pale pink V-neck shift was completed by a black pendant. Her look was 98% Goth, 2% sweet.

He 100% wanted to be closer to her.

Red tucked his head further into his hoodie, cursing that he had to wear that plus his beanie. Hard to remain covert with easily recognizable hair the color of molten lava.

Hard to hit the sweet spot between everyday student and serial killer with this getup. Smiling helped. He hoped. He'd considered brown hair dye for his brows and hair, but his sensitive skin failed the patch test. Rubbing the inside of his arm that still itched, he grimaced. If he had put that goop all over his head, his scalp would have peeled off by now. After that experiment, he had no time—or inclination—to risk temporary or semipermanent hair coloring.

So that left Red with a sweaty stakeout in Magnolia Ridge Mall. For the hundredth time tonight, he patted his lower back where the baggy hoodie hid the concealed Sig. He catalogued his other weapons. He kept a bead on Britt as she worked her way through the JT Armstrong department store. Earlier today, her visit to the fabric and craft mega-store had been a tedious two hours. Would it be too much to simply pick a shade of green and move on?

He knew the answer to that question. There were at least 326 shades and patterns of green at that fabric store. She'd looked at them all.

Now Red was finding out just how long someone could take two pairs of jeans, hold them up, test their appropriateness against various shirts, rub the fabric between fingers, and otherwise compare them. Answer: twenty-four minutes and counting for two pairs of jeans.

She didn't purchase either.

Half of her time was spent staring at the outfits like a platoon sniper calculating wind and distance while waiting for the perfect shot.

Did she have to run those fingers over every piece of fabric? Every time she touched a new fabric, he experienced that sea breeze *shushing* sound in a visceral way. He could almost taste salty ocean air and feel the warm sunshine.

Another peek over the children's clearance rack allowed him to identify the top of Britt's head. Tonight, her purple-streaked brown hair was pulled back in rows of silver clips, revealing her delicate features. The slight upturn of her nose was highlighted by the hoop on one side. Her dark lined eyes should have come across as edgy or angry, but on her it made her blue-hued irises glow. What about her lips? Red had so much intel about her mouth from last night, that the depth of knowledge constituted a conflict of interest.

He couldn't afford to lose focus.

Red glanced around. More witnesses in a public place, but still not out of the question for Lequire to make a move in this kind of location.

The store, with its sandpapery soft music echoing off the muted walls and its quietly chattering shoppers, would make it hard to pull off a kidnapping. A sudden chalkboard-scratch wail pierced the space around him, and he winced and spun around. The last time he'd been around toddlers … so many years ago in the foster home.

Hey, he knew how that kid felt. Five hours of shopping should qualify Red for combat pay.

He eased between two racks and squatted down to pretend to consider socks. How many brown shades were there? Another glance over the rack. Great. Now she had moved to lingerie. If he had to witness her stroking panties, then he would sue his employer for pain and suffering.

In a split-second his mind went from assessing strategic locations within this store to assessing what lay under her pink, thigh-length shift. What sort of bra swept over those soft curves? What undergarments went with the black tights, Doc Martens, and a pink shift? Black lace? Pink leather? As a fashion student, he needed to know if her foundation-wear fit the tough appearance she cultivated.

Memories of their steamy kiss mingled with his mannequin-obscured view of her exploration of sleepwear on sale. He knew that the fierce woman beneath the hair dye, piercings, and shitkickers could also melt in his arms.

A nail-drag sigh skimmed his hearing, and he got even warmer.

She was on the move again, to the petites' section. Of course. Selecting a few items, she disappeared into the fitting room. He scanned the area for any sign of danger. Anything out of place. Out of place? Like a dude in a hoodie lurking solo on the edges of women's athleisure in JT Armstrong.

He maneuvered close enough to the fitting room entrance that his sensitive hearing picked up on the rasp of fabric sliding against skin. A zipper made a lemony yellow *tick-tick* on its way up. Then came a penny-tasting *pop* of a metal snap. Another sigh. And a hum. With his virally driven ability, it was as if her lips rested mere inches from his ears.

Jumping at an overhead ping, he listened to the announcement: store was closing in fifteen minutes. Thank God they were almost done. He needed a snack, a cold shower, and a nap.

A flash of movement from the corner of his eye made him whip around, all senses on immediate alert. He ducked behind a rack of clothing. Two men in unbuttoned black blazers and black pants wandered in a nonrandom way through the center sale section, casting way too many glances toward the dressing room.

The evening's assignment rocketed from ho-hum to high stakes. Red's adrenaline pushed an icy hot wave through his veins, driven by the helicopter *whump* of his heart.

The blazers they wore? First of all, who shopped in Atlanta in blazers? Also, he could guess at the nature of suspicious lumps on the men's backs and hips. Lumps that rested in holsters and spat deadly bullets.

Red slid his hand over his lower back and retrieved his Sig. Tucking it into the front hoodie pocket, he kept a hand on it.

His training, driven by the virus, caused his muscles to tense. His nerves hummed like a high-tension electric line. Most people had a fight-or-flight response. The virus—and Red—only knew "fight."

Hunt's intel was dead wrong. Chances those men were shopping the latest summer trends? Zero.

A dressing room door clicked closed with a dull, moldy *thud*. Thick-soled shoes lightly *thudded* on industrial carpet as she came closer. Decision time. Explaining his presence to Britt would be disastrous to the mission. On the other hand: hell if he'd let those goons hurt her.

As she exited the dressing room, he remained hidden, keeping several racks of clothing between them, moving garments to the side, and peeking up at times to maintain line of sight.

The store pinged another cheery reminder that it was closing in five minutes.

She paused, then turned back to another rack.

Red ground his molars.

A sales associate strolled past Britt, mentioning the store's closing. Britt nodded absently and smiled, toying with her black pendant.

He groaned to himself as she kept shopping.

Over the next three minutes, the two men casually strolled until they had triangulated their positions forty feet from her on either side. The store lights dimmed to about fifty percent illumination.

Shit.

She turned toward the outer exit, but one of the men blocked her path in the tiled walkway between carpeted clothing sections. Her eyes widened and she spun around.

The second tall, bald man approached from the depths of athletic wear, put a finger to his lips, and held up his hand as if to tell her not to move.

Red scanned the store. Empty. Strangely empty. Like, *paid off* empty. He'd deal with whys later. The man that had motioned for her to stop now reached under his blazer.

Red's virus revved hard against his control.

Britt bolted.

She wove through racks, dodging in the general direction of the store's mall entrance, shoes thudding against carpet, then linoleum. Red ran parallel to her, staying hidden. An automatic metal grid clacked down over the exit with a mechanized thud.

Britt cast a glance from side to side.

The men casually strolled closer.

Red tracked them. He had to balance subterfuge with protection.

Her harsh, panicked breathing tasted bitter, like an overripe orange. Attuned to the sound now, he honed in on the breaths and her pounding heartbeat. This store had gotten far too empty, too quickly.

In the low light, one of the men made a hand signal to the other. Then the lights went out completely. Only emergency illumination with a bluish glow made the inside of the silent store visible. Red had the advantage in low visibility.

Britt froze in her tracks.

The men moved.

Chapter Ten

Tachi had warned Britt that her shopping habit was dangerous, but this terrifying situation probably wasn't what her friend meant.

The thunder of her heartbeat blocked out other sounds. Her crouch behind a clothing display burned in her thigh muscles, but no way would she stand and stretch.

She gasped, pressing her lips together to stifle the sound. Who were those men? Britt didn't care to find out. She had caught a glimpse of black metal, right before the lights went out. She'd seen Brady's gun enough to know the shape and dull, dark glint of a pistol. Sweat prickled her upper lip. What would happen if those guys found her? Her brain gladly provided her previews of possible Lifetime channel movies and *True Crime* murder shows, starring Britt. None had happy endings.

Britt peered out from behind a summer cotton dress draped over a plastic mannequin set back into a niche wall display where she hid. She pressed her lips together as she glared at the mall entrance's metal grille, firmly locked in place for the night. No exit there. She crammed herself as deeply into the small space as possible. *Think.* What about the door to the parking lot? A back employee entrance. One of those might work, if she could sneak around the men.

If the doors were locked? Usually they had deadbolts that could be turned. Otherwise, she could grab a Brannock shoe-fitting device on her way through the shoe section. That might work to break the door glass on the street entrance, if necessary. Defend herself. That heel cup would leave a mark, too.

See? A fashion degree was useful after all. A panicked bubble of laughter threatened to break free. She swallowed hard and trembled.

In front of her, one of the men slithered in and out of the racks, pushing at clothes on hangers that made high-pitched squeaks. She could just make out his broad shoulders and bald head in the low illumination from the store's emergency lights.

She crammed her fist against her mouth and hid behind plastic legs.

"Swear she was heading this direction." The bald man's low, gravelly voice drifted over to her poor hide. A direct glance in her direction and they'd see her.

Her legs shook. Calves quivered. She clung to the mannequin ankle until the figurine tipped forward. Swallowing a guttural gasp, she yanked the legs until the flat plastic footing *snicked* back firmly onto the platform.

"What was that?" bald gravelly voice said. Clicks of flashlights preceded bright beams piercing the empty store. "That her?"

She ducked and held her breath until the air burned in her lungs.

If they caught her … no. She couldn't think of that. Wasn't going to happen on her watch. If she could get a weapon, she'd at least make them reconsider killing her … or doing other things. She gulped again, her mouth dry.

A tiny, bizarre corner of her brain noted the irony of someone with severe anxiety thrust into such a terrifying situation. No amount of medication or breathing techniques would make these men leave her alone. She reached for the grounding exercise from therapy, anchoring her feet to the ground and then identifying something she could touch, smell, and see.

She could touch a cold mannequin leg, smell the

light scent of her sweaty fear, and see two men working their way through the racks in her direction.

Exercise failure. Once the men moved away, she slid out of the niche and wove toward the shoe section. She had to scamper from the petite section across an open aisle, and then hide again. How long could she evade these men in a locked department store?

Shoe section might have been a bad decision. Her legs shook as she stayed low. Shorter displays. More open space. She forced her lungs to slowly inflate and deflate. Anything to stay calm. For a split-second she detected a hint of pine and aftershave.

I wish.

No knight on a white horse or even a weird ex-military dude in mismatched sustainable clothing was going to magically show up. No, like so many things in her life, Britt would have to take care of this on her own.

A desperate will to survive was the only tool she had to work with as she duckwalked behind a sales rack, careful not to bump against any shoeboxes. Easing behind the register, she used her cell phone light to find the Brannock device. The metal width slides were tucked in, making it an oblong metal instrument. She clutched the weighted device. Note to self: metal heel cup side up if she had to swing at someone.

Murmurs and rustles of clothing filtered back to her location behind the counter. This hiding spot could work for a while—she could cram her body in the space under the register. But it didn't lead to an exit. What about the door behind the register? It likely led to a dead-end storage room. No time for dead ends. Only exits.

She tried to text Tachi. An error message flashed. Next, she dialed 911. Nothing. She checked the phone. No bars. No Wi-fi signal. Crap.

Time to move.

Silencing her nonfunctional phone, she slipped it in her pink shift and buttoned the pocket. Other than house and car keys, a maxed credit card, nine dollars, and a driver's license, all secured in the other pocket, she had nothing else to work with. At least the police would know her identity and terrible credit score. So, yay.

God, this was bad.

Sidling through the shoes to the more densely stocked sales racks in the center of the store, she froze as Gravelly Voice piped up less than ten feet from her.

"We're not getting anywhere. Get the infrared. I'm tired of this game."

Infrared. Heat. She could melt an igloo with the BTUs pouring off her. She whipped her head from side to side, mind whirling. How to disguise heat in a department store?

Under a register? That would probably be one of the first places they'd look. She peeked up over a rack for a split-second. No checkout counters, no nearby dressing rooms. Only circular racks of—her eyes widened—insulated winter coats. On final sale. End of the season. Hey, these might be 50% off. It might work.

Heavy treads grew louder as the higher-pitched man said, "It's on."

The infrared device.

She eased toward the racks. Last season's discounted outerwear loomed in front of her. She slithered under the coat hems. Nylon whistled too loud as she swept against the fabric. She froze. Didn't dare breathe.

"What was that?" Gravelly voice said.

"No idea," the other guy whined. From a brief glimpse, this man was taller and thinner, with a shock of dark hair.

"Scan over there, where I heard it."

Oh, no. She bumped her shin against the inner metal supports that made an X at the bottom of the display. Biting her lower lip against the pain, she looked up. The top of the rack was covered in glass, supporting a price stand.

Open. Visible.

"Is that a signal over there?"

She clung to the central vertical metal beam and stepped up on the metal X. Sweat tickled her temple but she refused to move.

The center of the rack got stuffy in a hurry with polyfill jackets and no air circulation. She'd stay here as long as necessary to evade those guys.

A clank and a clatter sounded in the far recesses of the store, like a display had crashed down. The men's heavy footsteps faded away. She sagged but remained upright, keeping a death grip around the central pole.

A hand snaked around her face and cut off her gurgled scream.

Chapter Eleven

"It's R—Al. Don't move," a low voice whispered next to Britt's ear.

A huge mass of a human body silently squeezed into the center of the rack, pushing her torso forward through the metal X. Every muscle in her body tensed.

His hand on her nose and mouth cut off air until stars sparkled in her vision. The shadows of dim light wavered beneath the rack's glass top as she stared upward. She clawed at his arm with one hand until he lowered it enough that she could draw breath into her nose. With her other hand she raised the Brannock, but he twisted her wrist until her fingers went numb. Without making a sound, he set the tool on the floor in an economy of movement in the limited space.

Then he curved his free arm around her waist, tucking her flush against his chest and pinning one of her arms to her side. She couldn't get a full breath, he had her wrapped so tightly.

The combined warmth of their bodies, plus the remnants of the store's last attempt to sell winter clothing in Atlanta, stifled her. Her finger brushed against a garment. Was that ripstop nylon? Down insulation? She gulped down an inappropriate giggle and tried not to shudder.

Heat poured off him. A scent of pine and aftershave filled the space, and little by little her muscles loosened until she was boneless. Somehow, Al was here. How?

She'd deal with that question later. Unless he worked with those men out there. No way. She tensed.

"I'm going to move my hand," he whispered. "Don't scream." It wasn't a request.

She nodded and he eased his hand away, but kept it cupped around her shoulder. He was probably ready to reload the facepalm if she made a peep. He relaxed his embrace so she could move her pinned arm.

"What's going on?" She pitched her voice low, holding the metal X with one hand while digging her fingers of her other into his corded forearm which was locked around her midsection.

His breath tickled the fine hairs along her neck, along with his glasses frame. "Do you trust me?"

"I don't really know you." She pushed against the vice of his arm. Didn't budge.

"Please. Britt."

New sound penetrated their hide. The men were coming closer again. She stiffened in Al's arms. He went still as a statue.

Mutters and scrapes of hangers on metal bars grew louder. She peered up. A flashlight beam swept over the glass. She couldn't breathe. Sweat trickled down her temple.

Al patted her shoulder. "I will take care of you. Stay here."

Not a good idea. He might be ex-military and willing to help, but gentle, Granny-helping Al was no match for two guys with guns. "Not safe."

"Only option." His warm lips brushed her ear.

"But…"

"Trust me." His rumbling voice vibrated through her spine, almost reassuring her.

What could she do? She wanted to help. To take action. To run.

Rapidly going through her choices, she came up with her only option: Trust Al.

"Want help?" She didn't want him getting hurt. Inching her foot along the carpeted floor, she bumped the

Brannock he'd set down. With that tool, she could make someone regret a few life decisions. Sucking air into her hot lungs, adrenaline surged and stiffened her spine. "I tried to call 911. I can try again."

He shook his head behind her. "Phones are jammed."

Who the heck jammed phones in a department store?

He gave a deep, nearly soundless chuckle she felt rather than heard. Like this life-or-death situation was funny. "Besides, I've got this situation under control."

Like it was no big deal for him to go after two armed dudes in the clearance section of JT Armstrong. Again, why was he here? Too many questions. Now she wanted to stay alive, if only to get some answers out of the guy.

"Stay here," he whispered, feathering a kiss against her temple. He gently peeled her hand off his forearm and planted it on the metal stand in front of her. Then he melted into the darkness with a high-pitched *shush* of ripstop nylon.

Britt's heart hammered loud enough that she couldn't hear anything for a minute. She clutched the rack. Two minutes. Three. Fleshy, low, gut-turning thuds were followed by smacks and stomach-turning crunches. She pressed her hand over her mouth. *Ooofs* and moans. Someone panted and coughed.

A thick metallic *click*.

Was that a gun safety? Instinctively, she ducked her head. Insulated outerwear wouldn't stop bullets. Her muscles quivered like Jell-O in an earthquake. Sweat dampened her hair and the strands clung to her neck.

Al was out there with those two guys. They had at least one gun. Maybe more. The gravelly voiced man answered her question. "Hold him."

Ice raced through her limbs. Rapid punches and slaps punctuated Al-sounding grunts. Over and over. It didn't stop until his bone-deep groan drifted back to her. Britt's stomach churned.

"Where is she, asshole?" one guy asked.

"Don't know what you're talking about." Al exhaled a long wheeze.

"The sister. We'll find her. You do know what Lequire will do when he gets his hands on her?" That gravelly laugh held no happiness. "Shit, it's easier to describe what he *won't* do to her."

Sister? Wait. What? She froze. Were they talking about Kiera or Reagan? Were her sisters in danger from these guys? She bit her lower lip to keep from whimpering. Her pulse raced. Mind spun. They wanted to hurt her sisters? Hell, no.

"Where would Lequire take her?" Al asked in a weak, thin tone, like the words and air came out through a clenched jaw. "Surely employees of the month like you would know that information."

What the crap? Al was chatting with the men.

Who was this Lequire person and how did Al know him?

Oh God. Oh God. Her brain struggled to put the pieces together. Nothing made sense.

"We're taking her to the safest place you can imagine. Top-notch security. And plenty of privacy." That grinding laugh turned her stomach.

"What's Lequire scared of, anyway?"

"Who knows?" A sniff, then the man continued. "All I know is he pays me well to produce results."

"What results?"

"Shut up. You're pissing me off."

The second guy's higher-pitched voice cut through the darkness. "What if we just take this guy in?

Boss can use him, too."

"No. We need the woman. I bet she'll come out if we hurt him." That last line was delivered with more volume. Making sure Britt knew what would happen.

An imaginary vise cranked down on her chest, pushing out air. Tears mixed with the sweat on her face. Al was a good guy, trying to help protect her from … who were these guys? Didn't matter. He didn't deserve to be hurt while she sat here.

"Let's see if we can flush her out," Grinder said.

Three quick punches and grunts, then a massive *thud* like a body had hit the ground. The whiny man screamed, "What the hell?"

Another flurry of sound and movement, and the entire circular rack above her shuddered as someone fell into it, crushing coats against Britt. She clung to the center pole, shaking so hard the glass rattled against the metal X support.

She had two choices: Stay here, panic, wait until the men finished with Al, then hide until they eventually found her. Or take action to help a good guy not die. She rested her forehead on one of the metal bars and took a few deep breaths. If she got out of here alive, Britt for sure was going to need a fresh round of therapy sessions.

Crouching, she lowered her trembling fingers until she encountered the metal fitting device. Could she do it—step in and help Al?

Another two quick thuds. Followed by several more. Britt knew math. Two against one wasn't fair.

A deep groan came from a few racks away. Sounded like Al.

Screw this paralyzing anxiety. Someone was being hurt and Britt was in a position to do something about it.

Scooting out between coats on the side opposite

the sounds of fighting, Britt blinked in the low emergency lighting. Large shapes lurched between racks of clothing. Glass shattered. Yowls and crunches prompted her to slide around behind one of the men and duck behind the pale legs of a ready-for-the-beach mannequin.

In the dim light, Al's tall frame blurred as he pushed one man back with punches, then turned and faced a bald man. A glint of metal preceded a booming gunshot. Her ears rang. Al dropped to a knee with a grunt, holding his side. Britt locked eyes with him. A tiny motion, but he shook his head.

Then the thinner man kicked Al in the lower back until he went down, glasses skittering across the aisle. Al didn't move. That was it. Britt had had enough.

Staying low, she crept near the coward who had kicked Al from behind. A strange calm came over her, steadying her grip on the metal. As the man reared back for another punch down onto Al's motionless, prone form, she braced herself and swung the tool. The satisfaction of metal crunching the side of his knee lasted as long as the dude's keening yowl. At least he left Al alone.

The man spun around with fists raised and hit the head of the mannequin which flew over into sportswear with a series of plastic *thunks*.

Britt faded into another rack of clothing. As the cursing man limped by, she ducked out and hit him on his lower back, the shock of impact jarring her arm up to her shoulder. The guy dropped to all fours.

Al raised his head and peered in her direction. "Get out of here! Go!" he panted.

Then the balding guy with the gun jumped on him, the butt of his gun coming down on Al's head.

Al crumpled.

Not fair. Wrong.

With no concrete plan but a definite goal, she rushed toward the attacker, ready to do whatever it took to get the jerk away from Al before the guy killed him.

"Hey!" she yelled.

The man stopped and stared at her with a perplexed expression that shifted into a nasty leer. He snickered, "Well, hello."

"Get away," she said, voice quivering.

The bald man kept his eyes on her as he dropped another fist onto Al's back.

Al dropped flat, then slowly pushed back to hands and knees, shaking his head as if to clear it. He struggled to kneel upright beneath even more spine-shuddering blows. The bald guy wasn't stopping. Britt had to do something. She stepped closer, just out of arm's reach.

"Quit it!" she screamed. Both Al and the attacker paused.

She brought the Brannock down with a crash on the guy's arm that held the gun. The gun and the fitting device skittered off across the tile floor.

"Goddamn it! Get over here!" The bald guy lurched for her.

She froze, no weapon handy.

His meaty hand clamped down on her arm.

Then, like a pissed-off, demented avenging angel, Al rose up and roared, a giant shadow in front of her, larger than any person she'd seen before.

Chapter Twelve

Red was handling things just fine until a deranged pixie appeared from behind the sales rack and clubbed the thinner bastard with that metal object. Good girl.

Red's concentration split between the attackers and the safety of the woman in question. Her tangy, rasping breaths of terror loosened his control over the virus. His vision tinted crimson, and somewhere in the depths of rational thought he recognized this color change as an end-game sign. Synesthesia took over. He experienced the deep bass salt-grinding breath of the bald dude, the tinny burnt-metal wheeze of the thin man somewhere behind him, Britt's tappity-tap frantic cold sleeting heartbeats a few feet away. His enhanced hearing coalesced every sense into deadly focus.

Turning Red into a living weapon.

The thin guy lunged for her.

Red's Morpheus Virus didn't give a crap that he was concussed and that his inner ear had reset the X, Y, and Z axes. Didn't care that a trickle of blood dripped down his temple. Didn't care that he was bleeding from a bullet hole in his side. Sure as hell didn't care how the surge of viral rage made him lose all control.

The virus had one goal: kill anyone that hurt Britt.

Red wanted one thing: to protect Britt and destroy anyone that touched her.

Teamwork made the dream work.

The bald dude lunged forward.

She yelped and reared back.

The mission became bigger than simple protection.

Releasing what constraints remained on the virus,

Red roared as he expanded to his full height and then some. Without his conscious control, the virus flowed freely through every cell of his body. Bones stiffened and muscles enlarged. His body stretched against his clothing, like a poorly adjusted Incredible Hulk. His extra ability to hear shot off the charts, swirling his sanity into the vortex.

Full synesthesia took over. All senses completely merged with his amplified hearing. *Oh, fuck.* Unable to think, he could only react and hope that he and viral buddy were on the same page.

The virus. Already, Red sensed his humanity slipping away in exact portion as his strength increased.

Antidote. Now.

No. Britt first.

He'd deal with sanity later.

Her safety was all that mattered.

Faster than he could comprehend, he threw several hard punches, whip-hot snaps that shot the bald guy back, launching him off his feet and onto his butt. Blood wet-penny pinged on the tile and glistened, tarry black. The man reached toward his hip.

Red's only coherent thoughts: Protect. Destroy.

Even as Red's blinding need drove him forward, his sensitive hearing picked up a high-pitched gurgle that smelled like a burning poker lancing fire through his ribs. He whipped around. The thinner man had his hands around Britt's neck. Her feet hung a few inches off the ground.

Terror rooted Red's feet to the ground. One wrong move and this man could snap her spine.

Britt's eyes rolled back, even as she clutched and clawed at the man's arms, kicking with those Martens for all she was worth.

Then her grip weakened. Kicks became light

swinging movements. Then her arms dropped to her sides. The man lowered her to the floor, but kept an arm around her upper chest. Britt's chin lolled forward, teeth meeting. That small, dull *clunk* registering as a thick moldy bread taste.

Red's heart stopped.

The man chuckled and dropped a kiss on her temple. He let go, but held onto the pendant which jerked her neck until the pendant chain snapped. She crumpled to the floor, her head hitting the tile with a gut-churning thud. She didn't move. The pendant followed with a tinkle of shattered glass.

The virus restarted his heart. His pulse hammered. "No!" The roar coming from inside of him vibrated every bone in Red's body, rattling the metal hangers on the racks.

Lunging with a desperate, instinctive grab, he pinned the thin man's arm behind his back. With a twist of Red's wrist, he crafted a satisfying and crispy dry-kindling snap. Ignoring the man's howls, Red cranked back his virally spring-loaded fist. Then let fly.

Blood spurted from the man's nose and lip as he flew back five feet and crashed into a square display stand. Deep moans satisfied both Red and the virus.

A spicy snick sounded behind him. Whirling, he spied a switchblade in the bald guy's hand. Red stood over Britt, one foot planted on either side of her motionless form. Those men would have to kill Red to get to her. Period.

Heat built in his head.

Britt's light wheezes excoriated him like rough lace against sensitive skin. Time slowed down. The movements of the blade through air became burnt steel wool raking his ears. Rage burned a habañero path of fire through what remained of his sanity.

Kill.

Wait.

Kill.

Never had he been this close falling over the cliff of sanity.

Britt wasn't moving.

Red would go beyond sanity if that's what it took to save her.

This was no longer a mission. This was *need.*

He was no longer a man. He was base instinct.

He was death.

Another uncontrollable snarl, and he walked right into the blade, shrugging off an acid-hot slash across his chest. The gut punch he delivered was aimed six inches beyond the man's spine. The virus lapped up the melodic squish of dense liver as it rebounded, followed by the agonized thin-pipe exhalation.

Before the bald guy dropped to the tiled floor, Red took a half-step back, teed up, and roundhouse-kicked the hell out of the man. Ribs snapped like acorns tossed on a campfire.

So satisfying.

He drew back for another kick, but that high, threadlike moan—hers—caught his attention and he spun, laser-focused on her needs.

In a flash, Red knelt next to her, clawing his way back to rational thought. "Britt?" The words ripped out of his raw throat. He lightly chafed her arms. He grabbed her ice-cold hands, and she pulled back with a grimace. His grip was too tight. He struggled to keep his touch gentle.

Even in the dim light and his crimson-tinted vision, he spied linear bruises marring her neck, and he fought the urge to rip everything around him to shreds. Collaring the virus triggered a stab of pain through his temple. Nevertheless, he fought for tenderness as he slipped an arm under her shoulders, cradling her on his lap.

Her gurgled whimper punched him right through his gut. Her eyes opened, but she didn't focus. Her face was a study in shadows.

"Al?" she rasped.

"Right here, sweets."

She lolled against his upper arm, eyes fluttering closed.

Out. He needed her out of this place. Pulling her easily up into his arms as he stood, he stepped over the motionless bodies on the floor. Didn't care if the men lived or died, as long as they didn't touch Britt again.

His vision remained maroon until he took some deep, cleansing breaths. Fought to push the virus down into the cage. Quickly assessed that he had retrieved all his weapons and that they were stashed and available. Focusing on Britt, silent in his arms, brought him back to sanity.

Damn, he needed an antidote dose. He had burned through the last dose far too quickly. Tonight had tested his limits. No guarantees he hadn't done permanent damage to his mind. No guarantee that any small threat wouldn't still push him completely over the edge. In his car, he had a dose. Hopefully, it would be enough.

Hopefully, the antidote wouldn't take away his ability to protect Britt. The trade-off had never been this terrible.

At the exterior doors of the department store, he retained enough rational control to keep from breaking the glass. Instead, he flipped the bolt on the door and again on the second similar door, like a logical, civilized human.

Once out in the open air of the mall's nearly empty parking lot, he jogged several hundred feet over to a loading dock where they could hide in a protected space while he assessed her condition. He glanced up. His teammates would have to take care of the video feeds. Easing Britt to the concrete, he leaned over to her. Half the little clips were missing, making pieces of her hair stick out in all directions. The black cardigan had fallen off one shoulder and he tugged it back up.

"Britt?"

"Mmm?" Her eyes flew open. "No!"

His tongue stuck to the roof of his mouth. He swallowed. "It's me, Britt. It's, uh, Al." His words tasted like sand. "You're safe now."

"Those men." Her hoarse voice strafed his raw nerves.

He glanced around them in the night. "Won't hurt you anymore."

"Because … oh my God." Her eyes, surrounded by smudged makeup, were luminous and wide. "Who are you?"

A sound made him whip around. Just a plastic bag skidding along on the breeze. At the far side of the parking lot, tree frogs chirped in the wooded area. The rumble of cars on the city road nearby registered in his hearing. "Long story. I need to get you to safety."

"No. I'm serious, who are you?" She tried to clear her throat but her voice came back croaky. "Why were they talking about my sister? Which sister?" No more glazed expression for Britt. Oh no, she'd gone from choked out to freaked out in the space of a few seconds. He couldn't blame her

"Are they okay? Al, tell me what's going on, please."

They had no time to chat. If either guy was

conscious, they could emerge from the mall or call for backup.

Speaking of which. He dialed a number on his phone and kept a hand on her shoulder as she sat up and swayed. He helped her lean against the loading dock wall and held up a hand to silently ask her to stay put.

Hunt answered. "Red."

"Problem, sir."

"Report."

Red explained the situation in three sentences, and ended with, "Get Stumpy to wipe the store security cameras, and send cleanup ASAP. We have until the morning to make it look like nothing happened."

"Roger that. Anything else?" The tight tone of Hunt's voice led Red to believe his CO had more to manage than Red's deteriorating situation. Didn't care. Britt was all that mattered to Red.

He took a few steps away from Britt, lowering his voice. "Things are FUBAR, sir. Send help."

"Roger that." Hunt ended the call.

Red flipped off the phone, turning in time to see Britt make a wobbly bolt for the parking lot.

Chapter Thirteen

As quietly as possible, Britt dragged a deep breath into her chest and slipped over the dock edge. And ran.

The memory of Al's rage-filled roar in front of the attackers drove her forward. The world tilted and her ears rang, but she stumbled ahead.

She reached the parking lot and turned right. Her beat-up car was parked right where she'd left it, center of the parking lot, in front of the store doors. She glanced toward the store, neck prickling, expecting to see those men...

She raced as fast as possible, fishing for the key in her pocket. Fifty feet to go.

Then she was flying, locked in the vise of Al's arms. Kicking for all she was worth, Britt worked to gain leverage. She connected with his shin and nailed him in the side with her elbow. He immediately let go with a pained grunt. Stumbling to her feet, she would have kept going, if he hadn't manacled her wrist in his big hand.

"Damn it, Britt. Stop." He shoved the phone in his back pocket. "You're going to get yourself killed."

"Because back there was safe?" She thumbed with her free hand. "Because *you're* safe?"

"You have to tr—"

"Trust you? You became a rage machine that basically dismembered two scary dudes like no big deal, and you think *they're* the problem? You want me to trust you? No way. This whole situation is not okay. I want out of here. Away from you."

Another grimace of pain twisted his face as she tugged against him. His shirt had a dark stain on that side. How badly was he hurt?

With a half-growl, half-curse, he pulled her chest against his chest and stood so that his back faced the store entrance.

"Listen. Please. You're in danger. I'm here to protect you."

"More answers. Now." Her voice came out muffled against his hoodie.

His head whipped around, a wild, almost feral, narrowing of his eyes. "We need to go someplace more secure. You're totally exposed. I'm not at full strength. May not be able to keep you safe." Another grunt when she wiggled. "Shit. Stop moving."

"You're wounded?" Not that she cared one bit. At all.

"I need to rest, and it'll improve." He eased away from her by degrees, a hard expression that chilled her blood. "Look, I'll explain it to you, but we must leave. Now." Those peaceful, earnest eyes, the quiet and unassuming guy she had met several days ago—it was all a compete sham, right down the to the glasses which he no longer wore. "Let's go to my car."

"Where?"

"Over there?" He pointed to a black SUV parked on the back row of the lot. Oh, yeah. That wasn't suspicious at all. Like, every single abduction show on TV that involved shady pseudo-government agencies had a large, dark vehicle and that was the last anyone saw of the victim. She really shouldn't have streamed all those *True Crime* shows.

She dug into the asphalt with the soles of her Martens. "No." As if she could stop him.

"Please?" The word rasped out of him.

"How do I know you're not making this whole thing up to kidnap me?"

"Because I could have kidnapped you at any

point before now."

Air caught in her throat. "Oh God." She coughed. "That doesn't make me feel better."

"It's true. Does that help?" He kept those arms around her, his heat bleeding into her chest.

"No. You better give me something else that'll make me believe you."

He paused. Grimaced. "Right." Al nodded. "Your dad is a supervisor at a post office. Loves playing pool. Only drinks Guinness. Your older sister Kiera is an accounting whiz who has a thing for dark chocolate. Oldest sister Reagan has a birthmark on her face and is happiest in the outdoors. You all called her 'Granola Girl' growing up."

The air whooshed out of her. Britt's head spun. Her knees went weak. She would have hit the asphalt if he didn't tighten his embrace. "How do you know all of that?"

"You're in way more danger than you realize."

Chapter Fourteen

A calculated risk, revealing family dossier information to Britt to prove his bona fides. Red didn't have to completely blow his cover to give enough data for her to understand the situation.

He was only partially dishonest to her tonight. He also was only partially honest with her before tonight. All this selective truthfulness, to manipulate her into cooperation. A nasty churn settled in his gut.

Red maneuvered the SUV onto a side street and fought to maintain focus as a lance of pain bolted through him. He sucked in a quick breath and splinted his forearm against the wound. At some point he'd need to assess injuries and take mandated rest.

Mission first. Protect Britt from Lequire's men who would stop at nothing to capture, hurt, or kill her. Strike that. Just *kill*. That shift spoke volumes about her value in this deadly game. An icy wave of hate washed over him.

"Hey, cool it on the steering wheel or you'll break it." She pointed at the leather creaking beneath his white fingers.

Easier said than done. Lequire's men had hunted down Britt in a public place. A compromised and altered public place, but still. What prevented another attempt?

Red.

"Hold on a minute," he bit out, wrestling back control of his virus. His muscles still twitched.

The abnormal instincts for vigilance and protection had fogged rational thought. His vision tinted red every few minutes until he blinked it back to normal. Circular breathing—in, out, in, out. Another few breaths and he could almost think again. Damn it, he was cycling too rapidly. He reached into the door well for the slim box containing the antidote doses. No. Britt would see. His fingers brushed the hard plastic container then rolled into a fist as he sat up straight.

Al glanced at her. "We have to get you to the hospital."

She touched her bruised neck and winced. "You're one to talk."

"I'm fine." He checked in the rearview once again.

"Clearly." Her jaw jutted out. "Then I'm fine, too," she said, her voice still raspy from what that asshat did to her.

"Please. Britt." The word was ripped from him. "Let me get you medical care." Going to a public place with documentation, questions, and identification could expose the team, but he'd take the risk for her welfare. Red's own mission goals had changed back in that department store.

For a few seconds, she stared out the windshield, removing the last few clips and finger-combing her tangled hair into something more tame. "Sorry, no."

"No?"

"Cost is too high. No way can I pay my bill."

He made a choking noise. "What?"

"You know how insurance works, right?"

"Of course." At one point, Red and his team members had the best insurance Uncle Sam provided— all medical procedures and tests fully paid for, in return for being a glorified lab rat. He checked the map on his phone, signaled again, and maneuvered the vehicle onto another city street. Like a normal driver would. In and out with his breathing once more. Normal. Calm. He turned his head briefly. "You have insurance, then you get sick, then you go to the hospital."

"Yeah, but first I pay out the nose because I hedged my bets, and enrolled in the high-deductible plan with huge copays." She rolled her head from side to side.

"I can pay for your care."

"You're a college stu—" She pinned him with a wide-eyed stare. "You're not exactly a college student, are you?"

His heart thumped. Too close to the truth. "I'm enrolled at SCAD Atlanta."

A snort and a shrug. "Then I'm not exactly injured. No hospital. What about you? Don't you need stitches or something?" When she reached toward his soaked shirt, he flinched.

"All good." Nothing about this situation resembled 'good,' except for the miracle that they were somehow still alive.

"Obviously. What with the blood soaking your sweatshirt and all."

"Britt, please. I can have a doctor come to you, free of charge. Would take a few hours or so but I can get him here. Please let me provide you with medical care. I can pay." Something deeper inside of him wanted to provide more than medical care, and he mentally stomped that thought before it could develop further.

"Thanks, but I'm not interested in owing anyone, anything. Especially not in a situation as freaky as this one."

He ground his teeth until his jaw ached. He could force the issue, but he'd already pushed too far this evening. Mission success depended on compromise and trust.

A truck followed them down a city street, and he tensed, changed lanes, and made a series of abrupt turns.

"Where are we going?" She cleared her throat and sighed, the sound rolling over him like a comfortable blanket.

"Right now? In a random pattern." He squinted against the streetlights.

"What?"

"Hold tight for a second."

She looked back over her shoulder and gripped the center console. "Is someone following us?" The glass-cracking tone of her voice gutted him.

He brushed his hand over hers. "Not if I can help it." He sped up, turned another series of corners in stomach-churning maneuvers, then quickly pulled into a parking garage and killed the lights.

"Al?" she whispered. "We should call the police."

"No police," he snapped.

"Are you a criminal?"

"The exact opposite."

"I don't understand."

"Hang on, Britt." Toggling the display on the dashboard, he tapped out a series of commands. A high-pitched whine shuddered through the vehicle.

"What's that?" Her sun-clear voice brightened the dark space.

"Long story, but I just changed the license plate and appearance of the vehicle."

"Like James Bond?"

"Kind of." 007's gadgets were child's play compared to what Stumpy could devise. The team also enjoyed a mystery benefactor supplying them with the latest tech. He tensed as a dark truck turned into the garage, headlights strafing their vehicle. The purr of the other engine was marred by a misfiring fuel injector, creating a unique rumble. "Get down." He winced at the movement as he cupped her head to gently ease her forward in the seat. He followed suit.

"This is not normal," she whispered. Beneath his

hand, she trembled. "Oh my gosh, they're going to find us."

He fought the urge to rush the truck and forcibly remove the people inside. *Stay calm.* In and out, he breathed. Over and over. "They won't see a dark SUV with the Georgia license plate. Just a boring, dented white family minivan from Alabama. Nothing interesting at all."

The truck passed by again, paused behind their vehicle, then exited the garage, the engine noise fading into the night.

As she sat up, her inhalation sliced his senses. "This is not okay," she said, reaching for the door handle.

"Britt. Stay in the car. There's a lot you don't understand…"

"Let me guess. It's complicated."

The air in the vehicle warmed. He needed her to understand enough to believe in his plan, but not enough to risk the team's safety. "Well. Yes."

"Tough toodles. I'm not an idiot. Those men are tracking us. They tried to kill us—"

"You."

She shot him an arch expression. "Were you not on the ground, gasping for air while they kicked the crap out of you?" Her tone of voice pricked at him like rubbing up against a cactus.

Of all the things she recalled about the attack, it was that part? "I was stalling so they didn't find you."

"And a good job you did of it, getting beat up, incapacitated, then shot. They found me anyway."

He puffed out his chest. "You were supposed to stay hidden."

"Couldn't sit back and do nothing."

He snorted. "I … I can't argue with you there."

"You were assaulted. So was I. So why aren't we

going to the police, which by the way, sounds like a normal, reasonable plan of action, and one we should have taken quite some time ago?" She sniffed. "It's my life, after all."

He gripped the wheel until his wrists creaked, then took a cleansing breath. It almost worked. He loosened his grip. "I'm with an organization that, ah, helps keep people safe." Once again, he dealt in half-truth.

"Military?"

He glanced in the rearview mirror and out the windows again. "Ex-military."

A minute-long pause. "That's it?"

"That's all I can tell you."

"So, no police?"

"Well. Our team technically doesn't exist. For a whole bunch of reasons, we need to keep it that way. Police would complicate things."

"Sounds like a convenient excuse not to call 911, but let's go with your explanation for a minute." She huffed. "Who were those men? Why did they mention my sister?"

"Those men are bad. My team is protecting your sisters and your father."

"What?" She rubbed her neck, then dropped her hands on her lap. "Hope the other people on your team are better at their jobs than you are."

Damn, her assessment stung. Fair. He had failed his mission today, but he was only a single operator defending an unaware target against a much larger and well-resourced organization. Asymmetrical warfare, if he ever saw it. "Hey, they didn't teach department store hand-to-hand combat in the military." He backed up and exited the garage, pulling onto the street with a lurch of too much gas pedal.

"Touchy." Her smirk and chin tilt bugged the hell out of him.

Britt managed to irritate nerves he didn't know he had.

Her presence woke up a few different types of nerves as well. Fine time to be thinking about anything other than the mission. He shifted in the seat.

Even with his body battered, exhausted, and hypervigilant, some small part of his brain remembered their kiss and how she felt in his arms. His brain reminded him in detail how he'd like to take things further with Britt.

"Look out!" she said, as he got too close to the curb.

He jerked the car back firmly between the lines. Red was in big trouble. He concentrated on driving slowly. Moseying along. Nothing to see here. Just a mildly dinged-up minivan from Alabama.

Another several minutes passed as he maneuvered the vehicle through the tangled grid of downtown Atlanta streets and the seemingly endless stoplights.

She broke the silence. "Where are we going now?"

"Safe house."

"What?"

"You'll need to stay in a safe house for a while."

"Like, overnight."

"Lay low for a few weeks. Maybe more."

City lights moving past cast her face in shadow and illumination, light and dark. "Then, no."

"No?" *No* wasn't an option. Did she not remember the recent beating and near-death experience? Hell, he hadn't even fully checked her for additional injuries. Great job of protector. As ineffective as when he was a kid in foster care trying to watch over the other kids in that house. Damn it. He rubbed his fingers through his short hair, the beanie long lost back in that store. He had to convince her of his plan.

With luck, his teammates would arrive in a few hours for cleanup.

By "cleanup," he meant getting rid of any evidence that he and Britt had ever been in that store. Getting rid of Lequire's goons if either one remained. Hopefully after his buddies painfully extracted useful information from those bastards.

"Uh, you're doing the steering wheel thing again."

She was one to talk, gripping the door handle like a lifeline. He kept his mouth shut.

"You can't go about your regular activities," he said.

"No can do." The lift of her jaw made his heart sink. As he opened his mouth to rebut her, she held up her hand. "Okay, I totally get the danger piece. I do. And, I guess, thank you for doing a job that I didn't know needed to be done."

He bit back a *harrumph*.

She continued. "Here's the situation. I have a few more weeks of school left. Heck, I have a senior project that needs to be finished. Soon."

"Project?"

"My fashion collection."

Of course he knew that. "With other people there?"

"That's the idea. It's a public fashion show. Big names in regional fashion—sometimes even national names—attend the SCAD show each spring. Many students have gotten their internships based on their collections."

"You can't do a public show!" he barked. No way could he provide enough security.

"Watch me."

It took an act of willpower to finally unclench his teeth so words could escape. "You don't get it."

"Yes, I do." She let go of the door and scrubbed her face with both hands. "But you don't understand how long and hard I've worked to complete my degree. What I promised Mom before she…" Her voice wavered, and somehow he stopped himself from reaching over to her. "You know how I mentioned about taking a while to finish college? Well, there's more to it than that. I've kind of drifted through my life so far. Mom and Brady's deaths threw me off course. I had to get some treatment." She waved her fingers toward her face. "But even with treatment, I'm a disappointment to my dad. A loser compared to my sisters." She raised an index finger when he opened his mouth. "Hold on. Listen. This degree is the one thing I've aimed for, stuck with, and have had any success doing. Before Mom died, her wish was for me to finish college. I won't stop now."

"You could start again next year." Alive.

"You don't get it. I need this. Finally. For her memory. And for me."

"You're not a loser." How could anyone think that of this vibrant, energetic woman?

"I want them to be proud of me. I want to honor Mom. I want the satisfaction of completing this goal, despite a lot of barriers. I have to stand on my own two feet and become successful. It starts with this step." She paused, her swallow prickling the skin over his scalp. If he didn't have extraordinary hearing, he might have missed the next words. "I have to be worth something."

Well, shit. He understood her line of reasoning. His entire childhood, validation was all he wanted from the rotation of foster homes. To be thought of as someone with value. Still, her safety was the highest priority. "First of all, you are worth something. More than something. You have value for being you, no matter what the degree is. Second, you won't be safe living out in the open."

"You'll be around, right?"

"Well. Yes."

"You're a specialist in protection."

"Yes."

"Okay, then. Stick close and protect."

"But. That's not the plan."

"It's my plan."

His head spun. What just happened? Did she somehow subvert the Morpheus Squad mission? "Wait—"

"Also, I want to know what the heck the deal is with those jerks back in the mall."

He blew out a breath, wincing against the sting of the wound on his side. Red was too tired to fight her relentless determination right now. "I can try to explain. Let's clean up and get secure first."

"Sounds good." The smug satisfaction in her voice reassured him not one bit.

Chapter Fifteen

His scowl said he wasn't happy about it, but Al did safely return Britt to her apartment. Before they exited the vehicle, he checked his phone, images flashing on the screen.

An uneasy sensation in her gut warned her that this whole situation was ridiculous.

Once inside, he held an arm back and motioned for her to stand next to the front door. He dropped the large black duffel bag he'd retrieved from the trunk of the SUV—no, cream-colored minivan—with a heavy thud on the floor, freeing up his hands to hold the phone in front of him again. He flipped through the images, then methodically checked all the rooms. Like he knew what was where.

Her apartment. Her bedroom. She peered at every corner of the living room. Nausea roiled her stomach. He'd been here before. He silently prowled through the rooms.

When he returned to the front door, she pointed a finger at the images on the screen showing very small black-and-white Britt from several angles. "You bugged my apartment?" The Britts in the pictures all waved their hands at the same time.

"Give me a minute, and I'll explain." He put his nose back in the phone.

She stomped the three feet over to him and tapped the case. "No. I'm done with this weirdness. You need to explain what's going on. Now."

He held up a hand, sparking bubbles in her vision. Those bubbles were half panic, half fuzzy head, half irritation. The math didn't add up. She didn't care.

"Britt. Please. I know it seems creepy."

"It *is* creepy."

Tense lines formed at the corners of his mouth. "Let me make sure systems are functioning and this location is as secure as I can make it."

Crossing her arms, she tapped her foot as he looked at more pictures. Then he texted something to someone and closed the app.

"Mind if I clean up first?" he said, eyeing her from head to toe. "We both probably should."

"Are you stalling?"

He lifted the hem of his shirt which was damp on one side, revealing an amazingly ripped set of abs. An angry red wound oozed blood.

"Oh my God, Al. That looks bad."

A shrug. "It's through and through." Like somehow that made it okay.

She'd entered an alternate universe. Her knees started to shake. "Yes, bedroom's that way, bathroom is … well, you know the layout, I guess." She paused. "Unless you need help with that."

"Might need to get a bandage on the exit wound." He shrugged and that boyish look came and went. "I don't want to bleed on your furniture when we sit down to chat."

Oh, no, he did *not* throw his injury out there as a guilt trip. After what she'd been through? With him stalking her. What about his lies? What about his protection? Damn it. She'd be dead if Al hadn't been in the store tonight. If he hadn't put his body in harm's way.

"Oh, for Heaven's sake." She preceded him into the bathroom and pulled out a small plastic box. "Sit." She pointed at the toilet seat.

"Yes, ma'am." In a smooth movement that stole her breath, he took his shirt off and held it in a ball on his lap. Heat rolled off him. A leather strap cut across his freckled chest, ending in a holstered gun that rested under his left arm.

She gulped.

Wetting a washcloth, she took a few test swipes around the bullet holes on his side and the deep cut across his upper chest. Tight muscles clenched, but his tense expression didn't change. She would know, since they were at the same eye level. He kept his lips pressed together while he stared at her, unblinking. Warmth climbed her neck, but she focused on cleaning the injury. She had no business considering his mouth was a few inches from hers. It only made her remember their steamy kiss from yesterday.

Yesterday. When she had no idea who—or what—he was. When he wasn't injured. When she wasn't concussed and her life wasn't in danger.

No business thinking about kisses. Or the muscles over his torso and arms that tempted her to trace a finger over each ridge and valley. Purely from a fabric draping potential, she was impressed.

Quit it. Britt put a dab of antibiotic ointment on a large square bandage and taped it to the front wound. She repeated the bandage-and-tape routine on the back.

Frowning, she said, "These have healed up pretty quickly for only occurring an hour or so ago." She trailed her fingers next to the cut that sliced over his hard muscles beneath his collarbones.

His skin rippled at her touch, and his chest rose quickly. He wrapped his hand around her wrist, holding her hand away from him. "I'm a fast healer." His hazel gaze didn't meet hers.

Well, he had a lot of secrets, didn't he?

She dabbed with water, dried with a towel, and added ointment and a few bandages over the deepest areas of the cut.

"Okay, let's talk," she said.

A quirk to the corner of his mouth made her pulse jump. "Here?"

The bathroom was far too close, too warm. He still had his shirt off. Her pulse ramped up, and his focus rocketed to her neck. Like he could hear the pulse pounding, but that wasn't possible, right?

She drew in a shaky breath and thumbed toward the living room. "No. There."

When she turned to go, he slid his grip down her arm, hanging onto her hand. That strong clasp remained gentle around her fingers. "I need to assess your injuries. What hurts?"

Pride. Lack of security for a safe future. Irritation at being told she couldn't have the life she wanted right now. The possibility of failure.

"Neck's a little sore, but some ibuprofen and it'll be good."

He lifted his hand to her shoulder. Easing her chin up, he growled.

"P-pardon?" she said.

"You have blood on the front of your outfit."

"It's yours." From when he had picked her up in the store and held her in the parking lot.

The rough pads of his fingers traced patterns on her skin, drawing goose bumps. As he went over the injuries, his touch stayed light. Remaining seated, he helped her out of the cardigan and his hands slid up and down each of her arms and lightly over her ribs. A quick pat of her legs finished the perusal. He pulled out a small flashlight and swung the beam over her eyes. "Anywhere else hurting?"

After-images of the light danced in her vision. "Lower back." She sighed. "My head and neck ache. No surprise."

Turning her by the waist, he then pressed lightly along her spine, hips, and the muscles from the top of her butt to her shoulders. Then he slid his fingers over the back of her neck and over her scalp. Once finished, he patted her shoulder and nudged her back around to face him, finishing the exam with light pressure over the sore front of her neck and collarbones.

"Bruises. Scrapes. I'm sorry they put their hands on you." Gravity and threat infused every word.

"Pretty sure that was their job."

He rested his hands on her hips. "Mine was to keep it from happening." With a blink, that narrowed, deadly stare flipped back to, well, less deadly. "I lost focus. Won't happen again." He clamped his mouth shut until a muscle popped on his tight jaw. "You probably have a concussion. You sure you don't want a proper medical exam and testing? Please."

"My insurance sucks. Besides, my vision is fine and the hearing is clearer now. I assume being in the military you know what to watch for with concussions."

"It's not the same as a CT scan."

"Cheaper."

He snorted. "Glad to be the discount option." Muscles of his neck flexed as he tightened his hands on her sides. "I don't like it."

She knew the decision wasn't the best, but it was the best decision for right now. "I'll have bruises and a headache in the morning. Think of it this way: if I was going to die, I would have done it in the store or in your car."

"That is not reassuring."

"Probably true."

He dropped his head and slumped his shoulders, muttering to himself as he slid his backpack onto his lap. His fist clenched and unclenched, like he wanted to reach into the bag. His chest rose and fell several times. Finally, he looked up. "Let's get cleaned up."

"Um."

"Separately."

"Yep. Give me a minute to wash up in here, then it's yours. My bedroom's right there, if you need to … unpack or whatever you … security people do."

When he stood to his full height, the bathroom got super small super quickly. He slid past, brushing against her as he exited the bathroom.

Chapter Sixteen

In the tiny bedroom, surrounded by the faint scent of hibiscus and the sound of water raining down on Britt's soft skin as she showered in the bathroom, Red plunged the needle into his upper arm and unloaded the syringe full of antidote. Thank God.

Damn it all.

Relief flooded him.

Sure as shit, like donning earmuffs, thirty seconds later his hearing dulled. He lost the ability to pinpoint Britt's exact location. His hearing remained more acute than normal humans, but it wasn't nearly as sensitive.

His tightly ratcheted muscles finally relaxed as the antidote tamped down the virus's effects. Thinking became clearer. More rational. Sacrificing full strength and sensory ability for sanity bugged the hell out of him in this situation.

At least he wouldn't lose his mind. Chalk one up for luck, because he had come way too close to losing himself tonight. Weariness settled like a lead apron, dragging at his frame. He needed sleep. He couldn't sleep.

Pulling a clean t-shirt on, he took care to cover his injury. Thanks to the virus, he healed far faster than most people. The antidote would slow down the process, but the critical portion of recovery had finished by now. Tomorrow, there would be no need for the bandages. Not that he wouldn't keep them on. Less to explain to Britt.

A quick check on his phone confirmed that Rodeo was en route to the department store. Back at base, Stumpy had hacked into the security cameras for the entire mall as well as the department store and pasted sham images and video loops to cover the incriminating periods of time containing Red and Britt's existence.

Stumpy might have erased Lequire's men from the feeds, but he saved a digital copy for the Morpheus Squad to analyze. Stumpy had mentioned that at least one asshole had survived, watching the guy stagger out of the store. That might have been who followed them in the truck. Red should have properly incapacitated them both, but at the time his entire world centered solely on Britt's survival.

Yeah, he'd gotten sloppy. Ignored protocol. At some point, this mission had become more than just an op. He ran a hand over the worn quilt on the bed. A flash of fantasy—Britt laid out on the mattress, a sheen of sweat on her soft skin, delicate arms reaching for him as she vibrated with a hunger. A bolt of pleasure laced with pain shot through him.

Loss of focus meant loss of life. He'd learned that rule in Special Forces, and he'd be damned if he would forget it again. He should get a teammate to take over. Someone who could be objective. *No!* The scream inside his head pushed him back, making the bed springs creak. He filled his lungs. Released the air.

He rolled his neck and shoulders, mourning the reduction in strength and stamina, but relieved that he was in full control of his impulses. At least he'd be less likely to hurt Britt.

In silence, he finished changing into clean pants, then mentally catalogued all exfiltration options and weaknesses for the apartment. He could only hope that the early detection system and Stumpy's overwatch with some extra special unpleasant goodies for any asshole stupid enough to try their luck, would be enough to protect Britt. He texted Stumpy to ask him to stay glued to the monitors for the next hour or so.

Red wanted to focus completely on Britt. He

should make her go to a safe house.

He also knew how it felt when personal choice was taken away. Knew what it meant when dreams and a future were at risk of slipping away.

Damn it. He'd have to do his job but on her terms. He'd served in the Middle East. Changing the standard op protocols equaled a recipe for disaster.

Red stalked in boots to the living room. No surprise, but Britt paced the space, in her typical constant motion. Fresh-faced from washing up, the lack of makeup highlighted every emotion playing out over her features. She had pulled the top half of her hair back, drawing his focus to her luminous blue eyes. She wore an oversized t-shirt, possibly her roommate's. The tights remained on. Her Doc Martens rested next to the love seat. She paused when he approached, her brows shooting up.

Then she crossed her arms. *Uh-oh.*

"Give me one good reason not to call the police on you, Al."

He mourned the fact that he couldn't properly experience the sensation of her voice's timbre caressing his skin. "Besides the fact that I saved your life." He took another step forward but stopped when she glared. God, her blizzard stare gave him frostbite. "Also, your sister doesn't want you dead. That's why I'm here. It's pretty simple."

"Which sister?"

"Kiera. Can we sit?" He lifted a heavy arm and motioned.

Her mouth drooped. "Is she okay?"

"Now she is."

"What?" She tilted her head. "Fine. I'd offer something to drink, but I'm still too mad at you to have manners." Her chin jutted as she flopped into a corner of the love seat. "Spill."

He hid a laugh. Barely. He settled as far away as possible for his own safety. Which was to say, way too close. Was he safe from her anger or safe from his driving need to encircle her in his arms and not let go?

She glared at him until he started to sweat.

Safe from the need to haul her into an embrace, then.

Clearing his throat, he began. "You know how Brady had worked for the Fallen Comrades charity?"

"Yes."

Red shouldn't be the guy to deliver this news. Britt's sister had protected her from the truth.

"Brady died."

"I know."

"Yes, but you don't know the whole story. He died as a result of his work with Fallen Comrades."

His fingers itched with the need to smooth that furrow forming between her brows. Her intake of breath came from a distance. "I don't understand."

"There is evidence that the CFO of Fallen Comrades, Beau Lequire, killed Brady."

That electric-blue gaze locked onto him. "What? Why hasn't someone gone to the police with this? We should get the FBI or law enforcement on the case." Her hands fluttered as she whipped her head around. "I need to call Dad. My sisters."

He held up a palm, like such a gesture could hold back the tsunami that was Britt. "Let me finish the story. Then we'll discuss next steps." He continued. "Kiera took Brady's death badly, as you probably know."

"We all did."

"Of course. But she had an additional stake in it. After the funeral, one of Brady's former teammates met with her. The teammate had … resources she didn't have.

He and Kiera cooked up a plan to infiltrate Fallen Comrades and discover the truth."

"You're kidding me. She never mentioned anything about a mission."

"She and the teammate spent almost a year undercover, infiltrating the Fallen Comrades charity. They found way more than they had expected."

Shaking her head, she said, "I don't understand. She emailed me a few weeks ago, enjoying her new job in Asheville."

"She's been here in Atlanta."

Her pretty mouth dropped open. "No."

A brief nod. "Kiera got proof of Lequire's crime. He had had Brady killed because Brady knew too much about how Lequire cheated vets out of their charity money."

"Really?"

"Yes."

She rubbed her upper arm with the opposite hand and whispered, "That's why Brady's dead, isn't it?"

"It's also why our teammate is dead, trying to protect the information he and Kiera stole from Fallen Comrades."

"Kiera?" she whispered. Those teary eyes swam on her pale face.

"She's safe." Barely.

His hand clenched and opened, grasping an imaginary weapon. He wanted to fight the shadows coming for her. He also wanted to hold her, to soften the blows of his words. However, she deserved to know the truth. "Lequire's crime wasn't only the diverting of charity funds or your brother's death. His father, the great Senator Lequire, is involved. Beau Lequire helped plump up his daddy's campaign pocketbook even more by cultivating a close and lucrative relationship with

Russian cartels."

"Cartels? Russians? Undercover missions? For real, this truly is like every Netflix series rolled into one. It's got to be a joke." Still, she glanced around and bit her lower lip.

Red shook his head. "All true. Lequire imports bad drugs. One in particular, Krokodil, is instantly addictive. Great for creating return customers. If that drug gets legs in this country, Lequire will ruin millions of lives, in the name of power and profit."

Britt paused. "I'm guessing if word of all the veteran-robbing and Russian drug-dealing came out, that would be terrible for Senator Lequire's political career, since his platform is tied to Fallen Comrades." Britt rubbed her forearms.

"Exactly. Also, his committee work in the Senate depends on his military connections." He pressed a palm into the couch cushion. For now, the sound registered as a sour, disappointed creak of old springs. "Public knowledge of his son's ties with Bratva would undermine his reelection bid."

"Bratva?"

"Russian mob."

She closed her eyes for a moment, rubbing her temples. Her lime-green nails were chipped and torn. Then she took a breath and pinned him with a clear, direct gaze that held him in place more surely than handcuffs or prison bars. This small woman had total control over a highly trained Morpheus Squad team member and she didn't even know it.

"Explain exactly how all of this involves me. And you. Those men?"

Skirting around the deepest secret Red had, he gave her the only information he could. "After Lequire blew up a house to kill Mateo, he tried to reach Kiera."

A gasp. "Is she okay?"

He turned sideways, bent a knee on the cushion, faced her squarely, and took her hand. He stroked the back of her delicate wrist with his thumb. The fine bones and smoothness of her skin beneath his calloused finger reinforced why he was here. "Yes, she's safe now."

"But?"

"No buts." A couple of glaring omissions, but the full story wasn't Red's to tell. Couldn't tell it without risking his teammates' freedom and very existence. "Kiera is a liability not only for Lequire's business empire, and for his strong desire not to go to prison. But also his father's entire political career is at stake. In short, Beau Lequire and his Senator daddy desperately need Kiera's silence and will do anything to get it."

"Crap."

He pressed a finger to her radial pulse. Too quick. Her shoulders heaved rapidly, pink jumper fabric moving up and down. "Britt. Lequire won't find Kiera. She's hidden in a secure location. But he can try to get to her in other ways."

"Through her family."

"Exactly."

Her brows shot up. "Reagan? Dad?"

"They have people like me looking after them." There was suspicious activity involving Reagan in the Smoky Mountains, but Red didn't want to add more worry.

"One of your ... people ... is with each of them?"

Sitting up straighter, he projected confidence. "Yes."

She tugged her hand away and rubbed the bruises on her neck. "Are they doing a better protection job than you are?"

Slumping against the back of the couch with an

exhalation of air, he muttered, "Ouch. You're blunt."

A shrug.

He rubbed his jaw, like doing so would brush off the irritation.

"So, you're here right now because Kiera is"— she waved her hand in the air—"somewhere else and safe. Lequire still wants her. So the bad guys are coming for me. Because if they have me, then maybe they'll get her."

"That's right." So many missing details. Later. He'd add them when he could.

"They must know who I am and where I live." A pulse jumped at the base of her bruised neck as she glanced around the living room, eyes wide.

"Thus the recommendation to go to a safe house and drop out of school."

"Not happening."

"Then you're as safe as we can make you right now." God, he needed that to be true. He also needed to check every window and security camera for the millionth time.

"I know an informed decision when I see one," she said.

"True." She needed to have the chance to participate in the mission for her own safety.

The half a minute she didn't say anything almost killed him. She tapped her chin. "Your granny?"

"A cover story."

"So you lied." After he nodded, she said, "Fashion student?"

He motioned to himself. No hip beanie. No glasses. Plain black t-shirt instead of a more cultivated patterned shirt. "What do you think?"

A silver hoop winked as her eyebrow lifted. "You're not the worst fashion student I've seen."

"Not the best?"

"Well…" She ran her fingers through the ends of her short blue and brown hair.

The barked laugh that erupted from Red shocked him. Even in these crazy times, at constant risk of exposure and recapture, with her life on the line, Britt made him chuckle. Her giggle in response bubbled through him, lifting the heaviness that had been weighing him down for the past days. If she believed him, then maybe he could still do his job.

Her laugh tickled the air around him. "This whole mess is ridiculous," she said after catching her breath. "It's not funny. It isn't. It's terrifying"

"I know."

"How are you involved, exactly? Didn't catch that part."

Stall. Think. "Is your roommate coming home tonight?"

"No. I texted Tachi a little while ago that I had someone staying. Seemed like the best idea for now. Her shift ends super late, and she will crash with one of her friends."

Why did it bother him that they had a system for sleepovers? It shouldn't. Adults all around here.

"So? Your involvement?" she asked again, pursing her lips. When she wanted answers, this woman was like a dog clamped onto a delicious bone.

Resting an arm on the back of the love seat, he brushed one finger over the skin at the side of her upper arm. As if maintaining contact somehow made his job easier. As if the connection would settle his virus down. Amazingly, he released another big breath and relaxed into the cushions.

Her presence did calm him. Considering her flitting, frenetic pixiness, that revelation was a shocker.

"Well?" she said.

As long as he didn't out the Morpheus Squad, his mission wouldn't be a total disaster. "The part about being ex-military. That was completely true. I'm now part of a private contracting group that handles security in situations like this."

"Situations where the police should have been called, oh, weeks ago?"

"It's more complex than you realize."

"How did your group know about Brady?"

"It's our business to help veterans. Covertly."

"That's a vague and dissatisfying answer."

"It's the only answer I can give."

"That's not good enough."

"I know." No apology. Britt's survival depended on her knowing the least amount of information about Morpheus Squad. However, Britt had been attacked and she deserved to understand the basics of the situation. "Here's the deal: if Kiera comes forward to the police, she runs the risk that Lequire will use his father's connections in law enforcement to gain access to her."

"Lequire's that rotten?"

"You've never seen anything so slick and polished, yet decayed to the core."

A nice, neat conclusion to the story would work well here. He let out a big breath and puffed out his chest. "Therefore, after tonight, you can see why it's recommended for you to go into hiding and defer your schooling."

"Not happening." She raised her hand at his opened mouth, and he clamped his jaw shut. "Look, I'm not stupid. This isn't a rash decision. I get the risks. But I'm not torpedoing everything I've worked so hard to accomplish because I'm scared of this jerk-face."

He almost choked on spit. "Pretty strong

language."

"I know worse." She tapped her chin again, the motion making him a little irrational, because he wanted that finger tapping his skin. Pausing, she looked at the ceiling and muttered to herself, "Mom." A deep sigh. "I promised. But it's my life versus my *life*." Her lips pressed together and his mouth went dry. Britt looked up at him. "You said another teammate was heading this way. And you said you have the apartment wired."

"Coffee shop and classrooms in school, too." He ducked when she flung a decorative pillow at him.

"That's an invasion of privacy."

"It was necessary." He shifted, wincing at the residual ache from the belly wound. "If it makes you feel any better, I'm sorry."

"I'd also like to not be dead. But finishing school is nonnegotiable." Her eyes shimmered. "I made a promise."

"It's not safe."

"I'm all too aware of that." She tucked a strand of hair behind an ear and he stared at her skin, wanting a taste.

His job had gotten exponentially harder. Instead of her hiding for several weeks, the bait would dangle out in the open. He still needed to keep his own existence and the team's existence secret. An impossible task. He hauled in more air through his nose and out his mouth, raising his hands. "Look, I understand where you're coming from..."

"First of all, you don't know where I'm coming from." Her blue eyes narrowed. "Also, you're like a peacemaker, aren't you?"

"I try to find common ground."

Rubbing the bridge of her nose, she mumbled, "My life versus my life." A heave of her ribs. "This is for

Mom and for me. Oh, man." She leaned toward him, resting her hand on his arm draped on back of the couch. The warmth of that light touch heated his entire frame. "Can you keep me safe until my collection is done next week?"

"The show?" Damn it. No. He couldn't guarantee safety in an unsecured situation. He studied her sweet, pleading face. Something flopped over in his chest. "I'll find a way." Hunt was going to have Red's head on a platter. Hopefully, Rodeo could support in this mess.

"That means a lot," she said on a deep sigh.

God help him, but the trust she placed in him made him feel ten times bigger and ten times more powerful than when the virus took over. He needed to succeed.

Not only because he wanted her to survive. He wanted to do for Britt what he couldn't do for his foster siblings years ago.

Damn it, he was in trouble.

She sniffed. "Sounds like a plan." Uncrossing her legs, she stood up, and he mirrored her movement. "Well, good night. You can crash on Tachi's bed. It's a disaster in there, so be careful of the rabid dust bunnies."

Oh, he knew all about that mini-hoarder space. He had more pressing matters to address, like his virally driven need to be close to her at all times. "I'm not sleeping there. I'm staying with you."

The sight of her jaw dropping satisfied him almost as much as yesterday's kiss.

Chapter Seventeen

No way would the walls of Britt's bedroom contain a woman, a huge man, and a duffel bag full of what she presumed to be a small arsenal.

He was right out there, in the living room. Waiting to come in here and occupy the same space as Britt.

The need for his presence chafed against her need for freedom and spontaneity.

The possibility that she might not finish college twisted her stomach into knots.

The reason why she might not finish frankly iced her blood.

So here she sat, with Al not twenty feet away. What did she know about him?

All she knew about espionage and spy craft she had learned from TV. He could be the bad guy in disguise. Unlikely, given the whole protection at the mall experience. She rolled her sore shoulders. The events hadn't been staged.

He'd saved her life.

Now he was standing. Right. There. In fresh clothing. With that clean soap scent wafting around from where he washed his face and arms after she'd bandaged him. Looking like he needed to act but wouldn't move until she gave him the thumbs-up.

She could scream for help. Why? Al hadn't hurt her. Quite the opposite. He hadn't made an aggressive move. Not that she'd mind, exactly. Even their kiss yesterday, she had initiated it.

That said, she didn't like the part where he had stalked her and lied. Not a good basis to build a trusting relationship. Crap, now she wanted a *relationship*? Britt traced a fingertip over her bottom lip, remembering the hard press of his mouth against hers. Once she moved past the lying part, she'd be okay with a repeat of the kisses from last night and might want to entertain something more intense in the near future.

God, had her standard dropped to the point where getting personal with a mystery guy who was involved in a shadow organization going up against the Russian mob, still made her toes tingle.

"Can I come in?" She jumped as his voice carried right over to her as he slowly eased the door partway open. Yet he didn't cross the threshold.

She stared at him, his form lit dimly by the bedside lamplight. The living room lights were off. She glanced around her small bedroom at the lovingly made but threadbare and mismatched items with a sigh.

"Britt?" His tone had a note of concern in it.

"No need to worry, Captain America. You can come in." As he entered, she leapt into the double bed and pulled the covers to her waist as she sat against the wall.

Al filled up the doorway space. His hazel eyes glinted in the low light. But he didn't move.

Despite the fact that she had on a tank top and shorts, his intense gaze raked over her like she wore nothing at all. Britt shivered, rubbed her upper arms, and pulled the blankets up to her neck.

"Um, so." Her mind churned with too many conflicting thoughts. "I'm not. We aren't sleeping. Here. Together. We're not going to..." She was no prude, but Britt recognized that she had just met this guy who hadn't told her the truth about himself. Now he lurked in her bedroom doorway. Boundaries needed to be set.

Stepping into the room, he held up a hand. "Don't worry, I won't be sleeping. "

A flush of heat burned its way up her chest and neck. "Wait. What?" Her stomach quivered.

"Sleeping?" His brows shot up. "Oh. No, that's not what I meant. Uh…" A gust of breath escaped him. "Although that would be…" He licked his upper lip.

Would be what? Fabulous? Awful? Strange? Earth-shattering? She gritted her teeth so she didn't blurt out, *Use your words, man!* His low voice made her skin vibrate.

With a motion, he said, "I'll be nearby but on the floor. Don't worry."

"Sleeping?"

"I don't sleep on missions."

"At all?"

"No."

She pulled her head back. "That's not possible."

"I'm well-trained." Matter of fact.

"Well, do you want a blanket and pillow for your not-sleeping?"

At his chuckle, she curled her toes into the fitted sheet. "I can snag them from your roommate's room if I need a little comfort."

"Are you trying to make me feel guilty?"

"I wouldn't dare," he snorted, the tight slash of his mouth relaxing.

What would it be like seeing this serious guy let loose and fully laugh, like total-body laugh? What would he look like in a completely relaxed state, all defenses down?

At the blast of images featuring his sexy, reclining, laughing body on her bed, Britt's muscles tightened into a completely non-relaxed state. She couldn't help it. Britt tracked him as he sidled the three steps around the foot of her bed and slid down until he sat with his back to the wall. He extended his feet under her bed. She inhaled deeply the faint scent of pine tree and soap that followed him.

He filled the room.

He filled her senses.

He rested his head against the wall and flipped the cell phone on, scrolling through pictures—all the cameras documenting every aspect of her life.

"Do you want to look?" He glanced up, the smooth, low tone of voice both calming her and electrifying nerve endings.

"No." She reached out and clicked off the lamp.

In the darkness, the cell phone screen cast his face in blue light.

"Britt?"

"Yes."

"I *will* keep Lequire from hurting you. That's a promise."

Chapter Eighteen

The nanosecond that the whispery, low murmur started, Red knew. His hearing might be blunted right now, but it still worked better than any normal person's.

He glanced at his phone. Just after midnight.

In the darkness, with outside lights filtering through the curtains, he stared at the small shape on the mattress. When the sheets rustled in a crisp, clean airy sound that sounded like leaves brushing against each other, he peered up over the edge of the bed.

Britt mumbled again and flopped on her side. Then she turned back toward him, her arm dangling off the mattress, like she reached for him, even in sleep. A shadowed cleft between the slight curve of her breasts above the low tank top neckline turned his mouth to dust. Then the sounds became louder with little moans and bats of her hand in the air.

"Britt?" he whispered, sitting forward.

She kept muttering. The thrashing got worse. Warm swishes of skin against cotton rasped against his antidote-dulled hearing. His sleeping virus stirred. Even in a suppressed state, it needed to protect her.

Red needed not to scare her.

He quickly pulled out his phone and flipped through the images of uninteresting security footage. Held his breath and listened as best he could for any abnormal noises outside the apartment: nothing. He mentally reviewed egress points from this room and calculated how quickly he could escape with Britt. Plan set. Premises secure.

Kneeling next to the bed, he tried to stay in a nonthreatening, crouched posture. The last thing he wanted was for her to wake up with a man looming over her. She'd had enough of that kind of terror tonight. "You're having a bad dream, sweets. Come on, now." Like he'd soothed many a crying foster sibling over the years. Anything to keep that one foster parent from noticing them.

He pushed his memories away and instead concentrated on the woman who had almost died tonight. If he'd been a half-step slower, this evening's situation might have turned out with a completely different ending. Even in the dim lighting, the shadows of bruises over her neck pissed him off, all over again.

Mission. Focus. He stared at the tangle of hair around her head, dark wisps against the light pillow. He swallowed. Mission. Focus.

"Britt?" He lightly stroked the back of her wrist. Her soft skin was cool to the touch. Holding back a desperate instinct to clamp down and hold on, he curled his fingers gently around her hand. Giving warmth and support, but not restraining her.

"Al?" Her voice broke.

Something in his chest broke right along with her. "Right here. Not going anywhere."

Scooting closer to the edge of the bed, she laced her fingers with his. With her other chilly hand, she touched his face. The tangy, carbonated scratch of her nails against his stubble sent liquid sparks through every nerve in his body. The weakened virus strained, wanting him to get closer. Red took a breath and mentally walled off the impulse.

He didn't move. Couldn't. She had immobilized him with the light touch of fingers on his cheek. Her tiny sigh glittered like prisms through stained glass.

Behind the mental wall, his virus urged Red to cover her with his body and never let anyone hurt this woman, ever again. His arms strained with the need to wrap her up and pull her tightly to him. Every sense zoomed in on her, to the exclusion of his job.

Then, after another sigh and movement, the blankets shifted. He concentrated on her face. In the filtered streetlight, her pale skin took on a bluish glow.

He swallowed again, a hard lump in his throat. His body responded to her. She was satin over porcelain over steel. God help him, but Red wanted her. Needed her.

No.

That's not why he was here.

As he tried to ease away, back to his corner, she hummed a soft note that tasted like summertime lemonade. She clamped her other hand over his wrist.

Damn it. What a mess. Every muscle in his body strained to surround her. Possess her.

His heart slammed against his chest. Air coming in and out of his lungs burned. He went through his biofeedback techniques to push down the baser impulses. Breathe: in, out, in, out. Concentrate on the assignment. He grabbed the phone with his free hand, scrolling again through the security images. The mundane activity might calm him.

His restrained hand would stay there as long as Britt wished it.

He rested his head against the mattress, his hand held by both of hers as she drew it to her chest. The warmth from her body seemed to flow into him. His thighs cramped in this kneeling position.

Red refused to move.

Chapter Nineteen

Britt's phone alarm jolted her awake: 6:00 AM.

Her muscles had locked up, mid-dream. Her arm wouldn't move. It was clamped down hard, like how that man grabbed her last night … right before he choked her out. Right before mild-mannered, nerdy fashion student Al turned into a stone-cold, counterattacking fighter. Her heart thudded against her ribs. She sucked in a breath, and her sore back muscles ached with the movement.

In the dark bedroom, reality shifted and danced like smoke in the wind. She inhaled the scent of plain, clean soap, laced with a hint of pine. Even in her confusion, that simple smell calmed her. Anchored her.

I'm not in that store with those men, she reminded herself, despite her heart's desperate flittering. She stared at the normal, familiar apartment window. *Not in the store.*

Tugging on her hand, she slid it from the warm grip of…

Al.

He silently reached up from his spot on the floor next to the bed, silenced the alarm, and flipped on the nightstand light, making his orange hair glint. Looking up from his seated position with his face less than a foot from hers, he blinked. Lines of fatigue bracketed his frown.

"How long have you been there?" she said, touching the back of her wrist where his fingers had been. She wanted to retain every bit of remaining warmth.

A shrug. "A while." His morning-rough voice made her insides quiver, as she banished her nightmare and woke up completely.

He was right here. In her bedroom. Not in the store. She peered around the room. No one else waited for her in the shadows. Just Al. He wasn't Al, the fashion student. This guy was Al, the secret, kind-of military guy. She knew nothing else about the person sitting inches away from her.

Sleep-confusion and lingering memories of last night's attack hit her all at once. A shudder ripped down her back. Her chest tightened. Air struggled to move in and out of her raw throat.

"Easy there, Britt." He hadn't moved but his voice soothed her, sure as if he had stroked her with his hands. "You're okay."

Flopping back on the pillow a few inches from where he sat, she ran her hand down to the edge of the mattress. Also warm. He must have rested his head there.

As swirling panic threatened to swamp her, she grounded herself.

Solid bed beneath her body. Her bed.

Lamp light. Familiar.

Scent of pine. Al.

The coo of a morning dove outside the window. Real.

Safe.

She turned her head to study him. He hadn't moved. He'd been there all night. Studying his earnest, open expression, she couldn't reconcile the image of this quiet, gentle man camped out next to her bed with the lethal professional who raged at the attackers last night.

"I'll give you a moment," he said, not breaking eye contact as he planted a foot under him to stand.

"Al."

He froze. Fatigue shadowed his hazel eyes. A muscle in his hard jaw jumped. "Yes."

Couldn't help herself. She reached out and he

leaned toward her. Britt brushed his stubbled cheek with her fingertips, the sensation shooting zaps into her belly. "I don't understand everything that's going on here, but … thank you."

That muscle popped again under her fingers. "Of course." His voice vibrated up her arm. "It's what I do."

The revelation punched her in the gut. "This is a job to you."

He opened his mouth. Nothing came out. Finally, he answered, "It's supposed to be."

His brows drew together as his expression went from lost and empty to detached and determined. His tightly pressed lips turned pale.

Not giving two damns about how crazy this situation was, Britt leaned over, closing the few inches between their faces. After one experimental brush of her lips over his hard, unyielding ones, she pulled away, studying him. His stony face tightened up even further, like a powder keg primed for a spark.

His eyes narrowed. He gave a nearly imperceptible nod and bent toward her.

When she propped herself on an elbow and kissed him again, the powder keg exploded.

In a blur of motion, he snaked a hand out to cup the back of her head. A growl preceded the onslaught of his kisses. His lips became all changing angles and varying pressure. Hot breaths were followed by low moans. With his other hand, he pressed her jaw until she opened for him.

At first she tried to keep up with his deep kisses, but his relentless probing and unstoppable movement overloaded her senses, like multiple movies running at the same time. Too much. Not enough. Every cell in her body became attuned to Al. His light pine soap scent along with his deep, possessive growls made her breasts tighten.

Then the world tilted as he went from kneeling on the floor to crouching over her, one knee on the bed, arms braced on either side of her shoulders. The mattress dipped under his weight. The light in the room receded as Al filled her field of vision, his big frame dwarfing hers, even as he held himself off her.

Had Britt known a simple *thank you* would yield these types of results, she would have expressed way more appreciation before now. *Wow.*

Even as he locked his mouth onto hers again, stroking her tongue with his, nipping, and sweeping his lips over hers … he held back. His corded arms locked out, rigid, suspending him over her. He didn't press against her. Didn't trap her. She was in a muscled cage that she could easily escape.

No, Britt wanted those arms wrapped around her, holding her so tightly that the only reality she knew was that of the possessive strokes of his lips and tongue. She wanted him to create a human barrier between the outside world and Britt.

Her universe was filled with uncertainty right now, but the one thing she knew for certain? She wanted more of Al. She wanted to forget the mind-locking fear of who or what stalked her. Forget about her chronic anxiety that was driven by a deep-seated fear of getting close to someone and then having that person snatched away.

Right this minute, Britt only wanted Al.

Latching onto his neck, she pulled her torso up until she brushed against his chest. Better. His answering groan as he slowly lowered himself onto her made her heart leap. The heat seeping from where their bodies touched, flowed through her, loosening her joints.

With his forearms resting on the bed, he steepled

his hands around her head, threading fingers through her hair. He still held most of his weight off her, but now they touched, chest to hip to thigh.

Beautiful, safe confinement. Perfect pressure.

He drew his head back and stared at her. Stark, wild hunger swirled in the depths of his eyes. He licked his lips. Was he waiting? No waiting. Not today.

"What?" she whispered.

He flinched, like her whisper physically affected him. He shook his head. Then he dropped a light kiss on her lips and rested his forehead on hers, his heated breath soothing and tickling the skin on her neck. He pulled back. "We shouldn't—"

The passion drained away by degrees. "Because of your mission?"

His Adam's apple bobbed. "Much more than that. Damn it. Way more."

"Tell me."

"Can't." He rolled his lips together and closed his eyes. Neck muscles tightened. Hands fisted in her hair and released. Chest rose and fell, over and over. Like he tried to regain control.

An irritated prickle that had nothing to do with passion and everything to do with being left out of the loop, built in her gut.

"Can't or won't?" she said. This was not a conversation she wanted to have while pressed up against him.

"Both." He sighed. "You don't understand, and that's for the best. It's not you, Britt."

"Whoa. For real, did you just attempt the 'it's not you' line on me?"

"Uh."

Bright stings of light popped in her peripheral vision, and her face burned. God, how could she be so stupid. This was his job, for crap's sake. "You can take that lame line and shove it."

"What? No," he sputtered, pulling back.

She instantly missed the pressure of his weight on her, his heat. She shivered.

That revelation spoke volumes about where Britt's head was. She studied his narrowed eyes and furrowed brow. Ah yes, she'd almost indulged in a stress-relieving bang. No connection, only fleeting comfort. Like therapy, but with more instant gratification. Great. He probably threw in some sympathy kisses. "You were being nice to freaked-out girl. I get it."

"That's not it at all."

"Then what?"

"I—" His mouth opened but no other words exited.

"Can't say?" More prickles, like a million mosquitos biting her. Irritating. Like Al's non-answers.

"Yeah." The intense glint in his eyes went dull. Flat. Empty.

"Okay." She pushed at his chest, as if she could move him. As if she could ignore the brick-hard muscles under her palms. "We're done here."

"Britt."

A hot wash of shame caught her off guard. Nope. She wouldn't feel embarrassed. She had gone for what she wanted in the moment. Nothing wrong with desire. They were both consenting adults. He was here as part of his duty. A job. She was here, going to … well, now she needed to avoid making a connection with someone who would leave after his mission was completed. The pattern: connection, trust, bonding, then the bonds being broken. Her fears, repeated again. Nope. Not going to risk it again. Better to avoid step one, connection.

Her stomach churned. "Please move."

"Sure."

Too easy. In a flash he stood next to the wall, the bed still recoiling with his weight suddenly gone.

His eyes hooded, he said, "About today's schedule."

She crossed her arms over the quilt she tucked around her. "What about it?" She peeked at her phone. Damn it. She had work in an hour and then an afternoon class. And God help her, but Britt needed to log time in the fashion lab, completing outfits before the fittings next week. See? No time for a tall, shadow operative who saw her as duty.

"I need you to stay here. In the apartment." He crossed his arms, making it clear how much muscle was in each bicep.

"Nope."

He reared back, like refusal wasn't an option. "Huh?"

More barbs of anger poked at her, driven by sexual frustration, residual fear from last night, prior mental health demons, and sore muscles. Britt was over this whole situation. Done with being told what to do and when. No more longing to connect with someone who was here only out of duty and who would leave soon. Everyone she cared about left. That was the one constant in Britt's disorganized existence.

"Was I not clear enough last night?" she asked. "Let me expand. I am going to work and then to school, like I do every Thursday. I have a life I need to live," she hissed. "I'm not in the habit of missing work or school." She rubbed her face. "Then I have to complete my collection. Which means I'll be in the lab today. It's for the fashion show coming up. Which I plan on participating in next week. In person. I'm sick of being underestimated. I'm sick of things I cannot control changing the course of my life."

"But this—"

"You said your job is my safety, right?"

"Yes."

"Well, my job is finishing college, completing my obligations as a productive adult, and freakin' living my life. I'll do my job. You do yours."

Chapter Twenty

Red tried not to stare at the bathroom door while Britt got ready for her day. Really, he tried. What he'd give for X-ray vision right about now.

The mouthwatering pings of individual shower drops tapping against her flesh tormented him. He uncrossed his legs as he sat on the worn couch. The position change didn't relieve the building pressure.

What the hell had he almost done this morning? Britt McNeill was his mission. An assignment. She was beyond vulnerable, and he needed to get that through his thick skull and not take advantage of the situation. He had to maintain complete focus on her welfare and ensure her safety. No distractions.

Britt was one big distraction in a tiny, hot package. Man, he'd only gotten a few tastes of her, but he wanted more. See, that was the problem. Because during that amazing space of time in the bedroom, not one brain cell had been focused on the safety of the operation.

She'd be safe in my arms, a small voice in his brain piped up.

Would she, though? Anyone who got that close to Red skirted danger in more ways than Beau Lequire's minions stalking her. The Morpheus Virus made him powerful and irrational—a terrible combination. If his screwed-up head flipped the switch from *worship* to *destroy*, then he would hurt her. Besides, his personal pre-virus baggage ensured that at some point he'd fuck up any good thing.

Post-virus baggage, on the other hand, took all that childhood trauma and inability to protect his foster siblings, and amplified and warped his need to protect, then mixed it with the knowledge that he would always fail. A prize-winning recipe.

His phone rang. Red glanced at his watch: 6:30 AM. Thank God.

"Rodeo."

"How's life in fashion world, bro?" When Rodeo spoke, it always sounded like the guy was laughing. But the teammates all knew the real scary-accurate military machine beneath the yuck-it-up, have-a-good-time veneer. Rodeo was a dead shot who would stare down ten armed enemies and pick them off one by one without breaking a sweat. Then he'd destroy them with his bare hands, just to keep his day interesting.

"Did you finish the cleaning job?"

Rodeo whistled low. "I won't lie. A few of those mannequins will never model athleisure again, but yeah, I hid the damage. Same with blood-spattered clothing. Good ol' Tide stain pen, some creative rearranging on the shelves, mandatory discard of factory damaged items—all taken care of. You didn't exactly try hard to stay neat and tidy when you were getting your ass kicked."

"Nope." Red sniffed. "Lequire's men?"

"One dead and the other terra incognita. Bloody footprints out the door suggested a limp."

Red's heart sank. "You took care of…"

"The leftover body? Of course."

"Security cameras?"

"Nothing to see here, ma'am. We've played this game before. Stumpy erased all footage that had you or Britt or those dudes in it. Replaced the feed with reruns. No one should be the wiser."

"What's the sitrep on Lequire?"

"Intel suggests that his people are focusing on Reagan."

"But?"

"Shoo-wee." He sucked in air. "That asshat is one squirrely son of a bitch, and I wouldn't put it past him to try for multiple targets." Muffled crunching footsteps and a dull rumble of semis on what Red presumed was I-75, filtered in behind his words. Must be leaving the store now.

"Didn't take him long to regroup after Kiera slipped through his fingers."

The walking sounds stopped. "Bro, he took a dose of virus."

"Hunt mentioned that. Shit. How'd it happen?"

"During our rescue of Kiera. Rat bastard unloaded a syringe full of Uncle Sam's finest cocktail into his arm." A whiz of sound and slap of plastic against skin came through the phone. Ah, yes, Rodeo and his ever-present yo-yo.

Red's gut clenched as he recalled the rush of power and loss of sanity when he received his carefully metered dose of the experimental virus. "What did it do?"

"Besides make him impervious to Gonzo's beatdown?"

"Impressive, yes. But what about other new and interesting skills?"

"Hard to say. It was early in the transformation." The extra little … quirks … that sometimes came along with the virus didn't always appear right away.

"Does he have any antidote?"

A car door opened and closed. Ambient outdoor noise ceased. "Didn't stick around to make small talk and ask."

"The whole situation sucks."

"Got that right. No idea what extra fixins he'll get with his dose."

"We have to stop him."

"That's Hunt's mission. It's the team's mission. But at this time, it's not your mission."

"Good point." Red glanced toward the bathroom door. "So. You're my backup?"

"For as long as our lovely CO can spare me. Your wish is my command."

He grinned at the bizarre image of Rodeo as a large, Black genie but with his signature cowboy hat. "Good. I need mandatory rest, but I can't take a break if I'm on my own. There aren't enough clones of me to stay one step ahead of Britt."

"That little gal too much for you?"

"Freakin' never stops moving."

"Could be fun, under the right circumstances." Rodeo chuckled.

"It's not like that."

"Isn't it?" *Poke, poke.* Rodeo's main purpose on the team appeared to be the role of the irritating younger brother figure. The thing that made the guy happiest? Getting under the skin of his teammates until someone flipped out. If Rodeo didn't have virally enhanced strength and reflexes, one of the Morpheus Squad guys would have flattened him and his big mouth. But Rodeo always pulled a "who me" and skipped away from conflict he created.

"I need you to take over until midafternoon."

"Roger. Can you transmit the camera access codes?"

He hesitated. "Yes. But keep it professional. No peep shows."

"My, my." He made a clicking noise with his mouth. "Want me to meet her? Show her my fashion sense? Maybe she needs a perfect model to dress and undress. A life-sized Ken doll!"

"Shit, Rodeo. Be a good covert operator and stay hidden." A metal-tasting squeak of the faucet being shut off in the bathroom, the rough and soft swipes of towel over soft skin, combined with Rodeo's charismatic drawl, triggered something primal and possessive in Red. He clenched his empty fist and swallowed hard. No, he sure as hell did not want Britt to meet Rodeo, the suave and outgoing teammate that all the women fell for. By some miracle, Red remained calm. "Can you tail her from the apartment in a half hour or so?"

"You know I love tail, bro."

Red ground the heel of his hand into his right eye until he saw stars. "Stay professional, man."

"Always. I'm professional at everything I do, especially when it comes to the ladies. Yelp reviews five out of five, all around."

"Seriously."

"We're good. Don't worry. Where's my first location?"

"Start at her apartment here, then coffee shop for work. I'll text you the addresses. Then whatever errands she runs. There's no pattern to her never-ending activity. Good luck. I'll pick up after lunchtime at our class together. I'm still a student here."

"How's Fashion 101 going?"

"About as well as can be expected."

"Any group projects with the coeds?"

"Screw you."

"I can gladly oblige." A pause and a chuckle. "Don't worry, bro. I'll keep your lady safe from asshole Lequire."

"She's not my—"

"Sorry? Bad connection." A tapping on the phone while Rodeo made fake static noises with his mouth. "Gotta go." Rodeo disconnected while Red ground his molars.

Not. My—

Then the bathroom door opened, and Britt flitted out in a cloud of clean water and some kind of flowery soap. She wore nothing but a towel wrapped around her and a chin-jutting you-want-to-say-something expression.

"Uh." His mouth wouldn't form words.

"Well?" she asked.

"Nothing," he mumbled, unable to keep from watching her sashay into the bedroom. He stared even after she shut the door.

Hell, this was shaping up to be a long mission.

Chapter Twenty-One

TGIF.

Ignoring her Al-shaped shadow all day yesterday had worn Britt out. Granted, he gave her some breathing room. No sign of him yet this morning. Guess he didn't think she was at risk of bad guys attacking her at the coffee shop or the fashion lab. Or maybe he was that good at hiding.

She'd seen him at yesterday's afternoon class and again for today's late-morning class. Face-to-face with Al again. Or face-to-mask, as the case may be.

The guy who sat at the desk next to her remained totally casual in his vigilant-protector-who-is-also-a-hapless-fashion-student mode. If she hadn't witnessed his deadly skills in the department store, she would never have guessed he had lethal abilities. She now could pick up on the nuances of his behavior. The extra quick turn of his head, the way he seemed to study his notes but instead monitored everything happening around him, gave him away. That, and the vigilant set of his shoulders until he dropped back into a slouch.

No, Al was the same, but harder. Despite his harmless demeanor, waves of heated tension radiated from him.

Britt flinched when he flicked a sideways glance at her. He blinked hazel eyes, then scanned the room from behind his new glasses. Also fake, like the rest of his getup.

Perhaps sensing a change, Jenna had recalibrated her approach to stalking Al. Apparently, Jenna had decided Al was more like a stone that she could wear down with a slow trickle of water. Every flip of her hair or lick of her ruby-red lips. *Drip-drip*. A brief touch of lacquered nails on his arm. An innocent question and a tittered laugh at the response. *Drip-drip.* Relentless tiny erosions on the stone that was Al.

Britt had seen the immutable force that was Al.

Little did Jenna know what a strange prize she would win if she succeeded.

Class ended, and Britt hurried out of the classroom ahead of Al and Jenna.

Not fast enough.

"Oh, Britt?" Jenna's high-pitched Southern lilt grated.

Damn it. She turned, ignoring Al, who casually hovered in that infuriating, not-hovering, Henley-clad way. "Yes."

"Good luck finishing your project. I mean, for a student supported by a grant, you've got some really … interesting … pieces in the collection. Way to go with the discount fabric, by the way. You can hardly tell." She peeked under false eyelashes up to Al, who smiled blandly. "This school is *so* inclusive, if you know what I mean? It's so good for people like us to be around less advantaged students and give them special scholarships."

God, Britt wanted to punch Jenna. Also, would it kill Al to step up and say something? Protection duties should extend to squashing spoiled bullies.

"The Challenge Scholarship was a competitive. Rumor is, you applied for it, same as me." Winning the SCAD Challenge Scholarship had made a difference in how much Britt had to take out in student loans, true. But it wasn't a handout. It was earned.

"Oh, but you had a leg up because of your financial need. Oh my gosh, so lucky for you!" She clapped her hands, glitter design on her nails glinting. Her congregating posse giggled and lapped up the fake praise.

Through gritted teeth, Britt changed the subject. "Yes, I'm looking forward to the fashion show. Are you working on your collection this weekend?" she muttered.

Jenna pulled her head back and pressed a hand against her chest, drawing attention to the plunging sweetheart neckline of her white KHAITE ribbed-knit top. Yeah, that shirt cost as much as Britt made last month at the coffee shop.

"Oh, I won't be in the lab," she gasped. "I have an event to attend at Chateau Elan tomorrow." At Al's quizzical expression, Jenna tittered. "Exclusive country club. Would you like to attend as my special guest, Al? You're the quality of person welcome there."

He blinked behind non-refractory lenses. "Um, no, thanks," he said, shifting his tote to the other shoulder. Hopefully it was so he could reach a weapon and fend off Jenna.

Britt smirked at the thought of Al and Jenna at the soiree. She could picture the club's packed event hall, filled with men in pressed white David Donahue button-down shirts, Zegna floral silk ties, topped by charcoal Hugo suit separates. There would be semi-bragging chit-chat about golf scores and State and local government. Handshakes and promises of business favors. Too-loud laughs. Accompanying them would be picture-perfect dates delicately fighting breathlessness and hunger in tight, unique-but-same little black dresses. There would be way too much jasmine and amber Chanel No. 5 perfume floating in a room where veneer smiles and air kisses were *de rigeur*. No, thanks.

Jenna flipped her hair off a shoulder. "Besides, I finished my collection ahead of time, so I get to celebrate. The models are flying in from LA and Paris next Thursday, right on time for the show. Oh my gosh, you'll have to meet them. They're fabulous." She paused.

"Though their rates are some of the highest in the industry." A shrug. "Hashtag: *worth it*."

"Hashtag *thanks, Dad*, you mean," Britt said under her breath.

Her gaze narrowed. "Just because you don't have funds to succeed is no reason to pull me down. Here we are congratulating each other. Fashion colleagues supporting fashion colleagues."

Nothing collegial about how Britt wanted to ram a shoulder into Jenna's ribbed-knit midsection right about now.

Al opened and then deliberately closed his mouth. Britt didn't know whether that meant he was smart or lily-livered.

Time to bail. "Bless your heart." A phrase Britt absolutely did not feel right this minute. "May you receive all that you have earned. Take care now." Thank God for years of observing her mother handle nasty, rude people.

Al wasn't standing up for her in this situation. Irritation needled her, making her skin itchy. Hey, his job wasn't to help her navigate snobs. He was tasked with keeping her alive. Big difference.

Before Jenna could respond, Britt turned on her heel and stomped toward the common area for lunch. She tamped down the tidal wave of anxiety that hit her out of the blue and left her trembling. Britt drew in a long breath, then exhaled as she mentally made a list of the final items before the show next week. Items, budget, schedule. Last push before the show. The finish line.

A last wish, fulfilled.

Not if Al had any say in it. He wanted to control Britt's every move. Stop her from finishing her work. She began to hyperventilate as she stomped her scuffed thrift store Martens.

Seemed like there was always something or someone in her way. Heck, Britt had gotten in her own way lots of times. Now Jenna's cattiness, then Al's meddling. How about catching a break? Life would be simpler if those two stayed out of her business.

Oof. She tripped on a step edge and caught herself. Man, Britt needed to chill. She did her sight, sound, and smell grounding exercise and took three long, slow breaths. Better. Marginally.

She walked into The Hub, the SCAD dining area, grabbed a packaged sandwich and bottled drink at random, and swiped her card. Glancing back, Al wasn't far behind. How about a little space? Would it kill him?

Or how about not so much space? A wave of warmth made her midsection quiver as she remembered how his sensual mouth felt against hers. How those strong arms felt wrapped around her, not enough to hurt but tight enough to assert quiet authority. If he wished, he could move her around wherever—and however—he wanted.

She didn't dislike the idea. Britt pressed her legs together.

Not going to happen. Concentrate on finishing the degree. Ignore the hot, weird undercover dude with an agenda separate to Britt's.

Hungry for more than lunch, she unwrapped her sandwich and took a disappointing bite of hummus and cucumber on dry pita bread. On her stroll to the fashion lab, a text popped up.

Tachi: **Got the evening off. Are we going out tonight? (disco dancing emoji)**

Pretty sure techno beats and large crowds didn't fit on Al's approved activity list. Britt glanced over her shoulder. He still hovered as a quiet, watchful shadow who hadn't helped her deal with a bully. All the restrictions chafed at Britt, and started to feel like imaginary shackles, ramping up her anxiety. Damn this guy and the whole situation.

She needed to release the tension building under her skin or she was going to lose her mind. Her favorite stress-reliever—dancing? With Tachi?

The mission. Danger. Making better choices. A twinge of doubt was quickly squashed by a wave of impulsive enthusiasm. Why shouldn't she have one normal night out?

Britt: **Does a duck say quack? Yaaasss!**

Guess what? Britt nodded her head and puffed out her chest. Al could always tag along if he had concerns about Britt's safety in an electronica venue with hundreds of mildly buzzed dancers where the biggest threat involved avoiding preppy dudes hitting on Britt and Tachi and witnessing some bad trance shuffles.

Heck, Al *should* come with. It would be good for him to loosen up some. Meet some people.

A little GNO wouldn't hurt, either.

Chapter Twenty-Two

God help him, what was Britt thinking, sauntering down the street from her apartment to the MARTA station at 10:07 PM with her roommate? Actually, Red knew precisely what they had planned, thanks to Stumpy's hack of her phone and the entire apartment having more bugs than a CIA covert supply depot.

Uber, MARTA, walking, a private vehicle—every mode of transportation had risks. She'd selected MARTA. At least he could tail her but remain inconspicuous.

He relaxed his tight control. Sounds flooded his auditory canals. Murmurs of the ladies' conversation brushed by him like melted butter on freshly baked bread. Behind their voices, an acrid sound of vehicle wheels on pavement turning at a nearby stoplight soured the sensory input. He scanned the city block and structures, as much with his ears as his eyes. Nothing. Yet.

Had she ignored everything he had told her about Lequire and danger? What the hell did Britt think she was doing?

She was attempting to live her normal life to its fullest. Something Red might want to try one day.

True, she looked edgy and sexy in a red-and-black miniskirt with crinkly material under it that made it puff out. She wore a cropped black halter top with a high neck that hid her bruises. The backless garment hugged her trim frame. Only a few bruises marred the skin of her back. She'd been lucky in so many ways. Her purple-highlighted hair was half pulled up, highlighting her elven features and making the silver hoops on her face glint in the streetlight. The whole look created an angelic and punk aesthetic that made his mouth water.

Still.

When he discovered what she had planned by, well, spying on her, he had phoned. His stern advice to stay home went over like a lead balloon. She had snarled about how he wanted to pick and choose when he provided backup, so she'd pick and choose when she needed backup, whatever the hell that meant. Then he got the "it's my life, I understand the danger, and I'm making an informed decision and taking back some control" thrown in his face.

Good God, she was pissed.

He couldn't argue with her logic. Much. He knew all about having no control over his life. CO Hunt wasn't an asshole about the rules, but every team member knew the consequence to everyone's lives if those rules didn't get followed.

Britt did agree to keep Red's presence and mission a secret from Tachi. He would take any win he could get.

She wanted to live her life on her own terms. Roger that. However, there was a difference between independence in safe situations versus dumb decisions in the face of known threats. This woman stomping toward the train in metallic booties had drawn a line in the sand. Britt McNeill had had enough and was Going Out, by God, and there wasn't a damn thing that Red could legally do about it. At least he'd have backup.

Right on time, Rodeo made brief eye contact with Red on the far end of the MARTA platform, appearing as if out of thin air. As the train approached, the whine of wheels braking on rails sliced through Red's mind. He panted, control slipping.

To regulate his response, he catalogued all infil and exfil points, including strengths and weaknesses of each. He confirmed the location of every weapon stashed on his person. Then Red took note of each person on the platform and on the approaching train. Listened to the world around him. Filtered sound in an orderly fashion. He detected no clicks of a gun safety. No mutters of people coordinating an ambush. No noises that didn't fit in the auditory soup swirling around him.

Once the doors opened, Red and Rodeo entered three cars back from where the ladies rode and separately worked their way up to the car behind Britt and Tachi. He and Rodeo picked different seats with a clear line of sight in all directions. Light passenger traffic this evening—no sports or major concerts downtown this evening.

Britt glanced back over her shoulder.

Red didn't mind Britt knowing he was present. She would expect it. But he didn't want to tip off the roommate. He also didn't want anyone to know about Rodeo, his proverbial ace up the sleeve for this mission.

His teammate sat, leaning against the wall of the train, a leg slung over two seats. He turned a small yo-yo over in his hand. The nonchalant posture didn't fool Red. Knowing Rodeo, the guy had identified every visible and theoretical danger and then calculated angles necessary to achieve a single-tap headshot to eliminate any threat. The guy wasn't just a good shot. He was a disturbingly accurate shot, thanks to the virus enhancing his already superior marksmanship.

At least he had ditched the ubiquitous cowboy hat, which would be as out of place in downtown Atlanta as substituting Frosted Flakes for grits and thinking no one would notice. Rodeo darted a smirk toward Red, one eyebrow quirking up, then returned to the guise of relaxing in broody solitude.

Despite Rodeo's lack of his typical Western attire

tonight, there was fat chance of his teammate going unnoticed. Without trying, Rodeo looked like the cover of *GQ Magazine* come to life. Red only knew that because he had flipped through that magazine recently as research for the mission.

Yeah, speaking solely from his newfound perspective as a fake fashion student, Red assessed that Rodeo had great facial structure, perfect skin, and a mug that begged to be photographed from any angle. Objectively model-esque. From the guy's short leather lace-up boots that likely hid a weapon or two, to the indigo jeans, to a tight t-shirt that let his biceps do all the talking, Rodeo knew he looked great. Smug bastard.

Shit, Red had become a fashion expert in the space of a week. He could now venture guesses as to the brands on each clothing item, and he'd be correct more often than not.

In a stunning turn of events, Red could now match separates. Testimony to Gonzo's and Stumpy's prep materials as well as Red's ability to absorb information in a hurry. Which in turn was testimony to the Morpheus Virus. Speaking of which, his shoulder blades twitched again under his too-warm combo of a tan button-down shirt topped by a denim jacket which contained communications and weaponry options.

Even Red's relaxed-fit khaki's bugged the crap out of him. Every movement was a whiskey shot *swish* of cotton blend arrowing right into his eardrums. No way could it be time for another dose of antidote. Too soon. If the virus got fired up, Red would reach that tipping point again. He hadn't planned to require another shot for a day or two.

The quarter-full train rocked and rumbled as it pulled out of the station. His ears rang with the thick thrumming, squeaking noise. Should he use the earplugs?

He slid a hand into his jacket pocket and patted the small pieces of silicone, craving the relief. Dreading the trade-off.

From his vantage point at the front of the car, Red kept an eye on Britt and Tachi, as did Rodeo. The guy might be all fun and games, but when he had a mission to complete, Red knew better than to believe the guy's devilish smile. Rodeo's focus was legendary. Throw in any excuse for him to shoot someone dead, and the grinning teammate transformed into one of the world's scariest motherfuckers.

Even now, his teammate shifted in his seat, checking the gun at his back. Knowing Rodeo, he had another pistol on his leg and a bunch of knives stashed all over his person. Rodeo was scary with any weapon.

"It's my life. I'm going out. If you're interested in your mission success, then make my life safe," Britt had said.

That's not how security worked, with Britt running all over town, exposed to Lequire and his goons.

Still, Red understood. Losing control of one's life sucked. Bouncing from foster family to family, rootless and adrift, his only life choices were like picking which flavor of dirt sandwich he wanted to eat for lunch. That asshole, Red's last foster father, had made those choices painfully clear years ago.

Thank God for his teammates—like brothers he'd never had. He glanced at Rodeo. The guy winked.

The team had made the decision together to take the experimental virus, to try and change the course of military conflicts with their augmented abilities. Gain an advantage. Prevent injury and death. Too bad the virus took away Red's freedom.

Actually, he had a choice. He could have stayed behind in that glorified military prison that good ol'

Uncle Sam claimed was a "voluntary testing center" and become a professional lab rat for the rest of his life. Instead, he escaped to blend into the shadows with the team. For what purpose?

To use their abilities to help other veterans and their families out of bad situations.

The endgame Hunt had in mind was less defined, but Red knew his CO ultimately wanted to destroy the Morpheus Virus and anyone involved in its creation and distribution. All that substance did was create monstrous puppets and even more monstrous puppet masters. In the wrong hands, the Morpheus Virus could tip the scales of global power.

He rolled his hands into fists until the joints popped.

"Penny for your thoughts." Rodeo mumbled, not looking at him.

Red leaned across the aisle of their nearly empty MARTA car, elbows on his knees. "Calculating how long this op will continue. When we'll encounter Lequire. Or if."

Rodeo glanced around. "Might catch a break. Hunt said Lequire's men had found Reagan this afternoon."

"Found?"

"Pele saw them on a trail cam."

"Damn. What about Pele?"

"Radio silence. I assume he's taking care of business. Tropical guy is resourceful."

"But in the Smoky Mountains?"

"Eh, some poison ivy is good for him."

"At least he's fearless." One of Pele's extra goodies from the virus.

"That's what makes me nervous." Rodeo buffed his nails on his shirt. "An abnormal lack of fear might not mix well with normal humans who are terrified."

"Reagan and Pele will do fine. It's selfish, but I hope they draw Lequire's attention away from us. Until then, we're on glorified babysitting duties."

"Great," Rodeo quipped.

"There are worse things," Red offered.

"Speaking of which..." Rodeo stretched up to full-seated height to casually scan the car behind them and in front of them, then slouched back down. "Sure that roommate doesn't need undercover protection, too? I'd like to volunteer to patrol her perimeter."

Red groaned. "Come on, man. No extracurricular activities. Mission focus."

"Hoo boy, you are so not one to talk."

"I'm professional."

"Dude, your face turns two shades redder with every little peek at Britt, and your pupils dilate and your blinking decreases. Not to mention the pressure wave on your jugular vein speeds up."

Gritting his teeth, Red muttered, "Could you not identify all the places where you can kill me?"

"Sure, but I'm bored and want to play," he whined.

"Lucky me."

"You have no idea." He stared straight ahead and flexed his pecs. "Maybe lucky roommate, if that gal plays her cards right."

"You read the dossier? She's a model and stuff."

He pressed a hand to his chest and pulled an offended face. "What are you saying, my man? Listen, I'm as close to a ten as our motley group of mutants will ever get." He grinned, broad and mischievous. "Bet she digs military dudes." He tipped his head toward the car in front of them. "She might like to check out my service weapon." He pushed his tongue against his cheek and waggled his eyebrows.

"Come on, man, stick to the mission."

Rodeo kicked back and crossed his muscled arms over his chest with a pout, not before scanning the train car again. "Spoilsport."

Chapter Twenty-Three

Al was nearby. Britt could feel it, like a sense of static before a thunderstorm rolls overhead. When would the lightning occur?

Glancing out the MARTA train window, she used the reflection to observe the few other people in the train. Friend or foe? She stared at each passenger, judging their behavior and demeanor. Did that older lady's cane hide a knife? How about those giggling teenagers pouring over the latest TikTok video? An imaginary finger of ice traced down her spine.

For a split-second she double-guessed her impulsive choice to go out with Tachi. Come to think of it, she had double-guessed a ton of decisions in her life. That self-doubt and anxiety were big reasons why it had taken so long to get to decide on her college degree and her life goals.

No more doubting. For once, she would pick an option and stick with it. This was Britt's life and she was an adult who could consider risks and benefits to her decisions. She smoothed her short skirt over her thighs. Brushed her fingers over a brow hoop.

A tiny voice asked if Tachi had a choice, if something bad were to happen? A sour taste of guilt answered the question.

Tachi was chattering about her upcoming shoot next week. Excited, happy. Animated. As she should be. "...and they want me to model summer fashions. If we get some good photos, they might use one for a cover! Can you believe it?"

"That's awesome, Tachi. You'll be fabulous." She struggled to stay present in the conversation. "Do you think there'll be some cute people there?"

"Models?"

"Or photographers, maybe?"

"Rule number one of modeling: never date the photog. Rule number two is don't even think about it with the other models. Lordy, they're as high-maintenance as I am!"

"I didn't know those rules existed." Britt laughed.

Tachi scraped her long, curly hair back off her face and fluttered dark eyelashes. "Actually, rule number one should be, never sleep with the casting professional or shoot director."

"Is that even a thing these days?"

"No idea. No one has propositioned me yet. Can you imagine?" She narrowed her warm brown eyes until they became glints as she studied Britt.

"Uh, I'm not sure the correct answer." Britt shrugged. "Yay?"

"Yes, yay. I get enough inappropriate advances from my patrons at the club."

"How could they not? You're athletic, artistic, and beautiful."

Tachi tapped her phone and held it up to her workplace's Yelp page with tons of five-star reviews. "Hottest plus-sized pole dancer in the greater Atlanta area, according to this *very* scientific survey." Her friend wasn't even bragging. Neither were the reviews. These were statements of fact.

Heck, Britt knew. She'd seen Tachi's skills on the pole and yes, her friend had impressive moves.

Britt leaned back on the seat. "Well, tonight is for us to blow off steam and enjoy moving to the music. It's necessary. Too much stress lately." If Tachi only knew.

"Oh, yes, darling. Use tonight to forget about that boy from the other night."

That boy. Yikes. Britt had made up a lame story

about Al coming over and then leaving. Anything to keep his presence on the down-low and protect Tachi. Unfortunately, the tale made Britt look pitiful and in need of a supportive girlfriend right about now.

Tachi could smell a charity case from miles away.

Before her friend could take a full breath and come up with a three-step plan to recover Britt's social life, the brakes squeaked as the train slowed. The recorded announcement came on overhead. MARTA Civic Center.

"Our stop." Britt jumped up and brushed the skirt down. Her look had drawn inspiration from Harley Quinn, with a two-layer skirt, black crinoline for the bottom layer and red satin over it. Enough coverage to be socially acceptable, but short enough to be super fun. She'd covered the darkest bruises on her legs and arms with dense foundation used in photo shoots. Thankfully, she had only light bruises on her back that weren't very noticeable. The neck bruises, on the other hand—at least she had clothing to cover them up.

Tugging the high-necked halter top and adjusting her small cross-body black Guess purse—the result of one fantastic day of thrifting last fall—Britt preceded Tachi out of the train. Out of the corner of her eye, she caught sight of two particularly handsome men walking slowly in Britt's direction but not closing the distance. They were both dressed in understated fashion but on-point for the club. One freshly shaved guy had sported red hair a few inches long, camel-colored pants, dark-brown Chelsea boots, and a distressed denim jacket that made his shoulders look even more solid than she knew they already were.

Al.

Her breath caught.

He lifted his chin toward the other guy then broke eye contact with her, pausing to ostensibly study the station map.

The Black man in dark jeans and a tailored t-shirt glanced her way with a quick grin, then brushed a hand over his hip. A blink-and-you-miss-it movement, but Britt had a pretty good idea that he stashed a weapon under that trim waistband. So, Al had help tonight.

The guys lingered behind as Britt and Tachi exited the platform and headed up the escalator to street level.

A ten-minute walk brought them to Midtown nightclub Amethyst, laser-light patterns illuminating a brick façade. A deep-purple door and cordoned line of patrons marked the entrance, just in case people couldn't find the place by the throbbing electronica bass spilling out into the street.

Once in line, Britt glanced around. No sign of Al or his partner.

A prickle snaked across her skin. She peered over at the busy, lit Midtown street. Groups of what looked like college-aged and early career businesspeople laughed and chatted at several restaurants' outdoor seating areas nearby. Two bars further down the street drew patrons in and had them lingering outside, laughing and smoking. No suspicious people.

A shudder hit her. No one resembled the men from the mall, as best she could tell with what little she had seen of their appearance. No one on the busy street this Friday night gave her any sketchy vibes.

No fear. No self-doubt. Britt wanted this evening out. She would trust that Al could do his job. She was going to enjoy herself tonight, bodyguard or not.

The bouncer paid zero attention to Britt and focused his attention on her roommate in her amazing bustier top and leather pants. With two fingers, he motioned Tachi to the front of the line, and Tachi grabbed Britt's wrist to tug her through the line.

At the front door, in those heels, her roommate towered over Britt and the bouncer.

Perfect height for him to check out her … ID.

Tachi did a smile/hair toss combo that worked like magic. With a half-hearted glance at Britt's ID, the bouncer sent them into the club.

The pounding bass and electric beats hit Britt full blast, vibrating her ribs, exactly how she liked it. She sped up her steps to the rhythm as she and Tachi wove through standing and dancing customers. At the bar, they returned the smiles of some well-dressed people around them and ordered drinks before finding an open couch near the VIP area. A clink of their glasses toasted the evening out.

The first few sips of an alcohol and fruit combo gave Britt that nice warm limb-loosening feeling that started in her neck and settled in her hips. Even seated, she swayed to the music.

"It's good?" Tachi asked with an arm thrown around Britt's shoulders, so they could talk over the soaring melodies.

Britt neck-hugged her roommate back. "Perfect end to a crazy week."

"I'll drink to that!" They tapped glasses again, sipped their drinks, and relaxed for a few minutes. The DJ's cuts were tight and people responded, packing the dance floor about thirty feet away from where Tachi and Britt sat.

Peering through the ever-moving crowd of happy club patrons, Britt didn't see anything—or anyone—out of place. Whoever tracked her wouldn't dare make a grab in a public venue like Amethyst. From the busy bar to the hopping dance floor in front of a renovated theater stage that housed the DJ and equipment, to the elevated clear spheres where dancers gyrated above the crowd, to balconies teeming with even more patrons, there weren't a lot of places to hide.

Speaking of. She scanned again. No sign of Al or the guy he was with. A chill worked its way down her spine. Fear? Or hope that she would see him here?

Whatever the mixed emotion, she wanted nothing to do with it. "Ready?" She finished her drink and waved her free hand toward the floor.

"You bet, darling!" Tachi shouted near Britt's ear, linking their hands together.

Weaving through dancers, they made their way to the middle of the dance floor. As hoped, the pulsing beat soon transported Britt far away from her worries. For a precious few minutes, her life boiled down to the blissed-out feeling of bass thumping through her chest. She let the music take her someplace else, where she didn't have projects due or bills to pay or strange dudes coming after her. A place where she didn't carry the weight of her mother's last wishes and her own anxiety. She moved her arms and hips in time with the rise and fall of the rhythms.

Even next to Tachi's flawless dancing, Britt felt sexy and free. She fed off the energy of the dancers and the music all around her.

Free. She skimmed her hands over the tight-fit open-back halter top. She spun around, enjoying the little swirl and flounce of her skirt. Even her shiny booties made her feel strong and confident. A few appreciative nods of dancers nearby in button-down Izod shirts boosted her self-esteem even more.

The strobes of light illuminated a group of men drifting over to dance around Tachi and Britt. The high-

and-tight haircuts gave them away, and the set of their muscled frames reminded her of Al. Those guys were probably from Dobbins. Marietta, Georgia, where the Air Force base was located, was not too far from downtown. The too-cocky swagger as a jeans-clad thigh brushed against her leg? Maybe another time. Britt just wanted to move in her own little bubble tonight.

She swayed close to Tachi, touched her friend's arm to get her attention, and tilted her head. At a nod from Tachi, they wove through the shifting crowd to another area of the dance floor. This area was not as tightly packed with people. She needed a little extra breathing room. They carved out space to move.

The back of Britt's neck prickled.

At the dark edges of the dance floor she caught a glint of hair, broad shoulders in denim, and the determined set of a wide mouth. Her heartbeat sped up to match the dance tempo. Al's shadowed stare slid off the other dancers to rest on her.

She sucked in a breath.

"Be right back, okay?" she asked Tachi.

"No problem." Her roommate currently had two guys triangulating on her. Tachi crooked a finger at both of them and laughed.

Britt worked through the maze of the shifting crowd until she reached a concrete pillar that supported the building.

Al leaned against it, one leg crossed over the other, full drink in hand. She'd bet money he hadn't consumed any of it. Also, she didn't buy the casual posture one bit.

"Having a good night?" he asked, expression grim.

Was it the relaxation of her drink earlier or did his words really create quivers deep in her belly? "Very.

You?" She tucked a finger under the cross-body strap where it connected with the purse at her hip.

"No. I've had to follow you across town. This is a challenging place to secure." He winced and touched the side of his face as the DJ made an announcement.

Come to think of it, Al did have the appearance of a caged, tormented animal. His head was on a swivel and he cringed a few times. Maybe he didn't like crowds. Or he knew this was a place he couldn't do his job.

She put her hand on his forearm as she leaned closer. "This is exactly what I needed tonight. A way to recharge and forget about this bizarre week. Let loose."

The way he raked his gaze over her from head to toe felt like a physical stroke of his hand. She shivered. Why had she been angry with him the other day? Couldn't remember.

"It's still not safe," he said. When a patron stumbled toward her, Al wrapped an arm around her to rotate them so her back pressed against the pillar and his body blocked traffic. The lava-hot glare he shot the stumbling man probably sent that dude right to the men's room to relieve himself.

Oh, yeah. Now she remembered. She was angry about the part where Al wanted to dictate her every move. Like right now. Then he locked eyes on her and licked his upper lip.

Her knees shook as she stared him down. Or up, due to her position against concrete and looking at his face, inches away from hers. "What part of all this isn't safe?" Britt quipped, no longer caring if she baited him. "None of these people are here to do harm. It's just a night out for them, too. Why shouldn't I have fun? Don't you want to have fun?"

"You have no idea." His low voice rivaled the bass beat as it rumbled through her bones.

If she was playing with fire, maybe she wanted to get burned, just a little bit. She knew this situation made no sense. Knew there was no future in it. But this was her choice to make. And his.

"Al?"

In the strobing lights, his pupils dilated, turning his eyes nearly black. He set the drink on the tray of a passing waitress. Then he rested both hands on the pillar next to her head, effectively creating a wall of … Al … around her. He leaned in, still not touching her. The space filled with heat radiating off his body and a light scent of aftershave. God, she wanted to close the distance between them, but she needed to know that he wanted to … play with fire, too.

He kept tilting his head, like trying to tune in to something and failing. His gaze flipped from her to around the room and back to her. Over and over.

"Ready to leave?" he said, this time biting his lower lip. Unfair. She wanted to bite that lip.

He moved his hand slowly toward her, giving Britt ample time to move. Thumping music buffeted her.

She held still.

He trailed a fingertip over her jaw.

Britt shuddered.

He swept the rough pad of that fingertip lower, to her covered collarbone. Rested his palm on her heated skin. Curled his fingers around the edge of her bare shoulder. His expression remained grim. Sure, he seemed interested and had all the right moves. But the tight set of his jaw didn't seem to match the mood. What gave?

"Britt?" he growled. "How about your place? Somewhere quiet. And safe."

Blinking, she shook her head like she needed to dislodge cobwebs. Something didn't jive. None of his moves felt natural. For sure, she wanted him to touch her more. She would love to go somewhere more private where she could taste him and make such a big, serious guy tremble.

This attraction had to be natural. And mutual. Whatever vibe she got from Al, not all of it was personal interest. There was calculation in each of his actions, almost like he was trying too hard.

Her lust-fogged brain cleared in a hurry. Pieces fell into place. "Not yet." Maybe not ever, if she couldn't separate his reality from her desire.

"You sure? We could have our own dance party." That line felt 100% fake. Al was a lot of things like hot, strong, and determined, but he wasn't a slick lady's man. At least, not based on her assessment over the past few days.

Realization hit her like a bucket of ice water. This guy was putting the moves on her to—wait for it—control her even more. No. Britt was in charge of Britt. This was her night. She had decided. No overprotective guard dog, no matter how tempting, would distract her.

However. He had a mission to carry out. She had only begun her evening. Let no one ever accuse Britt of missing any opportunity to kill two birds with one proverbial stone.

"I've still got some stress to burn off." She ducked under his arm. Breathlessly, she spun a quarter-turn toward him and asked, "Want to dance?"

A grimace creased his face as he dropped his arm, stood up straight, and faced her head-on. "Not my scene. Don't dance."

"You should try."

His neck flexed as his Adam's apple rose and fell. "You should take my advice and let's get you back home." *Let's get you back home.* Like it was a mission task to complete. Because it was a mission task.

"I'm not done here."

"I say you are," he growled, voice both caressing and abrading her.

"Sorry, but these are my choices to make. You didn't have to come out here. You can't create a scene because it's a public place and you're undercover."

"Now you're being unreasonable." He winced again at a super deep bass throb.

She threw her shoulders back and drew herself up to full height, which, even with her heeled ankle booties only put her at chest height with the guy. "Look. If you want to keep closer tabs on me, you know where I'll be," she said, thumbing behind her toward the teeming dance floor.

Before he could respond, she ducked behind a nearby group of laughing, dancing women and then zigzagged back through the crowd until she found Tachi.

"Everything okay?" Tachi asked, smiling as two admirers shimmied and gyrated close enough to rub up against her.

"You bet it is."

Chapter Twenty-Four

Red was in big trouble.

The earplugs had rendered him nearly defenseless, so he'd ripped those out and shoved them back in the jacket pocket. The noise in this place hurt like hell. Overloaded electronic beats hammered nasty, sour spikes of music into his head. He couldn't take much more of the squealing and shouting patrons, the sound creating a muffled background to the relentless sound drilling through the speakers. The virus flared, hating the sensory loss. It hated the limitless threats contrasted with his inability to identify true danger.

Britt's outfit didn't help Red's concentration. His Energizer pixie had transformed into a sexy dancer. Her short crunchy skirt showed off lean thighs that made his fingers tingle, so badly did he want to skim his way up her legs to her hips. He swallowed.

Her edginess with the ankle boots was offset by the slight curves hugged by her tight halter top. An expanse of exposed luminous skin on her back tempted him like nothing he'd seen before. The tie at the back of her neck enticed him to undo that scrap of fabric and peel the garment off, licking his way over the breasts beneath. Her nipples had turned into sexy, hard nubs when he had touched her shoulder.

He shifted his stance. That move didn't relieve the pressure like he'd hoped.

Damn it. Focus on the mission. Focus on threat avoidance.

Focus on anything except the silky skin that he'd only gotten a sample of. He couldn't give into this … whatever was brewing between him. God help him, he needed more of Britt.

The mission.

What mission? It was a joke of an assignment and a joke of an operator assigned to it. This woman confounded any standard protocol. His gut churned as he catalogued the various weapons stashed on his person.

This whole evening's security duty was FUBAR. Sure, Rodeo hung out nearby, fending off willing partners while remaining ready to jump into protection duties. This location, this situation. Pure disaster. Unsecurable. The only thing that had kept her safe up until now wasn't Red. It was straight-up dumb luck. That luck could run out any minute.

Red should have put his foot down and kept Britt from going out. A red clay-thick pounding pulse at his temple filtered through the techno music. He sucked in air and exhaled, logging ingress and egress points, and potential liabilities.

Everything in this place was a liability. Every. Damned. Thing. Red couldn't force anyone to do anything, not without committing a crime. Morpheus Squad didn't exist—not on paper. So he didn't exist. His job wasn't official.

Somehow, with Britt, things had gotten personal. Her relentless energy and independence and complete unwillingness to listen to him, had dug under his skin. A blended wave of irritation and sexual frustration knocked him back a step. What could he do?

Fair's fair. The best offense would be to keep the target off-balance. God, Red needed to make her feel as unsteady and unsure as he felt when he was around her. Unfortunately, this entire job and his own fucked-up baggage barred him from reaching out for what he truly wanted.

What he wanted was currently shaking her toned butt as a J. Crew wannabe spokesmodel sidled up behind her. Light glinted off the fellow's stiff, gelled hair. Red could hear the guy's salty low *mmm-hmmm* of appreciation as he checked her out.

Sound blended into a loud buzz of spicy rage when the guy put his hands on Britt's hips and swayed in time with her.

Red wasn't jealous. He had a job to do. Safety was job one.

For all he knew, that asshole could be part of Lequire's team. Could be a threat.

Sure as hell wasn't jealousy driving Red's decisions, because that feeling required emotional connection, and Red had every reason not to connect with anyone, ever.

Back to the mission. Of course Britt would be better protected if Red maintained a tighter perimeter. By perimeter, that meant he needed to be pressed right up to her tight body. Operationally speaking.

His virus rumbled inside him, either approving or egging him on—hard to tell. Red the man and Red the virally enhanced soldier blended together. Given the tension ratcheting up in the muscles of his back, the balance of sanity versus viral urges had started to tip again. It was way too soon. Damn it.

The guy on the dance floor took Britt's hand, lifted it, and trailed fingers up her arm until she laughed. Red's vision flickered crimson. God help him, but Red absolutely should not touch Britt in this state.

Virus didn't care. As if her presence out on the floor tugged invisible marionette strings attached to him, Red lifted a hand toward her. Leaned forward. He had to be in contact with her. Craved connection with a hunger that sent him reeling. Distracted him.

Distractions meant mistakes. Mistakes meant harm. Stick with protocols.

He had left mission protocol in the dust long ago, right when she ran smack-dab into his chest in the hallway that first day.

He pushed away from the pillar.

Shouldering through the crowd, Red ignored offended yelps as he bumped people on his way to the knot of dancers. A quick glance up on the balcony revealed Rodeo's position where he observed the crowd and Red. The Morpheus Squad guys were particularly good at identifying physical changes in each other when the virus took off. His teammate's crossed-arm stance and vigorous shake of the head guaranteed that Red would catch hell for what came next.

Didn't matter what percentage of the impulse came from the virus or from Red. He was no longer the quiet peacemaker, thinking about a problem, then negotiating to find a solution.

The man dancing behind Britt gripped her hips and eased her back against him.

Negotiation over.

Red's vision bled until crimson strobe lights pulsed against crimson house lights. Sound roared. The virus inside him raged, battering against Red's skull, as if it wanted out.

Red would be damned if that well-dressed, preppy little bastard smeared those hands all over Britt for one second longer. Purely as a security issue.

He grasped the man's wrist and applied the perfect amount of pressure. Any angry protest disappeared right when a bone started to crack, the burnt-popcorn sound making Red's mouth water. Focus and cold control abruptly returned, and his world tunneled down to the two people in front of him, one of whom needed to step the hell away from the other one.

"Dude?" the guy sputtered as he jumped back.

"What the fuck? Back off."

Britt's eyebrows shot up, sparking glints off the hoops, a surprised smile quickly morphing to shock as she studied Red.

Red lifted a shoulder and leaned in close to the sweating man. "My turn. Get lost."

"Fuck you. I was here first."

Calm. Control. Red tamped down the virus. Hard. His unbreakable control would not crack. Not today. "Leave." He squeezed once more on the man's wrist until he yelped and snatched his arm back.

"You're nuts."

Red leaned forward and threw every bit of viral insanity into his voice. "You have no idea what I'm capable of, friend."

The man backpedaled and disappeared into the crowd.

Red turned and faced Britt. A small space had cleared out around the two of them. In the strobe lights, he could guess at the target of her pissed-off expression, and it wasn't her dance partner, Scooter McDougal, or whatever that shit's name was. Tough. Red had a job to do. If she insisted on staying in danger, then he would stay in it with her. Simple enough.

"May I?" He managed to grit out the civility.

With a jut to her chin, she turned her back on him and undulated toward other dancers.

The virus was having none of it.

Red caught her hand. *Control it*, he prayed. *Don't hurt her*. More gently than he thought possible, he spun her toward him. "You *had* offered." His vision still misfired, tinting everything red, though it was improving. Something about the connection with Britt calmed the virus. He blinked once. Twice. Then stared down at her.

She sucked in the hoop on her lip, that tiny action

shooting blissful tightness into his belly and lower.

"But you said, and I quote, 'I don't dance'." She wrinkled her nose.

Words became more fluid as the connection with Britt fueled his ability to calm the viral urges. "Why don't. You show me. How." Bending down, his breath shifted the hair next to her ear. As synesthesia amplified, that millimeter of a *swish* sound of hair moving against fabric sounded like vanilla merengue cookies tasted. Delicious. "Let me know if I'm doing it right or not." He gave the lightest lick to her ear.

Her sharp intake stung like bubbles of a fizzy root beer. Every sense folded and blended until all he experienced was Britt in front of him. Good God, they were both in trouble.

The proper protocol when impaired or disabled: call for backup. He turned his head enough to glimpse Rodeo leaning over the railing. Waiting for the signal. Watching.

Red didn't give the signal.

Instead, he trailed his hand down Britt's bare arm. Her skin was satiny-soft. That simple contact further calmed the overwhelming viral impulses to protect, surround, defend. Touching Britt revved up other impulses. Red could maintain control. He had to.

When she turned away from him, he thought he'd screwed up again.

Then she slipped her arm out from under his and gripped his wrist. Britt backed up to him, her hips keeping time with the music that Red could process once more. She brushed against him tentatively at first. Nerve endings sparked to life where they connected. Her small hand held his wrist prisoner. The whisper of the skin of her back against the rough denim jacket, arrowed warmth right into his chest. The bruises visible when her clothing shifted, sent a virtual dagger into his gut. This woman. Injured on his watch. His tense arms shook with the need to wrap her up and not let go.

Britt swayed with the music's throbbing beat, tugging lightly on his wrist until he matched her movements. She pressed his palm to the dip in front of her hip bone and repeated on the other side, resting her hands on top of his. He shook with the overwhelming need to clamp onto her. To tear the clothing from her and touch every inch of her. Every muscle tightened, wanting more contact. To surround her more. He needed more of Britt. Somehow, he kept time with her undulating body.

His pelvis pressed against her butt became the place where Heaven met Hell.

He tightened his fingers, the tips digging into her softness mere inches from the juncture of her thighs. Her high-pitched sigh cracked, nearly slicing him in two. Instead, he curled his shoulders around her and lowered his head until her hair tickled his chin.

Bass beats and melodies flooded the space around them until Red's entire world became a two-foot radius of his body trying to surround Britt. The rock of her hips against his focused his senses.

His world narrowed down to the smoky rum tasting sounds of Britt's small frame grazing his. Trailing his hand up her arm, he leaned away long enough to sweep a palm across her bare back, bumping over the purse strap that went from one shoulder across her body to the other hip. He traced the edge of a bruise that peeked out over one shoulder blade. Then he rested his fingers on her fabric-covered neck, thumb toying with the halter tie. He fought for control over a virus that wanted him to grab, to hold, to clamp down.

Control it.

Then, good God, her hands slid back to grip the

tops of his thighs, making the muscles twitch and bunch under her lightest touch, even as their bodies continued to sway. Her fingers rested too close and way too far away from what he needed. She relaxed into his chest, and he responded by cupping the front of her shoulders and drawing her tighter to him.

He brushed his lips over her hair, taking in the scent of hibiscus. Red nudged her head to one side with his chin, and she complied. He pressed his mouth over the skin between her ear and the angle of her jaw, tasting the snare drum percussion beat of her pulse under his lips.

What mission?

For how long they moved like this, him all but locked around her, Britt molding into his body, Red had no idea. All he knew was that the sense of connection, of rightness, nailed him in the solar plexus. His Goth pixie had turned him soft.

She rubbed her butt against him.

Okay, not soft. Not even close. He swallowed. At some point the ill-conceived plan to seduce her into staying by his side for safety had turned into a dangerous game, and she might have outmaneuvered him.

He brushed his lips against the shell of her ear and absorbed her full body shudder. So satisfying. Another nip and he felt her groan reverberate through his sternum, crashing into him like ocean waves.

"How much longer do you want to stay here?" he asked, throwing in a nip of her earlobe for good measure.

Another shudder. She craned her head up and back at him. "What did you have in mind?"

"I'd like to see how we move together … in private." Okay, that might be laying it on a little thick. But did it work?

"Mmm. That's a pretty bad line."

Oof.

Then, her satisfied cat smile soothed his virus as something deep inside of him settled down. She stroked his thigh, edging up so tantalizingly close to what he wanted. A scrape of her nails on cotton pants fabric made his belly tense. "Is this part of your job, too?"

He stumbled at a surge of light-headedness, the toe of his shoe bumping her heel. "What?"

"You. Me. Here." Her shoulders rose and fell, and his hopes rose and fell along with her. "You're on the clock, right?"

"Damn, Britt. I *want* to be right here. With you."

"That's not an answer."

He maintained the verbal judo. "It's an honest statement. I want you. It's that simple."

Britt paused, and his heart stopped for the full ten seconds before she answered. "Then carpe diem. I'm all for it!" She laughed and pressed a thumb right at the junction of his thigh and groin, half a millimeter from a testicle.

Red saw stars.

How the hell was he supposed to survive the trip back to her apartment?

She turned to face him and wrinkled her nose at him. "Let me tell Tachi we're leaving."

The definition of *loss*: the moment she stepped away from him. Red even leaned forward, his body straining to maintain contact.

While she spoke into Tachi's ear, Red texted Rodeo: **Going back to apartment. Monitor roommate. Then watch apartment perimeter if possible. Stay away.**

Glancing up, Red was rewarded with a brisk salute and a flash of a white grin. Then his teammate disappeared.

As he put his phone away, Britt stepped up to him. A wrinkle of her forehead was followed by her nibbling her lower lip with even, white teeth. Which of course sent a bolt of *bite me* right through Red.

He held out a hand and tried his level best to remain neutral and nonthreatening. Anything but desperate. "Ready?"

Several beats of music went by. "Let's go." She laid her palm on his.

Chapter Twenty-Five

What the hell was Britt doing?

Two days ago, she had been pissed off at the guy, and her immediate priority was finishing her college degree and fulfilling Mom's wishes. Then there was the other priority of not being dead. Now she wanted to jump into bed with him?

Priorities change.

Eyeing the tall guy leading her toward the exit, her heart fluttered in her chest. She rolled the upper lip hoop under her teeth. No, she didn't need to jump into bed with him. Didn't need a bed. Any workable surface in a semiprivate location would do.

At what point had she become so impulsive?

Okay, fair enough, impulsiveness wasn't exactly a new phenomenon for Britt.

Confident decision-making as a step to personal growth and overcoming anxiety? She'd taken that self-improvement step to a whole new level tonight, thanks to the mouthwatering man who had nearly made her come on the dance floor by doing little more than kissing her under her ear. What else could he do with that mouth and those hands? Britt stumbled. Al tightened his grip, keeping her upright.

Once out of the club and away from the throng of

people, he repositioned them so he walked between her and the street. Then he draped his arm over her shoulders and pulled her into his side. Warmth and the wafting hint of aftershave loosened her limbs.

After a small, intense glance at her, the muscles of his arm bunched as he cupped her shoulder. He kept his head up, almost on a swivel. Scanning. Monitoring. Anticipating danger.

Despite her lust-hazed brain, Britt realized the stark reality: impulsive interlude aside, her life remained in danger. At her shiver, Al pulled her more firmly against him.

"You okay?" his voice rumbled through her chest wall where they were pressed together.

"Sure thing. A little chilly."

He stepped away, shrugged out of his denim jacket, and helped her into it. "Do not touch anything in the pockets. Please."

"Don't you need the items?"

Al patted his leg and brushed a hand over his lower back and under the arm opposite her. "What I need is attached to me."

She sighed as the fabric's warmth from his heated body seeped into her skin. The garment's cuffs hung past her hands. "Thanks. So warm."

Without looking down, he grinned. "I know other ways to warm you up." His smile froze, and tight lines bracketed his mouth.

Heat climbed her neck. The guy might be a fashion disaster, but he wasn't without basic pickup skills. "Want to share those ideas?" she asked.

"Rather show you." That low, calm voice melted her insides. He slid his arm back around her shoulders once more. "No answer?"

"Not one that's fit to be said aloud."

A dry chuckle, but came across as hollow. "I like that." The tone of voice was off. Unnatural.

Something about his vigilant, concerned expression, cadence of words, and the content of what he said, didn't add up. Britt's neck prickled again. He was pushing without pushing, but still steering her.

No one steered Britt.

"Wait." She stopped in her tracks. "You're distracting me? With sexiness?" she asked.

He leaned down, a pretense of nuzzling her hairline and sending goose bumps down her spine. "We're being followed." That voice, once smooth and sensual, now abraded. As she stiffened, he shushed her. "Don't look around. Don't stop. We'll be at the MARTA station soon. It's only 11:30. The train schedule timing should work out."

"How do you know that?"

"Memorized the schedule. Almost there." He brushed his mouth against her temple and said, "I need you to walk a little faster. But casually."

Easy for him to say. Britt forced her shaking legs to turn over faster. Where did the sexy flirting stop and mission start?

Someone stalked them.

Her stomach churned. She had made another bad decision on impulse tonight.

Taking her hand, Al led her down the stairs to the platform. They moved a hair faster than socially acceptable. A handful of passengers played on cell phones or leaned against the tile walls as they waited for the train.

Too much open space. No place to hide. She felt the imaginary sting of laser gun targets pinning her body.

"It's okay," he murmured, turning so her back pressed against a wall of tile. He stood in the way of any threat. "Breathe. Stay calm." His strong presence and warm voice wrapped her in a cocoon of safety.

Strong and warm.

He was doing a job.

The guy had gone from seduction champ to ice-cold professional in the space of mere seconds. With his arms snaking around her, he pressed against her waist and she yelped.

"Shh." He used the move to dig into the jacket pocket and palmed a black object.

Gun.

"You said the weapons were on your person."

"Less noticeable if I access the jacket pocket," he breathed.

A metallic squeal made Britt jump. Train approaching.

Al pulled her alongside the train, stopping at the second-to-last car. As soon as the doors opened, he pressed his palm to her back as she entered.

Two Black women, maybe early twenties, also entered the car and sat at the back, giggling and snapping photos on their phones. A middle-aged Latino-appearing man in a security guard-type uniform took a seat near the front of the car then promptly crossed his arms and rested his chin on his chest. A gaggle of various styled college-aged people huddled in a group of seats and chatted together.

Normal people, going about normal activities. Her head spun.

Al positioned them near the door on a center-facing double seat, again draping an arm over her shoulders and pulling her close. This time the gesture wasn't affectionate. Hard tension in his muscles felt like pressing up against a hot brick.

Every time his head lifted and turned to scan the

car, she felt his muscles shift and bunch. He never stopped monitoring. His hand rested on his thigh, gun hidden beneath his palm.

The train pulled away from the station in a smooth whoosh and gentle rocking rumble.

Maybe they had lost the guys following them.

"Shit," Al muttered, his head whipping up.

Chapter Twenty-Six

Red had sent instructions to his teammate at the club. If he could safely leave Tachi, then Rodeo was to meet at Britt's apartment, ready to support.

Red was going to need support.

Three men in varying shades of black-and-gray nondescript clothing stood in the last train car, their exact appearance through the safety glass obscured by the movements of the two cars. His hearing ability was superior, but the dull rattle and faint squeaks of the moving MARTA train masked any conversation. When the men took three strolling steps toward Red's car, he didn't need a second invitation.

"We need to move. Now."

The electric-blue fear in Britt's wide eyes made him feel a million feet tall and miniscule at the same time. Her gasp of air brushed against him like velvet, but rubbing against the fabric's nap. Rapidly, he calculated exfil options, distances, steps. He forced his racing thoughts to slow long enough to methodically evaluate plans.

Got it. He brushed an ankle against the other one to verify the gun and knife stashed there. Gripped the gun in his hand. Weapons ready. Now, to buy some time.

The overhead voice alerted the next stop coming up. He checked his watch. One minute to the next station. Their stop. He leaned away from Britt, pulled his phone from a pocket, flipped open an app, and hit a few buttons.

A sudden fifteen-second period of darkness both outside and inside caused a few passengers to murmur. He tugged Britt through the doors connecting cars, then stayed low and rushed through the next two train cars.

Still dark. They entered another car and kept moving forward.

Trying to disappear like his teammate Curly, Red pretended that the passengers ignored their behavior. If only he could be that lucky. As it stood, Stumpy would have to scrub the MARTA security system until it didn't know what day of the week it was recording.

The lights came back on.

Reaching the first car, they sat down right as the train pulled into the Midtown MARTA station. Doors whooshed open. A few passengers exited and hurried away. Red peered behind him, counting the seconds. He spied the men working their way through the car behind them. Checking seats. They hadn't seen Red and Britt yet.

Go out. The doors are closing. Sure enough, the men rushed out in a group and scanned the platform.

Twenty seconds.

Hand pressed against her neck, he kept Britt's and his head bowed, like two lovers whispering together.

The doors stood open, tempting him with the gasoline-scented scratches and squeaks of street noise coming from above the platform.

Stay or go? He tapped his foot, counting.

Muffled conversation and scuffs lasered sound into his ears. One footstep clicked, crisp, like bacon. A hard leather-soled shoe. Another footfall made a grinding, gritty-tasting crunch of gravel embedded in lug soles that protested the heavier weight placed on them.

A mutter.

Then a matchstick-scented laugh.

Ten seconds. Red glanced through the window between trains.

The three men stepped back into the car, facing in his direction. Two moved toward the doors connecting the cars. The doors in front of Red started to slide closed. His pulse spiked.

In one fluid movement, he grabbed Britt to him with one arm nearly lifting her off the ground, stayed low, and in three steps, turned sideways and slid them both out of the closing train doors. Two furious faces filled the window of the car as the train pulled away from the empty platform.

That left ... one very angry bald, white dude. With a gun. Ah, the fellow from sportswear at JT Armstrong. He'd recovered well. Too well.

"Get behind me," Red said, gripping his own gun as the train disappeared down the track.

Yep. Good luck to Stumpy with erasing and replacing the MARTA security camera files, because this scene was about to become must-see TV.

Britt's fingers fisted his shirt but she hung on, matching him as he took deliberate steps backward.

The man grinned and raised the gun.

Shit.

He recalled the layout of this station. If Red could get Britt up those escalator stairs to street level, they had a chance.

Making a ruckus was low on Red's list of response options.

A safety clicked. Not his.

Red fired, hitting the guy on the side of his chest. Not center of mass. Damn it.

The return shot didn't do much better, but kudos for nailing Red's thigh. Fire burned through his leg as the bullet made a high squelching sound, passing through and through at a gazillion miles per second. A yelp from Britt. Had she been hit? Damn it.

He pulled the trigger once more.

Off-target, damn the blinding pain from Red's

leg. The dude stopped and leaned over, a hand pressed into his chest wall, his arm hanging at his side. A few seconds—that's all Red had bought them. The man groaned and stood up again, hatred and pain etched on his meaty face.

"Run!" Red yelled as the man raised a shaky hand with the gun still in it.

Britt dashed up the escalator, and he followed, obscuring the guy's target, and moving slower, as his leg tried to collapse on him.

He adjusted control of the virus, exchanging clarity of thought for amplified strength and abilities. The virus flared, surging to the injured area, and beginning the healing process. Not fast enough.

As they emerged to street level, Red scanned the area and pulled Britt along with him, trying to mask the limp. He glanced down. Hard to mask the spreading dark patch on his upper khaki pants leg. He glanced back, catching a glimpse of the man's sandy hair as he emerged from the station at a slower pace. But relentlessly moving forward.

Red scanned his surroundings. City blocks, closed businesses, few cars, and fewer people out at this hour. Less ability to blend in. He couldn't formulate a plan quickly enough. Thinking took too much effort with the virus surging.

Humid evening air cooled his sweaty forehead.

"This way," he gritted out, pulling her down a short alleyway.

Britt's ice-cold hands gripped his wrist. "Are you okay?"

He clamped his jaw against the slice of pain as he stepped down on his injured leg with a *clunk* on a thick iron-tasting manhole cover. "Fine. For now." He could barely form sentences. He needed her safe. The damned virus needed her safe and it didn't care about the price to reach that goal. Red retained a tight rein on his sanity and hung on for dear life.

His vision winked crimson.

Limping a few more blocks, he led her into yet another alley and ducked behind a dumpster full of spoiled alcohol, rotting vegetables, and damp cardboard. Not ideal, but it would work. He sucked air into his lungs and did his damned best to compartmentalize the pain lancing through his leg as he pressed Britt next to the rusted metal bin and stood in front of her.

He hit a button on his phone. "Rodeo?" he said, keeping a hand on Britt's shoulder.

"Hey, got some half-time details, party boy? Is she the freak in bed, or are you?"

"Shut up, asshole." The words hissed out through a tight jaw. "Problem."

"Shit." The switch flipped and Rodeo became a cold, calculating operator in a half second. "Sitrep."

"Shot at, successfully."

"You or Britt?"

"Me. We're safe right now. What's your location?" Red sucked in air as his leg muscles spasmed.

Rodeo's voice came through musical background noise. "Club."

"Where's the roommate?"

An atypical pause. "Dancing with two new guys who joined her shortly after you left. Seems to know them. Lipreading looks like she might go home with them." Was that a weird tone to his voice?

"Probably a good idea."

"Do you want me to follow?"

"Yes. But we need you." He turned back to Britt. "Tachi's going home with some guys."

She nodded. "Darius and Chaz. Modeling friends.

She texted earlier that she'd crash at their place."

He caught her extra intake of breath. That was his girl, planning to have the apartment for a night of … nothing. He groaned. "They good?"

Britt's brows rose. "Of course." Like it was routine. Whatever. Not Red's business.

Rodeo's curse came through the phone. "I bet those pudknockers will … look after her all right. I don't plan to stick around to see if they decide to play 'hide the salami: deluxe edition'." Again, Red's hearing picked up a lime-sour tightness to Rodeo's voice. "What do you need?"

"Lequire's people are on our six."

"Shit."

Right now, Red reckoned he had a half-hour, tops, before more of Lequire's men cased this area. He had less time than that if he didn't stop bleeding. He was, frankly, fucked.

One glance at wide-eyed Britt, and a moment of clarity nailed him in the gut. God help him, he would get her out of this situation. Unharmed.

As much as he hated the exposure there, he did have security monitors set up at the apartment as well as stashed supplies. "Rodeo, what about the apartment?"

Wind sounds without dance music now came through the phone. Guy must be jogging.

"CO would tell you to go to ground."

He glanced at Britt. "Safe house?" A quick shake of her head. Damn it. "Apartment," Red gritted out.

"Stay hidden for another half-hour," Rodeo said, barely panting, the asshole. "I'll lock shit down, tight."

Red wasn't above begging. "Are you sure we can't hide you somewhere, Britt? Please."

For a split-second the determination in her gaze wavered. Then she studied his face. "Apartment. School.

Safety."

"Goddamnit, Britt." When she opened her mouth, he pointed a thumb toward the street. "Shh." She crossed her arms and jutted her chin. He searched the city night sky as if he could get some help from the heavens dealing with this woman. Nothing appeared.

"Shoo-wee, bro." Rodeo whistled low. "You've got a real cooperative damsel in distress, Prince Charming. Let me know if you want me to try the 'Rodeo approach' with her. She'll gladly stay in one location. But not one position."

Red's head buzzed painfully at the thought. "Come on, man. Make this op work. Find a protocol that fits."

His teammate replied, "A protocol? Seriously? We've been as successful as a Chihuahua trying to fuck a football, for all the good these damned protocols are."

"Roger that." He paused. "So, what's next?"

"Shit on shit, bro." Rodeo blew out a breath and muttered, "Fine. Here we go again. Good ol' Rodeo, cleaning up everyone's damned mess. Again." He sniffed. "You're killing me here, Redhead." He paused. "Resources: you've got security measures, early alerts on perimeters, and tons of media feeds in place in and around the apartment. And me. If we can't protect it with those layers, then go to plan B."

Plan B. Which meant screw whatever Britt wanted and put her in protective custody against her will for as long as it took.

She was free to choose. For now. If they went to a secret safe house, she'd have to buy into the entire plan, which meant torpedoing her degree and her life. She'd never agree. Which meant she'd have to go kicking and screaming. Which, technically, would be felony kidnapping.

She'd hate him.

Hell, they were screwed.

No other viable option right now. Apartment it would be. "Roger that. Thirty." He put the phone away and took a step toward her. The bum leg nearly gave out.

"You're shot," she gasped.

"A little bit."

She grabbed his arm and damn him, but the connection did wonders for his fortitude. "A little bit *shot*?"

"Give it an hour or two. It'll be okay."

"Before or after you bleed out? You've got a weird way of looking at things. You want to sit down or something?" She tugged on him, but he waved her off and planted a hand on the concrete building wall instead.

Then she started patting him down everywhere. Pain mixed with pleasure in a bizarre way, especially when she encountered the soaked leg of his pants, dark dampness on lighter fabric color in the low lighting of the alley.

"You're still bleeding."

"Gunshot wounds do that."

She blew a stray piece of hair off her forehead. "Can I call an ambulance for you?"

"No." Already the virus was healing him. He'd be 100% functional by morning.

Next step: make it to the morning.

"Al?" She kept her hand on his arm, as if she could support his body with hers. The mere thought made him smile.

"Yes." No, he would not laugh at her fierce scowl.

"Should we be going somewhere?"

"We will soon. My teammate is locking down your place."

She frowned. "I know you think I'm making a bad decision."

He rolled his lips together, then blew out a lungful of air. "Britt. You're an adult. You have the information required for decisions."

"Not all of it."

"You have what you need to know."

She snorted and glared at him, her irritation made way less effective due to her standing next to a dumpster, in a midtown Atlanta alley, wearing a cute flippy skirt and his oversize denim jacket. Nothing made sense.

"Are you sure I can't do something for your leg?"

He recognized a subject change when he saw one. "It'll be okay."

She rubbed her hands up and down her denim-clad upper arms, the rough rasp of her palms on the fabric sweet and smoky. "Al?" She pointed at him, her finger shaking. "That was a bullet meant for me." The waver in her voice got his attention.

"Britt—"

"Do you know how many things have been shot at me in my lifetime, not counting in Nerf guns?"

"No."

"Two." Her voice cracked on the word like a ceramic vase shattering.

"Damn it." He snagged her arms and pulled her into his chest, trying to surround her with warmth and safety, but knowing full well that anything he did right now would be temporary and inadequate.

Despite everything, she seemed to still trust him as she relaxed against him. That trust might be the only thing that would get them out of this situation in one piece.

Trust.

Unfortunately, his entire existence here, with her,

was a lie. Her tremors condemned him.

Although he had literal insanity coursing through his veins, he still wanted her to understand. He needed to explain why her questions about him were on the right track. Why she should fear him. Why things didn't add up.

But Britt knowing anything about the team and the Morpheus Virus meant that her value as a target for Lequire would skyrocket, along with that guy's determination to extract information and then silence her.

If she knew about the Morpheus Squad, then she had the power to destroy Red and his entire team.

Her knowing the full truth would also put her entire family at risk of destruction.

Chapter Twenty-Seven

"We'll head to the apartment in twelve minutes." After scrolling through an app, Al stowed the phone but remained leaning against the building.

Where her hand rested on his arm, every muscle of his turned to iron, but Britt didn't mind. At least he could stand. Maybe it wasn't as bad of an injury as she'd thought.

"We're safe?" she asked, once again double-guessing her decision to go out this evening, and double-guessing her decision to stay and finish her degree. Foolish? Maybe. But these were her choices to make, and after years of self-doubt Britt needed to stick to her guns for her own confidence. She would feel safer in her apartment, surrounded by familiar things, and with Al and his friend nearby. She had to finish college. Had to gain that closure and fulfill her dream and Mom's wishes. Needed to succeed in something in her life.

Problem was, Britt wasn't explaining this background logic to Al very well, and she recognized that it made her look like a flighty, terrible decision-maker.

Logic wasn't driving this decision-making bus. Anxiety, grief, regret, fear—those emotions steered her. At least she'd been through enough therapy to realize that fact. Her thoughts churned as she searched his face and stared toward the street.

After another period of time, he brushed tendrils of hair back from her face, sending a different kind of shiver down her spine. "Time to head out. Coast is as clear as it can be. My teammate will patrol tonight."

"What about you?"

"I need to stay in the apartment with you. Close

enough to respond to a direct threat." He glanced down at her, eyes dark in the shadows. "If that's okay."

At least he asked her permission this time, even though giving her a choice was an afterthought. It was hard to argue with him. Her thoughts whirled. Waves of panic crashed against her. Nothing like being shot at to ramp up anxiety. Great.

Focus on something solid that she could contribute to this situation. "We can clean up your leg." She peered down the dark alley and over to the lightly traveled midtown street. "Any idea how we're getting back?"

"Not MARTA."

In the midst of almost dying—again—Britt laughed despite herself and leaned her forehead against his biceps. A deep drag of his pine and aftershave scent fortified her. She'd been assaulted twice this week and Al had stopped both attacks.

After another minute, Al pushed away from the wall with a grunt. A glimmer of pain creased his brow. "Let's go."

She winced in sympathy as he came up short on his first few steps.

Staying close to the shadowed wall, they exited the opposite end of the alley onto a secondary street. He hurried her into a nearby parking garage where he texted something on his phone to a guy named Stumpy who was a "cleaner," then proceeded to break into a sedan and exit the lot.

"Are you sure this is okay?" she asked, a police booking photograph with her holding up a number flashing through her mind

"You have an alternative?" he snapped.

"Uh. No."

He rested a fist on the steering wheel and blew

out a long breath through a tight mouth. "Sorry to bite your head off. I'm usually even-keeled."

"It's been a heck of an evening."

The ride to her apartment complex proceeded in silence, through a winding, roundabout route. No nasty surprises, thank God.

After confirming that the area was safe, he parked off the street in another apartment lot and quickly got out of the sedan. Britt did the same, following him the long way around to finally reach her apartment complex and up the side stairs. She prayed they didn't encounter any tenants at this hour. The dark patch of blood on his khakis would be a lot to explain.

Once in the door, he quickly surveilled the entire space, methodically checking each room. Took all of sixty seconds, but she felt more secure for his effort.

Fear hit her followed by a bolt of anxiety, and she pressed her palm against the front door, sucking in a deep breath. They had survived her bad decision to go out. Barely. Panic gripped her neck and squeezed. She couldn't breathe.

The floor was solid under her feet. She stood up straight to ground herself.

What can I see? Love seat.

What can I hear? The low buzz of the refrigerator.

What can I smell? Damn it … pine and Al. She inhaled.

When she opened her eyes again, Al stood right in front of her. Watching her. Waiting.

The hammering of her heart sped up. She needed concrete activity. Needed to make a decision. Move forward.

"All right, get in there," She forced lightness into her voice and pointed toward the bathroom. "Let's get that cleaned up." Playing with the hoop on her ear, she said, "Seems like we've done this before."

His quick smile didn't make it up to the tight lines around his eyes. Was he running on adrenaline? He should sit down and rest. Put pressure on the injury. Something like that, right?

"Better if I take care of this one." Holding up a hand, he waved her away. "It's not too far from a personal spot, so…"

Warmth crawled over her skin. The only thought she could clearly articulate was the one she couldn't speak: boxers or briefs? Inquiring minds wanted to know. "Okay. You know where the first aid kit is, from, ah, the other day."

"Got it."

Lacking anything else to do, Britt took off the jacket and laid it and her purse down on the table. Then she made a few sandwiches. Because, after midnight, why the hell not?

A few minutes later he exited the bathroom.

Oh, hell, no. Boxer-briefs, then. Great-fitting ones at that were not quite covered by the tan button-down shirt. Of course he couldn't wear the ruined, bloody pants. But, wow. She tried not to stare, but his legs were corded with lean muscle and dusted with dark-red hair.

An elastic bandage wound around his upper thigh. No blood visible. That seemed like a good sign. He didn't seem to be in pain. At all.

Her mouth had gone dry and God bless her, but she couldn't stop looking.

"Britt?"

"Sandwich?" she blurted out.

In bare feet, he didn't so much walk as stalk over to where she stood next to the small kitchen table. The air left the room. She'd seen his ability to reduce armed men to comatose lumps on the floor, and now with the unmistakable evidence of his strength in his forearms and legs, Britt had two conflicting thoughts. One: she couldn't imagine anyone making her feel safer. Two: she had zero chance to take any action if he objected. The guy could stop her easily.

Funny, though, he didn't intimidate her. Didn't lord his size over her, like many guys did.

Al intrigued her.

"I'd love a bite," he said, licking his lips.

Was it possible to faint from sexual craving, because the hunger in his baritone voice almost pushed her over.

Wait. Was this more of his act, like before? Damn her brain, but she couldn't tell real sentiment from fake.

She handed him a sandwich and a Coke from the fridge. "Couch or kitchen table?"

"Couch." He groaned as he eased into the cushions and stretched out his long legs.

The shirt rode up.

Oh, God.

Her mouth went dry. Well. Al certainly had the whole … package.

They chewed through PB and J in tired silence, Al's jaw working each bite thoroughly, with focused intensity. He licked his lips with a tiny tired sigh, the only sign that he was mortal. He took another bite.

For the first time in her life, Britt was jealous of Jif and Smuckers. Mouth dry, she sipped her glass of water and tried hard not to peek. Tried.

Seriously, though. All of him was *right there*. What about mission readiness? Seemed like he should have pants on.

He gave a smirk as he caught where she was looking. "Sorry for casual attire. The go bag is in another vehicle. Rodeo will bring it by later."

She stared at the half-eaten sandwich on her plate. Al had taken two bullets for her in the past couple of days. He'd killed or maimed grown men. She knew nothing about him.

On the other hand, yes, she would like to jump him. On the whatever hand it was, could Britt truly trust her decision-making abilities right now?

She sighed, and he whipped his head over, eyes locked on her. Okay. Weird reaction. Damn it, Britt was so tired of double-guessing herself. Ground the situation, ground the anxiety. What could she see?

A sandwich-eating guy who had been freaking shot, not an hour ago.

Who wore boxer-briefs.

Britt uncrossed and crossed her legs, the crinkle of crinoline too loud in the small living area. At the sound, he stared at her legs for a split-second and swallowed.

"Penny for your thoughts." His low voice made her libido do a backflip.

There weren't enough pennies for what was going through her mind right now. Talking business might provide a needed distraction.

"Just … processing everything that's happened this week. What about my sisters and Dad? What is this world I'm in?"

"My colleagues are looking at them."

"Can I speak with my family?"

"It's not a good idea. I mean, yes, if you absolutely must, it's your choice. But it's better for their safety, the less you know and the less you communicate with them right now."

"I don't love that."

"It's temporary."

"Sure." She took a half-hearted bite and chewed.

"The team will resolve this problem."

The *problem* being a powerful man who lived in Atlanta and who wanted to get to Kiera, even by hurting Britt, Reagan, or Dad. "Yeah. To be clear, this"—she motioned at the half-clothed man and her small apartment—"was totally not on the vision board for how my last semester would go."

"I'm really sorry." Al said it like a guy who understood having his whole life upended as well.

A minute, then two, passed in silence until he ate the last bite of sandwich and balanced the plate on the love seat armrest. He glanced at her. The heat coming from him in the confined space made her want to snuggle up next to him. She wanted to do more than snuggle.

Good decisions, Britt. Clapping her hands once, she pushed to her feet. "Anything else to eat?"

His lids dropped to half-mast. "Maybe later."

Damn.

"Um." Needing something to do that didn't involve jumping on his lap and twining herself around him, Britt took the dishes and empty glasses to the sink.

A few minutes passed with the sounds of water and clinks of secondhand Corelle dishware.

"Britt." The voice came from right behind her, and she jumped, dropping the dishrag.

He swept a warm hand over her bare back and shoulders, drawing goose bumps.

Gripping the sink edge, she closed her eyes. His touch felt so good. *Make better decisions.* "Yes?"

"I meant what I said earlier today about coming back here with you…"

Good God, wasn't he wounded? On a mission. This was business. Then his warm breath feathered the hair at the back of her neck.

No way. She wasn't falling at this guy's feet. He'd have to prove he wanted her as Britt, not as a mission target to distract. Right now, he was in way too much control for her to completely believe his motives. She took in a lungful of air and blew it out, staring at the kitchen drapes covering the window in front of her.

"This isn't a game, Al."

"I don't play games."

Damn. "Please don't—"

He stepped away, the air around her cooling the exposed skin on her back from the halter top. "I won't do anything without your say-so. I swear. Mission or no mission, I hope you realize that by now."

He wasn't wrong. He was just … persuasive.

It was still her choice.

God, in a perfect world she wanted him pressed up to her. Needed to feel safe in his arms. Needed to feel worthy of honest interest. Wanted to explore his body. Taste. Enjoy. Connect. Feed the hunger that continued to build. She wanted a few hours where her life hadn't been upended, her future uncertain.

Dropping her head, she bit her lip. Now who had questionable motives? She couldn't use him just to satisfy her own needs. But what if his needs and hers truly were mutual?

Britt dried her shaking hands on the towel and reached back for him, like in the club. His fingers brushed against hers, the lightest, most breakable touch. She couldn't look at him. Not yet. Too many thoughts and conflicting needs swirled inside of her. Her therapist would have a field day with the fact that she wanted him but couldn't face him in a moment like this.

In Britt's logic, the fear that someone would leave her decreased if she didn't have to confront the person head-on. Vulnerability decreased if she wasn't face-to-face. See? Just saved her an hour-long session and a hundred bucks. Britt was nothing if not thrifty. A lump formed in her throat. The connection of his fingers curling against hers almost broke her.

Screw anxiety. Screw her baggage. Screw self-doubt. "Closer. Please," she whispered.

In a whisper of movement, he pressed against her backside. Kneecaps to thighs, pelvis to butt, abs and chest to the bare skin of her back. Warmth flowed from his rigid frame into her trembling one. She tipped her head back until it rested against the shirt-covered chest. His heart thudded hard enough to feel it through her skull.

"Al, I want—" Fear stole her words.

As she peered up at him, the kitchen light threw his face into stark planes and lines. He tilted his head down, lips hovering at her temple. "Say it." He loosely grasped her fingers. His other hand rested in a loose fist on the kitchen counter on the other side of her. She gripped the counter with her free hand.

He didn't move, even when she shifted from foot to foot, brushing her butt against his erection. He did, however, growl, deep in his throat.

That growl. That was what she wanted, and so much more. "I want you, Al."

"Good." He brushed his nose along her neck.

"Wait."

He froze.

"This is real connection, right? N-not for the mission." Her heart rattled against her ribs.

"Britt." Her name sounded so good rumbling through his lips. "God help me, but this is a real connection *in spite of* the mission." Spoken like he fought his own inner conflict.

Talk about having the data needed to make an

informed decision. "Oh," she breathed.

"Yeah. Oh." He remained motionless, until every nerve ending quivered with the need for him to touch her. "You need to give me the go-ahead."

Had she dented the metal of the sink with her grip yet? "Yes." Her voice cracked on the single syllable.

A tiny lick at the top of her ear sent a shudder down her spine. Oh God—

He slid his hand up her bare arm to the halter fabric that covered her neck, to cup the side of her head. In a deliberate, slow movement that she could easily pull away from, he squeezed his hand into a fist of her hair, tightening nearly to the point of pain. Then he used that grip to tilt her head. Her knees went weak when that hot tongue laved her ear. Damp warmth combined with his breath and the nips of his teeth clinking against her earrings which sent sparks over her sensitive skin, all had her hanging onto the sink like it was a float saving her from drowning in an ocean of lust.

Somewhere in the back of her mind, two brain cells not involved with pleasure finally made a connection. "Aren't we. Surveillance?" she gasped out.

Another nip of her ear came with a hint of pain, followed by a lick to soothe the skin. "Good point. Don't move." Air cooled her back. Britt froze for a minute, then glanced around. He had disappeared.

A minute later, Al exited the bathroom with his cell phone and laid it face-down on the kitchen table. "There. Should be fixed."

"What?"

"No digital feed from inside the apartment right now. No one can see or hear us."

That was a good thing. Right? She turned and leaned her hip against the sink, studying him as he stood next to the table, legs slightly bent as he balanced on the balls of his feet. Always ready for the mission.

Was his interest real?

A check at the boxer-briefs answered the last question. No doubt at all. Her mouth went desert-dry.

His eyes narrowed. In three strides, he was in front of her, not quite touching but so close.

"Can I kiss you?" His head cocked to one side, like he heard the tiny whimper that welled up in her throat.

Her head swam. The guy was still asking her, like he wasn't sure of her answer?

Through a lust-clogged brain, self-doubt, and anxiety, Britt realized something amazing. Even in this messed-up situation involving military dudes and power plays, where she was a glorified pawn, where her future rested on finishing up college while in danger, this man gave her something she didn't have: control. A choice.

Fixated on his mouth, she decided to put it to the test. "What if I said no?"

He took a step back, hands up. "I would stop. Immediately."

"What if we were past kissing?" Stopping was the furthest thing from her mind, but Britt needed to be in control of something in her life right about now. This might not be a secure situation, but she needed to feel secure in her own decisions.

"Past kissing? As in, while I'm licking every inch of your body? About to be buried deep inside of you until you scream?"

Oh, God. Heated liquid pooled at her pulsating core. "Th-that. Sure."

"No questions asked. It would be difficult, but I would stop." He licked that lower lip, making her own tongue jealous. "If you don't want this—us—then I will step away. No questions asked. No hard feelings." He grimaced. "Maybe 'hard' isn't the right term."

No kidding. "So."

"This is your call." He rolled a hand into a fist, then released it. Twice.

"I do want this—us. I just needed to know—" Her cheeks warmed. Since when was Britt afraid of open communication with a partner? She glanced at his careful, neutral posture. She couldn't make full eye contact. It was too much.

She was afraid of open communication because for the first time in years, she had allowed herself to connect with someone on a level that made her feel vulnerable. The flip side of connection was her fear of abandonment.

The part where she had almost died this week, twice, amplified her fear. Nothing was certain in her world. Nothing except the two people standing in her apartment, facing each other.

His voice bridged the space between them. "You're safe, Britt. No one can see us. No one will come in here. No one will hurt you. I will see to it." The words came out like a promise wrapped up in a terrifying threat.

Not a threat to Britt, though.

He hadn't moved. Hadn't imposed his size and his will on her. He tipped his chin and raised an eyebrow, inviting her to make a first move.

Her breathing sped up. Fine by her.

Britt closed the space in a gasp of air and took two fistfuls of his shirt, drawing him easily down to her mouth. The brush of her lips against his was meant to be a warm-up, a taste, to see if they were on the same page.

The page exploded.

Britt burned. Her mouth tingled as she stood on tiptoes in her booties, wanting more.

Al growled low and snaked a corded arm around

her waist. With his free hand, he cupped the back of her head, lightly trapping her in the sweetest of prisons as he arched her back and nudged her lips apart with his.

She sighed as he swept his tongue into her mouth, changing angles, nipping, tasting. His touch sent quivers from her head down through her belly and into her toes. She pressed against him, her short skirt crunching against his boxer-briefs. Too much clothing.

God, his kisses were like discovering the answer to a question she didn't know she needed to ask. He locked her in his arms and plundered her mouth in the best possible way. Instead of suffocating her, his deep, intense kisses still gave her air to breathe. His sexy grunts lent her fierce strength to press against his mouth, insisting on more. Dragging her fingers up behind his neck, she stretched to meet him, kiss for kiss.

He didn't disappoint. The rough and smooth of his tongue swept patterns of pleasure until her knees gave out on her. Al braced his legs shoulder-width apart and his arms tightened, not a painful grip but solid, stable.

Somehow they ended up with Al half-sitting on the back of the couch, drawing Britt between his thighs, into the heat and hardness there. The trail of his rough fingertips over her bare back drew out shivers. Brushing his fingers lower, he skimmed the sensitive skin peeking out between the hem of her top and the skirt's waistband. Then he slid his hands around to undo the lower clasp of the halter top. He scooted her shirt up, inch by agonizing inch, until he brushed the underside of her breasts with the rough pads of his thumbs.

He lifted his mouth away for a second. "Britt." His breath came out harsh, like he'd finished sprinting a mile.

Following suit, she ran her hands under his shirt. Curling her fingers in the sparse hair overlying the hard ridges of muscle, she smiled. "Yes?" Which turned into a long gasp on the "s" as his thumb flicked over a sensitive nipple.

That grin of his. Not so much happy as determined. Possessive.

Promising more. Demanding more.

God, she wanted more.

She couldn't relieve the pressure building in her hips, and shifted, restless against him. The ridge of his erection hit the perfect spot between her legs.

"Careful," he growled.

Reaching behind her neck, Britt untied the knot, letting the shirt fall off. "I'm tired of being careful." She grasped his narrow hips.

His rasping indrawn breath triggered butterflies deep down inside of her.

Then he slid his arm around her and she leaned back, knowing he would hold her steady, giving him access.

Oh yes, she thought, when his hot mouth latched onto a breast. Every one of his muscles tensed as he held her.

She sensed that Al held himself back, like an engine revving in neutral.

The vehicle was tuned, fueled, and waiting to jump into "drive."

Britt slid her hands up his ridged torso, then slowly back down past the waistband. She put one hand on the gearshift.

Chapter Twenty-Eight

Foreplay for most normal people didn't create stark terror that they would accidentally rip the limbs off their partner.

Red took another breath and tried to get hold of the viral impulses. Unfortunately, Britt got hold of him first.

His eyes rolled back in his head as she stroked him through the fabric of his briefs. Her fingertips drifting over the stretchy material, sounding like silk over leather to his ears. Tasted like thick spices. Smelled like desire. Senses coalesced again, tinting his world red. Red needed more. The virus needed more. Pronto. Minus the underwear.

Gentle. He had to be gentle. Even now, he was losing control of the amount of force he applied when gripping her upper arms.

She squeaked but didn't stop the action of her hand on him. "Why are you holding back?" She ran her thumb and fingers up and down his covered length until his vision went blurry.

"Don't want to hurt you," he gritted out. God help him, he would keep her safe in all respects.

"It would hurt more if you didn't share all of yourself," she murmured.

No way did she truly understand what she asked, given the kind of creature that stood in front of her. "I'm physically stronger than you, Britt." An understatement. He was stronger than nearly anyone in this universe. The words tore out of his throat as he swallowed. "I could cause you pain."

"I will feel pain if you don't kiss me again." Her voice was like he imagined expensive champagne would taste—layers of delicious bubbles and flavors tempting him to drink deeply, again and again.

He opened one eye. With her hand still resting on his hard erection, she smiled, catlike, arching her back and enticing him. Her light skin was marred by the bruises on her neck. His rage spiked, quickly followed by the need to replace injury with pleasure. He would give the lady what she wanted. Anything.

Licking his lips, he bent his head. "Can't have you suffer, then." He laved one tight breast with his mouth while he rolled the other nipple between his fingers. Her gasp ran down him like a cool breeze, invigorating, enticing. He needed more oxygen than his body could obtain.

As he sucked her nipple between his lips and flicked his tongue over the tip, she clenched her grip on his neck, shooting bolts of is-it-my-turn right through his dick.

"Al," she breathed.

What she'd give to call him his actual name. Secrets. This entire experience was built on half-truths. A twinge of guilt nailed him in the solar plexus.

Hey, he couldn't change the facts of the situation, but he could focus on the here and now. Right now he wanted to taste every bit of the woman squirming in his arms. The throb in his leg from tonight's injury faded away, replaced by a different kind of throb.

He lifted his head from her chest and kissed her deeply until they both panted. "What do you want, sweets?"

"I want you."

He smiled. "Be more specific. You're in control tonight." He palmed her breasts, panting as his fingers pressed into the softness. *Don't let me hurt her.*

God, he hoped his transfer of control to her

wasn't wishful thinking. Even now, with an iron-willed grip on his baser viral impulses, he continued to run that knife's edge where he could lose his ability to restrain the virus that begged him even now to throw her on the floor, spread her legs, and plunge in as deeply as humanly possible. And never stop until she had been marked as his, inside and out. The virus wanted release, relief, completion. It wanted Britt. Now.

The viral need left little room for what she wanted, and Red would be damned if he wouldn't focus on her desires at this moment.

The way she ducked her head and smiled wasn't innocent. That little gesture held the promise of a plan in mind. Red tilted her chin up. "Tell me what I can do for you. To you."

"This is so much…" Her wavering gaze brushed past him then away. Her soft voice nearly drove him to his knees. She blinked. "Can we use the back of the couch?"

Anything she wanted, he would make it work. "How?" Of course, Red had plenty of ideas, but he needed to fulfill her wishes.

After a pause, she stepped away from him, reaching under that short skirt to pull off the scrap of panties. All Britt had on was her short, crinkly skirt. And those silver booties. Then she leaned forward on the couch, looking back over her shoulder as if for approval.

Oh, he approved all right. Ever muscle in his body tensed, wanting to grab her, to stroke her. To be inside of her.

God help him, but her lean, smooth thighs disappeared under the skirt. That damned skirt had tempted Red all night long with what was hidden beneath. Even now, it still concealed his view of what he wanted most, but he was one step closer to finding out.

When he didn't move, she gave a small groan and straightened up, pushing away from the couch. "Um, my bad. This is silly. Never mind."

"No. Hell, no," he growled. "Go right back where you were. *Please*." He bit his thumb as she looked back at him. "I want to take it all in, how smoking hot and sexy you are. How lucky I am. All of it."

"Okay," she said, and he inhaled that one smoky incense word.

In this position, Britt willingly made herself vulnerable as she continued to watch over her shoulder, eyes wide. He recognized the gift. Trust. Safety. There was nothing that could compel him to betray her. Ever.

Stepping forward, he wrapped his hands around that tiny waist, absorbing her shudder at the first contact. Then he took his sweet time stroking every inch of her back, arms, and sides. He ran a hand up her neck, gripping her hair and tugging her head back. His arms shook as he controlled his strength. When he bent to kiss her shoulder, Britt's knuckles whitened on the cushions. Her rib cage expanded and contracted, more quickly now. Little sighs and moans drifted back to him.

He wanted to give her pleasure, more than he wanted air.

For one night, he wanted something for himself, too. He wanted to be the reason why she felt safe and cherished. For one night, he wanted to exist in a world far from the reality they faced.

As he slid his hands lower over her narrow hips, he crushed the skirt fabric in his fists with a delicious, buttery popcorn crinkle. With superhuman effort, he quelled the urge to rip the garment off her. Instead, he stroked her butt and the backs of her lean thighs.

The tiny caramel moan whetted his appetite even more. He slid his foot between her legs and gently kicked them apart. Still he couldn't see what he wanted, thanks to that damned skirt.

He let his fingers discover her instead.

Slowly. He wanted to savor her. He bent the knee of his good leg, scooting her into an even wider stance. Nothing stood between him and her sweetness. The air crackled between them. His quick breaths and hers blended in a spinning carousel of need.

Take her now, the virus screamed at him, like some base Neanderthal.

No. Slowly. "Britt."

"Please," she whispered.

Trailing his fingers up the inside of her leg, he encountered the warmth and liquid he craved. When he ran a finger between the satiny soft folds, she gasped and swallowed. As her head dropped forward, he tugged back with the fist in her hair, keeping her upright and looking back at him. She whimpered, a sparkling diamond sound raining over him. He feasted on those tiny noises. Wanted to hear them again and again.

Vision flickered crimson and normal. Over and again. *Hold it back.*

Finally, he released his grip on her hair and drifted his hand to rest between her shoulder blades. He pressed her forward, so her chest rested on the back of the couch and her butt lifted up. "Put your hands out to the sides."

She did so, and the image of her spread out for him, with all the trust involved, with Red knowing who—what—he was. The gift of this situation nearly drove him to his knees.

He leaned over, trailing kisses down her back to the skirt's waistband. All while pressing his fingers between her legs. Inching inward. Watching for any hesitation.

A sigh and a moan? Excellent.

How about that reset of her sexy legs a few inches wider with a bit more tilt of her hips, giving him even more access? God help him, but he loved it. Every instinct screamed at him to hurry the hell up.

Not going to happen. He didn't care about any bastard virus coursing through his tainted veins, there was no way Red would miss any chance to bring her pleasure.

When Red dipped a finger fully into the pooled heat, she cooed his fake name. His erection threatened to punch through the fabric containing it.

He used his thumb and other fingers to flick over her nub and stroke up and down the soft folds, even as he continued to press and withdraw his finger, stroking her deeper and deeper. He increased the pace until her hips bucked. Grabbing a handful of sexy butt, he stilled her movements so he could touch what he wanted.

Another roll of her sensitive nub, and she panted, "Oh my God."

"You can call me Al."

Her half-laugh, half-gasp broke the tension long enough for him to slip a second finger into her slick hot tightness. Things got serious in a hurry. He moved in and out, pressing along the rough patch in her vagina. Her legs quivered, but he held her up with his other hand which gripped her hip.

"I've got you, sweets," he growled. "Don't move. I've got you."

"If you keep doing what you're doing, oh God, I'm going—" Her whole body shuddered, vaginal muscles clenching around his fingers in a hard, fast rhythm that made the tip of his dick twitch in jealous response.

The fabric beneath his waistband developed a

small dark, damp spot. Damn it, he wanted to be inside of her so badly.

Her shudders tapered off until she hummed and sighed, the sounds tasting like gumdrops on his starved tongue. Casting a coy glance over her shoulder, she blinked slowly and smiled. "That was amazing. Are you waiting for another invitation for round two?" She wiggled her hips, her butt moving beneath the bunched-up skirt. "No worries. IUD in place. Clean bill of health on a recent checkup. You?"

"Same. Clean, I mean." Damn. No time to discuss that he was sterile, after being "voluntold" by the military docs to get a vasectomy due to the DNA-altering virus in his system. He couldn't form the words, but bottom line: no way would Red expose her to something that could harm her. He reached back to the kitchen table under the phone, pulling out a foil package. Shucking off his briefs, he tore open the package. A few crinkles later and the condom covered his raring-to-go erection.

A glance up and down her petite frame made him hesitate. Would he hurt her? Not if he was careful. Not if he went slowly.

Her folds still slick, he stroked her again until she started to purr under his touch. Using her lubrication to coat his condom-covered dick, he eased into her, then paused.

Britt whimpered and wiggled.

Shit, he wouldn't last long under this kind of torture. *Go slowly.* Any concerns about hurting her went plumb away when Britt sat back on him, sheathing him in one blissful move that almost caused him to lose consciousness. Their twin groans filled the room.

God, she was perfect, gloving him like she had been tailor made for him. Inside, her warmth enveloped him and clung like her body didn't want to let him go.

The feeling was mutual. He could do this every minute of the rest of his life and never get enough.

He eased away until he had almost withdrawn completely, then, as if they were two poles of a magnet, he surged forward and she pressed down on him

The rhythm and intensity increased, skin slapping against skin, and the virus flared, hungry and desperate to have all of her. Red panted as he drove deeper, with looping thrusts, nearly picking her up off the ground with each swivel of his hips. He ran a hand up her back and down one of her outstretched arms, to lace his fingers in hers. Even now, she remained in position, trusting him to give her pleasure. He would never betray that trust.

Her cries mixed with his lower growls and blended until he couldn't tell where the sound came from. He cupped a breast, easing her torso up and back as he pulled her to his chest, still moving inside of her, faster and harder with each thrust

With one hard thrust he suspended her off the ground for a second, driving his dick impossibly deep inside of her as she cried out and shattered around him. Easing her feet back to the ground, he pushed with two more strokes and followed her over the edge, her muscles milking him as he came apart inside of her.

For the first time in forever, all extraneous sound disappeared, leaving perfect clarity of his senses centered on Britt. Stepping back briefly to slip out of her, Red then picked her up, holding her limp, flushed body against him, like he could never let her go.

Chapter Twenty-Nine

In the early light Saturday morning, Britt snuggled her naked body into a cocoon of solid warmth. Last night was amazing. Al was amazing. How had she thought he was a quiet, reserved guy? After last night, that illusion was gone. Wow.

Even though she was in a place of uncertainty with her life and her future—hell, her safety, too—she had still asked for what she needed. God bless this man, but he'd given it to her, with interest. Then he'd taken care of her afterward. Al had held her boneless body as he tucked her into bed. Only, they didn't sleep until after another few rounds of mind-blowing sex.

Rubbing her legs together, she winced at the delicious tenderness in her hips. Worth it.

She froze, thinking. The next logical train of thought which entailed logistics like meeting each other's friends, house key privileges, and cohabitation? None of that would ever happen. Not with his line of work. Not as long as Beau Lequire hunted her.

She was his mission, for Heaven's sake.

Hell of a mission.

Who was Al, really? She tensed. Staring at the gray morning light against the window, she frowned.

"You're thinking so loud I can hear it." His breath feathered her hair and gave her vagina total amnesia regarding being sore.

She rolled over, her head resting on his arm. A firm, strong biceps flexed as he adjusted position to stare down at her.

"I'm thinking you're a terrible fashion student," she said.

That quick, broad grin created warmth in her

chest that spread out to her fingers and toes. He winked. "At least you don't think I'm terrible at other things."

"Like … dancing?"

Twining the fingers of his free hand in hers, he half-shrugged. "Sure."

"Fair to middling skills there."

"Glad it's not a job requirement." His chuckle vibrated the bones in her chest. "I'll try harder next time."

She snuggled into his warm chest and he released her hand to tug the quilt around her shoulders. "Try any harder and one of us will need medical attention."

Whatever he was about to say was lost at a knock on the door.

Like a light switch flipped, every muscle in Al's frame went tense, and he pressed a hand on her chest. "Stay here." The playful light in his eyes changed to a calculating and lethal squint.

It would take one fist, one flick of an arm, and he could kill someone. The guy was dangerous. She couldn't suppress a shiver.

What waited outside that door? She held her breath.

Sliding noiselessly from the bed, he paused long enough to draw on underwear and a shirt and palm his gun. Then he stalked out of the room.

No limp. Hell of a recovery from a gunshot wound twelve hours prior. Two gunshots this week. She frowned.

The thudding of her heart drowned out all other sounds. The spot where he'd pressed his hand tingled with heat from his palm.

The click of a door filtered back to her.

Then she heard low, male voices. Were they the men from JT Armstrong, back to finish the job? The guys from the MARTA train? Her breath rasped in and out of her mouth. Her heart hammered on ribs double time. She gripped the bedding, calculating how quickly she could open the bedroom window and how bad it would hurt when she fell three stories to the ground to escape.

More murmurs. A chuckle. Al.

No. Britt wasn't going to cower under the covers like a big chicken. She tiptoed around the room, pulling on sweatpants and a tank top. Crouching next to the bedroom door, she held her breath and listened.

"…look, Magic Mike, I know you've gone and lost your entire goddamn mind." The new voice reached her.

"Keep it down. Besides, you got a better idea? Just give me that dose already and monitor security while I recover." That was Al, his low voice laced with anger.

"Hard to monitor security when you turn off the feed, bro." A pause. "Here you go."

"Thank God and damn it." Al grunted and blew out an audible breath. Then two more breaths.

"Ears drying up?"

Huh?

A groan. "Yes. Damn it."

None of this conversation made sense.

"You're on mandatory rest," the other guy said.

"I'm good."

"Hoo, boy, I bet you are." There was laughter and a hard edge behind that voice. "Look, we can't totally secure this location, and when I say 'we,' I mean 'me,' because you're damn near useless right now. You need to exfil. Now. Come back fresh as a daisy."

A pause. "Can't."

"Look, Red. I can see you enjoy playing house while making your O face, or whatever the fuck you're doing here. But you're operating outside of factory safety specs."

Red? Must be the color of Al's hair. A nickname.

"That what Hunt said?" Al asked.

"That's what I say. Hunt is off, trying to find Pele and company."

Al pulled his head back. "Where are they?"

"Unknown. I'm not on that mission, bro." The other man's voice lowered. "Your objectivity is compromised. I'll step in."

"No! Would it kill you to keep your voice down?"

She flinched.

"The fuck I will." An *oof* sounded, like someone got poked, hard. "Do not fuck up her life, Red."

How much did she really know about the man she'd slept with? Britt trailed a shaking finger over her lips. Damn it.

"I know the risks."

"Yet you're still willing to take them? That's cold, bro. After her sister and Pele…"

Britt burst out of the bedroom, stumbling as she caught sight of the tall, muscled Black man from last night's MARTA station standing toe-to-toe with Al. Both men had their fists clenched. She recovered and stomped over, looking straight up at the man. "What about my sister?"

Al's eyes narrowed. "I told you to stay in there."

"Those words did come out of your mouth." She popped fists on her hips. "You might have a magic pelvis, but that doesn't make me obedient to your command." Okay, that last statement was not entirely true after last night. Semantics.

Al's jaw dropped.

The other man snorted. "Oooh, I like her." He went from angry to flashing a charismatic megawatt smile and swagger so quickly that she stumbled back a step. "Rodeo. Nice to make your acquaintance, ma'am. So sorry you got stuck with this pudknocker." He held out a hand. "Let me know if you want a *real* man protecting you. From head to toe."

Al shoved a palm over his face and dug with his fingers, like he wanted to scrape the skin off.

She giggled. "I'm Britt McNeill. Guessing you knew that already."

The Black man's smile, while easy and confident, contradicted a calculated narrowing of his eyes and flick of his gaze over her and around the room, similar to Al. Must have to do with the training.

Her hand disappeared in his, but he kept the grip firm but gentle. Like he held strength in check. Like Al. Heck, both men could be on a fitness magazine cover with their twin sets of corded arms, Al's crossed as he stood in an aggressive, angry stance.

After several more pumps of her hand, Al reached out to separate her hand from Rodeo's. "Enough canoodling."

Rodeo pressed a hand to his chest and reared back in mock horror. "What? Red, that right there is called being polite. You should try it sometime. You'd do much better with the *lay-dies*, bro," he drawled the word.

Al's face was beet red.

Britt pressed her lips together to keep from laughing. After a few moments, she frowned and faced him. "Red?"

"It's my ... name. Kind of. Damn it." For some reason, he appeared not as tall. Really tired. Must be the slump of his shoulders.

Her world tilted. "Wait. I haven't even been calling you the right name?" Seemed like something to know prior to having brain-exploding sex. Prickles of irritation formed over her neck and shoulders. What other important pieces of information had been left out?

He had lied about his name. Britt didn't have time to address the mounting anxiety. Filled with a hefty dose of self-doubt, she couldn't concentrate on her grounding technique.

Rodeo piped up. "It's just his nickname. Besides, if this big schlump was getting sexy times, he wouldn't care if you called him Berniece or Bartholomew. The guy's a monk." He fished out a small purple yo-yo from a pocket and sighed, almost like it was a relief to hold it.

"Shut. Up. Rodeo." Al—no, Red—raised a clenched fist.

Britt choked and stumbled back a half step.

Rodeo darted a glance from Britt to Red and raised his eyebrows. "Roger that." He whistled low, brows raised. With an inward roll of his mouth, he sent the yo-yo up and down the string, the soft, rhythmic whizzes breaking the silence.

Red's broad chest rose and fell. "My name is Alfred."

"Tell her the whole name." Rodeo rocked up on his toes like a kid with a secret he was dying to tell. A very big, muscled kid.

Red scowled. "Alfred E. Newman."

Britt frowned.

"From *Mad Magazine!*" Rodeo burst out.

She thought for a moment. "You're named after that old parody magazine?" she asked.

Rodeo studiously used the toy to do an intricate rocking basket maneuver, all while pulling an *uh-oh* face.

Red glared at the top of Rodeo's bent head. "Yeah. The big-headed guy on the cover. My birth mother's last name was Newman. She had a hell of a sense of humor, sending her redheaded baby off into

221

foster care with nothing but that name."

Covering a laugh in a cough, she managed to respond, "Well, it's unique. So, now you get called Red because of…" She motioned toward his head.

"That, and also it's the end of Alfred."

Rodeo whispered loudly behind a hand. "It's because of the hair. It's like a fire truck."

"Shut it, man," Red growled.

In a high voice, Rodeo quipped, "Not scared of youuu."

Britt sobered up. "Hey, what were you saying about my sister? Which one and what's going on?"

A quick glance between the men, but she saw it: a silent decision about what to say, made in a split-second. *Oh, no.*

"Your sister, Reagan…" Rodeo began.

Her temples throbbed. Ears buzzed. Her stomach felt like the moment right before the zero drop of bad news. She knew all about that feeling. It had happened with her mother's terminal cancer diagnosis and when Britt found out about Brady's death. "Tell me."

"Some of the team are en route to pick Reagan and Pele up at the rendezvous point," he said.

"I don't follow."

"They've been out of communication since yesterday. Deep in the Smoky Mountains in an area of the park no one visits."

"That doesn't sound good," she said. "What's she doing so far into the mountains?" Reagan worked at a camp on the edge of the Smokies, so hikes weren't unusual for her. Bushwhacking cross-country wasn't her typical activity, though.

"Lequire's men tried to kill her yesterday."

Britt took a step back, only to find Red's solid frame behind her. He cupped hands over her shoulders.

She didn't know this man. She stepped forward and his hands dropped away. "And?"

"She escaped with Pele. They're on the run."

"Oh." And what? There was nothing Britt could do. Couldn't go help. Couldn't call police. What would Britt say? A mystery group of people was helping her sister escape the guy who might have killed her brother because her brother had discovered the guy was scamming millions of donors and stealing funds for veterans. Britt didn't have proof, and now her sister was in danger, so please send help to this large area of forest. The police would so not believe her.

Rodeo rubbed a thumb on his chin, like he wanted to say more but didn't. He returned to running the yo-yo up and down the string.

Red's voice broke through her spinning thoughts. "The guys will take care of her. Pele's the best. She'll be okay."

If the reality of their situation hadn't completely sunk in after last night, it did now. "Can you let me know when something, um, happens?"

Rodeo shot her a tight smile. "Will do, ma'am."

"Are Kiera and Dad okay?"

"Of course," Rodeo said.

Silence. A few vehicles moved up and down the street in front of the building. Light traffic on a Saturday morning. Some birds chirped in the trees outside the back of the apartment. Normal sounds. Nothing threatening about them.

"So, what now?" she asked.

Red stepped in front of her, filling her field of vision but not touching her. "You need to vanish."

Her head was shaking before the answer made it out of her mouth.

"That's what this team does best. Disappear." He

rubbed his neck. "It's the safest thing to do."

Crossing her arms, she paced. Then she stopped, spun on her heel, and faced both guys.

Rodeo's eyes widened and he muttered "Oh, shit."

"We've been over this. My opinion doesn't change just because you … we…" She huffed. "It doesn't change."

"But—" Red interjected. When Red opened his mouth, she stepped right up to him. Out of the corner of her eye, she caught Rodeo looking anywhere but at Britt and Red.

She took a deep breath. "I hope you understand." She stared at Red. "This degree is something I've worked my ass off to accomplish. My mom's dying wish was for me to complete the degree. Nothing, not a jerk face businessman who's too scared to take care of his own dirty business and picks on innocent people, will stop me."

"Can we hire her?" Rodeo piped up.

Red's head whipped back. "No, we cannot." He turned back to her. "Don't fight me on this one, Britt. We can't keep you safe if you're out there. My team cannot control all the variables."

"I get it. That's called life. There are no guarantees. These are weighted decisions."

Red's brows slammed down. "You don't understand. This is different. You have to trust me."

She sputtered, "Trust a guy who lied about everything? Are you for real?" Everything felt off-balance. Logic fled. Her anxiety took over. Her heart pattered and palms sweated. "It's still my life. How about this for a serving of reality? I will accept the consequence of my actions. I understand the risk. There's no liability for you. No one will blame you if things don't work out perfectly. That way, you can still fulfill the duties of your *job*." She spat that last word.

"You're not a—" he sputtered to stop at her finger pointing at him.

"If you value your life, don't complete that sentence."

Rodeo studied the rug like he was cramming for a textiles final.

Which left Red, gape-jawed and turning, well, red. "This is about your safety. I can protect you, within reason."

Standing between these two tall, massive men drove home the point. She motioned toward herself. "I get it. But just because I don't have big, bulging muscles or fancy guns doesn't mean I'm a wimp."

Red shut his mouth with an audible clunk of teeth. "I never said—"

"Dude," Rodeo muttered, still looking at the floor. "Bail the fuck out of this conversation, ASAP."

Red crossed his big arms. "Fine."

"Fine?" Britt studied the angry slash of his hard mouth. Was this a trick?

Red spat, "How much longer?"

"How much longer do you have to be here, babysitting, stuck with me?" Fear drove her words faster than she could think them. Half her brain was horrified, half still felt helpless. Britt didn't like either. "You know the answer. The show is next Friday. Once that's done, I can pass the semester without showing up for another class, if necessary. The collection is my senior project. My final exam." Tears stung her eyes, but she refused to give in to the overwhelming panic that bubbled up in her throat, choking her. "That's more than four years of work." During which her mother and her brother had both died.

Her memories of college and memories of their deaths wove together. Unravel one and they all might fall apart.

Last year, her world had shattered and somehow, Britt had gotten the professional help needed to build herself back into a functional adult again.

Running a hand over his head like he wanted to rip out the hair, Red half-turned. "Rodeo. What do you say?"

The big guy's teeth gleamed. "I'm all for helping people meet their life goals in spite of assholes. Hunt's incognito right now, so I'll make the executive decision. We can pull twenty-four-hour shifts. I don't require sleep."

"You're not a robot."

Rodeo's stare dropped the temperature in the room twenty degrees. "I can make it to Friday for the right reasons, bro."

Britt's heart leapt.

"Damn it. This is a bad idea," Red muttered, rotating back to Britt. "No more big risks. Clear all activities with me or Rodeo. Got it?"

Every instinct wanted her to tell him where to shove his dictator attitude, but deep down, she knew he had her best interest at heart. "All right."

No one moved for a solid minute.

"So. Go team?" Rodeo tucked the yo-yo back in a pocket and held his hand, palm down out between them. "Don't leave me hanging."

"I'm going to take a shower." Britt ignored Rodeo and dug a finger into Red's rock-hard chest. "Does that fit into the plan?"

Red's eyes hardened, then glinted. "Only if I can inspect your progress. For safety."

"And, I'm done here." Rodeo stared at the

ceiling, palms up. "Why me, God? Do you hate me? Why would you make me work in conditions like this?"

Chapter Thirty

Her life wasn't perfect, but it was close enough for Britt as she strolled the few blocks to school for some fashion lab time that Saturday afternoon. Rodeo had watched over the apartment while Britt slept for another few hours. Al—no, Red—had rested in Tachi's room.

Fine, it was a second nickname. People had multiple nicknames all the time. It was one more issue in a long line of issues for Britt.

The emotional roller coaster over the past few days had left her exhausted, drained. In Britt's world, hope seemed to always get ruined by self-doubt which in turn was driven by anxiety. Over the past year, she had worked through her anxiety. The self-doubt had improved. Then she met Red, the first person in years she'd made a meaningful connection with and trusted. Roller coaster car going up, up, up.

Turned out he had lied to her. Everything about Red was a lie. Her sister was in danger. Lequire hunted her family. The roller coaster car plunged straight down.

Despite this bizarre personal and family situation happening, Britt could still see the finish line for this next step in her life. There were people who would keep her safe until the show next week. That's all she needed.

The lightness in her step had very little to do with the hulking, sulking guy in fake glasses next to her who walked faster so she would keep up. Red whipped his head up at the sound of a car door closing. After a beat, he returned to the slouchy student posture.

Yep. Britt could chalk up yet another impulsive decision for the books. Nothing like sleeping with a guy who led a secret life. Oh, no. In Britt's world, just jump his pants and figure it out later. God, she was an idiot.

Later. She'd process her bad decision-making later. Right now, Britt had a project to finish and bad dudes to avoid. No handsome slab of overprotective male would distract her from that goal.

Unless it was like last night. What a distraction. She curled her toes. From here on out, she would focus on fashion.

She adjusted her backpack and tugged at the untucked denim shirt. One of her favorite outfits when paired with the lightweight cotton red gingham skirt. A nod to pioneer aesthetic, right down to the brown ankle booties.

Red had his ubiquitous hair-covering beanie on, even in the spring sunshine. The end of March in Atlanta had turned warm. She lifted her face to the sun and took a deep breath. The daffodils along the walk to school bloomed, and the bright color lifted her spirits even more.

Less than one week. One more project. One chance to show everyone what she could do with some fabric and her creativity. Her chance to make her family proud. Maybe her chance to have an entire career that she'd never thought possible.

A buzzing sound, and Red fished out his cell phone and touched the screen.

"Huh…" He stopped.

She paused with him. "What?"

"The team extracted Reagan."

Gripping his forearm, she said, "Is she safe?"

"Yes." He cupped a hand over the screen and squinted at the text. "She has a broken arm and is a bit banged up, but is going to be okay."

"Oh, no. What happened?"

"No idea." He read further. "Pele's hurt but they

think he'll recover. They're both in our compound."

"That's good, right?"

He pulled her into his side and dropped an arm around her stiff shoulders, like they were a couple. The pretense hurt as much as the strong band of muscle locked around her. She peeked up as he scanned the vicinity.

A muscle jumped in his jaw. "Good that she's safe and Kiera's safe. Bad that Lequire is running out of targets."

"Oh." Her stomach sank. "*Oh*."

With a squeeze of her upper arm, he slid his arm down to her lower back and applied gentle pressure. They needed to keep moving. She was catching on with the unspoken messages.

"Six more days." He stowed the phone in a back pocket with his free hand. "We should be able to spare another teammate to help here, and an extra person for your dad. More personnel would be good."

"You seem tired, even after the nap. You might need a break."

"Tired? Because of—uh, yeah. The mission and all."

"Thanks for understanding."

He rolled his neck and rubbed it. "I don't have to like that your safety is at risk, but I get why this is important to you. You'll finish your project, come hell or high water."

She glanced at him as she hurried toward the campus building. "I know that none of my plans were part of your original mission. This means a lot."

"I know what it's like to have a life you've created from your own two hands. I know what it's like for that to be taken away." Then he clamped his mouth shut.

Of course. He'd been a foster child. Again, she didn't know additional details, because it made way too much sense to get to know the person she was sleeping with before the sleeping occurred. Britt shook her head. This mess would take a while to untangle. No risk of her therapist going out of business anytime soon.

They walked through the building and up two flights of concrete stairs to the lab. Two students she recognized from other senior project disciplines—sculpture and photography—passed them in the hall. Britt's heart fluttered. She was eager to put the finishing touches on the outfits in preparation for the fittings this week. The music, lighting, timing for her part of the show—she had so much to consider. But first, she had to get the collection perfect.

The zip in her step matched the thrum in her veins. So close. This final project would be fabulous. Britt would prove that she wasn't at SCAD because of charity. She was here because she had earned her place with talent.

She opened the doors of the empty fashion lab and walked past sewing tables, clothing forms with pinned fabric, and racks of clothing. Approaching the corner that housed her project, Britt stopped. Stared. Rubbed her eyes and looked again. Draped over the table, sewing machine, and clothing rack?

All of her show's clothing. In hundreds of tiny, cut pieces.

Chapter Thirty-One

Red frowned as Britt skidded to a halt, color draining out of her face. Instantly, he went on alert, positioning himself to cover her, scanning for danger.

No one else was in the room. He listened with his antidote-diminished ability. Damn the limitation. Peering at the table, he didn't understand what he saw. Shouldn't there be finished pieces of clothing?

She made a choked, gurgling sound and walked two halting steps forward, picking up random fistfuls of fabric. Ragged pieces drifted back to the tabletop. A button clinked against the metal table and rolled onto the floor, out of sight.

She opened her mouth. No sound came out.

Half turning in his direction, the electric blue of her eyes lasered into him. Desperate. Pleading. Layered with pain. Her mouth gaped.

Oh, shit.

"What the … I don't … It's. All gone," she gasped.

He reached for her, but she ducked away, rushing around the table. With jerking motions, she held up more pieces, then let them fall between her fingers.

"My project. Oh my God."

She staggered a few steps and thudded her back against the wall, sliding down until she sat on the concrete floor right in front of floor-to-ceiling windows. He didn't have the heart to tell her it was an unsafe location to collapse.

Her harsh gurgles got his attention. Tears rolled down her face. That blank stare of desperation gutted him as he sat down on the floor next to her.

"What happened?" she said, dropping her head

into her palms. "What happened?"

"I can find out—" He dug for his phone, took one look at her, and abandoned the task. "Come this way, sweets. Away from the window." Tugging her into the vee of his legs, he pulled her quaking body flush against him, hugging her tightly to his chest, surrounding her with as much of himself as he could. He wanted her to draw strength from him.

To what end?

Damn it.

To no end. There was no future.

For the present, though, Red sure as hell would help by any means necessary. Even now, the silent shakes of her shoulders twisted his heart in ways he had never experienced before.

"It's ruined," she whispered.

The vulnerable voice coming from this sparkling, bold woman triggered a heated rage that slowly grew deep inside of him until it threatened to boil over.

"I can find out what happened," he finally said.

"Really?" Her voice cracked on the word.

He pressed his lips to the crown of her head. "We have surveillance cameras set up here."

He took the sniff and a nod as permission. Drawing his knees up to better bracket her with his body, he settled her deeper against his torso. The way she turned to one side and sagged against him, cheek pressed to his chest and both arms clutched around his midsection, both terrified him and made him feel a million feet tall.

"When were you last in here? Yesterday afternoon?"

A nod.

Pulling up the app, he scrolled back through video feeds of this room over the past day. Black and white images filled the screen. Britt leaving in the early evening yesterday, before she went out to the club. More hours passed with a few students working at their stations. Then late last night—no, this morning—he caught flickers of movement on the screen. He backed up and slowed down the replay.

Just after midnight a woman wearing a dark Balenciaga hoodie entered the lab, headed right over the Britt's table, and cut into the fabric for ten minutes with a pair of scissors. She even took extra time to distribute the piles of ruined clothing evenly over the surfaces. Once finished, the woman set the scissors down next to the sewing machine and walked out. He caught a wink of pale hair, perfectly manicured long nails, and enough of a facial profile for identification.

Jenna.

Britt stared at the screen with Red. "What the heck? Seriously," she said, a sob tearing out of her. "Why would anyone do this? To me? I'm no one."

"I'm sorry." He snaked an arm over her chest. "This meant a lot to you."

"I need to go to the school with this video."

He shook his head. "You can't, sweets. It raises too many questions."

"What?"

"The mission. Your safety. My team."

Her shoulders dropped. "It'd be real nice to mess up her project over there." She lifted her chin with a sigh. "Yes, I realize that revenge would get me nowhere." Turning her head, she nuzzled a cheek on his upper arm, the movement sweet and sad at the same time. His sleeve became damp where her face rested. Damn it, he wanted to fight this battle for her. He couldn't.

"Four years of work. Gone." She trembled and gripped his forearm.

He checked the current feeds to ensure the perimeter was clear, tapped out a message to Rodeo, then set the device on the floor. "I don't know what to say. I'm so damn sorry."

"Nothing to say."

In silence, they sat in the empty room with Red propped against the wall and Britt in front of him. His butt went to sleep on the concrete. Didn't care. He wouldn't move until she asked him to.

Every few minutes, he brushed his fingers over her hair. Patted her arms. Anything to make her feel connected. He knew that hopeless, alone feeling all too well. Knew the need to be supported by someone in a dark time.

So they sat together in the quiet, empty room.

Thirty minutes later, the doors burst open, and Tachi ran up to them, dark eyebrows lifting and long wavy hair flying over her shoulders as she leaned over. "Oh, honey." She glanced over the ruined clothing, eyes narrowing. "I am so going to kill whoever did this."

Sauntering in a second later, Rodeo leaned a hip on the table.

Letting Tachi take over consolation duties, Red extricated himself and stood up, stretching his back. He walked over to where Rodeo stood.

"Bro, whoever did that … this is some cold-ass shit." Rodeo motioned at the worthless piles of fabric.

"I'll say."

"At least now you don't have to convince her to stay and finish the project."

Red leaned into his teammate and growled, "Speaking of cold, that's a dick thing to say."

Hands went up. "Whoa there. Don't climb all over my lovely ass for stating the obvious. This is still a job. At least, for one of us."

Red clamped his teeth together until he regained control. Thank God he'd taken the antidote this morning and could think clearly. "Sorry, man. It's just … this family can't catch a break. This wasn't even because of Lequire."

"Good point." Rodeo peeked over Red's shoulder. "What are those two doing? There's a lot of whispering and sniffling and head petting going on."

"Jealous?"

"Naw. I could have any woman rub my head and whisper to me, any day of the week."

"So you claim." Red crossed his arms. "Any woman?"

The guy's eyes darted back to Britt and Tachi still in the corner. "Of course."

Red's snorted response was interrupted by Tachi. "Come here, guys." She was sitting next to Britt, an arm thrown around her shoulders. "You know who did this?"

"We do." Red nodded.

"Then we're calling campus security and turning that person in."

"No, we can't do that." Britt locked eyes with Red.

"That's total crap. Why not?" Tachi scraped her long hair back and glared at the men.

Britt sniffed. "We just can't."

"Not following. How about fill me in here, fellas? Things have gotten weird ever since Tarzan here dragged me out of the apartment fifteen minutes ago."

Rodeo froze.

A shrug with her free shoulder. "What? It's true. The guy didn't explain anything, just kept grunting 'Let's go,' like repeating simple words made the situation clearer. If he hadn't mentioned Britt, I would've used my self-defense moves, thinking he was some kind of unhinged kidnapper." She wiggled her sneaker-clad feet in front of her. "I have fabulous aim."

Rodeo snorted and lifted his chin. Then he stepped back, hand drifting over his groin.

A hiccup of laughter from Britt broke the tension in the room. "Good God, my life. Red, tell her the basics of my family stuff and this mission."

He shushed her and waved a hand.

"You heard me. Tachi is my roommate, so she's basically family. If you two are going to hang around for a while, she needs to know why."

"Danger, bro. Danger," Rodeo said under his breath.

Red considered his options, then relented. "Okay." He sketched a brief overview of the situation, leaving out tons of details. "So you see we can't reveal our camera data without exposing our operation."

Tachi leaned her head back on the wall, her sculpted features set in a determined expression. When she opened her eyes, the intense glint made Red want to stand up straighter. It was a similar expression his teammates wore when they had to carry out an impossible mission. "May I personally maim Jenna? Pretty please." She nudged Britt.

Off to the side, Rodeo rubbed his chin with a bemused half-smile.

"Tempting." Britt gave a small nod of approval. "Won't solve the problem." She rubbed a hoop on her ear. "Look. We need to make peace with the fact that my course of study and career just ended right here. Today. There's no way I can do this show now. I can't recreate the entire collection in time. Some of those fabric pieces had to be special ordered. Besides, Red was saying it was too difficult to provide security for the show with teen models. Too many moving parts. This disaster is a sign from God. Game over." Her shuddering sigh echoed a growing ache in his chest.

The rubbery *thunk* of the toes of Tachi's sneakers against each other filled the empty space. She tapped a perfect red nail against her lower lip and hummed. Rodeo stared at her like a starving squirrel eyeing the last acorn in the forest.

Tachi got up and sauntered over to Rodeo, posing next to him, shoulder to shoulder. "What do you think, Britt?"

Rodeo swept his assessing gaze over Tachi and raised his eyebrows, flexing as he brushed his big shoulder against hers. "I know what *I* think, baby."

When Britt giggled, the ache in Red's chest eased.

"Jesus, take the wheel." Tachi looked at the ceiling then pinned Rodeo in place with a glare that should be weaponized. "Hey, eye candy with the empty brain box. Keep the stares up here." She put one finger under his chin and he flinched. *Uh-oh.* "No talking unless it's meaningful contribution to this discussion. Brilliant minds are at work here." When he opened his mouth again, she held up a hand. "Ah-ah-ah. Zip it."

Rodeo froze. Sure as shit, the guy shut his big mouth. Wow.

"So?" She spun back toward Britt, motioning toward herself and Rodeo, who was still rocking back on his heels in stunned silence.

Red stifled a laugh.

"What do you think?" Tachi waved in Red and Rodeo's general direction. Red held his breath. He had a bad feeling about what was developing.

"About what?" Britt said.

"How do I look next to him, image-wise?" She struck another high-fashion runway pose and then held up both thumbs and index fingers to make an imaginary camera. "Think: runway still shots for your portfolio."

Britt's eyes went wide. Her shoulders straightened as she sat up straighter. "No. Are you serious?"

"He could pass. He looks good. It might work," Tachi said.

"Baby, I always look exceptional—" Rodeo's sentence ended with Tachi's elbow in his ribs and a deep *oof*.

"Your high opinion of yourself is not the point. What did I say about talking?" She catwalked straight over to Red and rested her upper back on his shoulder. Casual. Fashionable. "How about here?"

Red's gut twisted into a knot as he struggled to understand.

"No." Britt exhaled. "Maybe. Could it work?"

"I could train them."

"In a week?"

"Yes."

The pieces of this awful plan started to come together for Red in a damned hurry. *No.* He opened his mouth but no words came out.

"Yes?" Britt's brows shot up.

Tachi made a slow-motion clap. "Yes."

No. Red's mind spun. He couldn't—

"But by Friday?" Britt asked.

"The boys can help with other tasks." Tachi tossed her hair back over a shoulder and shrugged. "Not like they have any other plans."

"Um, hello? Yoo-hoo. Over here." Rodeo raised his hand. "May I have permission to ask a question of the delicate genius, please and thank you, ma'am, baby?"

Tachi's snort was the only indication she heard him. She smoothed her hand over her curvy hip and continued to face Britt. "I'll clear my schedule starting now."

"Tachi, you can't. Your job."

"Looks like a family emergency to me, darling."

Red grabbed the edge of the metal sewing table. Good God, this out-of-control train to Destination Unknown had just jumped the tracks and showed zero signs of slowing down. What about Beau Lequire? What about maintaining safety, security, solutions? The mission.

Red pivoted in Rodeo's direction, extending his hands, palms up. Rodeo shook his head and mouthed, *What the fuck*? He motioned for Red to go ahead and say something. After a second, Red cleared his throat. "If we're discussing any schedules, the team needs to be involved for operational planning purposes."

Britt scrambled to her feet before Red could reach down and help her. "Tachi, what about your shoot? Work? You can't just—"

She paused and popped a hip to the side, hand pressed on the curve. "Well, of course I'll take time for the shoot, but the rest of the week I'm yours!"

They carried on as if Red had never spoken. If he didn't have the antidote onboard, his virally driven anger would be popping by now. He opened his mouth again.

Tachi held up her hand while dialing her phone, walked ten steps away, said three or four sentences, hung up, then repeated the process again. She sauntered back, shoving the phone in her back pocket.

Red scratched his head. Damned beanie. Damned situation. "Stop. What the hell is going on?"

"We have a solution." Tachi sashayed up and clapped Rodeo on the shoulder, making him startle. The cords in his forearms bunched as he fisted his hands. Red knew the tell: Rodeo was furiously suppressing the virally driven violent response to unexpected stimulus that triggered the fight-or-flight response. He was hanging on. For now.

Details mattered on this mission. However, Red craved Britt's watery-eyed, half-smile of sheer hope as she nodded.

"You still have those other sketches?" Tachi asked her, stepping away from Rodeo.

Britt toyed with the hoops in her ear as she walked in front of the sewing table, back and forth. "Rough ones. Never fully developed. Back at the apartment." She trailed her finger on the surface, then stopped. "This is insane. Six days. Six models. Who else can we…?"

Tachi walked up to Rodeo. They were only a few inches apart in height. His nostrils flared as his wide eyes remained riveted on her face. How close to the edge was he running? Red almost intervened. Like all the virally enhanced team members, Rodeo tended to overreact to direct confrontation or invasion of personal space.

Tachi turned to Rodeo and Red. "Do you have any other buddies who are built like you? Who would pair well with models like me?" She motioned at her statuesque frame.

Rodeo puffed out his chest. "For perfection like you, babe, there is no one else quite like me. No need to look any further. I'll pair with you right now."

"Okay, funny guy. Listen, just because I'm smoking hot and give you the time of day doesn't mean I'm into you. Get your brain out of your pants and focus."

Rodeo's brows furrowed. "I don't follow." His voice came out almost pitiful-sounding.

"Me neither." Red shrugged.

Britt's blue eyes danced. "Yes! There are more.

Red said they could free up more teammates to help."

Alarm bells clanged in Red's brain. Whatever the women were cooking up had *bad idea* written all over it. "Whoa. What's going on here?"

Britt rushed over and hugged him around the waist, the action fierce and perfect. He couldn't stop his arms from snaking around her small frame. "Oh my gosh. I might still pull off the show. If you'll help me."

Warmth spread through him at the easy way her arms encircled him. He would give her the world to continue this feeling. He'd give her time, materials, his left arm. Anything. "Of course, but … what do you need?"

"More of your friends. And a few more of Tachi."

He might have the best hearing in the world, but he must have misunderstood. "Huh?"

Britt leaned back, a determined glint in her eye. "I'm going to use my alternative collection. It's your lucky day, Mr. Fashion Student. You and your buddies just *became* the show."

Chapter Thirty-Two

The rest of the weekend flew by in a rush of whirling activity.

The four of them returned to the apartment to regroup and plan. Britt pulled up and printed out old designs she had mocked up a year or so ago, but had discarded in lieu of her plan for a teen line of clothing. While the guys communicated the change in plans with their commander, Britt and Tachi brainstormed and updated the sketches to prep for cutting and sewing.

The new theme: *Hope Greater Than The World.* Ambitious. Perfect for the biggest Hail Mary in SCAD's history.

Tachi's relentless, confident approach to her modeling career had inspired Britt's theme when she had created the old sketches. Never in a million years had Britt expected to put a collection together with such short notice. As for finding big and tall models? The guys had to bolster security. Betting money was on Lequire making a play for her. More teammates were headed to Atlanta and Britt could use them in the show.

With Tachi's network, it looked like she would get two more plus-sized female models.

Britt's heart soared. She had a chance to fill her allocated slot in SCAD's fashion show. She still controlled her destiny.

The dilemma of finding money to buy fabric was answered when Red silently opened his wallet at the JOANN Fabric store counter on Sunday. Large bills. No questions, no hesitation.

With grim expressions and tormented huffs, Red and Rodeo carried two precarious towers of bolts and accessories out the door and to Rodeo's black SUV.

Britt's ears rang after hours of sitting in front of a chugging sewing machine that Sunday evening. She'd kicked off her ballet flats many hours ago, but kept the scarf in place to hide her fading bruises. Thank God for the comfy A-line skirt and t-shirt ensemble today. Easier to work in.

Tachi had volunteered for light sewing duty at a nearby table. Even Rodeo had contributed, sewing buttons. Sure, his learning curve was slowed by poked and bleeding fingers. Not to mention an inventive string of curses.

Red patrolled constantly, never stopping. He either monitored the camera feeds on his cell phone, or he walked a circuit through and around the building. A few other students came and went during the weekend, putting finishing touches on their collections, oblivious to the danger surrounding all of them.

There was no intel about Lequire. Radio silence. Their teammate Gonzo would join them soon. When Dad arrived in town for the show, there would be additional teammates protecting him as well.

Reagan wanted to attend but agreed to stay in the compound for safety. Of course, Kiera couldn't attend. She made way too tempting a target. Dad had volunteered to record Britt's portion of the show.

Her stomach flipped and quivered. God, Britt didn't want to disappoint her family. She scrubbed her burning eyes and straightened out her spine with a few satisfying cracks. Oh, man. Midnight. The fashion lab had been empty for hours.

Monday morning work in the coffee shop was going to suck. Not as much as class and facing Jenna. Her palms grew clammy in anticipation of confronting her saboteur.

"Need a break?" The low voice came from

behind her and vibrated through her entire body. Red. He'd become a steady anchor in the whirlwind of her life.

Poor guy didn't understand how a show got put together, all the steps involved, or collection development. The one thing he seemed to understand was that Britt needed this project to succeed. She needed one thing to call her own. Needed to fulfill Mom's last wish. Britt's degree. Her pride. Her destiny on her own terms.

"Let's call it a night," she said.

Tachi and Rodeo had left a few hours ago, returning to the apartment where Rodeo had patrol duties.

"Whatever you need." The sensual weight of his quiet words was unmistakable.

Wasn't she mad at him for something? Lying? Omitting the truth, but still. He had made up some ground by supporting her. She stared at his firm lips, his clenched jaw, and that intense stare.

Libido flared in the aftermath of this weekend's creative frenzy. Warmth pooled in her belly.

Suddenly taking a breath took effort. "Anything?"

His rough finger pad trailed up her arm, drawing out goose bumps. "Literally anything."

Not taking time to think, she turned toward him, stood on tiptoes, fisted his Henley, and kissed him until they both gasped.

"Damn, Britt. Don't you ever get tired?" Little lines crinkled next to his hazel eyes.

"Does that bother you?"

"Never. I could get used to an Energizer Britt."

She leaned back and bit her lower lip. "If it's too much…"

With a growl and a wild shake of his head, he

smashed his lips onto hers, opening her mouth, and tangling his tongue with hers until her knees shook. He pulled back, drawing air like he'd run a race. "It will never be too much."

"Good." She slid her hands under his shirt, encountering the chest holster strap over hard muscle.

He shuddered. Good. Britt ran her fingers down over the ridges of his stomach muscles and under the waistband of his cargo pants, to drift over the curve of his hard butt. Cargo pants. On trend ten years ago, dated now, but ideal to hide his guns and knives.

At some point, hanging out with a fully armed guy whose sole duty was to keep her alive had become a normal day for Britt.

Speaking of fully armed...

She encountered the ridge of his hard erection, pushing against briefs to rise almost above his waistband. A flick of a belt and a button gave her access to push the briefs down so that she could stroke and cup him.

"Damn it." He fished out his phone with a shaking hand and ran through the app, turning the fashion lab cameras off and deactivating the badge reader outside the door so no one could enter. He dropped the phone on the metal sewing table with a loud clatter.

"All clear?" she asked.

"Yes."

She smiled up at him until his eyes widened as she encircled him firmly. She ran her thumb over the smooth and damp head of his penis. Sweat beaded his upper lip. A squeeze on his heavy balls had him clenching her upper arms tight enough to make her yelp.

"Sorry," he panted. "Damn, you don't mess around, do you?"

A quick stab of doubt made her pause. "Would you prefer it if I were coy and shy?"

"Hell, no. I love everything you're doing and how you're doing it." He shuddered again when she stroked his length. "Obviously. My main concern is logistics." He eyed the high sewing table. "How do you want to do this?"

Lifting a leg and sliding her bare foot over his calf, she rocked against him. "Fabric cutting table?"

"Roger that." He pulled his briefs and pants loosely around his hips, boosted her up, and she wrapped her legs around him, the skirt bunching up over her thighs. Every step as he walked across the room rubbed his erection against her core. Hard warmth and polyester knit created a terrific friction combination. Who knew?

Resting her butt on the laminated cutting table's sturdy edge, he slid his garments back down and groaned. He slipped off her lightweight scarf. "At some point, we should try using something like a king bed, sweets."

"Kind of conventional, don't you think?"

"Hell, if you want acrobatic sex in zero-G, I'll do my damndest to make it happen for you." He braced his arms on the table, leaning in close. Licking his upper lip, he said, "Don't let me hold back your creativity."

Invitation accepted, she pulled him to her. The sweep of his tongue into her mouth demanded and promised more. She dropped her head back, giving him all access as he nipped and licked over her lips and neck and the vee of her t-shirt. He cupped her breasts in his warm hands through the shirt, and she shivered.

Then she floated backward. His hand under her neck supported her until she rested on the table, legs dangling over the edge, skirt up around her hips. With a hook of her panties using his finger, air cooled her heated flesh.

"Hot damn. Midnight snack." He knelt. His warm

breath teased her entrance until she squirmed. "You're mine now." He held her thighs with his iron grip, opening her to him. She tried a test movement. Nope. Couldn't move.

God, she needed him to touch her, to relieve the pressure building, to do … something. She gave a frustrated squeal as she reached for him.

Red ducked out of the way, chuckled, and planted his mouth on her sensitive skin. Relentlessly, he licked between her folds in long strokes. Then he groaned deep in his throat and sucked her clit, creating pressure that took her right up to the edge of pain. Right when the pressure started to sting, he stroked downward with his tongue and into her core. Again and again. She panted. It was too much sensation, too much connection, her senses overloaded. Her head rolled from side to side as he continued to nip and lick, using nothing but his mouth to give her the sweetest torment. Pressure built down deep in her belly. She laced her fingers with his, their hands joined on top of her thighs.

He lifted his head. "You still good?"

"Maybe. Yes. I don't know. Please." She couldn't form words. "Red. More." Was that her high-pitched begging voice that cracked on his name?

"Happy to comply." The glint in his eyes spoke volumes. Her desire lined up perfectly with his own agenda.

He pressed her legs back even further and growled. "Damn, sweets. You are so beautiful. Amazing." Bending down again, he flicked his tongue over her folds and clit until she whimpered. He stood briefly. "Look at me, Britt." She opened her eyes and was rewarded with a view of him putting two fingers in his mouth to wet them, then thrusting both fingers into her.

Her view of the overhead fluorescent lights dimmed when his fingers curled toward the ceiling as he stroked her interior vaginal wall. Gasps burst from her mouth in quick succession. She clung to the edge of the table.

He pulled his fingers out, crouched down, and licked her clit again.

Quicker, deep thrusts of his fingers took her over the edge as Britt combusted in a full body climax that turned her vision dark for several whirling seconds and left her unable to catch a full breath. "Oh my God," she panted. "Red." She tried to lift her head and reach for him, but her body refused to respond.

He sheathed himself in a condom, swept his fingers inside her again, and withdrew to coat the latex in her wetness. Then he licked his fingers clean. "I will never get enough of you, sweets. God, you're beautiful." He teased her sensitive folds with the tip of his erection. "I want you so damn much." He swiveled his hips and drove in to the limit of her body, stretching her in every direction. "You feel so good."

"Agree," she gasped.

Bending her legs up, he dug his hands into her thighs and pulled her into him. The skin where they met heated and rubbed, creating the best friction in the universe.

"Red!"

"Yeah." He eased out, then slammed back into her, over and over, until sweat rolled off his creased forehead.

Tension climbed a new ladder inside of her. Higher and higher, he pushed her. The rhythm and depth increased until she rocked her head from side to side. When he leaned over, Britt grabbed the back of his neck and tugged until he roared, dropping his mouth onto hers and kissing her until his breath became hers. Still, his hips kept moving. How much more could she take? He kept driving her upward. Higher. Faster.

With a spark of light, she came apart again, gripping his t-shirt fabric, clenching him inside as he followed her over his own cliff. Aftershocks raced through her body. Each little movement or swivel of his hip sent delicious shudders through her pelvis.

Resting both forearms on either side of her head, he didn't move. He was still seated inside of her, in amazing, heated connection. Her ankles were still locked around his waist. He bent down and kissed her, sucking her lower lip into his mouth.

He pulled back a few inches. "Britt. You're amazing."

"My thoughts exactly."

A pause. "Can I stay with you tonight?"

"In the apartment?" Because that was the plan with the security detail.

"In your bed."

Chapter Thirty-Three

Despite being an Energizer Bunny, Britt's batteries were 100% drained on Monday morning.

Fabric cutting table sex in the fashion lab. An amazing experience but exhausting.

Britt would have loved to climb all aboard for more rounds with a hot and hard man like Red, but fatigue got the better of her. She remained in his arms for the entire night, waking up five hours later in the same position as when she'd fallen asleep, surrounded by his big frame and muscled limbs. The alarm blasted her back to consciousness. Time for work. Then school.

Her jaw tightened as her back teeth pressed together. She'd have to confront Jenna today. Damn it.

With a groan, she turned off the alarm on her phone and pushed to a sitting position. Or tried to. A big, warm arm around her midsection stopped her.

"Morning." The sexy rumble of his voice woke her up faster than a double shot of espresso.

"Mmm." Giving up against his corded embrace, she nestled into his chest and shoulder, like she belonged there. Warmth flowed into her from where her back pressed against his firm chest. He nuzzled the skin of her temple, tickling her hairline.

She sighed and glanced around the small room.

Too comfortable. Too perfect. Too temporary, and Britt knew it. Once this business with Lequire ended, Red would be off on another mission. He had his own life to live, after all, and she wasn't part of that life.

But what if they *could* have a future together? Not that he'd offered or that she had asked. Besides, she had her career to build and a bad guy to avoid. Also, Britt knew her own life patterns all too well.

Step one: Survive.

Then: Connection or cherishing..

Later: Vulnerability

Always ending with: Loss.

That was the pattern, and only her family members and a few rare relationships made it past step two.

Maybe she could break the pattern. When had this grab-life-by-the-horns encounter with a sexy man turned into a longing for a type of relationship she'd never considered possible?

She should ask him. Communicate openly. What a novel idea. Doubt hit her in the midsection. Could she ask for what she wanted? Risk rejection? For a split second she couldn't breathe under the crashing weight of a wave of brain-whirling anxiety.

After a lungful of air and a deep sigh, she pushed until he let her go. She sat on the side of the bed, facing away from him.

"You okay?" he asked.

She rubbed her face, like she could scrub away all the bad junk in her life. "Peachy."

A rustle of sheets and then the bed dipped.

Don't touch me, don't touch me.

"Britt?" He sat next to her, fully naked. *Oh, come on.* That was unfair.

She stared at the floor. "Yep."

"What's going on?"

It would be so simple to share her worries. Air out concerns. See if there was a chance for a future together. Determine if he even wanted such a thing. Discuss issues like two normal adults. Simple, but difficult to do with severe anxiety.

The choice might not be hers to make. Or his. He'd said it before: he worked on a covert team that had to remain below the radar. There had been no mention of any of his work or life beyond this mission, and rightly so.

But the thought of a future without Red in it didn't sit well with Britt. At all.

Panic pushed to the surface, cracking rational thought and logic into disorganized pieces, making clear thought difficult

After throwing on a long t-shirt to feel less vulnerable, she stood and spun around to face him. "What's going on?" She clicked on the lamp. "Bad week. Long days. Almost died. Twice. On the verge of failing a college degree I have worked so hard to complete. Missing Brady and Mom and wishing they were here. Sleep deprivation. Have I forgotten anything?"

His auburn eyebrows shot up. "Well." In the yellow lamplight, his eyes glinted. Always assessing. Calculating. Because this whole situation was a damned mission for him. "Ah, anything we should talk about?"

"You are not pulling a freaking counselor move on me. I've stomped people for less." At the wiggle of the corners of his mouth, she pointed. "Don't even think about laughing or you'll be my next victim." It was a funny comment, but her ears buzzed. An avalanche of emotions broke loose and snowballed in her exposed, exhausted state. "I'm also wondering where"—she waved her hands toward Red still sitting nakedly on the side of the bed—"this is going."

His brows rose. "Um." He tugged on boxer-briefs and a t-shirt in an efficient and muscular movement.

"Or *if* it's going anywhere." When he didn't answer, the words came flying out. "My anxiety-fed brain is going ninety miles per hour thinking about logistics of a relationship with a guy whose job is undercover work. How would I introduce you to family?

Where would I live? Where would you live? Where would we work? How much time would you have to spend on the relationship—are we talking about you coming home on weekends or every few months? Would I be jealous or scared while you were away?" She rolled her lip hoop against the other lip.

"I don't know—" he haltingly started.

She held a hand up. "No need to answer any of these questions. I'm just letting you know where my head is." She paced two steps then paused. "Wrapped up in all those thoughts are longstanding fears of being abandoned. My therapist thinks I haven't gotten over Mom and Brady's death and those losses are still affecting me, and she's probably right. So then I circle back to the part where you might not even want to deal with this mess"—she knocked on her head—"and walking away might be the best decision you can make."

Silence filled the room for several thudding heartbeats of time.

"Britt, I want to have a future with you." The words shredded from between tight lips. He didn't meet her gaze. "But it's not possible."

She knew the truth of his words but they still landed like a slap to the face. Britt sucked in a quick breath. "Got it. Besides, how normal of a relationship would we have anyway? This whole situation has been weird from the start, from the stalker dude out there to not knowing your actual name or occupation to needing to have a guard dog with me all day long."

The guard dog in question recoiled, pulling his head back. "Hey."

"Hey, nothing. As much as I like you and I might like … what we're doing together … this togetherness is not normal. Look, I've earned a normal life. A life where

I call the shots. A life without babysitters or death threats. I deserve a college degree and a chance at a career, damn it, and a somewhat predictable partner who doesn't leave. These seem like very reasonable asks." A sad, painful gulp followed that last statement. "The fact that it's taking such a colossal effort to reach any one of these goals is pretty much the definition of *insanity*." To be fair, part of why it had taken so long to finish college was Britt's flighty fault, no question. She'd own that piece of the irregular puzzle of her life.

His low voice elicited a shiver. "What I want is you, but my job has restrictions—" In the glow of the lamp, the muscled ridges on his shoulders and torso tensed in stark relief, reminding her of the sheer strength taking up space in the room. Reminding her of the reason he was here.

She was his mission.

She glanced down at the fabric of his briefs. He was semi-erect. God*damn*it.

Sour disappointment mixed with a burning desire to lose herself in his powerful thrusts until she didn't care about her failure-to-launch life and difficulty completing the next step in her future. Britt knew full well her overstressed brain exaggerated key parts of the situation and drew illogical conclusions, but her anxiety had taken over. She shook her head. "Look, never mind. Oh man, I'm babbling. Just … go back to sleep or whatever. I have to go to work, which is an activity that exists in my normal life. It's something tangible that I can succeed at doing." The words tumbled out before she could stop them. "Normal life—you know, where people aren't shooting at me and covert military groups don't exist. Where my sexual partner has a past and a future."

He reared back like she'd walloped him.

In some place way deep down inside, she

recognized the unfairness of that comment given his history as a foster child and wanted to take back her words, but her fears and insecurities kept pushing her. "God, I've had about as much weird secrets to last a lifetime. I can't take any more." She lifted her hands. "Would it be too much to ask that I have a normal life with normal problems and normal relationships?" She blinked tears and swallowed hard. "Why is this so hard to accomplish?"

His voice, low and under icy control, scared her more than if he yelled. "Normal life is not an option for me or for you right now. I'm sorry." His Adam's apple bobbed and neck muscles shifted. "Straight talk: I want you. I would love to have a future with you. I don't see how that is an option, and I won't torment you by confusing the situation. I can promise that as soon as this mission is over, I will be out of your life forever. It's a job requirement."

Well, crap. Not the answer she wanted, but the answer her wary heart had anticipated. Her eyes burned and her throat hurt like it had swollen shut. She couldn't breathe. The light in the room went dim.

Not now. No. Britt wouldn't have a full-on panic attack in front of Red. She forced air in and out of her windpipe. She felt the floor beneath her feet, saw the man in her bed, smelled the light scent of his aftershave. Grounding helped. Marginally.

She glanced at his stony expression, but his eyes showed a glint of pain. Britt didn't have the emotional capacity to take back the unfair words she'd said, even though she wanted to.

The only thing Britt knew with 100% certainty was that she had four days to pull a proverbial rabbit out of a hat. One power-hungry CFO stood in her way of the only life goal she'd ever been remotely able to complete.

This secretive guy in front of her who had saved her life and given her so much pleasure would not be part of her future. End of story.

"Britt…"

"Nope. All done here. Too exhausted. Too stressed to deal. I'm sorry that's the case. I'm sorry if I was unfair." She glanced at the big man sitting on her bed. "Look, if you wouldn't mind, can you make yourself a little less … here? I know you have a job to do, but I can't think straight with this much closeness. Which isn't healthy, since there's no future for us. Heck, the past and the present we have are pretty crappy."

"I never asked for a future." His voice chilled her skin. "I can't help my past."

Oh, God, she'd made him think his past impacted her current messy self. "It's really not your—"

"No need to finish that statement, Britt." Gone was the warm lover who made her scream his name and who put himself in harm's way to keep her safe. "I respect your concerns. They are valid. I will focus on my work. That's the professional behavior and protocol I should have been performing all along."

In the space of two haggard breaths, the man in front of her changed into a cold, mission-driven machine. The shift made her chest ache. Wasn't that what she wanted? Emotional distance?

Britt wasn't happy with either outcome—distance or closeness. What the heck? Nope. Her irrational, exhausted, anxiety-driven brain shut down and refused to process any more. A shower and breakfast. That's all that she wanted. And for this week to be over. As much as it hurt, she needed emotional detachment to protect her own heart.

Her eyes burned. She wanted to sink into his arms and sob. Instead, Britt clasped her hands together. Hard.

"Red." She waited for the tiny nod to indicate he heard her. "Can you do your job without being three inches away from me at all times?"

"Yes." White lines bracketed his hard mouth. "It's not as easy, but yes."

"Sounds like we have a plan." She spun on her heel and closed herself in the bathroom. Hopefully the sound of the shower would drown out any sniffles.

Chapter Thirty-Four

O. Kay.

Hell, what the hell happened? Red paced in the small bedroom, trying to piece together the past few minutes that had started out like watching a blissful sunrise but instead turned out to be a nuclear bomb exploding.

He shook his head and replayed in painful detail the memory of their times together. Had he pushed her or crossed boundaries? Misinterpreted anything? No, she had encouraged him. He had made sure Britt initiated each level of intimacy.

Had he taken advantage of his position as her protector? It was the nature of the job to get close to a target. He'd never gotten this close to his mission target in his Special Forces or post-virus Morpheus Squad work. As a potential romantic partner he was as good as radioactive, thanks to the virus.

The presence of the virus made him even more undesirable as a partner than he would have been without it.

She had said, *"Where my sexual partner has a past and a future."*

He could be proud of neither. Without the virus, he still brought his history as a foster child with no parents and no solid past. With the virus, he had no future. He had nothing of value he could bring to any long-term relationship. Certainly not one with an amazing woman like Britt. The sex might be outstanding, but eventually his virally driven need to remain close and protect her would be stifling. That, combined with the limited career options available for a government-hunted, weaponized soldier with an uncertain life span.

Hell, he no longer had the option to have children, thanks to the recommended mandatory vasectomy.

All his personal issues didn't matter.

Britt was stressed and her feelings were real even if her views were clouded. He of all people should know how thoughts became warped in a difficult situation, or in fear for one's life and the lives of those they loved. Not having control over an existence was stressful. Growing up in those terrible foster homes had taught Red that lesson more than once.

He knew firsthand how power dynamics screwed with people's emotions. In this situation, sure, he had ensured Britt's consent, but the fact remained: he technically retained the upper hand based on his strength and his inside knowledge of the situation.

God help him. What had he done? He had tried to develop a relationship in an impossible situation, during a mission. His gut clenched. Hurting Britt was the last thing he wanted to do.

There were other last things he wanted to do with her. To her. Which was part of the problem. He'd lost objectivity and focus.

He paused, picking up a soft noise coming through the lemony plinking shower sound in the bathroom. He shook his head, unable to discern it. He should be out there in the living room, guarding her. But the prospect of facing Britt terrified him in a way that had never scared him before. He resumed pacing.

If he continued the way things were, Britt would eventually resent him. *If* he continued down this path. What a joke. He was on the path, right up until the path had dead-ended here in this apartment several minutes ago.

To salvage her future, he needed to stay away

from Britt.

To keep her alive, he had to remain close.

Damn it. He rested his forehead on the closet door. As for that fashion show? He grimaced. Red wanted nothing to do with prancing around in whatever outfit she dreamed up.

But he'd promised. The team would help her finish the project. A dangerous plan, but also it was fair. Lequire's hunger for revenge wasn't her fault.

Every teammate understood a life without choices. Red certainly did. He would help her finish the show. It was her future at stake.

As soon as that damned show ended, Red would make sure she went someplace safe until they untangled the mess with Lequire. Then he'd leave her the hell alone.

A hard knot closed his throat. No contact with Britt. He was going to be sick.

The mundane task of reviewing current infil and exfil plans kept him functional and focused. Barely.

Pulling on the rest of his clothes, he removed all the personal items and equipment he'd brought to this apartment. Except for the surveillance monitors and a few hidden weapons—he would leave those here until the mission ended. He would do his job but stay at arm's length from Britt.

Then Red slipped out the front door.

Chapter Thirty-Five

"Careful what you wish for" never seemed so prophetic as right now, as Britt got ready to finish her work shift and go to class Monday. Alone.

After her meltdown, blowing up at Red this morning, there was nothing else to do but drag herself through work. Lattes got mixed up with Americanos, and half-caf no-creams became triple-soy with extra shots. Toward the end of the shift, Britt collected less tips than usual, but had amassed a heaping helping of regret that made her chest feel caved-in. At times, she had to fight to take in a full lungful of air.

Despite the emotional roller coaster, the fact remained that her life was in danger and Red held the line of protection around her. Wherever he was right now. If she hadn't told him to back off, Red would likely be in this coffee shop right now, innocently drinking his second cup while she completed her shift.

She cleared a table and set down the empty dishware in the kitchen. Scone crumbs clung to her hands and she washed up, not registering water temperature, but merely going through the cleansing motions.

"Customer at one of your tables," another waitress called as she collected a muffin and eggs.

Britt glanced at the clock on the wall. Thirty-five minutes until her shift ended. She peeked out, half-expecting Red or Rodeo to be sitting at her table. Nope, just a businessman wanting breakfast, like any other patron.

She sighed and turned off the water, drying her hands on the apron that covered her knee-length black knit skirt and floral Lucky brand long-sleeved t-shirt. Completing the look, the white Topshop sneakers had been a risky choice, what with the chance of spilling food all morning. Sucking in a big breath, she stood up straight and set her shoulders. She could do this. She could get through this week.

Where was Red? Probably tracking her from across the street.

With a sigh, she pulled out the server iPad and walked across the half-empty coffee shop. "May I take your order?"

The man held up a hand and finished talking on his phone.

Britt gritted her teeth. She peeked at his fashion choices as she waited for him to wrap up his loud, Very Important Phone Call. He wore gleaming brown Louboutin oxfords without a scuff on them. That gray suit, double-breasted with not a crease to be found, looked like an Armani, based on the cut and the four-button cuffs. Appeared to be a wool, silk, and linen blend for the warmer spring weather. She fought an impulse to rub the material between her fingers. Silver cuff links on crisp white cotton peeked out under the blazer sleeves and boded well for the size of her tip.

The guy must work out, judging from the cut and breadth of the suiting as well as the cords of muscles on his neck. Even the hand tapping a pen with impatience was broad and strong as it flexed and moved. Several knuckles were red and bruised, like Red's after the department store fight. Where both she and Red had almost died. She swallowed hard.

Frowning, she glanced at the man's smoothly shaven face. Bruises dotted his temple and stony jaw. MMA fighter, maybe? She peeked at his normal-appearing ear. Didn't MMA fighters have messed up ears from getting hit there? Britt was no expert.

Before she could kill more time crafting a make-believe story to explain his background, he barked a goodbye and put down the phone with a definitive *thud*. When he swiveled his head to her, his expression went from tight rage to an engaging grin in a split-second. With the combination of his icy blue eyes, a gleaming smile, and thick hair that was perfectly mussed, she rocked back on her heels at the impact his appearance had on her.

"Good morning, Britt."

She froze. Her heart scampered a million miles per hour. How did he know her name? Should she know him? Oh, God. "How? What—"

He crinkled his nose in a handsomely disarming manner and pointed. "You, ah, have a name tag right there. Sorry if I offended." His Southern drawl dragged out the words like thick Karo syrup.

Name tag. Of course.

"I … got it. Yes."

He reached out but didn't quite touch her. "Having a rough day?" Tapping the back of his phone, he added, "Because I am." He made a dramatic and handsome sigh. "Actually, the person on the other end is now having a worse day." A fleeting twitch made his left eye and an eyebrow scrunch.

"Hmm," she gave a noncommittal noise and held up the pad. "What can I get you?"

His assessing gaze cooled a few degrees, but then he broadened his smile to compensate, almost like he tuned an instrument. "Pretty lady like you should not ask questions like that to guys like me."

Kind of gross. Kind of flattering. She didn't know whether to bat her eyes or wash her hands again. "Um."

"Say, do you know anything about the Rodgers Building?" He straightened both cuffs to one half-inch of white fabric showing with a peek of cuff link visible on each side. "I've got a meeting there in an hour. Not sure which way to go."

He could literally tap on that phone he'd been barking into and pull up a map.

Maybe he was nervous about the meeting or trying to be friendly. Not like she could fault anyone for that. Britt would be friendly back, because, frankly, she liked good tips. "I believe it's down the street to the left one block, then a right onto Peachtree Circle. Not Peachtree Street, which is what we're on now." A laugh bubbled up. "That's not confusing at all. I'm not sure if I helped or not."

His warm, deep chuckle came out a half-tone wrong as he shook his head. "Darlin', you gave me exactly what I needed this morning."

Before Britt could try and figure out what he meant by that, he provided his order. As she walked back to prepare the custom coffee with extra shots of everything, the muscles of her neck prickled, as if sensing that he was watching her.

Turning back, she stared across the room. No one looked up. The man's head was down as he typed on his phone, like any other customer. Nothing sinister. Just a businessman—she paused—softly whistling a tune while he probably pulled up emails and waited for his breakfast croissant and coffee. Great. Now she saw danger everywhere, including her customers.

A few minutes later, she returned to his table. "Here you go." She set down the cup and plate with a cheese croissant in front of him. "Anything else I can get for you?"

A half-second later that media-ready smile creased his face. He shot her a handsomely boyish look. "See, I had an inappropriate answer in mind but thought better of it." His eye and eyebrow twitched again. Could be he had a nerve or muscle injury. He curled a hand into a fist on the table, then deliberately laid his hand flat but this time slid it onto his thigh. "Maybe later." He set out a twenty and pushed up from the table with a fluidity of movement that appeared at odds with his big frame.

"I'll get your change."

"No need. Seeing your sweet smile while you served me and stood here, not a foot away, within arm's reach, was well worth the investment."

Britt didn't know what to say to that.

The man strolled out of the coffee shop, whistling again.

He had left his drink and croissant behind.

Chapter Thirty-Six

Damn it.

Red had lost an hour of video feed. Class was starting soon. He fake-relaxed on the sidewalk bench across from the coffee shop, fighting through the fake video loops playing on his phone while keeping an eye on Britt's workplace.

A large man in a suit exited the coffee shop, whistling a tune that Red couldn't place. The guy looked somewhat familiar. Rodeo called, catching Red's attention.

"Did you fix the camera feeds?" Red asked.

"Yes, Stumpy fixed it just now. Shit on shit, bro. Lequire's been in the coffee shop!"

"Damn it." Red jumped to his feet, ready to run to Britt. Was she okay? Should he go after Lequire? That must have been him in the business suit, leaving the shop. Hell, that guy was way bigger than the mission photos indicated.

Stop. Think. It damn near killed him, but Red forced himself to stick with mission protocol. Process the situation logically. Assess infil, exfil, options, liabilities. Determine priorities.

Logic and standard process went out the window where Britt was concerned.

Rodeo continued. "The feed came back up a minute ago. There that asshat was, talking with your girl."

Not my girl. "Did he do anything to her?" Because Red would kill the man if he had hurt Britt.

"Appears to have chatted with her and then ordered a croissant and coffee with all the fixins, tipped well, and left. I'm calling this in to Hunt." A low whistle came through the phone. "Damn. Lequire. Here, in broad daylight. Shit, that fucker has gotten huge. No telling what the virus has done to him. He's only had it for a week."

Red peered down the street. Lequire had disappeared.

Was he sending in his minions to this location, now that he'd identified Britt's whereabouts? Every muscle in Red's body tensed, ready to sprint.

Britt. Red needed to get close to her. Now.

"I'm closing the distance to target," Red managed to say between a clamped jaw as he stormed across the busy street toward the coffee shop.

"Stand by for Hunt's orders. Stay close to your girl."

Not my girl.

She sure as hell isn't going to be Lequire's girl, either.

Chapter Thirty-Seven

Settling into her late Monday morning class seat, Britt pulled out her laptop.

The temperature dropped in the room with that too-loud tittering laugh.

Jenna sauntered in and sat in her usual spot near the front of the class. Flipping her hair over a shoulder, she glanced back at Britt and froze. The smile turned plastic. *Busted.* God, Britt hated Jenna's entitled hiney, even encased today in Brunello Cucinelli distressed jeans. The superb fit was likely tailor-made. The Fendi pinstripe shirt completed the causal ensemble that probably cost the same as six months of Britt's rent.

All that junk about forging forward and not seeking revenge went right out the window when Jenna gave Britt a manicured wave and a wink.

The top of Britt's head was about to steam right off into outer space. She gripped the edge of her desk and hung on. Before she could take inappropriate action, who entered the class but Mr. Fake Fashionisto himself. He sat down right next to Jenna, without turning his head toward Britt at all.

The first minutes of lecture registered as nothing but the buzzing of gnats in her ears. Britt tried to think of something else besides poking sewing needles into her classmate. She had been tough on Red this morning, but then again he hadn't been forthcoming with information. She cringed. Seriously, *that* was the alternative topic her brain wanted to consider? She swallowed. A few rows up and over, she spied Red sit up straight, head angled toward her. Weird.

"Whatever," she muttered.

He glanced back. Like he heard her.

Above his denim jacket layered over a Henley shirt, the skin of his neck flushed.

With effort, she concentrated on the class. She still had to pass two exams later this week. She needed to finish the brand-new fashion collection before Friday. Her mind spun. Not enough time and too much to do.

Sucking in air became a problem. Her heart thumped, fast and constricted beneath her ribs. The squeeze in her chest accompanied racing thoughts of how the hell she was going to pull off everything this week.

What about after this week? The beating in her chest sped up. She gripped the edge of the chair.

The burning in her eyes had to be from lack of sleep.

Minutes or hours later, who knew, the class finally ended. Britt zipped up her backpack and swung it over a shoulder. A few steps and she drew even with Red, standing next to his seat. He stiffened and his hand moved toward her then stopped.

His hand dropped to his side.

Jenna was quickly shoving items in her bag.

"How's it going?" Britt said, way too brightly.

Jenna stiffened. "Excellent. Had a wonderful party at the country club this weekend. Made some amazing business connections for after I graduate. You know. The usual types of things," she babbled, then stopped and pasted a plastic smile on her face.

Britt would pay good money for a free shot at popping Jenna in her perfectly created nose. "So. Are you excited for the big show?"

With a snort, she said, "Looking forward to seeing everyone's collections."

"Me too!" Britt lightly brushed Jenna's arm and Jenna jumped like she'd been branded. Britt ignored Red's palpable stare. He was a large, silent shadow nearby. "Well, let's hope everything goes perfectly at the show. No speed bumps, right?"

"Well—" The laptop clattered to the floor. Jenna scrambled to pick it up, her fingers slipping twice before she clutched the computer to her chest.

"You know what's been great?" Britt fought to keep her voice calm and steady as she poured on a bless-your-heart saccharine charm that would have made Mom proud.

Jenna narrowed her eyes and tossed her blonde hair back over a shoulder. Her entourage gathered around her, breathlessly waiting. "No."

"It's so cool how we get to change our minds at the last minute. See, I'm going in a totally different direction with my show. A better direction. You could say I've been inspired by a remarkable turn of events!"

"Um, that's nice." She patted her bag before lifting it off the desk, and smiled at her friends. "You all waiting on me?"

A few bland replies.

Britt plowed ahead. "Yes, it is *so* nice to have the flexibility and a fantastic creative spark, and thank you for saying so."

"I didn't say so."

"Of course you did." Britt twined her fingers into the backpack strap. "Hey, I can't wait to see your collection up there on stage. Like you said: colleagues supporting each other and all, am I right? Hey, good luck with Design of the Year. Once people hear about your hard work … refining …other classmates' designs … I'm sure you will be in the obvious choice for that award." With a wink at Jenna's gape-mouth expression, Britt nearly skipped as she left the classroom. Only a few steps into the hall, the taunting didn't feel so good.

Damn it, Britt wasn't a jerk. Dishing out

snarkiness satisfied for a few minutes, then … nothing. The tension dripped out of her limbs and she slouched her way to the next class, eyes burning.

Red had watched the whole thing. At least he would know she didn't limit her bad behavior to him.

As Mom used to say: *Pretty is as pretty does.*

Britt had not been very pretty at all back there. Mom would have been so disappointed. She gulped.

"You were kind of rough on her," Red's voice floated down to Britt.

"Oh, look, you're there." Without looking up, she muttered, "She deserved it, and more."

"Not arguing with you. I'm still amazed how you didn't destroy her project in return. Would have tempted me, if I were in your shoes."

Pulling her head back, she gave him a side-eye. "What are you getting at?"

"You're better than her, head to toe, inside and out."

"And?"

"You don't have to stoop to her level." His half-smile did not make her heart flutter. Not at all. "Sometimes the best revenge is success."

A sour taste coated her tongue. "Thank you, Counselor Red."

"Britt, we need to talk about this mor—"

She held a hand up before they entered the next classroom. "Here's the deal. I said not-nice things early this morning, and I'm sorry. I could have voiced my concerns better, and I'm going to own my behavior and apologize. However, it doesn't make the facts of our situation less true."

"Yes, but you need to know—"

No way were they having this conversation here, in the hall, this week. "I have no extra energy to spend on dealing with us, with whatever this is or isn't. It's going to be an act of God if I finish everything I need to do. So please, give me some space to work."

There went that clamp of his mouth and guarded expression. Classic Red. One nod, then he pushed the door open for her to enter.

Still a gentlemen in the face of her lack of courtesy.

Chapter Thirty-Eight

True, Red wanted to talk with Britt. Have a heart-to-heart discussion. Figure out a way to apologize for his part in the mess of her life. Even apologize for all the stuff he couldn't control, but wished he could—for her sake.

He trudged upstairs to the fashion lab, a few steps behind her. Interpersonal communication wasn't why he stuck close to her after class. It wasn't even because he wanted to torture himself either, with the light scent of hibiscus and her sighs that electrified his skin.

She needed to know that Lequire was here and had gotten too close. Britt knew her life was at risk. Knew he would target her. If Red and Rodeo performed their mission properly, then she would go about her day as if her life was normal.

If that asshole in a suit had gotten his hands on Britt, Red would have gladly taken action, risking exposure and the military recapturing him. At this time, Red had to stay close enough that he wouldn't irritate the piss out of Britt but not leave her vulnerable.

Even now, hours later as he sat on the stool opposite Britt's sewing station, flipping through the digital video feeds from cameras planted all over the school, her workplace, and her apartment, she glared at him as she stitched another hem. Despite Britt's prickly demeanor, she managed to look casually sexy in white sneakers, a black skirt, and a fitted long-sleeved t-shirt.

"Careful," he said. "You'll catch your finger in the machine."

"Yes, sir." She made a weak salute. "Always looking out for bodily harm, I see," she muttered

In a snit, didn't even come close to the mood

she'd been nursing all day long.

"Can I help?" he tentatively asked. She might be tiny, but her wrath was terrifying. Mostly because he cared what she thought.

She stared at him for long enough to make him sweat. Damn it.

Blinked those big, blue eyes. "Accessories."

He pulled his head back. "What?"

"I…"—she whipped the material off the machine—"need"—she snipped a thread—"accessories." She laid the material out next to another piece of fabric on the table.

"All right. Where do we get them? I can send Rodeo."

Cutting another pattern, the crinkle of paper and *skrunk* of the scissors against the metal table made his ears tingle. Damned virus had started ramping up again. He patted the backpack. Syringe ready, for when he was ready to sacrifice tactical advantage for sanity.

"Hello?" She waved her hand in front of him.

"Huh?"

"Some help you are. Never mind."

"No, seriously. Let me know what you want and I'll make sure you get it. Anything." He froze. Damn it.

She stared at him. Breathed. Pupils dilated. Two heartbeats passed.

The tiny dart of her tongue against her lip gave it away. "Will you now?" she murmured. Pink tinted her cheeks. "No. What I mean is that *I* need to go get accessories to complete my designs." She looked over at classmates several tables away, working hard on their projects. "If you want to do your job, you'll have to come with me."

"Let me coordinate with Rodeo. Do you know where you want to go?"

"Mall."

"Again? Are you serious? No."

A tight smile. "Fine. Thrift shop in Midtown. It's a thirty-minute walk."

"Terrible idea."

"Then you can drive."

He scrubbed his face. Another unsecured location. "Can you send a list of what you want?"

She shook her head. "I'll know it when I see it."

What kind of answer was that? He ground his back teeth.

"If I can't find what I'm looking for there, then yes, we're going back to the mall, and you'd better not kill anyone this time," she whispered.

"Shh."

A rise of her chin and a shrug told him her opinion of this mission. She'd gone from scared to pissed and now appeared to be heading straight for reckless. If he didn't reel her in, she'd be in even more danger.

He walked over next to her and with the pretense of looking at a pattern, leaned down, listened to the raindrop sweet taps of her heartbeat—because he liked to torture himself—and said under his breath, "Lequire contacted you today."

"What?" she nearly shouted.

Classmates looked up and stared.

She covered up the lapse. "Oh, I didn't know it was your birthday this weekend!" She pounded his denim-clad biceps. "That's great!" The other students went back to their work. Dropping her voice, she said. "What?" Her eyes locked onto him and widened.

"At the coffee shop."

A pause as her brows went up. "Oh my God, the man in a suit. That was him?" she whispered. "He was huge. Looked like a WWF fighter gone corporate. It was a very nice suit. Wool blend, I'm guessing."

"That was him."

"But in the pictures on the Internet, he wasn't a big guy. Kind of thin and smarmy."

How much could he tell her about the Morpheus Virus? That info was need-to-know. "He's, uh, been working out."

"Or on something."

Too close to the truth. Red rolled his own corded shoulders. He had no room to judge. Well, other than the fact that unlike Red, Lequire lacked the training to handle the virus, and the damned virus had turned Lequire into an unstable ticking time bomb, wired backward. One wrong move and *boom*.

"What can I do?"

"About Lequire? Nothing. Leave that to Rodeo and me."

She brushed bangs off her forehead with a shaking hand. "He got close." The knuckles on her other hand turned white as she gripped the scissors.

"Too close." Red leaned over and tapped the back of her hand. "It won't happen again. We'll keep you safe."

She released the stranglehold on the implement. "Yeah." The tough-woman act slipped. For a split-second, he saw through the cracks. Stark fear. The look of someone about to walk a tightrope for the very first time. Without a net.

A blink, and her steely-eyed determined façade slammed back down in place. Good. He could work with tough and single-minded.

"Screw. That. Guy," she said.

He nodded. It was her life. He got it. "Okay."

"Okay?"

"Let's go shop for accessories." He began typing

frantic messages to Rodeo to prep the site.

Chapter Thirty-Nine

Damn her bizarre existence, but there was something particularly sexy about a fake fashion student who was really a military dude pretending to shop for knockoff fashion jewelry at downtown Atlanta's largest thrift store.

Red held up a matching set of bracelets and a necklace. Chunky fake gold and diamonds sparkled. "Yes?"

"Sure. If you're eighty, still wear White Shoulders perfume, enjoy polyester blends, and have Jiffy Pop hair."

"Huh?"

"No. The correct answer is 'no.'" She rifled through the rack and laid a few items on the glass countertop. "These might work for the ladies' outfits. Now I need some dude jewelry."

The twist to his mouth triggered a laugh.

As he shook his head and backed away, she leaned forward. "Yes. I said Dude. Jewelry. Tasteful. Guys wear embellishments all the time. The look we're going for is Confident Guy."

"As opposed to?"

"Mafia Pimp or New Jersey Shore Wannabe."

He snorted. "You want my opinion?" His dark-red brows rose.

"Nope. Just hold my stuff and look pretty."

A half-smirk flashed. "Yes, ma'am."

She walked to another display stand. "Here. Let's see how this looks." Like a fool, she got close to him, and on tiptoes, held a thick, fake gold chain up. His pine and aftershave scent tempted her to lean closer. To lick. To nip. To do all the other things that came after those actions.

Jewelry. Okay, the simple chain worked. Subtle, but would still add to the luxe yet casual look she wanted to create.

Studying him under her lashes, still holding the chain, she realized Red would look great no matter what she draped around his strong shoulders. Her hand drifted down his chest, dipping into the ridges of muscle. She clutched the chain in her other hand and leaned against him. Solid. Supportive.

Her hand dipped lower, to his hard belly.

He shuddered. Balled his hands into fists. He met her gaze. The irises were nearly black. "What are you doing, Britt?" he said through a tight jaw.

Good question. Wasn't she mad at him? More like mad at herself. Mad at her situation. Mad at her life. And frankly scared, nervous, and stressed, which brought out all of her best behaviors.

As she skimmed a fingertip under the band of his jeans, he sucked in air and froze. She was being cruel. Red was doing his job. She had set boundaries, and now she wasn't honoring them. Also, she knew the score: he was on a mission. His presence here was just business.

His jaw worked, ropes of muscle on his neck shifted when he swallowed. He didn't take his half-mast eyes off her for a second.

What if this wasn't only a job for him? What if she could make peace with the fact that any relationship with him had an expiration date? Well, wasn't that an interesting idea.

As she slid her hand along the inside of the waistband, warmth built up in her hips.

"Damn it, Britt." Only, he didn't sound mad. Frustrated, yes.

"Red."

Sliding her hand toward the front of his belly, she stopped, her wrist manacled by his hand. "You go hot and cold. I'm trying to keep up. We had a whole meeting about how we're not an item and we have no future together, not ten hours ago."

"I. Yeah. I get how frustrating that is. I'm sorry." How could she put into words the overwhelming need to be with him, how much she wanted him on a physical and emotional level? There wasn't a way to ask that didn't sound like she was using him.

She *used* him for security.

She *wanted* him for being Red, a good guy who had some demons but who wanted nothing more than to protect her. He seemed to accept Britt's own demons, and together they just … clicked.

If by *click* she meant *filled a piece of her heart she hadn't realized was missing and that they spontaneously combusted together during amazing sex*, then sure. They clicked.

Britt looked up at him. "You're right. I've been all over the page for a lot of reasons. Your opinions and feelings are important here, too. Truth matters here."

He flinched, then blew out a long breath, the muscles of his chest shifting. His growling words rumbled. "God help me, I want you so badly, I would chew off my own arm if that's what it cost to be with you again. But I don't want there to be any confusion of lust versus the emotions from this mission."

She rested her forehead on his chest. His warmth seeped into her, giving her strength. She leaned back and locked her gaze with his. She could do stark honesty. She owed him that much. "There's a difference between the man and the mission. I want the man. All of him."

Every muscle tensed. "You sure about that?" A flicker of pain flashed across his face.

Through her anger and confusion early this morning, the close call with Lequire, the 24/7 stress, battling her anxiety, and second-guessing her entire life, the one thing Britt knew for certain was she had a connection with Red that she didn't want to end. Not yet.

A tiny voice added, *maybe not ever*.

Did her relationship needs and desires just crystallize right this minute, right here in the Midtown Thrift Mart, over the discounted cubic zirconium collection?

"Britt?" She felt more than heard the word.

"Yes."

"You sure?"

Holding his gaze, she said, "I'm very sure. I want to try for whatever future there is, even if it's only for another few days." She paused. "After my back-and-forth, I need to ask you the same thing. You get an equal vote."

The five seconds of contemplation felt like hours. "You're like a living tornado and the bravest and sexiest person I've ever met. I can't get enough of you."

Oh. My. "Red, you're solid, and patient, and … yeah, so hot." Heat bloomed where her thighs met.

A crimson flush betrayed his calm words. "Are we really going there? Here?"

She glanced around, gauging the customers and some options. "I mean. It's not very busy today, so…"

He barked a quick laugh. "Oh hell, that's not what I meant," he gritted out. Exhaling, he kept hold of her wrist, the grip firm but not painful. "Relationship developing. In this store."

"Isn't it obvious?"

"The last thing I want is to hurt you, and even in the best of situations, I don't know if pain is avoidable. Also, I don't want my own ass handed back to me again.

Sorry for the extra step, but you need to be very clear with what you're asking of me, of yourself. Of us."

The world seemed to collapse until it was the two of them in the back of the shop. A few customers milled around near the front of the store. "I'm a messy person on the inside. I have issues, and I want to continue working on them. You're amazing to be with, like a counterbalance for me, but so much more." She gulped and maintained eye contact, pouring her heart into the words. "I've never wanted to be as close to someone as I have with you. If you're okay with it … I want you, Red. Now. For as long as this lasts." Even saying the words made her limbs go liquid.

His grip tightened a fraction. He rested her hand against his chest. Under her fingertips, his heart thundered. His jaw worked for a solid minute before he spoke. "Here's the deal: you must want me for who I am, right now. Not for who I never was. Not for who I cannot be. Not for any promise of a future. Yeah, I know that's not the most enticing deal." He swallowed. "You gotta want Red, the messed-up undercover dude pretending to be a fashion student, who is modeling fake jewelry in broad daylight, because he would do … anything you ask." He rubbed the back of her hand with the rough pad of his thumb. "To be clear, I need you more than I need water or air. No question. But I will suppress what I want if that's what it takes to keep you from you being hurt. Is that clear enough?"

"Crystal."

"Hell, Britt…"

God, she loved how he said her name. Half-blessing, half-epithet. She dipped her hand lower until she brushed against his thick erection, hard and heated beneath his cargo pants.

He shuddered. "Not here. But soon." His breath

flashed hot against her neck, even as he scanned the store around them.

"Got ideas?"

"Hell, yeah, I've got ideas." He straightened up and removed her hand from his pants. "First of all, I think you should go try on some clothes."

Try on clothes? Her lust-filled brain struggled to keep up. "What?"

"In the dressing room. Try. On. Clothes," he growled.

"In the ... oh. *Oh*. Really?" Her heart pattered.

He flipped through his phone images and typed a message, then led her through the racks of purses, socks, and scarves. A nod. "Rodeo's covering us and taking care of store feeds."

They headed toward the women's changing room. "Wait." She pulled back against his light grip on her hand.

"What?"

"Look at the store demographics. Where do you think we'll have the most privacy and attract the least attention?"

His brows drew together as he turned in a circle, taking in the female-only shoppers milling. He caught murmured conversation and the metal scratches of hangers. "Men's dressing room."

"It's pretty normal for partners to take a look at the outfits guys try on. "

He changed direction and grabbed several items at random en route to the dressing room.

The deserted men's dressing room. Bingo. Her heart raced. Were they really going to do this? Here? A tingle built low in her belly and grew. A girl could hope.

They stepped into the last stall. A door. A bench. A mirror. Perfect. He hung the garments up on the hooks.

Not taking his gaze from her, he deliberately closed the door and locked it. He shrugged out of his jacket and hung it on another hook.

Then it was all about her hands needing to be on his body and vice-versa. As she worked his belt and zipper, he pulled up her skirt and yanked down her panties. Cool air on hot skin made her squirm. Red's touch seared her as he traced wonderful fire, skimming his way up her thighs to settle a possessive hand on her core.

After kicking off a shoe and pulling a leg out of his pants and briefs, he sat on the bench and guided Britt so that her legs dangled on the outside of his thighs. Then he moved his legs apart, spreading her open. The mirror's view off to the side featured his fingers digging into her partially clothed butt.

"Hold on here." He guided her hands to his shoulders and she gripped his bunched muscles through the Henley fabric.

Then he slid his feet apart once more. The sensation was fantastic.

"Amazing," he breathed. "I have to touch you." He bunched the skirt at her waist and stroked her exposed skin, dipping a finger into her wetness and over her folds until she bucked against him.

She didn't want him to stop, but the sensations swamped her. Then he shifted his legs again, creating such a sexy burn in her inner thighs. She shuddered.

"That's more like it," he whispered, sweeping his thumb over her clit while he added a second finger to the internal strokes.

She whimpered and clutched at his shoulders. "Oh my God, Red."

"Glad you know my name. So hot, coming from your mouth."

He pushed the rhythm faster with tiny, wet sounds and their panting filling the small space.

"I want you so much," he said.

Her arms shook as she clung to his shoulders. "How much?"

He withdrew. Winked. Licked his fingers. Then slowly pressing upward, this time with three fingers. The stretch of his strong hand working her sparked stars in her vision.

"Oh my God…" Every inch of her body quivered.

With his free hand, he gripped her butt, holding her in place, straddled over his legs, and balanced by her grip on his shoulders. He had become her anchor point.

With each stroke, he pressed further until she stretched to accept him up to his knuckles. She couldn't close her legs, couldn't stop the relentless press and release of his hand into the place where she wanted him the most. Light dimmed and she bit her lip.

He leaned forward and kissed her deeply. Pulling back, he murmured, "Are you okay?" He wiggled his fingers inside the tight glove of her vagina, and her muscles clenched. Then he rubbed the pad of his thumb against her clit.

"Ah," she panted. "When you do that, yes, I'm very okay."

"Not hurting you, sweets?"

"Red."

"Yes?"

Facing him fully, exposing every piece of herself, she stared into his hazel eyes. "Give me more."

His lips curled back from his teeth. "Good."

Then he increased the pressure with each thrust of his hand. He kept her grounded with his hand on her hip.

He leaned forward and caught her lip between his teeth with the next kiss, as he drove her higher and harder with his fingers deep inside of her. The world around her tilted and swirled.

She clenched and shattered, and he covered her mouth with his and muffled her cry as she shuddered over and over on his relentless fingers. Her arms had become so heavy, and she sagged. But he supported her.

A few minutes later, he pulled his hand away and stared at her as he licked his fingers clean.

Chapter Forty

Having sex in a dressing room was not part of any mission protocol. Hell, at Red *had* stuck close to her.

The image of Britt, beautiful mouth open, panting, lips wet from his kisses, her body limp in his arms, fired up every protective instinct. That image repeated itself on the mirror as he watched the arch and flex of her back and hips as she came. He could replay that scene forever and it would never get old.

The virus had woken up in a hurry, gnashing at the chained control he had, wanting to mark her, claim her.

Shifting, Red fished for a condom and tried to rip it open with shaking hands. Britt hummed and smiled, her neck and cheeks flushed, as she plucked the packet from him, tore it open with her teeth, and slowly unrolled it down his dick, fisting him in her small hands as she went.

Her touch short-circuited his brain.

Scooting to the edge of the bench, he cupped her butt and drew her toward him and up until she perched over his dick. A few inches separated Red from Heaven.

Her kiss drove his need higher as he entered her mouth in an echo of what he wanted elsewhere. Her musky scent of desire made him as dizzy as if he'd spun in circles for five minutes.

She slid down over him, still wet. The delicious stretch of her body fit him perfectly. They both groaned.

"Finding what you need in here?" a store clerk asked. Damn it, he had barely heard her enter the dressing room area. That bastard virus had one job: help Red hear shit. It had gone out to lunch today.

Britt clapped a hand over her mouth, brows raised, trying hard not to laugh or moan, with him sheathed inside of her.

It was all Red could to do to form coherent words. "It's the perfect fit, thanks for asking."

"Let me know if I can take out anything else for you."

"Oh, yes. Will do, ma'am." He caught himself before he exploded with laughter.

The clerk's light footsteps faded away. Red held his breath, listening carefully, straining to perceive anything else over the pounding pulse in his ears. His dick throbbed in time with his heart.

Britt giggled, then gasped as he swiveled his hips. Her eyes went wide. "Oh my God."

"Where were we?"

"I believe you were trying something on." She bounced, drawing him in deeper inside with a mutual gritted gasp.

He lifted her until he had almost pulled out, then leaned back and lowered her, driving in again, up to the base. He stifled her cry with his mouth, absorbing her sexy moans. With her chest pressed to him, she panted right along with him. He couldn't stop the quickening rhythm and he braced himself to improve leverage.

Biting her lower lip, she threw her head back and a whimper escaped.

"Sweets, you're beautiful."

"I love what you do to me, Red," she gasped. Her restless hands roved over his neck, scratching, pinching him. "God, I love this connection."

So close to the words he never thought anyone would say to him.

He thrust upward and pushed her onto him. It was impossible to tell where her body stopped and his started. Everything about this felt so right.

Red increased the pace, until he could feel the

tight tingle of release building up in his balls. He grunted with concentration as he begged his body to wait for her, even as he covered her cries with his mouth. Shit. He needed more. Needed her.

Clenching his arms so tightly that he could feel her ribs creak, he slammed up into her one more time, setting off the chain reaction he craved. Her entire body shook and her legs tightened against his. He gave several more soul-wrenching thrusts until he followed her over the edge of oblivion.

No question about it. He knew right that moment, that he would destroy the world and torpedo his entire existence and his sanity for her. The virus agreed. Red would annihilate anyone who dared hurt her. Anyone.

Even if that person was Red.

His sanity slipped.

Chapter Forty-One

Heck of a shopping trip this afternoon. Britt wouldn't mind catching another sale tomorrow. But as much as Britt craved sex with Red, she had to finish her collection. She looked around the nearly empty fashion lab.

Hanging another completed outfit on the rack, she checked the clock. Almost midnight. It was technically Tuesday. Three more days to go.

As she stretched her back with a satisfying crack, she glanced over at Red. The guy had disappeared this evening, and Rodeo took over babysitting duties for a few hours. Truthfully, Red's teammate was better with a needle and thread, but she still preferred the man who made her want to try on another outfit in the dressing room. Wow. What a turn her life had taken over the past … week?

Even now, Red scrolled through the images on his cell phone. Cameras and motion detectors documented this strange reality show that featured Britt.

Three days to finish the project. Then what kind of life would she have? What kind of life would they have? No. There wasn't a guarantee of *they*. She had to come to peace with that fact.

His head came up. Eyes locked onto hers. Burned into her. They were in the room alone, her classmates long gone hours ago. She might be hungry for the guy, but her gritty eyes informed Britt that she'd better get some sleep or she'd be in trouble for tomorrow's classes.

"Done for the night?" he asked.

"I'm sure you're tired of sitting here."

"That's not why I asked. I will stay here as long as you need to work." Funny, after he had returned from his break this evening, his frame or energy or whatever that intangible quality, seemed different. Less tense. He was still tall and broad but somehow seemed smaller. More … tired.

Before he had disappeared, his vigilant movements didn't stop for a second and he kept one hand on her at all times, like he had to stay in contact with her. An undercurrent of violence for anyone who came near her vibrated the space around them. After he returned, that undercurrent and intensity had ebbed. His movements were slower, more deliberate. Of course he must be tired, but fatigue didn't explain what she noticed.

Mysteries to solve another day. She had a clothing line to finish.

"You're right. I can't do any more tonight," she said, locking a drawer that held her tools and accessories and carefully folded garments. An extra step she never had to take before having her work destroyed.

Britt knew she was tired because it took too much energy to get pissed at Jenna again.

Swinging a backpack over a shoulder, she inclined her head toward the door. "Ready?"

"Always."

Her cheeks warmed.

He held a hand up. "Wait for a second while I update Rodeo." Tapping out a text, he waited for a chime. "He'll be in position in four minutes. One more check of the cameras." A frown, more scrolling, then he stowed the phone. "Clear."

The unspoken *for now* hung heavy between them.

"Shall we?" He patted his back.

Right, because gun. Because Britt needed protection. Because she needed to finish what she started. Was she being selfish? Stupid? Probably. On the other hand, no jerk threatening her family would stop her from completing her degree and fulfilling Mom's last wishes. Family.

"What's wrong?" Red hovered at her shoulder as they exited the fashion lab. The hallway echoed with their steps.

She waved a hand. "Nothing. Tired."

If he wanted to say something, it never happened.

A loud bang rang through the hall, and Red heaved Britt into the wall, covering her body with his own.

Chapter Forty-Two

Damn it. Where was Rodeo?

Red hadn't detected the threat.

He listened. Muffled sound. This evening's antidote impaired his extrasensory hearing. He rolled his shoulders. The antidote also reduced his strength close to non-enhanced levels.

Without the virus, he might not have the goods to keep her alive.

At another clatter he dragged her into the men's bathroom and pushed open the door of a stall.

"Lock the door. Stand on the seat," he hissed as sweat rolled down his temple. He shook his head to loosen control and try something—anything—to get the viral boost back. Of course it didn't happen. He couldn't even triangulate position of that sound.

The idea that he couldn't do his job scared the hell out of him. He punched in a text to Rodeo, silenced the phone, and shoved it in a back pocket. He pulled out the Sig.

Britt's wide eyes were the last he saw of her as he backed away. He clicked off the bathroom light and exited. Even without his heightened hearing, he knew his steps were all but silent. At the end of the wide hallway another squeak drew his attention. A heavy footstep.

Rodeo should be close by now. Good, because Red needed backup. Or a witness.

He sped down the hall, ignoring the art and portraits hanging in displays on the walls. The dim fluorescent light gave a flat, whitish-purple cast to everything in the midnight hour.

Another sound came from right around the corner.

As Red raised the gun and prepared to go on the offense, his friend's drawl drifted down the hall.

"Nice evening, isn't it?" Rodeo asked.

"Well, yes." A male voice, higher pitched. Younger?

"Hawks gonna make the playoffs this season?"

A snort. "I wish. They stink this year."

"I hear you. Maybe they'll get some good draft picks. Better luck next season." A few smacks of skin on skin followed by a snap. "Take it easy. Have a great night, bro."

"You too."

Red relaxed his grip, held the gun behind him, and peered around the corner. Custodian. The young man, walking away from Rodeo, dropped the mop handle and the loud clatter rattled back to Red. Mop handle. Red hadn't been able to tell.

Damn it. Red's nerves were shot, his virus was useless right now, and he couldn't save his own life, much less Britt's.

Two dark eyebrows shot up as Rodeo's gleaming grin brightened his mug. "Howsit?"

"Eh."

"That's what I thought." Rodeo approached Red, his casual stride belied by the tight set of his shoulders and his ever-assessing eyes. "Britt?"

Thumbing over his shoulder, Red said, "She's back there."

"Alone?"

"There was a loud noise this way." They walked quickly down the long hall. "What the hell do you want? I can't be everywhere at once."

Hands up, Rodeo snorted. "Defensive much?" He wiggled a hip. "Not criticizing, only motivating."

"Damn it. I know."

"Mission getting to you?"

"Something like that."

"Mission target getting to you?"

"I'll never tell."

"Got it." Rodeo stopped cold. "Hey." He pointed at the far end of the hall.

A flicker of movement, and then it was gone. Of course Red didn't have Rodeo's targeting ability.

"What?" Red asked.

"Someone ducked out of a room down there. Where's Britt?"

He pointed. "In the bathroom. Down there."

They took off at a sprint. Lights were on in the bathroom. Damn it. Rodeo covered the door. Red checked under the stalls, then banged on one stall door.

"Britt?"

"Red?" When her voice broke, it took all of his restraint with it. He ripped the door off the metal hinges, denting the metal where he gripped it.

Britt stood frozen on the toilet seat, hands braced against the walls, face bloodless, still wearing her backpack. She didn't move.

"Are you okay, sweets?"

"Yep. Sure. Fine." The words came out of her mouth, but her body told a different story.

"What happened?"

"Lequire was here," she said, voice shaky.

Rodeo ripped out a curse with eloquence that made Red jealous.

Red held out his arms and hugged Britt to him as he carried her, backpack and all, out of the small space. Her entire body trembled.

"Did he hurt you?" He set her on her feet and patted her from head to toe.

A jerky shake of her head. "Right after you left, a

man came in here. Flipped on the light. Used the urinal. Washed his hands. Then he started talking. Sounded like Lequire from earlier today."

He tucked her next to him. Anything to maintain contact. "And?"

"Said that he will enjoy destroying the Morpheus Squad. What's Morpheus Squad?"

"Shit," Rodeo spat. "He knows." He paused. "Now *she* knows."

Her shoulders rose with a big breath. "Mentioned that now that he had some 'special goodies,' he could play the game even better. This time he'd win." She looked up at Red. "What did he mean?"

"He's just an unhinged guy, that's what," he said, darting glances all around as he forced a fist to open and close, over and over. He assessed exfil, infil, options, liabilities.

"I think there's more to what's going on, and you need to tell me."

He glanced at Rodeo. His friend lifted a palm up. "You have to tell her, but not here."

"Tell me what?"

God, every well-laid plan, every secret, ever illusion of secure life for Red—and possibly for Britt—unraveled in front of him.

"Soon. We'll talk in a safer place. Please." She had to hear him. Had to cooperate.

Rodeo stared at him, mouth pressed into a grim, hard line. "Bro, exfil. ASAP."

"Roger." He looked down at Britt. "Let's get back to the apartment, okay?" At her hesitation, a jolt of adrenaline made him stammer, "Trust me."

"Really?" She rounded on him, pulling out of his embrace.

Over her shoulder, Rodeo's silently mouthed *oh,*

shit made Red want to laugh. Almost. But he didn't, because they were in some serious crap here, standing in a bathroom, where a lunatic chock full of unchecked Morpheus Virus who possessed God knows what special ability, played cat and mouse with Britt's life.

"Work with me on this one, please, sweets."

The ten seconds that passed were some of the longest Red had ever endured.

"Fine."

"Fine?"

She waved her hand toward the door. "Sooner we go, the sooner you can tell me what other secrets you've been hiding."

Chapter Forty-Three

Britt walked straight into the apartment, not bothering to close and lock the door because, heck, she had ex-military secret … whatevers … for that job. She headed straight to her room. She flipped on the lamp, sat on the bed, crossed her arms, and dared Red not to follow her.

True to his determined and solid nature, he hesitated only a half-step before entering. He closed the door and dropped his backpack and hers on the floor.

How could there be more secrets? A lead weight sensation pulled at her stomach.

A guy she'd been intimate with kept more things from her. For Britt intimacy wasn't only about sex. It involved trust, vulnerability, communication. For the first time in years, she had dared to connect with someone despite the fear they would be taken away. She had done the one thing that terrified her most, especially after watching her mother suffer and die and finding out her beloved brother had been killed.

Her trust had been for nothing. "Spill."

He rubbed his lower face. "You don't beat around the bush, do you?"

"Nope. Let's do this. I'm tired, grumpy, and feeling threatened because, well, I *was* threatened. Now I find out there are secrets on top of your lies. This, after even more amazing sex today. It's like my brain and heart just went through a blender. And guess what? I've got to get up in the morning and keep slogging through all this crap. You'd better make this revelation brief so I can get some sleep."

"Well, okay." He remained a few feet away from her, like she was radioactive and he shouldn't get too close without special equipment.

Red opened his mouth. Closed it. Then he went to his backpack, unzipped the main compartment, and dug around deep in the bag. He pulled out a small black case and unsnapped the fastenings. Two syringes full of pale-yellow liquid rested on foam. Four spaces were empty.

"So, you do drugs?" she asked, heart pounding hard enough to clang in her skull. Maybe this wasn't such a good idea, forcing him to reveal what he obviously worked so hard to hide. At least not in a confined space like her bedroom.

Another hesitation. "Sort of, but not."

"Don't you dare play the Sphinx here." She pointed at him. "Be clear. Now."

"Fine. I'm infected with a virus that will make me go nuts if I don't take this medicine."

She reared back. Knock her down with a feather. Virus? Like an infection?

"Uh, concise is nice, but you need to expand a little further."

His tight smile held no happiness. He clicked the case closed and returned it to the bag.

"Know how I told you I was in the military?"

"You lied."

"No, that's the truth. I was Special Forces. Morpheus Squad. We all were, including Rodeo." He paused. "Including your brother Brady."

Time stopped for five seconds. Her heart clenched. "Wait, you were Brady's teammate?"

"Yes."

"You never thought to mention that?"

"Oh, I thought about it several times. Couldn't say anything. That detail was need-to-know." He paced a few steps in her tiny bedroom. God, he took up all the space. "After Brady's accident, the team volunteered for an experimental treatment that could make us stronger, faster, and, well, harder to kill. Every guy in the squad volunteered, because…"

"Of what happened to Brady." Realization dawned on her.

A curt nod. "We saw firsthand how having a tactical advantage could make our operations more successful. Less of our buddies would go home injured, or in a body bag."

"Makes sense. So far." Her mind still reeled with the knowledge that he was Brady's teammate.

"The treatment wasn't, uh, FDA approved. It had been rushed through testing, but because of the challenges the military was having in combat theaters, a few higher-ups involved in the drug's development were willing to take the risk and do a live trial of the virus. Since our squad volunteered, the Army researchers called it the Morpheus Virus."

"They tested it on you guys." That sensation of the ground falling out from under her grew stronger.

He poked a thumb into his chest. "Guinea pig number one right here. We all rolled up our sleeves like good soldiers and took the virus. Within minutes, we were stronger, faster. Then our mission success rate went through the roof. We performed exactly as the brass had hoped."

"But?"

"You know the saying, 'if something sounds too good to be true'?"

"Literally living that phrase, right here, right now."

He rolled his lips together. "Two things happened. One, most of us developed an extra goody. Like, I have super-sensitive hearing, Rodeo has amazing vision and aim. Stuff like that."

"That sounds helpful. What was the second thing?" Something told her she didn't want the answer to that question.

"There was a price. We were powerful and deadly and we all came back from every mission, even if we had been shot. The virus healed us quickly."

"Also a good thing."

A nod was followed by a flash of pain creasing his features. "The cost for becoming a super soldier was our minds."

"I don't follow."

"The stronger the virus got in our system and the better we performed, the more the virus pushed us beyond the spectrum of normal human behavior. We became unpredictable, dangerous, erratic." He ended on a whisper. "Animals acting solely on instinct."

She had watched him decimate the men in the department store. That raw, unchecked anger had scared the hell out of her. There had been a reason for that behavior. Red was a living lethal weapon who rode the knife's edge of insanity. Great. She shoved her shaking hands under her legs. "But you have a cure?" She lifted her chin toward the case in the backpack.

"A temporary antidote that controls the slide into insanity. Slows it down. There's a difference."

"Will it ever … stop working?"

"No one knows. I'm the fastest cycler, meaning I must take the antidote every few days to keep it in check. Other guys are different. Some can go up to almost a month between doses. It also depends on stimulus."

"I don't follow."

"If we're stressed or in a heightened emotional state or pushed to use our virally enhanced skills, then the virus burns through the antidote quickly and pushes us to a critical level."

"Critical, meaning insanity."

"Yes."

"You've been … stressed … recently. In a heightened emotional state."

He pinned her in place with a mere look. "That's an understatement."

"So, just take more antidote."

"Not that simple." He pushed off the wall to pace. Or stalk. "When I take the antidote, my performance edge disappears. The super hearing I depend on fades back to normal. My strength drops to near human levels. In short, I can't be as effective in protecting you."

"But you don't lose your mind."

"Great choice, huh?"

She jiggled her foot until she caught him staring, and stopped. A new, awful thought occurred to her. "The virus. Is it contagious?"

Red's pause gave her zero confidence. Finally, he said, not looking up, "We don't know."

There it went, the ground completely out from under her. Britt's throat clamped shut. Her head spun. "So, I could be…" she choked out.

"Probably not. Doesn't seem to be transmitted through casual contact or through sex. But I have always used protection when we…"

The wave of dizziness hit her, full force. "Oh God. Oh. My. God."

He dropped onto a knee in front of her, reaching out, but not touching her. "I would never put you in danger, Britt."

She toyed with her ear hoop and rocked back and forth. "You did. By not letting me know the risks." Never had a choice. Damn him.

A flinch. "You're right. We can't risk our secret getting out, so the teammates aren't allowed to tell anyone about the virus. That's not an excuse, it's an explanation of why."

Why he had lied to her.

Britt's policy of not getting too close to anyone ever again? Not trusting her heart to be vulnerable? Damn it all, she should have stuck with it, because right now, every fiber in her body hurt. "So, like, you could have kids, right. With the virus and all?"

Resting a forearm on his bent knee, he looked up at her. "One more piece of information, and then I don't think there are any more unexpected information bombs to drop."

Against every instinct, she leaned forward. "There's more besides the top-secret radioactive STD?"

He rested his other fist on the edge of the bed. Still, he didn't touch her. "It's not like that."

"You don't know that for sure." She dropped her forehead into her palms. "Go on. What could be worse?"

He cleared his throat. "Your sister, Kiera. She had a baby."

"Come again?" No way had Britt heard him correctly. She'd have known if Kiera was pregnant. Right?

"Last week, in fact. It's a really long story."

She managed to stammer as her thoughts spun, faster and faster, "Is she all right? Is the baby okay? Who's the father?" Left out again. No one had told Britt anything. *Protect Britt. Keep Britt focused on the task in front of her and hope she can finish it.* Her ears buzzed.

"The baby appears healthy."

"Appears? Because..."

"The father was one of us. He has the Morpheus Virus."

"Who?"

"Jake, one of Brady's closest friends in the

squad."

She nodded, recalling the quiet man and schoolmate of Brady's who attended her brother's funeral. Which Red did not attend. "Jake grew up with Kiera. I know him. Is she okay?"

"It does not appear that she or the baby contracted the virus. Our physician can't find anything wrong with the baby."

A baby. Something Britt had never thought about personally for the same reason she hadn't been able to truly consider a long-term, deep relationship with anyone. It took more trust and vulnerability than Britt could handle.

"So, if I ever got pregnant..."

"You can't." His ears turned red. Cute, if it weren't for the fact she wanted to kick his ass and also run away from him. "Well, not by me. The researchers recommended that anyone who took the virus should get a vasectomy for exactly that concern. No one knows for certain what a child born with the virus will be like."

"You got snipped?"

His hands went up. "Hey, everything else still works."

And how. "Jake didn't get a vasectomy. Why did you do it?"

"He got one after having sex with Kiera, because putting her at risk freaked him out." Red kept kneeling and scrubbed at his face. "I personally never wanted anyone to risk this damned virus for themselves or for a baby." He ducked his head, not meeting her eyes. Guilty. Good. He should be. "But also because I have no family, came from nothing. And there's nothing holding me anywhere, but I have to stay in hiding because the government wants all of us to go back to being lab rats held prisoner in the testing facility. My career options are both limited and endless. I wouldn't want a child born to that kind of life."

"Wow," she breathed, like her opinion mattered at all. Fine, he used condoms. Still. That's information you give your partner *before* taking them to bed.

Come to think of it, very little of their sex involved a standard bed. She shivered and shoved her legs together. Excellent sex. Not enough pre-sex disclosures.

"Any more secrets you want to share?" she asked.

"No. Isn't that enough?"

Her laugh came out fractured, like puzzle pieces were two different sizes. "Here I thought your secret about being an undercover operative to protect me from a madman intent on revenge was a big bombshell. Boy, was I wrong."

"You're not wrong. How could you have known?"

"How? You open that big mouth, say words, then close the mouth. Pretty simple."

His face could have been carved in stone.

Rubbing her chest, she tried to ease the ache there. Didn't help. "Wow. You've done a great job screwing with my mind. Screwing with more than that, really." Her heart, damn it. She rubbed harder. Still didn't help. "Goddamnit, I'm so stupid."

"No. Britt. It's my fault."

"Is it? Maybe some. But I made the biggest and worst decisions on my own. My parents always said I was impulsive and one day it would bite me in the ass." Her laugh sounded like nails rattling in a metal can. She hit herself on the chest with a hollow thud. "Good ol' Britt, making a bad choice. Again." Air burned in and out of her windpipe. She was dizzy. The exercises, she should do therapy exercises. Ground herself.

Floor beneath her feet. Bed beneath her body.

She could hear a truck idling in the parking lot.

She could see a man standing two feet away from her.

She could smell his scent of pine … damn it.

Her eyes burned.

A minute passed with only their breathing audible. Well, audible at least to Britt. Who knew what Red heard?

Finally, he cleared his throat. "Where do we go from here?"

"You're asking me?" A manic bubble burst in a half-giggle, half-sob. "Fine. You have one job to do. Finish it and then get out of my life. Forever."

"What if—"

"Keep me safe until I complete the one thing I've truly wanted to accomplish. And yeah, even if it's a dumb decision, it's my decision. I'm not stopping two feet short of the finish line, so you can take whatever new recommendation you have and shove it." She drew in a breath and stared at his intense hazel eyes. "Oh my God, you were going to try and convince me to stop."

"It's a viable option."

Of course it was. If her goal had put her family in danger, then sure, she'd quit. It would suck, but she'd do it. But if her family didn't attend, then the only one at risk would be Britt. And anyone else at the show.

Good God. "Can your people keep my dad and sisters safe, wherever they are?"

"Yes."

She leaned over to check the time on her lock screen. Just past midnight. "It's super early Tuesday morning. Can you keep Lequire in check long enough for me to survive until the show on Friday?" She whispered words she never thought she'd have to say. "Can you keep me alive until then?"

A muscle popped in his jaw. "I will do that."

"Are you sure, because you kind of sucked at other stuff you said you could do."

His mouth closed with a clunk and his voice came out as a hard whisper. "Yes."

The shaky breath seared her windpipe. "After my project is finished, I'll go hide until you've finished whatever you need to do. For a while. I can't put my whole life on hold for this insanity. But out of respect for Kiera's life and Brady's memory, I'll lay low so you can take out Lequire and his shitty company."

"Then…?"

"Then I never want to see any of you people again."

Chapter Forty-Four

Later that Tuesday morning, Britt woke up from what she loosely termed "sleep." More like tossing, turning, and counting dots of streetlights cast on the ceiling.

As she padded in her shorts and sleep t-shirt to the bathroom, she froze. A man sat on the couch. She backed against the door, chest heaving. This roller coaster of fear needed to stop.

The Latino guy smiled, dimples forming as thick, dark brows lifted to meet a sweep of dark-brown hair that fell over his forehead. With two tanned hands held up in the air, he stood up slowly. He was several inches shorter than Red and Rodeo, which was to say, still tall. He was powerfully built and due to a few lines on his face he appeared a few years older than Red. "Don't shoot. I'm a good guy."

She snorted. "If you're related to Red, then I'll believe the 'good' part when I see it."

The guy tilted his head. "Ooh, *mi chicka*, has Red been *estupido* again?"

Couldn't help it. A giggle erupted, and she couldn't stop it.

He took a few steps toward her, beefy hand outstretched. "I'm Gonzo. I'm a good guy."

"You said that already."

"Ah, it didn't seem like you heard me the first time." He dropped his empty hand.

"Hmmph." She looked around. "Where's Tachi? Why are you here?"

"*Loca bonita* is still sleeping." He whistled low. "Though she yelled at the boys yesterday, and now Rodeo's too scared to come back here, so I pulled on-site security duty. *Caramba*, but did she give Red and Rodeo an earful last night. That woman, she's fabulous but scary."

"To who? You people?"

"Never seen Rodeo shake in his boots like that. But not me. I'm cool under pressure with the ladies." Gonzo buffed his nails on his shirt. "My opinion? It's good for Rodeo to get taken down a notch or two. Take stock. Read a self-help book to learn more about his mistakes. Personal growth. That kind of junk."

Despite herself, Britt smiled. The action felt good on the tight muscles of her face that moved like nearly dry clay shifting. "So, you're here to…?"

Gonzo leaned against the back of the couch and crossed his thick-soled boots at the ankles. "The big question is, how much of my amazing fashion expertise and skills do you want me to contribute to finish your project?"

"You're into fashion?"

"Surprised?" He pressed a finger to his lips. "Don't you dare tell anyone, but I am exceptional in every way but especially in the fashion department. I outfitted your sister with the best pregnancy outfits that the Sylva, North Carolina, big box store had to offer. Don't even get me started with your niece. That little *chickita* is the most fashion-forward two-week-old the world has ever known." He glanced back over one shoulder then the other and dropped his voice to a whisper. "My vision for her style motif was 'Smokies sunrise,' and that child is the cutest child in the universe, dressed all in pastels and lace, thanks to my eye for 0-3-month-sized fashion."

After her jaw hit the floor, another laugh burst out of her. "Oh my gosh," she said. "You're hired. I need help. We have less than three days to outfit a bunch of models and I'm still sewing outfits. I've needed a decent shopper to get odds and ends. Red's useless." She gulped against the lump as her eyes burned. She blinked hard.

A hard glint formed from within a narrowed gaze, then he flipped back to a dimpled smile. "Of course he's useless. He's not Gonzo." His easy manner relaxed her. He shooed her with his hands. "Now go do whatever womanly things are required to begin your day. You are going to take the fashion world by storm, come Friday."

Britt nearly skipped to the bathroom. For the first time in a long time, she felt a new emotion: hope.

Chapter Forty-Five

As much as Red wanted to stop hurting Britt by staying away from her, he couldn't stay away. Student Al had classes to attend Tuesday. With Britt.

She stared straight ahead as they walked up the stairs to the classroom. The rigid set of her back didn't freak him out nearly as much as her utter silence. This woman was plotting.

If she was smart, she'd stay far away from him. If he was smart, he'd help her meet that goal very soon.

A piece of him still wanted the chance at a future with her. Another piece of him told him to leave her the hell alone before he hurt her even more.

How could he even consider a future together? His damn resume had three items on it: Special Forces, supersonic hearing, and human lab rat. Not exactly long-term relationship material.

One look at her delicate and determined profile and he had his answer—complete this mission and then bail the hell out of her life.

The way his gut twisted at the thought of never seeing her again, must be because of coffee on an empty stomach rather than anything resembling an honest emotion.

At least he was a solid twelve hours beyond receiving the latest antidote dose. That meant his hearing had improved. In his current heightened emotional state he would burn through this dose rapidly. He had to concentrate to avoid growling at anyone who got too close to Britt. Even now, his hypervigilance had climbed a few notches since she left her morning shift at the coffee shop. Every movement, every noise, all ratcheted up his need to protect her.

Which was ironic, when Red considered that he was one of the people who had hurt her over the past week.

In the next class, and he took his seat several rows over and pretended to take notes. Instead, his hearing tuned in to every tiny noise, scrape, sigh, and cough. Everything and everyone was a threat to Britt until proven otherwise. He wanted to claw his sensitive brain out. Damn it, was this how it felt to lose his mind? He couldn't concentrate on anything besides her safety.

Many hours later, he was ready to crawl the walls of the fashion lab. Too many giant windows. Too exposed. Too many people milling about. Thank God for Gonzo who come by to help. When Gonzo departed with a list of items Britt needed, Tachi sauntered in, a shoulder-slumped Rodeo following behind her. Must be a story there, but hell if Red cared right now.

The two women conferred, their voices rising and falling as they held up different pieces of fabric and draped them over Tachi. Then Britt motioned Rodeo over and pinned material on him. The sight of her hands on his buddy's chest made Red's hands curl into bone-creaking fists.

Red had no right to be jealous or possessive or anything other than professional when it came to Britt.

Sticking this close to her, after all they had experienced, knowing they never would have that connection again, was a special kind of torture. Even now, he had to adjust his jeans to address the lack of space. The gentle sway of her hips in that cute fake leather thigh-length skirt made him want to do recon to check what lay beneath the fabric. Instead, he uncrossed his legs, trying to take pressure off and sent texts to his teammates.

No more information about Lequire. No sightings. Nothing. Unnerving radio silence.

Three more days. Today was Tuesday. If Red could keep Britt alive until Friday, she'd be done with the show and could walk away from school with her degree attained. Alive.

Three days was an eternity when it came to an op.

He rolled his shoulders. Damned virus itched for action. Frankly, Red agreed. He'd love to destroy Lequire once and for all. He pushed to his feet and strode over to the trio of fashion experts.

"Oh, good," Britt said with a clinical flick of her eyes over him and back to the table. Her tone said anything but *good*. At least she acknowledged his existence. Barely.

He shoved his hands in his jeans pockets. Nope, didn't help the situation down there. Damn it. "How is the project coming along?"

Rodeo peered at the groups of students working across the room and said in a *sotto voce*, "Well, I'm the sexiest ex-military model the world has ever known."

Tachi rolled her eyes. "Hasn't even signed a contract, but he's already the biggest diva I've ever seen. Next thing, he'll be asking for his own dressing room and organic treats on his makeup table."

"A few packs of beef jerky works fine for me, ma'am," he quipped with a wink.

Tachi sucked a tooth. "I can see it does."

Out of character for the guy who never shut up, Rodeo opened his mouth but no words came out.

"Your turn." Britt held up a bolt of green heavy cotton blend to Red, not quite touching him. "What do you think, Tachi?"

"Looks a lot better than on Slim Jim over there."

Rodeo flapped a hand. "Hello, I'm right here."

Tachi sighed. "That's too bad."

Britt stifled a laugh. "So, a casual jacket in this material and pants in this canvas fabric is what I envisioned," she said. "Never thought I'd be designing for ease of weapons access."

"Shh," Red hissed.

She lifted her chin toward the chugging sewing machines that other students operated. "No one can hear us except you."

Rodeo snorted.

Red glared until his teammate turned away and pretended to select clothes from the rack.

"Stand there," she instructed him. "Ready?" Britt asked Tachi.

Her roommate brandished a pad and paper. "Go."

With clinical expertise, Britt extended the measuring tape and called out numbers. "Neck, 17.5 inches. Arms up, please. Chest 46. Arms down. Sleeve length 37." Like a moron, he dumbly complied as she moved his limbs and body around. "Turn. Neck to waist 21. Turn again. Waist 34."

When she reached around him at the waist, he inventoried stashed weaponry to try and take his mind off her proximity and floral scent. He started the count again when she knelt, her face level with his … service weapon.

"Hold still, please." She reset the measuring tape.

Rodeo snorted. Asshole.

"Hip 44. Length. Inseam…"

Red put out a hand. "Whoa, there."

"What? It's for the project. And your comfort. You don't want the pants to bind, do you?"

Rodeo's eyebrows shot to the sky. Tachi's arched glance kept his teammate silent. Smirking, but silent.

Tachi resettled the pen on paper. "Continue."

Hell.

Britt fluttered fingers at the top of his inseam and pulled the tape down.

Desperately, Red calculated fuel usage for the average Humvee going twenty miles per hour in hilly terrain at an altitude of 2500 feet above sea level. In fifty-degree weather.

"Inseam 34." Britt pushed to her feet, and he caught her at the elbow to help her up. Staring at his hand, she grunted, "Hmmph."

"Nice numbers, Pudge," Rodeo quipped.

"You have no room to talk, Jack Links." Tachi chewed the end of the pen and took a menacing step toward him. "You want me to share your own fluffy numbers with the class? Or are we going to be body positive and accepting of all shapes and sizes?"

"All," he said in a sullen voice.

Britt hid her smile. "Do we have Gonzo's numbers?"

Tachi nodded. "Yes, and I have Kim and Damaris's numbers ready to go."

"Are we done?" Red asked. He couldn't take much more of this proximity.

The stare Britt gave him would have withered a lesser man's balls.

Rodeo pursed his lips as he backed away. "Hoo boy."

Britt looked at Tachi. "One more outfit tonight, and two tomorrow afternoon and evening? Ready for fittings on Thursday. Barely." She rubbed her eyes.

Red called over, "Hey, Rodeo, pull the blinds. Sun's going down."

"Roger."

"Hey, guys," Tachi said, tapping the notepad with

her pen. "Don't forget runway practice tomorrow afternoon."

"I know how to walk," Rodeo muttered.

Tachi scowled. "The two of you definitely do *not* know how to walk on a runway."

"How is that different than regular walking?" Red asked.

Rodeo piped up, "Do you want us to run? I can run."

"Jesus, take the wheel," she muttered before rounding on him. "You two walking a runway is like watching Frankenstein model thong underwear. You look like this." With a scowling face, she did a stiff, stomping stagger, complete with pulling out an imaginary wedgie.

Britt and Tachi burst into laughter. Red could feel his mouth turn up. Rodeo? Not so much.

"Work with me, fellas," Tachi said. "We have forty-eight hours to turn you goobers into runway models. There are entire classes on this subject. I need you to learn enough to hold yourselves together so you blend in during the show."

Rodeo pulled out the yo-yo and sent it down the string. "Hold ourselves together." He snorted and puffed out his chest. "Baby, you should see me hold things together. I'm the king of composure."

She stood a foot away from him, with her arms folded over her ample chest. "Are you now?"

The yo-yo got stuck at the bottom of the string. He quietly re-rolled it and stashed it in a pocket.

Red shook his head down and counted the hours until the show. He returned to his compulsive scrolling through the security cameras. He needed to forget inseam measurements and avoid tracking Britt's every movement, every sigh, each quick deft movement of her fingers.

Because down that path lay literal madness.

Chapter Forty-Six

"Hi, sis." Britt gripped the phone Gonzo handed her Tuesday evening before he disappeared with a soft click of the apartment's front door closing.

Tachi and Rodeo were driving over to see Kim and Damaris and inventory what accessories they could add to the project. Red sat in Tachi's bedroom, twenty-some odd feet away, with his extra special hearing.

There was nothing such as privacy these days. Britt sighed. "How are you, Reagan?" She leaned against a love seat cushion, a shaking hand pressed against her cheek.

"Better now, knowing you're safe."

Okay might be a stretch. Britt's safety remained in question and her heart was battered, but she would survive. "This situation is a lot to deal with." Tears pricked her eyelids as she changed the subject to one she could discuss without going to pieces. "Hey, what happened to you last week?"

Reagan sighed. "A little hypothermia, a long trail run without enough food or water, bad people shooting at me. The adventure ended with a Samoan falling on me."

"What?"

She laughed, warm and spontaneous. Classic Reagan. "It's a long story."

"You're okay now?"

"Arm's broken, but it'll mend."

"Wow." She chewed a thumbnail. "How's Kiera? They said she had a baby. I had no idea!"

"Me neither, she kept all of us in the dark. Both Kiera and Mattie—that's what she's calling her little girl—are both fabulous."

"Gonzo said Mattie was the world's cutest baby."

Her sister's chuckle came right through the phone like a big hug. "He's not wrong. She's beautiful!"

Britt needed to get to the point of the call. She hauled in a big breath. "Sis, I need you to stay away this Friday."

"No way! I wouldn't miss your senior project for anything!"

"Listen to me. I think you might get hurt if you come here."

"Have you met the rest of the team?"

"No. Just Rodeo and Gonzo." Air got stuck in her chest. "And Red," she stammered.

A pause. "So. Anything you want to talk about?"

Britt pinched the bridge of her nose to keep from crying. "No."

"Seriously? Talk to me."

"I'm just super tired, Reagan. It's another long story, probably like yours. I can't wait for this all to be over and get back to our normal lives."

"Me too, sis. You have no idea how much I want that."

"So, you're not coming, right?"

"If I do attend your show, I'll have Pele right there with me." Reagan's voice changed when she said the man's name. Something more happened on the Smoky Mountain mission, than an escape from Lequire's men. Britt would put money on it.

"Please don't. It'll just stress me out more." She pressed the phone to her ear and whispered, "I'm scared. I don't want anyone else being hurt. But I need to finish this degree for me … and for Mom." Her heart pounded as she glanced around. "I'm not making the right decision here, am I?"

"Old Reagan would say to play it safe. However, life is sometimes too short for playing it safe. When that nasty Lequire guy takes away your choices? Forget it. Be smart, but don't let that jackass ruin your future." She chuckled. "I say get your degree, Britt. Let Red and the teammates do their jobs. They know how to keep you safe."

A bubble of a sob hit her, and Britt took a moment to pull herself together. "Thanks, Reagan. That's really helpful." A big shuddering sigh. "You're still staying away, right?"

A few seconds' pause. "I don't like it, but I'll stay put if it that's what you want. Just know that I'll be cheering you on when I watch the video. I know what this project means to you. You've worked hard for this degree and it's been a journey to get here. I'm proud of you. We all are."

Britt sniffed. "Thanks."

"Oh, sweetie. I wish I could give you a hug. Kiera wants to hug you, too."

Tears rolled down Britt's cheeks. "It's almost over. Another few days left in this week that will not end."

"Trust the guys. They will do whatever it takes to protect you and keep you alive."

Britt whispered, "That's what I'm afraid of."

Chapter Forty-Seven

Red's Wednesday morning shaky truce breakfast with Britt, Tachi, and Rodeo started off fine. Until the ricochet of a vehicle backfire outside the apartment sent Red and Rodeo diving to cover the ladies.

Britt's soft body caged beneath Red tormented him as he counted down the minutes for Gonzo to give the all clear. Any danger would have to get through Red first. Nearby, Rodeo similarly sheltered Tachi. A quick grin and a thumbs-up told Red all he needed to know about his teammate's not-so-unpleasant experience as a human shield.

A backfiring car. Damn it. When it came to Lequire and his next move, the other shoe hadn't dropped today, but at some point, it would. How and when, no one knew yet.

Yet.

Britt pushed hard to complete her work, and Red had no idea how she did it. The woman had worked for several days straight on only a few hours' sleep each night. With endurance like that, she'd make a hell of a Special Forces soldier. Her relentless schedule kicked Red's butt. Even with the virus onboard, reducing his baseline requirement for sleep, Red was tired.

Two more days to go. Mission almost completed. He couldn't lose focus yet. He wanted this mission to end. Did he?

He didn't know what his life would be like once the mission ended, not seeing Britt. He inhaled, his nose buried in her hair, and the floral scent tormented him as much as the sound of her citrus sweet breaths as she lay tucked in beneath him.

Gonzo's text came back: **All clear.**
In Red's world, nothing was clear.
****

A day later, Britt couldn't keep her eyes open for Thursday's class, Fashion 399: Concept Development. She propped her forehead on her hand for a few seconds.

"Ms. McNeill?" The words cut into her unconscious state. "Ms. McNeill?"

She jolted, whipping her head up. Tittering and murmurs filled the classroom. Was she drooling? She rubbed her mouth. Even Red looked amused, sitting next to Jenna. Whatever.

Britt figured the best tack was to fess up. "Sorry. I was resting my eyes for a moment. Show's coming up this week. Retooling my collection."

The professor pushed glasses up his nose. "You're going in a different direction for the fashion show? Last minute?"

"Yes. I ... changed the collection I was going to present a week ago."

"Why?"

Do not look at Jenna. Do not look at her. "It became obvious that I needed to take some risks and stay true to my vision. The result is way better than what I had originally planned. You could say that I was inspired."

Now she could glance over at Jenna. The woman looked like she had sucked an entire lemon. Good.

"Well, we all look forward to sharing in your vision," the professor said. "Until then, I do need you to pay attention."

"Yes, sir." Not much else she could say.

Pinching herself on the leg and biting the inside of her cheek when sleep threatened to overtake her, Britt remained awake for the rest of the lecture. Couldn't remember anything the professor said, but at least she did the courtesy of not dozing off again.

When she dragged her sorry butt up to the lab, she stopped short a few feet inside. Red bumped into her from behind. Following too closely.

"Sorry," he muttered.

Pointing, she breathed, "Wow. What's that?"

There, on her table space in the corner sat a massive bouquet of flowers. Red and white roses burst from the sparkling crystal vase.

She turned to the few classmates present. "Did you see who brought this?"

Head shakes and shrugs.

Strolling to her work area, she set her backpack on the floor. "Did you do this?"

"No." His brows drew together. "Wish I'd thought of it."

Well, then. "Maybe my sisters sent it since they couldn't come to the show."

Red's posture went rigid and his eyes narrowed as he swiveled his head. He grabbed her hand as she reached out. "Don't touch it."

"Ow."

"Sorry." He rubbed his thumb over her wrist, sending inappropriate tingles up her arm. Weren't they past this response? They had both moved on. "May I?" He examined the arrangement. Plucked the card out of the gold holder.

The envelope had a foil seal on it—not the usual for a commercial florist delivery.

She studied the beautiful flowers and the vase. Britt wasn't a fine arts major, but the vase looked fancy. Really fancy. Wouldn't surprise her to see a Waterford acid stamp at the base. If true, the vase itself could be worth nearly a thousand dollars.

Something was dead wrong. A tilt of vertigo hit her.

Red opened the envelope and they both peered at it.

All the best for the spectacle. What is the true price of fashion? I look forward to finding out. Yours, Beau.

The air left the room.

Red caught her with an arm around her waist and pulled her into his solid chest, holding her up and turning his back so the other students wouldn't see her reaction. "Damn it."

Stars crowded her vision. Breaths rasped hot in her throat. Too harsh. All the security had been wasted. She'd been so confident they could pull off this event. Things had been so calm and safe, especially with the additional help.

Then Beau or his underling simply waltzed in here and dropped off a giant floral arrangement. Taunting the tight security in a move meant to shake her to the core. The move worked.

Her heart skidded in her chest, too fast. She dug her trembling fingers into Red's corded arm. Solid. Warm flesh over hard muscle grounded her. She concentrated on the stability of their connection.

She sucked a breath in. Out.

She could see Red's denim jacket.

She could smell his aftershave.

She could hear the low growl rumbling from his torso.

Breathe. In. Out.

Her hand on his arm. Solid. Stable.

She fought back the clawing panic.

With his free hand, he fished out his cell phone

and hit a series of buttons. Set down the phone. Ran a hand up and down her upper arm. "I'm here. You're safe."

For now. Then the tremors started. She made a choking sound. Couldn't swallow.

Success was never going to happen, was it? Not in a way that protected both her family and the team.

"Can you sit on your own?" he whispered. "I don't want to draw more attention."

She nodded and he eased her onto a tall chair with a back and scooted her up to the sewing table. Moving the arrangement to the far corner of the table, he returned to hover over her shoulder, hand on her back. She didn't have to look to know he was scanning the room.

Every muscle in her body burned, tense and drained of strength. The act of holding her head up took too much effort. Why was she pushing so hard to finish this task? Britt had forgotten why it was so important.

"What am I going to do?" she whispered.

Red's voice wove a net of support around her. "Right now, you're going to smile and act normal," he said under his breath. "Then we'll assess next steps."

The heat from his body seeped into her. She concentrated on her exercises until sparkles left her field of vision. Fishing out a bottle from her backpack, she swished cool water in her dry mouth and managed to swallow.

Then Gonzo strolled into the lab, casual as you please, if you didn't know to look beyond the dimpled smile to the deadly glint in his eye.

"*Que paso?*" Like any other day. Nothing to see here. He took up a subtle position on her flank.

Red gave him an efficient three-sentence recap that chilled Britt's blood.

She fiddled with the hoop in her earlobe. "What am I going to do?"

Gonzo's head tilted as he studied her. "You, *mi amiga*, are going to put on an earth-shattering fashion show tomorrow, that's what you can do."

Britt huffed. "You're joking, right?"

"You're joking, right?" Red echoed.

Gonzo partially turned so he could scan the lab, his dark stare meeting her eyes. "Never fear. I'm here to help."

"It's a bad idea, Gonz," Red said.

Gonzo's brief dark and lethal expression made Britt lean away.

"No *cabeza de pinga* is going to threaten good people like you. Not on my watch." The fabric of his black-and-green button-down strained over the biceps as he formed two huge fists.

Britt glanced at Gonzo. "Do I want to know what that means?"

A snarl smoothed into a tight grin. "No, you do not, *mi fashionista*."

She blinked. "Just like that?"

"Exactly. We're bringing more resources for the party tomorrow."

Red rumbled behind her, remaining close. "Resources?"

"Rivera will be occupied with Britt's father, who by the way is as stubborn as his youngest daughter here. He could not be convinced to miss the show for all the world. For models, we've got Rodeo, me, and unfortunately this guy." He made a flicking motion with his thumb and finger. "Eh, win some. Pele's coming tomorrow afternoon, hopefully without Reagan. Something about McNeill ladies not listening to common sense. Stumpy's got us tech-ed out to the max." He grinned. "So, yes, we will cover all the bases so that you have a fabulous show, or my name's not Gonzo."

With a sniff, Red muttered, "It really isn't 'Gonzo'."

"*Silencia*, Alfred!" he said with a chopping motion that almost hit Red.

Britt giggled.

"Fine. 'Gonzo.'" Red threw air quotes. "Bases covered. Final decision is Britt's." He leaned forward, bracing his forearms on the table next to her, and turned his head to search her face. "What do you want to do?" his words feathered the skin of her cheek.

She shivered, then sat up straight. "I'd like to sleep for about a week," she said. "But I'm kind of pissed that this Lequire guy is messing with my family and interfering with my life."

"And?"

"Kind of would like for him to go screw himself, if you want my honest opinion."

"Get it, girl." Gonzo gave a thumbs-up with a rakish grin.

"Is that the worst decision ever?" she asked Red.

Red clenched his jaw, glanced over at Gonzo, then back to her with a nod. "Remember what I said before. You've had things taken out of your control. You make the call." A sincere, if not sad, smile took him from good-looking to breathtaking in a split-second.

Damn it, how her stupid eyes burned. "Definitely leaning toward the *screw that jerk* category."

"Let's make it happen," Gonzo piped up. "We're locking down security. You have beautiful people coming in for fittings. Miss Tachi needs to teach some people how to be models." He waggled his eyebrows. "Not me. Wait until you see my fierce walk." He continued behind his hand. "Lunks like Red here? Good luck getting any sort of sashay out of him."

Her laugh caught on a sob, and both guys awkwardly patted her on an arm and back. This wasn't happiness, but close enough for now.

Chapter Forty-Eight

Friday, 7:31 PM. A little less than an hour to go until the show.

The constant tremors in Britt's hands had less to do with mainlining caffeine since late last night as she pulled the all-nighter to end all-nighters … and more to do with real fear that her collection would bomb today.

That, and the part where she might die.

Her shoulder blades prickled.

Britt was java-juiced to the point where she would sprint faster than a cheetah if anyone startled her.

Speaking of close, she hadn't seen Red since this afternoon's dry run of the show. He hadn't exactly hidden how much he didn't want to participate, and she couldn't blame him. Modeling wasn't for everyone, and it kind of sucked that he had gotten coerced into walking. It was the only way he could help her succeed and still do his job. The teammates would be so exposed, but they brushed off her concerns.

Gonzo, for his part, kept switching gears between helping Britt adjust the outfits, ribbing Rodeo, and checking himself out in various mirrors. He flirted with Tachi's model friends, Kim and Damaris. The ladies held their own next to the tall, muscled guys. The show's theme, "Hope Greater Than The World," required a big production, and Britt felt dwarfed by the military guys with their solid muscle, beautiful Tachi, and her similarly statuesque and curvy model friends. The amount of sheer gorgeousness here tempted Britt to make a comparison to herself.

Came up short. Literally. She tugged at her canvas skirt and green faux-leather tank top embellished with Swarovski beads. Her metallic booties finished the ensemble. Her outfit was similar in design theme to that of her collection pieces. She looked nothing like the impressive models, though.

"*Que paso, bella fashionista?*" Gonzo sidled up to her collection's backstage prep space and smiled at their reflections in the mirror. He bumped her hip with his, gently.

Behind them, activity swirled and excited voices rose and fell as each designer's collections took shape in small groups across the backstage area. Three steps above the backstage floor, a curtain concealed the raised main stage's backdrop and catwalk. Forward in the main modern theater space, the catwalk was elevated a few feet from a concrete floor. Spectators occupied four tiers of seating cubes along either side and at the end of the catwalk, where models could turn right, left, or do a crossover from one side to the other and then exit stage left. The best seats were those next to the stage, where fashion scouts had taken up residence with their phones ready to snap photos of the collections.

They would post images of their favorite looks on social media and scout new designers for fashion houses. Britt gulped. Her collection would get almost instant feedback—good or bad, along with her future career opportunities.

There were twelve senior collections being shown today, and as the Challenge Scholarship winner, Britt had the prime slot to close the show.

The backstage area had been partitioned off for each collection's models to prepare. Even with the separate spaces, there was a carnival atmosphere throughout. Even a portly and hunched custodian in the corner seemed to get into the spirit, smiling and sweeping in time to the music piped in from the main stage.

"Nothing's up." Fingering the hoop in her ear,

she sighed. "Tired. Nervous. Jittery. Glad this is almost over." She darted another glance over her shoulder. Models milled around, student hair and makeup artists touched up the models, and designers flitted around, nervous energy feeding on itself with chatter increasing in pitch and volume.

"I think it's more than 'nothing.' First of all, we've got your back. He put an arm around her and followed Britt's gaze to the models who stood in a circle around a preening Rodeo. "Second of all, you are a beautiful woman, inside and out. Even more important, you created this collection. None of us could do that. None of these other designers, either." His eyebrows rose. "Your collection is on point!"

The corners of her mouth lifted. "I know, but..."

"You have something to fear from these other lovely ladies? Or from the other designers?"

Hesitantly, she drifted a fingertip over her crystal-adorned glam faux-hawk and said, "No."

Gonzo met her gaze in the mirror with a frown. "Oh, you think a certain someone will want these women over you?"

Too close to the truth. "Moot point, Gonzo."

"I disagree."

"Doesn't matter. As soon as this show ends, I need to disappear. Alone. That's for the best, considering everything."

"The best what?"

"His job. My future. His safety. My family. The virus." She held up a hand and turned her back on the mirror. Gonzo dropped his arm to the side as he propped a hip on the table edge. "Doesn't matter. He's not here." Shaking her head to clear it, she asked, "Is everything else ready on your end?"

Gonzo peered out over her head to visually sweep

the backstage area. "Your male models are packing considerable heat. Some of our planted audience members as well. Stumpy's got visuals and communication in place. Rivera won't leave your father's side. We're ready for anything."

She shivered. "As long as no one gets hurt."

"We'll take care of safety." He went from vigilant soldier to a cute guy with a dimpled smile. "And you, go present the best fashion collection any student has ever produced."

"How are you so good at fashion?"

"What? Surprised? Because I was Special Forces? Army? Expected to be macho?"

She laughed. "It's unexpected, is all."

"I helped raise my younger *hermanas*. We poured over fashion magazines and never missed *America's Next Top Model*. That Tyra and Jay Alexander, they gave good pointers."

"Well. Your expertise is my advantage!"

She glanced at the clock on the wall. Forty-five minutes until everyone would line up, first collection to last, followed by another walk at the end where each designer traveled the catwalk with one of their models at their side. Her model was supposed to be Red. "Thanks for the pep talk."

"It's nothing." He turned and waved at Kim, the tall, laughing honey-blonde standing next to Tachi. "If you'll excuse me, I need to do some networking. To maintain my cover, of course."

"Ha."

He sauntered over to the group. Britt was all but forgotten.

Almost.

Jenna, her blonde hair pulled into a tight French roll updo with gold lame flecks on her face and neck, strolled by. "Still going to try and do a last-minute show?" she asked. For such a pretty woman, when she opened her mouth, she became ugly.

"Of course. You inspired me to try a different idea. And wow, is it going to be fabulous."

Jenna tilted her chin, looking down her nose. "Looks kind of work-casual to me. So last years' collections." She fake-yawned. "I mean, it's good if you're targeting Target or DressBarn. It's important that all walks of life have accessible fashion. Not everyone can afford luxe items." Patting her gold shift, she smiled.

That outfit seemed like gold overkill, but Britt recognized that she had no objectivity where Jenna was concerned. Instead, she bit her tongue. "I'm betting on my vision." She hoped. Untested clothing patterns and materials. Untested models. Untested fashion designer. Death threats. What could possibly go wrong?

What she meant to think was, how many different ways *could* it go wrong?

However, Britt had bigger fish to fry than worrying about Golden Girl. "Hey, you have a wonderful show. Your collection is beautiful. I'll be rooting for you."

Jenna froze on what looked to be a snotty retort. Stared. Gaped like a largemouth bass. Turned and stumbled as she walked away.

Wow. Britt never figured magnanimity could double as a weapon. Tuck that tidbit away for future reference.

After another fifteen minutes of tuning up Tachi and Kim's outfits with last-minute hidden pins to tuck the fabric just so and adjusting hair and makeup, Britt stood and stretched her back, catching a glimpse of a familiar face.

"Dad!" she called out, hurrying toward him.

Gonzo and Rodeo casually flanked her, but kept their distance.

Dad had on a light-blue long-sleeved button-down shirt, a navy sweater vest, and gray woolen pants. Yes, her father had worn his postmaster uniform to her fashion show. She grinned. He'd even slicked his thinning hair in what could best be described as "male newscaster chic." Quintessential Dad.

He reached out. "Hi, honey."

His bear hug brought tears to Britt's eyes as she inhaled his Brut aftershave—a scent she associated with him as long as she could recall. She clutched him, panic ramping up. She didn't want to let go. She scanned the venue. How could she put him in this danger?

He patted her on the back, harrumphed, and pointed behind him. "This is Luis Rivera. Just started working at my post office. Turns out we both like beer, pool, and Atlanta Hawks basketball." His brows shot up. "And he's ex-military, too, like me."

Rivera had on loose-fit jeans, a tan button-down shirt, and casual lace-up brown leather shoes. Britt didn't buy the getup for a minute. She'd bet a rack of clothes that he had tactical weapons stashed all over him.

The tall, lean Latino man stuck out his hand with a tight, brief smile. "Nice to meet you, ma'am. I'm, uh, not a big fashion fan, but the reward of going to a round ball game tonight? Hooah, I couldn't pass it up." He paused. "Uh, sorry. I mean, I'm sure the show will be nice, too."

Dad beamed—as much at his friend as Britt.

A glint in Rivera's steely gaze. Britt knew the score. The teammate's awkward schtick was for show. He was here on business, pure and simple. The business of keeping her dad safe. Good.

A tight vise she didn't realize had wrapped

around her chest, loosened up a notch. Dad would be okay. Rivera would see to that. Dad was here. He'd get to see her achievement.

"Thanks for keeping Dad company, Luis. I hope you enjoy the show and the basketball game." *Please keep him safe*, she tried to convey with her eyes.

"Will do." He elbowed her dad. "Hey, Sean, do you think they have popcorn for events like this?"

A grimace. "I don't think so." Dad sighed and blinked, rubbing his hands together. "There might be fancy drinks at the reception afterward. We could sneak one now."

"Dad!"

"Fine. I'll wait until later." He made a kind of *aw, shucks* arm move and pointed with a thumb. "Right. Enough talking. I want to get a good seat." He beamed at her. "I wouldn't miss your show for the world, honey. I'm sorry to hear your sisters couldn't make it."

Another hug, laced with relief. "That's okay. They had important things to take care of. But thanks again for coming, Dad. It means a lot."

"Can't wait." He had no clue about anything to do with fashion. Heck, he really had no idea what her major entailed. Yet, here was good old Dad, always supportive of his kids, no matter what.

He and Rivera strolled out of the backstage area like two peas in a pod, chatting about basketball stats as Rivera pantomimed a free throw.

Britt stood by herself. Checked her watch. Twelve minutes until the show started. Her heart pounded and palms grew clammy as she stared around the room.

The models clustered in a group in her section. Tachi and her friends practiced removing the jackets to reveal the surprisingly sparkly tank tops beneath as well as Gonzo's accessories he had purchased the other day. Gonzo had even insisted on sewing on a few fun silver four-leaf clovers "for luck." They surprisingly looked great on the women's tops. Britt's collection was meant to inspire day-to-evening fashion with a few simple adjustments.

Hopefully a designer would see the vision. Heck, every year scouts from New York and LA fashion houses sat on the front row of the SCAD spring show. For good reason. Typically, one or two fashion students got offered an internship at one of the major designers. Careers had been launched from this very catwalk.

That outcome was too much for Britt to hope for, given how quickly she had thrown together this collection. Her main goal was to get a passing grade and graduate.

Next goal: disappear until this mess with Beau Lequire and his creepy fixation on Kiera was resolved.

She rearranged the order of the models once more, since they were a model short. Disappointment created a sour taste in her throat. No, the show should work fine. They were professionals. Well, the women were. The guys had some of the worst struts she'd ever seen, but here's hoping their bulging muscles and handsome swagger made up for whatever they lacked in runway skills.

Still no Red.

In case she had wondered how he felt about her. About the show. About everything. A lump formed in her throat.

She concentrated on the solid ground beneath her feet for several seconds, trying anything to stay calm.

"Heard you needed an extra model." The warm voice slid down her spine. How had he snuck up behind her?

Spinning around, she sucked in a lungful of air. Red wore the collection's slim-cut canvas pants that emphasized his muscular legs but still hid at least three guns or knives, black loafers that gleamed, and a dark-green jacket hinting at the tank top beneath—also concealing another gun. His short hair had been somehow gelled into a handsome fade with a bit of volume on the top. A bit of irregular skin hinted at the tiny neck microphone each of the men wore, camouflaged with special effects makeup and rubberized skin-mimicking material. Clean-shaven, with broad shoulders, the guy looked good enough to nibble on. She inhaled the fresh aftershave and unique pine scent he had.

"Hey," she managed, ignoring Gonzo and Rodeo's twin brow-raised expressions.

"Hey yourself." He propped a lean hip against a nearby chair. "Reporting for duty."

"You hate this stuff."

"It's important to you, Britt. So I'm here."

Chapter Forty-Nine

Red wanted nothing to do with this whole scene. Strike that. He wanted nothing to do with the show. He wanted everything to do with Britt, but had no right to even ask her out on a coffee date, much less consider anything that resembled a relationship or, God help him, a future. He'd screwed with her life enough. Some damage could not be repaired. The sooner he left her in peace, the better off she'd be.

That said, no way would he abandon her at the eleventh hour of her dream coming true. Her future career hinged on success tonight. Damned if he would sabotage it by dropping out. Her life depended on his team's success.

Red wanted to remain close, which fired up his virally driven protective instincts. But he'd held off taking the antidote today. Then he had to stay away, so that his need to safeguard her didn't burn through his tenuous control before the show. Already, her presence in this crowd of people stoked his protectiveness.

God, she was cute, in her metallic booties that highlighted lean legs which were only partially concealed by a structured canvas skirt similar to the pants and skirts her models wore. That forest-green tank top with crystal beads hugged her in all the right places and tempted him to lick the exposed skin.

Tachi had styled all the ladies' hair, Britt included, in matching poufy styles, finishing their looks with polished makeup that featured dark eyeliner and shadow. Britt was the perfect edgy pixie. Sexiness in a fierce, tiny package that could knock him over with a mere glance.

When the lights dimmed, he gave her upper arm a

quick squeeze. "It's going to be fine. We're professionals."

Her wavering smile didn't reassure him. Whether she was scared because of the fashion show or nervous about Lequire, he couldn't tell. Patting the compact Sig hidden in a special pocket inside his pants waistline, he clamped his jaw shut. He would keep her safe.

A screen on a wall showed images from the main stage. Music pulsed in the background. All the seats in the SCAD event venue were full. People lined both sides of the catwalk and were seated several rows deep. Audience members held cell phones. Stumpy had his work cut out for him, snagging and obscuring images of the team before people posted them online. Word was, Stumpy had control of the nearby cell towers and school Wi-Fi so any data being sent would fail. From there, he'd backtrack into the originating phone and swap out faces before the person hit "send" again. If all else failed, he could temporarily jam all transmissions. Impressive.

Red watched on the monitor while Professor Janssen, their Fashion 399: Concept Development instructor, stepped out on stage to the sound of fading chatter and rising applause. He introduced the show and the collections, giving the audience an idea of what to expect. Then a twenty-minute video presentation highlighted each student designer's college career. Red took the pause to assess the environment around him. Nervous energy. No furtive movements or abnormal sounds detected.

Red joined Britt and the other models.

Tachi caught his eye and winked. "Glad you could join us."

"Looking good, Alfred," Rodeo piped up from over her shoulder before facing Tachi. "I still think we should have a stomp-off."

The dark-haired beauty pulled her chin back and laughed. "High heels or not, I would beat all of you guys."

"Care to make it interesting?" Rodeo grinned.

She nodded, giving his hand one solid pump. "You're on. What do I get if I win?"

Rodeo puffed out his chest. "I'm the one that should be asking that question."

Britt looked up into the group of beautiful and supportive people around her. "Okay, everyone. You know what order to line up? Feeling good about the crossover at the end of the catwalk?"

Rousing yesses.

The models from the first four collections ascended the backstage stairs. Energetic, slick electronic beats thundered through the building as the first group confidently took the stage to more applause. Like in the club, the loud noise obscured Red's hearing acuity. He shook his head, trying to clear it. Didn't help. The virus pushed against him to change location and take Britt with him. He fisted his hands and surveyed the space, going through infil, exfil, options, and liabilities. Too many liabilities. Damn it.

He activated the flesh-toned earpiece adhered behind his ear. As a bone-conductive piece of advanced tech, it allowed the teammates to still hear ambient sound in addition to receiving direct communications input. The skin-colored throat mic, also tiny and nearly invisible, rested flush against his skin.

As the first collection started to walk, the stage manager signaled for the next four collections to line up.

Britt motioned for everyone to lean in. "Hey, you all look fabulous. Thank you for helping me pull this off," she said. "And … um, go team?"

"Go, Team Britt! Best designer at SCAD! Drinks

afterward!" Tachi said, putting her hand in the middle of the group and elbowing Rodeo to follow suit. The other models stacked hands and gave a big shout, and to Red's satisfaction drew nasty glares from Jenna's aloof New York City-based professional crew across the room. Behind that group, over on the far wall, a janitor in glasses clapped in time with the beat, the broom resting on his shoulder, and a gleaming smile on his weathered face.

"Break a leg, fashion plate." Rodeo smirked at Red.

Red couldn't hear much else over the noise. Auditory overload. The virus clawed at his mind. No. He would hold his shit together for Britt.

Jenna's glimmering group of female models silently lined up, arms stiff at their sides, hair pulled back in severe buns. Too much of one motif, if you asked Red. But hey, he was only a fake fashion student, not a real one.

The house music morphed to something classical-sounding with a moderate beat as Jenna's models made their appearance. A roar of the crowd answered Red's question. Apparently gold was in this year. Who knew?

After a minute, the first models to have walked began to re-enter backstage from a side entrance elevated by a few stairs above the rest of the backstage. As they returned, one model from each group returned to the original entry to the stage, and stood next to each designer in preparation for the finale.

Could he seriously do this? Twice?

The stage manager waved the final four collections up the back of the stage.

"You all look fabulous," Britt's voice quavered over the rolling beat. She looked almost green, and Red wanted to hug her. She descended the stairs to watch the video feed with the other designers and wait to make her own entrance. He nodded at her small form surrounded by other student designers. Safety in numbers in the few minutes it would take for the teammates to walk on stage and return backstage. Thank God Stumpy had an eye in the sky fixed solely on Britt. Should be a hidden team member somewhere nearby as well.

His skin crawled.

He had one more job, and by God, he'd do what he could to make Britt's dreams come true and then keep her alive.

Tachi and Rodeo would get their chance to face off, as Britt had designed the show with the male-female models entering from opposite sides of the stage, going down the catwalk together, turning out at the end of the catwalk, then crossing over each other's path for a final pose, before both exiting at the side of the catwalk to return backstage.

Through an opening in the curtain, Red watched the stage.

The moment before Tachi stepped into the spotlight, her shoulders went back, head came up, and a sly almost-smile lit up her face. She strode out in heels and canvas capris like she owned the place. Rodeo followed suit from the other side of the stage in leather shoes and regular length canvas pants, tipped an imaginary hat at Tachi, much to the screaming excitement of the crowd. Those two beautiful people oozed charisma and chemistry, and the audience loved it. Tachi and Rodeo took their time strutting. Halfway down the catwalk, Tachi slipped off her structured jacket and hung it on one finger over her shoulder. The green tank top shimmered in the theater lights, drawing gasps and flashes of cameras.

Upon reaching the end of the stage, they lifted

their chins at each other, spun apart, walked five paces, turned back, and gave their best fierce pose-off. Tachi popped a fist on her hip and Rodeo made a show of wiping his brow at her perfect posture and angles. The crowd went wild.

Rodeo, resuming the long-limbed, slightly slouched model posture, crooked a finger at Tachi, who strutted right over to him. They hit one more pose and then exited the catwalk.

Down behind the stage, Britt stood in front of the monitor, hands clasped over her chest, eyes shimmering. She deserved to savor every wonderful minute of her collection being presented to the world. Next up, Kim and Gonzo strutted to similar enthusiastic reception.

Red's heart thudded. He waited for his cue, then stepped out right as Damaris mirrored his movement. The stage became a deafening blur of house music, crowd noise, and his heart pounding in his head. Was that glint of metal in the audience a gun? He couldn't hear himself think, much less detect a safety's click. Every step took him farther away from Britt, and his virus strained against the separation. As he entered the catwalk, he scanned the audience and glimpsed Rivera and Britt's dad a few rows back, as well as Pele on the other side, wearing a fashionable cape. According to the plan, Curly would be in the audience, too, likely utilizing his ability to blend in and become no one. Or he was the backstage team member in support. The guy was a ghost – everywhere and nowhere at the same time.

The rest of the crowd was varied. The lights illuminated the bright colors, diverse clothing textures, sparkling accessories, and smiling audience members. A face in the crowd caught his attention. He almost stumbled. The face didn't fit. Smiles all around, except for one audience member scowling. Guy in sunglasses.

You know what they say about people who wear sunglasses indoors? Either blind or an asshole. Red would put money on the latter. The guy looked at his watch. Had Rodeo or Gonzo picked him out? Pele or Curly? Red stared for one beat too long and didn't move his lips to mutter into the throat mic, "My three o'clock."

Red tried to walk as Tachi had taught him, arms swinging but contained, hips forward without swaying, with the "deep thought" slightly squinting expression. He slowed as Damaris slung her jacket over a shoulder, revealing a semifitted green tank with silver accents that went well with the canvas deconstructed skirt that somehow managed to swirl. Finally, the end of the catwalk appeared before him, and he hit his mark right along with Damaris, turned out for five paces, spun back, posed, paused, and then crossed over again. He waited for Damaris to do her final pass on the end of the catwalk before she joined him to exit the stage together.

He nearly ran. All he wanted was Britt. He needed to reach her. His heart thudded.

In the backstage area, he dashed down the few stairs and hurried over to where the designers lined up with their models. He searched for Britt. Where was she? His ears buzzed.

Backstage, Gonzo and Rodeo kept Tachi and her model friends together and off to one side. Red met his teammates' eyes. Rodeo blinked once. All good, so far. Gonzo looked around then back to Red. One blink as well. Red kept a hand on his thigh and moved toward the return stairs on the other side of the stage to take up position there.

Where was Britt?

Red scanned the crowd of glittering, constantly moving models, fashion staff, and designers. The virus clawed at him, needing to connect with Britt. Toward the service doors at the far end of backstage, he could still see the quirky janitor who had worked his way to the back of the space. The guy limped and swept, occasionally bobbing his head to the music with that occasional smile. Out of place. Alarms went off in his mind.

Red needed Britt. Now. His head swiveled back and forth, sanity clawing for purchase. His vision flickered crimson.

Right before he started shoving people to create a clear path, a hand pressed against his palm, fingers lacing through his. As he looked down at Britt's smiling face, the emotional distress response driving the virus dropped several levels. He could breathe again. His amazing Britt was right next to him. They were a few minutes away from pulling off this crazy op.

Red and Britt followed the other model-designer sets up the stairs behind stage right until it was their turn. As last designer to present, Britt walked out on stage to cheers and applause, Red right next to her, motioning as if to show her off to everyone. Red's chest swelled as she beamed and looked around, then up at him. God, the woman glowed from her blue eyes, to the crystals in her hair, to the sexy and fierce skirt and tank top, to those metallic booties that made him think fondly of a certain couch.

She smiled up at him. He would remember this moment forever. His heart soared.

They had completed the mission.

Over the top of her head, Gonzo stood in the wings of stage left. A sudden scowl flashed over his face. He stared out into the audience then back at Red. His teammate's spine had gone rigid. Gonzo blinked twice. Made a quick hand signal. Red's heart dropped. Fuck. He had to be physically in contact with Britt. ASAP. Didn't care if it broke a fashion show rule.

Keep it together. Get her to the end of this show. Alive.

Hurry.

He offered his arm to Britt with what he hoped was an insistent but appropriately broody-model expression. Thank God she accepted it without question, tucking her hand around his elbow. He could yank her into his frame in a split-second, if need be.

Red's back muscles twitched as he walked Britt to the end of the runway. They stopped and she released his arm to clap and wave at the audience, giving Red a chance to peer around. Those few inches of distance made his sanity slip.

Two other men, obvious in how similarly they dressed in black, stood near the guy with sunglasses. Was that who Gonzo signaled about? Were there more?

"Two additional tangos in black, near first one," he muttered, transmitting to the team.

Something else niggled at Red's memory. Something that didn't fit. The audience members seemed out of place, sure. But there was more.

Red retucked Britt's hand against his arm and guided her from the end of the catwalk around to the backstage area. She'd done it. His heart swelled with pride.

He couldn't stop looking at her trusting, beautiful face. She was his strength. His weakness.

His concentration split.

The music continued, though not as loudly. The house lights slowly came up along with the backstage lighting. Murmurs of cheering, laughing, shimmering models and designers mixed with chattering of the members of the audience who started to filter into the backstage area. Maddening cacophony swirled around him, thick and tarry, blocking his ability to discern individual sounds. He fought for clarity. Couldn't think.

"Britt!" Tachi waved and beckoned her to their knot of models.

Red paused, not letting go of her.

Gonzo appeared from the stage left wing. "You want me to monitor up here?"

"Yes until we're secure."

"Roger that." Gonzo turned to Britt and hugged her. "Best show I've ever walked in. You knocked it out of the park, *mi fashionista!*" He quickly returned to a vigilant stance.

Britt laughed, but hung onto Red's arm. She tugged him down the stairs, flitting through the crowd.

Something in the scene didn't fit for Red. He couldn't pick it out with his hearing. Too much noise. Looking over the heads of most of the crowd, he scanned the space again and again. Britt dropped his hand to run over and hug Tachi. He kept an eye out for the crystal-studded purple hair bobbing in the crowd. Hard to do, given her height.

Nothing seemed out of place. No targets honed in on her.

Rodeo tugged Tachi toward the far end of the backstage area, their heads bent toward each other in what looked like intense conversation, punctuated with some mutual waving of hands.

A few minutes later Gonzo breezed by Red. "We're going to the after-party, right?" He didn't wait for an answer, but beelined over to Kim and Damaris where they chatted with Britt.

Red exhaled. The Morpheus Squad had gotten Britt to the finish line.

Mission accomplished.

His neck and back muscles relaxed.

A white gleam jogged his memory. A broom.
Oh, shit.
All hell broke loose.

Chapter Fifty

Project done.

Britt walked around in a daze, heart leaping, somehow feeling amped and exhausted. She'd actually finished!

Tachi hugged her, and then sidled away toward the back of the room with a grinning Rodeo. They made the perfect fashion power couple.

Professor Janssen walked up. "Wonderful collection, Miss McNeill. The juxtaposition of fabric type to create structure yet movement to the viewer's eye, flawless. Thematically, it was pitch-perfect." He clasped her hand then let go. "I'm told that scouts from Khaite and Ralph Lauren showed significant interest in your designs!"

"You're kidding!"

"No. Your vision fits perfectly with their planned fall collection. Let me know if you need a reference." He excused himself to mingle with other students, models, and their families.

Wow. Britt stood in the middle of the crowd, unable to stop smiling.

Standing about twenty feet away, Jenna looked like she sucked another lemon as she stared at Britt. Her models exuded boredom as they removed their accessories and packed up their bags. Jenna's parents and a few friends came up to congratulate her, but the atmosphere in that section of the room was chilly. She had surrounded herself with cold statues, not real people.

Britt smiled at her motley crew of beautiful, unique, happy people. She was so proud. Eventually, she'd need to find Dad and visit with him and his new buddy, Rivera. She breathed a massive sigh of relief. Dad hadn't been hurt.

Lequire hadn't shown up.

Britt wanted to collapse into a boneless lump and sleep for a few weeks.

Over the top of all the people milling around her, she spied Red slowly moving through the crowd. He literally rose head and shoulders above most everyone else. His wink and smile sent a jolt right through her.

Didn't realize until right now how much his opinion mattered. Didn't truly realize until right now how much his safety mattered, too, along with everyone else who helped on this project.

Her body felt light as air. She'd done it. Finished. She would graduate. A bubble of happiness fluttered in her chest. Catching Red's gaze again, she gave him a brief, shy wave. Then he frowned, and his face turned to furious stone as he opened his mouth, as if to yell.

Blood drained from her head to her toes. Several loud cracks pierced the world, and a light exploded above Britt. Red howled and reached out to her, like he could bridge the thirty-foot distance between them with sheer will alone.

Britt covered her head and cowered as glass shattered around her. Screams rippled through the room. Everyone started running in all directions.

Britt stood up and tried to run, too, but in the press of people, she caught an elbow to the jaw and a hand to the back. Stars sparking in her vision, she went down on a knee. The crowd banged into her from side to side as they rushed toward any exit.

Tachi? Red? The models? Where were they?

More loud pops and screams came from the main theater.

Dad? Oh God.

The room had cleared out by half already as

people bottlenecked through the backstage emergency exits.

Was that someone whistling nearby? Seriously?

Heart pounding against her chest, Britt tried to stand, only to get knocked sideways again, this time by a person with a massive frame. A hard forearm clamped around her midsection, turning her scream into a wheezing gurgle. She dug her fingers into the fabric of the sleeve. Black Italian wool blend. Distinctive four-button cuffs. Armani.

A wave of nausea hit her as the grinning face of Beau Lequire filled her peripheral vision as he leaned his head down.

"Game over, pretty lady. Told you the next time we met, I would win. It's for keeps now. You're going to help me now." His gleaming, too-broad grin triggered a clench of terror deep in her gut. "I have a business to run. My Daddy has an election to win. The McNeill ladies are in my way. You're mine."

Britt struggled, but the grip he cranked around her cut off air until her lungs burned. Total bull. This was not how her day was going to end. This was not how her college career would end, dragged away in the clutches of Mr. Nasty Armani. No way.

So what if she wasn't as strong as Beau. She could slow him down. The heels of her booties could do some damage. She extended her foot and flung it backward as hard as she could, connecting with a thud that vibrated up her entire leg.

"*Ooof.* Damn you." He readjusted his viselike grip, still suspending her off the ground. Air exited her lungs and did not reenter.

With her unpinned arm, she reached back and clawed at him, the movement awkward and weak. A familiar shout reached her buzzing ears. Then a blurred impact like a torpedo hit Beau and the force transmitted into her. Beau staggered and dropped her. She flew across the concrete floor and thumped into the wall. Her head swam, and she laid there, watching the world sideways, too stunned to get up.

The backstage area had nearly cleared out of fashion students, models, and audience members. All that remained were four men dressed in black suits who she didn't recognize. They attacked a tall, tanned man with dark hair. The janitor circled them.

The janitor? What?

Then the hunched man straightened up, ripped off a covering on his face to reveal a hard jaw and a flattop haircut, and brandished the mop handle like a baseball bat.

"Tee one up, Pele!" he commanded, his voice rough and low.

Pele? Reagan's Pele?

Pele rotated and kicked, sending the man with sunglasses toward the flattop guy. "Roger, sir."

The former janitor showed zero emotion as he swung the mop handle and connected with the sunglasses-clad man. The guy dropped to his knees. That mop handle had to be reinforced with something.

What about Red? Britt pushed to an upright position against the wall. She should run. She couldn't figure out how to get her legs under her. Mental cobwebs slowed every thought.

Through the fog, she spied Red. He had done that thing where he got super big and terrifying, like in the mall. His face turned crimson, and his eyes bulged. Giant fists curled as he stood at full height in front of Lequire.

Unless the light played tricks on her, Beau Lequire had gotten bigger, too. His shoulders strained against the suit, corded neck muscles rippling.

Lequire thundered a hammer blow onto Red, knocking him flat to the ground. Red's head bounced with a sickening *thunk* on the concrete floor and he didn't move. Lequire strode forward and kicked Red hard enough to lift and move his limp body more than four feet. Closer to Britt.

Lequire snickered as Britt crawled toward a motionless Red.

"Pretty lady, why are you in the way? You McNeill women just don't know any better."

He lurched and planted his foot.

Britt threw herself on Red's chest. The kick intended for Red glanced off her ribs, driving the air out of her with a sick *crunch*. Pain blinded her. She couldn't breathe.

"Move away. Your turn will come soon," Lequire's slickly soothing voice had the opposite effect on her.

Finally, the air returned to her lungs "Get out of here!" she screamed. "Haven't you done enough?" Didn't care if she sounded dumb. Didn't care about the insanity of the situation. Just cared about Red not dying.

"Pretty lady, do you want him to live?"

"Yes," she gasped. "Please."

He studied her with a broad grin. "Oh, my." The man's bloodshot eyes bulged as he loomed over her. "Do you want your sisters and father to live?"

"God, yes. Don't hurt them."

"Well. Today's your lucky day. I'm going to make you a one-time deal. Come with me and I won't kill him or your family members." He reached under the suit coat and pulled out a dark object.

At the sound of the gun safety clicking, her fingers and toes tingled then went numb.

Over on the other side of the room, those two

teammates now fought three attackers.

Where was Gonzo? Rodeo? Hadn't Red said there might be one other guy from the team here, blending in? That was probably him, the janitor.

Dad?

Oh God, no help was coming. She glanced up.

Unwavering, Lequire pointed a gun at Red's forehead.

Even if the two teammates broke off their attacks now, they wouldn't make it over here in time.

The puzzle pieces of her life slotted together in rapid succession. Her career and degree were important. Her freedom was important. Truthfulness was important. But the man beneath her, who had sacrificed himself time and again to protect her was more important. Britt would protect him, no questions asked.

Britt didn't have a future with Red, but at least she could do her part to make sure Red would have a future. The distinction sent cold calm through every cell in her body. She knew what to do.

With a brush of her trembling lips over Red's, she pushed off him and turned toward Lequire. He pointed the gun at her.

"You promise not to hurt him?" she asked, pushing up to her stand in front of Red so she blocked any bullet.

"Why would I lie?" His left eye and eyebrow twitched.

She swayed on her feet. "That's not an answer."

"Scout's honor. I won't kill him."

"Or my family members?"

Heat made his eyes glow avid as his nostrils flared. His face twitched. "I don't need them dead, just silenced. If you're with me, they won't talk." He held a hand out and made a come-hither motion. "End this madness now. Save this boy. Let's go."

Another glance back at Red's motionless form broke her heart.

"All right." One rib-jarring step, then two, had her gasping. Lequire clamped onto her wrist until the bones creaked. Her knees buckled at the blinding pain.

"Oh, sorry, dear. Don't know my own strength. Yet." That nasty laugh turned her stomach. "I look forward to finding out. Maybe you can help me experiment with all the things I can do in this new and improved form?" He tugged her to his side, pinning her next to him with his iron-hard arm. The gun remained in his other hand.

Britt didn't move.

He dipped his head down and licked her earlobe then inhaled. She almost threw up.

"Oh fuck, but you smell a little like her. You look like her, too."

A wave of nausea hit her. This guy was talking about Kiera. He must be obsessed.

He inhaled deeply. "We are going to have so much fun while I get what I want from you. Your sister will destroy the evidence and leave me be. Then I can concentrate on my import business and foreign relations and making Daddy proud again. But not before you and I have some fun of our own." His hot breath seared her skin. He lightly bit her upper cheek. "You might be the sweetest McNeill of them all. Mmm. Delicious."

Couldn't help it. A sob broke out of her mouth. Lequire laughed as he dragged her toward a side exit.

A roar, like that of an enraged bull, made her ears ring.

Lequire spun around, turning Britt with him.

Red barreled toward them at a screaming, dead run.

Lequire fired, hitting Red point blank in the chest, not once, but two times. The impacts slowed him down, but Red's momentum carried him forward, ripping Britt away from Lequire as Red fell. He pinned her under him.

Red had been hit. Oh God.

She couldn't breathe with his heavy frame suffocating her.

The weight lifted as Lequire grabbed the back of Red's jacket, flexing his torso backwards at his lower spine. Red's slack arms dropped down to Britt.

Red's eyes snapped open, looking at Britt. He pressed his gun into her hand where Lequire couldn't see.

A wide smile. "Get him, sweets," he whispered.

God help her, she laid on the ground, aimed past Red's shoulder, and did exactly that. First shot missed wide. Second shot caught Lequire in his chest.

Lequire dropped Red onto her, crunching the air out of her once more. Red's arms and legs immediately came around her like a giant cage of muscle. He palmed the gun and held it away from her, then rolled multiple times, coming to rest with him crouched over her.

Craning her neck, she spied Lequire as he held his side. Red bloomed over the portion of white shirt visible between the suit lapels. He backed toward the door, cursing and eyeing the rest of the room. "We're not done here. I might not have a McNeill, but I've got my plan B and they are going to suffer. You still lose." A gurgling cough, then he was gone.

What did he mean, plan B?

Silence. Britt craned her neck just in time to see the flattop janitor guy and Pele dump the fourth limp figure on top of a pile of three other bodies.

The man barked out information, obviously in command, "Rodeo's missing. Roommate, too."

Pele cursed. "Roger."

"Find them. I'll deal with these deadweights until Curly finishes his cleanup." The leader turned toward Britt.

Pele dashed out of the building.

Speaking of deadweight, as much as she liked the security of Red holding her, she couldn't breathe within the clamp of his arms, crushed beneath his two-hundred-plus pounds frame.

"Red," she whispered as her vision went black.

Chapter Fifty-One

Red lifted his head and peered around him, unwilling to move until he knew Britt would be safe. Then he braced his elbows on the floor, holding some of his weight off her. She didn't move.

God help him. No! He searched for wounds, bleeding. Nothing. His vision was coated crimson. Sound and fear swarmed like wasps in his mind. The virus lashed at him, taking over thoughts and centering them on Britt.

He sat on his knees over her, chafing her arms. "Sweets, wake up. Please."

Suddenly, she gasped, drawing in huge draughts of air, then clutched her chest and moaned.

Britt. Alive. He ran his hands over her ribs feeling the telltale give along the crunching bones. A few broken ribs. She was alive.

Lequire was gone, thanks to her good shooting. His heart thudded as he looked at her sweaty face, her mussed hair, her blue eyes wide and terrified.

He cupped her face. "Britt?" he asked, waving off Hunt, who promptly snorted and began muttering into his throat mic while he paced nearby.

"You've been shot. I saw him shoot you there." She lifted an arm weakly, then let it fall.

The crimson tint to his vision faded. "You're getting looked at first."

"Oh God, the ribs are sore, but I think otherwise I'm okay. You need help."

He untucked his shirt, revealing a thin piece of plastic that molded to his chest. "Best lightweight products the US military can provide. It was a bitch to get these tailor-made in time for our outfits. The designer was running behind schedule."

She lifted a shaking hand to touch the two dents from the bullets. He'd have awful bruises, but at least he hadn't exploded a lung or whatever lived under those two locations.

"You could have..." she murmured.

Pushing hair back from her forehead, he smiled down at her as he eased her to a sitting position. "But I didn't. Thanks to you standing up to Lequire. Oh, and that stupid move jumping on top of me to save my life?"

"Yeah?"

"Don't ever do that again. My heart can't take it."

"Wait. You've got to be kidd—"

"But it did distract him so I could reach my gun. Way to go, Britt."

The shimmer of tears in her eyes caught him completely off-guard. He was unprepared for the effect it had on him. A virtual fist formed in his chest. He helped her to stand up with him, not willing or able to let go of her. Not yet.

"God." She put her arms around his chest.

He encircled her like he never wanted to let her go. Damn it, he was in deep.

The way she shuddered in his embrace made him want to hang onto her for that much longer. He tightened his hold, but at her yelp of pain, he let go. "What?"

"Ribs. Oh my God. Lequire."

"You need medical attention." Red's vision blinked back to crimson. He would punish Lequire for hurting Britt. "You're safe now." He rested his hands on her shoulders. Couldn't bear to lose contact. Needed to keep his body close enough to protect her.

"That's your job, right?"

"Sweets, this hasn't been a job since I met you." Just because he couldn't exist in her world didn't mean he had to lie.

"What?"

"You have no idea. This whole time, I've wanted you and wanted to protect you for my own selfish needs."

"Red," she breathed.

Hunt interrupted them, barking, "Are you two done playing pattycake?"

"Not now, *sir*," Red gritted out, keeping his focus on Britt.

"Well." She leaned in and rubbed her cheek against his bicep. "I have to go hide now. I promised."

"Of course. We will get it set up." Knowing it was the last time he'd ever touch her, he let his hands slowly slide off her shoulders as he stepped back. The distance hurt way down deep in his gut, like a part of him was getting ripped out. It was also the right thing to do. "Um, the guys will take care of everything. Hunt, she needs medical eval."

Britt ignored the CO. "I'd like to hide with you, actually." Pink tinged her cheeks as she ducked her head. "If that's an option."

His knees almost buckled. "What are you saying?"

"You're the one with supersonic hearing." She twirled the ear loop and didn't say anything for a minute. Finally, she started again. "Hear me out. First of all, I am still pissed that you hid the secret of the virus from me."

"Totally within your rights to be mad about that."

"But…" She paused and stared at him.

"But?"

"The thought of walking away from you hurts even more."

"What?" he said, like he'd learned to speak only yesterday.

Twining her fingers together, she said, "Uh,

unless. You don't want me around. Which I totally understand. I was kind of mean a few times this last week."

"You had good reasons, and you didn't have all of the information you needed." He had to shake his head to make sure he'd heard her correctly. "Britt," he whispered. "Listen, I can't imagine a world without you. I want you with me. But what kind of life can we create together, with the weird universe I live in?"

She licked her lips. "Aren't you getting ahead of yourself?"

"Huh?"

"We don't even know if there is a future to be created. But you know what? I'd be up for exploring the possibility."

What was he hearing? "No."

She frowned. "No, as in *no way and leave me alone*?"

"No, as in I don't deserve you. Any of this. A chance at a future with you."

"Likewise. I have my own demons, you know. I'm a lot of work."

"You're worth it. We're worth it."

"I'm not saying that our future is a lock," she muttered.

He held up his hands. "Of course not."

"I'm saying I don't want to give up yet. You … I realized how much you mean to me. I want us to try. That is, if you want to."

"Britt, you bring light into my small, dark world. I can't ask you to step into that world with me."

Her blue eyes pinned him in place. "What if I was the one who asked? Would you say yes?"

"Yes. God, yes." He framed her face with his hands. "Listen to me, Britt. I am falling in love with you.

Sweets, I am no one. I come from nothing. I have no future to offer. No kids. No assurance of sanity down the road. It's a horrible deal, and one I could never ask of anyone, much less someone as wonderful as you."

"So you'd rather I be miserable?" She crossed her arms.

Somewhere in the back of his mind, an alarm bell sounded. "No?" Was that the right answer? Damn it. This felt like a trap.

"Then I want to try for happiness. For us. With you. For as long as it lasts." She let her arms hang at her sides. "If you want the same thing, Red."

He kissed her until he couldn't tell where his lips stopped and hers started. Only that the connection was so right. He lifted his head. "You can call me Al."

Epilogue

The day after leaving the Atlanta fashion show, Hunt stood in the main room of his Morpheus Squad's Ashe County, North Carolina, base. Familiar faces—minus one—locked onto him as he set down his pencils, placing them exactly parallel to each other and perpendicular to the edge of the big table which held stacks of marked-up maps and blueprints. He considered his words carefully.

"Here's the situation. Team, we completed Mateo's initial mission to infiltrate Fallen Comrades and secure evidence of Beau Lequire's crimes against our brother-in-arms, all while protecting the McNeill family. Thanks to Kiera, we now have the intel to demolish Lequire's corrupt business including his drug trade and along the way put a real damper on Senator Lequire's reelection campaign."

Kiera held a sleeping Mattie in her arms, the baby wearing one of the many pink outfits with fluffy trim that Gonzo had purchased shortly after the baby arrived at the compound. Jake hovered at her shoulder with a determined and fulfilled expression. Hunt swallowed. Never thought he'd feel fatherly pride for the success of one of his teammates.

He continued. "Mateo's mission was Project Morpheus, Phase 1: Gather intel. Protect the McNeill family." He rubbed his jaw. He couldn't ask this group to take yet another massive risk.

The work wasn't completed yet. Hunt had pressing issues as well as long-term goals to accomplish and needed his team all-in for the next stage.

"Over the past few weeks, we extracted our people and civilians from some FUBAR situations."

Reagan grasped Pele's hand in her non-casted one and glanced up at him, meeting his gaze with a warm smile that he returned tightly.

"We don't know the end game for Lequire's viral infection. We don't know what that large of a dose is doing to him or will do to him. According to Britt..." Hunt motioned toward the small woman tucked securely under Red's arm. "Lequire plans to hurt our people as deterrent against us exposing his crimes. If we don't stop him, I assess that his next step will be to sell the Morpheus Virus to the highest bidder, ramp up imports of the Russian drug Krokodil, and invite his Bratva buddies to help hunt us down. Or use Senator Lequire's government connections to use the military to reach us."

Murmurs of disgust came from his team.

"What can we do, sir?" Rivera asked, nodding toward the McNeill family's patriarch, Sean McNeill, whose stunned and rapt expression toward Mattie reminded Hunt that the guy had just discovered he'd become a grandfather. Mr. McNeill had agreed to remain at the base until all three of his daughters and his granddaughter were safe from Lequire's reach.

"Team, if we go get Rodeo and Tachi, we risk capture by Lequire, exposure in general, and recapture by Uncle Sam. I won't order any of you to take part."

"Fuck that moron, boss," Gonzo blurted. "With respect. Sir." His Adam's apple bobbed. "We have to get our boy."

"And Tachi," Britt piped up, chin raised.

Hunt almost smiled. Almost. "Anyone who wants to stay home, I will not fault you one bit. Each of us has everything to lose."

"Gonzo gave us a way to track them. Once they leave their current shielded mobile location, I'll have a position and can run schematics within an hour," Stumpy said, leaning on his cane. "Goddamn it. Special Forces soldiers don't leave teammates behind."

Voices of agreement filled the room. Hunt nodded. This team might be made up of damaged souls, but when rubber hit the road, they risked their lives for one another.

He infinitesimally readjusted the pencils to perfect alignment, then pinned each person with an assessing stare. "Decision's been made to release the information we currently have that proves Lequire's crimes. Once we do that, it will prompt Lequire to act against Rodeo and Tachi and to come for us. All of us. We have to get to them first." He pressed his hands to the table, applying the exact same pressure on each set of four fingers. "Is everyone here ready to embrace the suck on this mission?"

Silence descended over all of them, until Mattie shifted and gave a light, contented snore and a baby fart. Most the team members smiled or chuckled.

Jake shrugged. "At least one of the team members appears unconcerned about embracing the suck. Sir."

"Yeah. What are we waiting for, boss? Let's go get our boy and his gal." Gonzo snapped his fingers. "Easy-peasy."

Around the table each person muttered agreement, some putting hands in fists, others giving hard nods. The McNeill family members stood fiercely, ready to help.

Hunt unrolled a large paper and picked up a pencil, tapping the eraser on the tabletop. "All right, team. Let's start Project Morpheus, Phase 2."

The End

Author's Note

When I was a teenager, Mom taught me how to sew my own clothes, and I remember spending hours putting together some crazy patterns and outfits! (Come to think of it, I might post some of the worst/best handmade looks in my newsletter!) Thanks to Mom, I learned how to cut patterns and loved experimenting with different fabric types. Then I had a cousin attend SCAD (Savannah College of Art and Design), and hearing about her interesting classes and her creative classmates fascinated my non-artistic self.

When it came time to write this book and I needed an unconventional heroine and an unconventional occupation type, those experiences drove my character's background and journey.

The idea of synesthesia has always fascinated me, and I've touched on it with prior virally enhanced Morpheus Squad members. But in this book I could really play with the synesthesia phenomenon by using Red's unique hearing ability. There are people in this world who truly experience sound in the form of other senses.

The closest I have ever come to synesthesia was at times while playing piano, I could tell the "texture" of the musical passage, whether it was dry, heavy, sparkly, floral, etc. Whether that's true synesthesia or musical interpretation, I'm no expert to say one way or another. I do recall a few times when I accompanied a violin quintet, and I swear that at points in their playing it sounded like people talking to me. Again, I don't think that's synesthesia, I believe that is the mimic of a violin bow stroking violin strings creating a similar vibration as vocal cords, and it was super cool. I kept looking over my shoulder, thinking someone was talking right behind me. It was the music!

I'd love to hear if my readers have any personal experience with the synesthesia phenomenon, and more importantly, if my research and fictional liberties seem to jive with the experience. As always, this is a researched work of fiction with input from various subject matter experts, but any errors are my own.

ACKNOWLEDGEMENTS

Biggest of thanks to my agent Jana Hanson who believed in Project Morpheus from the start in 2019 and kept pushing me to make it better, while working to get this series published for readers to see!

Thank you to eagle-eyed Diane Wiggs who served as one of my most valued first readers.

Massive thank you to all of my readers and fans who have waited patiently for each of the Project Morpheus books to come out, and for the ARC team with your enthusiasm and time spent reading and reviewing my books. You all rock!

If you're reading this and haven't signed up yet for my newsletter to get a chance to receive advanced reader copies and hear the latest scoop on my writing projects, please do so here:

https://tinyurl.com/58887jsu

Lastly, to my readers, there *will* be a Project Morpheus Phase 2. I hope you'll come along for the ride!

JILLIAN DAVID

EVERNIGHT PUBLISHING ®

www.evernightpublishing.com